The desperat  **turned Travis**

He longed to hold ... everything would b ... empty promise. And once she was in his arms with her soft body pressed into his, comfort wouldn't be the only thing on his mind.

He wanted to kiss her, had wanted to since the night he'd first laid eyes on her in the Passion Pit, though he hadn't admitted that to himself then.

Now the desire was entangled with his need to keep her safe and help her find her son.

HARD RIDE
TO DRY GULCH

BY
JOANNA WAYNE

blackprint CPI, Barcelona

Published in Great Britain 2014
by Mills & Boon, an imprint of Harlequin (UK) Limited,
Eton House, 18-24 Paradise Road, Richmond, Surrey, TW9 1SR

© 2014 Jo Ann Vest

ISBN: 978-0-263-91365-1

46-0714

Harlequin (UK) Limited's policy is to use papers that are natural, renewable and recyclable products and made from wood grown in sustainable forests. The logging and manufacturing processes conform to the legal environmental regulations of the country of origin.

Printed and bound in Spain
by B

Joanna Wayne was born and raised in Shreveport, Louisiana, and received her undergraduate and graduate degrees from LSU Shreveport. She moved to New Orleans in 1984, and it was there that she attended her first writing class and joined her first professional writing organization. Her debut novel, *Deep in the Bayou,* was published in 1994.

Now, dozens of published books later, Joanna has made a name for herself as being on the cutting edge of romantic suspense in both series and single-title novels. She has been on the Waldenbooks bestseller list for romance and has won many industry awards. She is also a popular speaker at writing organizations and local community functions and has taught creative writing at the University of New Orleans Metropolitan College.

Joanna currently resides in a small community forty miles north of Houston, Texas, with her husband. Though she still has many family and emotional ties to Louisiana, she loves living in the Lone Star State. You may write Joanna at PO Box 852, Montgomery, Texas 77356, USA.

A special salute to mothers everywhere who know
what it's like to love a child unconditionally.
A smile to my grandchildren who bring endless joy
to my life. And hats off to my editor, Denise Zaza,
who has worked with me through almost
sixty books. Here's to sixty more.

Prologue

Faith Ashburn emphasized her deep-set brown eyes with a coat of thick black liner and then took a step away from the mirror to see the full effect of the makeup she'd caked onto her pale skin. The haunted eyes that stared back at her were the only part of the face she recognized.

Her irises mirrored the way she felt. Lost. Trapped in a nightmare. The anxiety so intense the lining of her stomach seemed to be on fire.

But she'd go back out there tonight, into the smoke and groping, the stares that crawled across her skin like hairy spiders. She'd smile and endure the depravity—praying, always praying for some crumb of information that would lead her to her son.

Cornell was eighteen now. Physically, he was a man. Mentally and emotionally, he was a kid, at least he was in her mind. A trusting, naive boy who needed his mother and his meds.

Faith's bare feet sank into the thick mauve carpet as she stepped back into her bedroom and tugged on her patterned panty hose. Then she pulled the low-cut, trampy black dress from the closet and stepped into it.

The fabric stretched over her bare breasts as she slid the spaghetti straps over her narrow shoulders. Her nipples were covered, but there was enough cleavage showing to suggest that she'd have no qualms about revealing everything if the offer appealed to her.

Reaching to the top shelf of her closet, she chose the bright red stiletto heels. They never failed to garner the instant attention of men high on booze, drugs and the stench of overripe sex.

Struck by a burst of vertigo, Faith held on to the bed-post until the dizziness passed. Then she tucked a lip-stick, her car keys and some mad money into the small sequined handbag that already held her licensed pistol.

Stopping off in the kitchen, she poured two fingers of cheap whiskey into a glass. She swished the amber liquid around in her mouth, gargled and then spit it down the drain. Holding the glass over the sink, she ran one finger around the edges to collect the remaining liquor. She dotted it at her pulse points like expensive perfume.

Her muscles clenched. Her lungs clogged. She took a deep breath and walked out the door, carefully locking it behind her.

Six months of going unofficially undercover into the seediest areas of Dallas. Six months of questioning every drug addict and pervert that might have come in contact with Cornell, based on nothing but the one shrapnel of evidence the police had provided her.

Six months of crying herself to sleep when she came home as lost, confused and desperate as before.

God, please let tonight be different.

"ANOTHER BACKSTREET HOMICIDE, another trip to see Georgio. I'm beginning to think he gives a discount to killers. A lap dance from one of his girls when a body shows up at the morgue without identification."

"And the victims get younger and younger." Travis Dalton followed his partner, Reno, as they walked through a side door of the sleaziest strip joint in the most dangerous part of Dallas. Georgio reigned as king here, providing the local sex and drug addicts with everything they needed to feed their cravings.

Yet the rotten bastard always came out on top. His rule of threats and intimidation eliminated any chance of getting one of his patrons to testify against him. Not that they would have had a shred of credibility if they had.

A rap song blared from the sound system as a couple of seminude women with surgery-enhanced butts and breasts made love to skinny poles. Two others gyrated around the rim of the stage, collecting bills in their G-strings.

A familiar waitress whose name Travis couldn't remember sashayed up to him. "Business or pleasure, copper boy?"

"What do you think?"

"Business, but a girl can hope. Are you looking for Georgio?"

"For starters."

"Is it about that boy who got shot up in Oak Cliff last night?"

Now she had Travis's full attention. "What do you know about that?"

"Nothing, I just figured that's what brought you here."

Travis had a hunch she knew more than she was admitting. He was about to question her further when he noticed a woman at the bar trying to peel a man's grip from her right wrist.

"Let go of me," she said, her voice rising above the din.

The man held tight while his free hand groped her breast. "I just want to be friends."

"You're hurting me."

Travis stormed to the bar. "You heard the woman. Move on, buddy."

"Why don't you mind your own business?"

"I am." He pulled the ID from the breast pocket of his blue pullover. "Dallas Police. Back off or I snap a nice metal bracelet on your wrist and haul you down to central lockup."

A thin stream of spittle made its way down the man's whiskered chin as his hands fell to his sides. Wiping it away with his shirtsleeve, he slid off the barstool and stumbled backward.

"She's the one you should be arresting. She came on to me," he slurred.

Travis studied the woman and decided the drunk could be right. She was flaunting the trappings of a hooker, right down to a sexy pair of heels that made her shapely legs appear a mile long.

But one look into her haunted eyes and Travis doubted she was looking to make a fast buck on her back. She had a delicate, fragile quality about her that suggested she'd be more at home in a convent than here shoving off drunks. Even the exaggerated makeup couldn't hide her innocence.

If he had to guess, he'd say she was here trying to get even with some jerk who had cheated on her. That didn't make it any less dangerous for her to be in this hellhole.

"Party's over, lady. I'm calling for a squad car to take you home."

"I have a car."

"Get behind the wheel and I'll have to arrest you for driving while intoxicated."

"I'm not drunk."

He couldn't argue that point. She smelled like a distillery, but she wasn't slurring her words and her eyes were clear, her pupils normal.

"I don't know what kind of game you're playing or

who you're trying to get even with, but if you hang around here, you're going to run into more trouble than you can handle."

"I can take care of myself." She turned and started to walk away.

Travis moved quicker, setting himself in her path without realizing why he was bothering.

He looked around for Reno, but his partner wasn't in sight. He was probably already questioning Georgio, and Travis should be with him.

"Look, lady. You're in over your head here. I've got some urgent business, but sit tight for a few minutes and I'll be back to walk you to your car. In the meantime, don't make friends with any more perverts. That's an order."

She shrugged and nodded.

He stalked off to find Reno. He spotted him and Georgio a minute later near the door to the suite of private offices. When he looked back, the woman was gone.

Just as well, he told himself, especially if she'd gone home. He didn't need any more problems tonight. But even after he reached Reno and jumped into the murderous situation at hand, he couldn't fully shake her from his mind.

Whatever had brought her slumming could get her killed.

Chapter One

Four months later

Travis adjusted the leather-and-turquoise bolo tie, a close match to the one his brother was wearing with his Western-style tux. The irony of seeing his formerly Armani-faithful attorney brother dressed like this made it hard for Travis not to laugh.

"I never thought I'd see the day you got hitched to a cowgirl."

"I never thought I'd see the day you showed up at the Dry Gulch Ranch again," Leif answered.

"Couldn't miss the wedding of my favorite brother."

"Your *only* brother."

"Yeah, probably a good thing you don't have competition now that you're building a house here on the ranch. On the bright side, I do like that I get to wear my cowboy boots with this rented monkey suit."

Travis rocked back on the heels of his new boots, bought for the conspicuous occasion of Leif's wedding to Joni Griffin. He'd never seen his brother happier. Not only was he so in love that he beamed when he looked at his veterinarian bride, but his daughter, Effie, would be living with him for her last two years of high school.

The Dry Gulch Ranch was spiffed up for the ceremony

and reception. Lights were strung through the branches of giant oaks and stringy sycamores. A white tent had been set up with chairs, leaving a makeshift aisle that led to a rose-covered altar where the two lovers would take their vows.

Most of the chairs were taken. Leif's friends from the prestigious law firm from which he'd recently resigned to open his own office nearer the ranch mingled with what looked to be half the population of Oak Grove.

The women from both groups looked quite elegant. The Big D lawyers were all in designer suits. The ranchers for the most part looked as if they'd feel a lot more at home in their Wranglers than in their off-the-rack suits and choking ties.

In fact, a few of the younger cowboys were in jeans and sport coats. Travis figured they were the smart ones. Weekends he wasn't working a homicide case he usually spent on a friend's ranch up in the hill country.

Riding, roping, baling hay, branding—he'd done it all and loved it. A weekend place on the Dry Gulch Ranch, just a little over an hour from Dallas, would have been the perfect solution to Travis. Except for one very large problem.

Rueben Jackson Dalton, his father by virtue of a healthy sperm.

"Time for us to join the preacher," Leif said, jerking Travis back into the moment.

He walked at his brother's side and felt a momentary sense of anxiety. He and Leif had been through hell together growing up, most caused by R.J.

It had been just the two of them against the world since their mother's death, and they'd always been as close as a horse to a saddle. Now Leif was marrying and moving onto R.J.'s spread.

Oh, hell, what was he worried about? R.J. would never come between him and Leif. Besides, the old coot would be dead soon.

The music started. Leif's fifteen-year-old daughter started down the aisle, looking so grown-up Travis felt his chest constrict. He could only imagine what the sight did to Leif. Travis winked at Effie as she took her place at the altar. Her smile was so big it took over her face and danced in her eyes.

Travis looked up again and did a double take as he spotted the maid of honor gliding down the aisle. She damn sure didn't look the way she did the last time he'd seen her, but there was no doubt in his mind that the gorgeous lady was the same one he'd rescued in Georgio's sleaziest strip club four months earlier.

He'd spent only a few minutes with her, but she'd preyed on his mind a lot since then, so much so that he found himself showing up at Georgio's palace of perversion even when his work didn't call for doing so.

All in the interest of talking to her and making sure she was safe. In spite of his efforts, he'd never caught sight of her again.

Travis studied the woman as she took her place a few feet away from him. She was absolutely stunning in a luscious creation the color of the amethyst ring his mother used to wear. She'd given the ring to him before she'd died.

It was the only prized possession Travis owned—well, that and the belt buckles he'd won in bull-riding competitions back when he had more guts than sense.

The wedding march sounded. The guests all stood. Travis's eyes remained fixed on the maid of honor. Finally, she looked at him, and when their eyes met, he saw the same tortured, haunting depths that had mesmerized him at their first meeting.

Travis forced his gaze away from the mystery woman and back to Joni and Travis. He wouldn't spoil the wedding, but before the night was over he'd have a little chat with the seductive maid of honor. Before he was through, he'd discover if she was as innocent as he'd first believed, or if the demons who'd filled her eyes with anguish had actually driven her to the dark side of life.

If the latter was the case, he'd make damn sure she stayed away from his niece, even if it meant telling Leif the truth about his new wife's best friend.

The reception might have a lot more spectacular fireworks than originally planned. Travis was already itching for the first dance.

Chapter Two

So far, so good, Faith decided as she concentrated on putting one foot in front of the other. She had to hold it together and not let her emotions careen out of control. Any tears shed tonight should be ones of joy.

Unfortunately, she'd forgotten what joy felt like. Cornell had been missing for ten months now and she seemed no closer to finding him. Her nerves were ragged, her emotions so unsteady that the slightest incident could set off the waterworks.

Had it been anyone else who'd asked her to be maid of honor in her wedding, Faith could easily have said no. But she couldn't refuse Joni, especially after the way Joni had stood by her when Cornell first went missing.

Joni was still concerned, but as the weeks had turned into months, she—like Faith's other friends—had moved on with their lives. Faith understood, though she could never move on until Cornell was home again and safe.

As for the cops' theory that Cornell had left home by choice, she was convinced it was pure bunk. Sure, she could buy that Cornell had gotten mixed up with the wrong crowd. He was extremely vulnerable to peer influence.

And she wasn't so naive as to believe it was impossible

that he might have experimented with drugs. A lot of kids had by age eighteen. But never in a million years would Cornell have left home and shut her out of his life—not of his own free will.

Wherever he was tonight, he was being held against his will or—

Here she went again, working herself into an anxiety-fueled meltdown.

This was Joni's big night. Surely Faith could hold herself together for a couple hours.

Her glance settled on Leif Dalton. A boyish grin split his lips, and his dark eyes danced in anticipation. A sexy, loving cowboy waiting for his beautiful bride. Joni was a very lucky woman—if it lasted.

For Faith, marriage had been one of life's major disappointments, enough so that she had no intention of ever tying the knot again.

She switched her concentration to Leif's brother and best man. Tall. Thick, dark hair that fell playfully over his forehead. Hard bodied. Ruggedly handsome.

And familiar.

She struggled to figure out where she'd seen him before as she took her place on the other side of Leif's daughter. Faith had missed the rehearsal celebration last night and arrived at the ranch only minutes before the ceremony tonight.

But she'd definitely seen him somewhere.

The tempo of the music changed and a second later the bridal march filled the air. Sounds of shuffling feet and whispered oohs and aahs filled the air as the guests rose to their feet for their first sight of Joni in her white satin-and-lace gown.

Adorable twin girls, their curly red hair topped with pink bows, skipped and danced down the aisle in front of

Joni, scattering rose petals. Lila and Lacy, Leif's three-year-old half nieces, whom Joni bragged about continuously. Faith wouldn't be surprised if Leif and Joni didn't start a family of their own within the year.

Faith stole another quick glance at the best man. Her heart pounded.

All of a sudden she knew exactly where she'd seen him before. In a Dallas strip club. He was the sexy cop who'd come to her rescue a few months back. The cop whose orders she'd disobeyed when she'd cleared out before he could ask too many questions.

He wouldn't be nearly as easy to dodge tonight.

Talk about spoiling a wedding. One word from the groom's brother about where he'd met the slutty maid of honor and Joni would figure out exactly why Faith had turned down every Saturday-night invitation to meet her and Leif for dinner.

Joni would worry about Faith's safety. Worse, if she couldn't persuade Faith to give up her visits to the criminal underbelly of Dallas, she'd insist on getting involved. No way could Faith drag Joni into that.

Steady, girl. Don't panic.

There was a good chance the hunky, nosy cop wouldn't connect her to the woman he'd met in a strip club months ago. For one thing, she had on tons less makeup. For another, she wasn't braless. She was just Joni's maid of honor.

Besides, he'd originally figured her for just another woman on the make, or perhaps even one of the off-duty strippers. No reason for him to have given her another thought.

Play this cool, leave at the first opportunity, and the cop would never guess they'd ever met.

"Surely you're not thinking of sneaking out without a dance with the best man?"

The husky male voice startled Faith. Poor timing. She'd already stepped out of the tent and was about to start down the path to the parked cars.

Except for a brief conversation when Leif had introduced them after the ceremony, she'd managed to avoid Travis all evening.

She flashed what she hoped was an innocent-looking smile. "I'm not sneaking anywhere. I've said my good-byes to the happy couple."

"It's still early. The party is in full swing."

"Yes, but it's a long drive back to Dallas."

"So why drive it? The guest rooms in the newlyweds' ranch bungalow aren't fully finished yet, but I'm sure R.J. can put you up for the night. From what I've seen of his house, there are plenty of spare bedrooms."

"So I've heard. Joni invited me to stay over," Faith admitted. "But I really need to get home tonight."

The band returned from their break. A guitar strummed. The lead female singer in the country-and-western band that had kept the portable dance floor occupied all night belted out the first words to an old Patsy Cline hit.

Travis fitted a hand to the small of Faith's back. "One dance before you call it a night?"

Her brain issued a warning, but the music, the night and even the tiny lights that twinkled above them like stars overpowered her caution. Besides, Travis showed no sign of recognizing her. What could one dance hurt?

They walked back to the dance floor together. His arms slid around her, pulling her close as their bodies began to sway to the haunting ballad. His cheek brushed hers. An unfamiliar heat shimmered deep inside her. She dissolved into the sensual sensations for mere seconds before her brain kicked in again.

She hadn't felt a man's arms around her for years. No wonder her body had reacted to the contact.

She pulled away, putting an inch of space between her breasts and his chest and points lower. The warmth didn't fully dissipate, but her breathing came easier.

By the time they finished the dance, she was almost fully in control. "I really do have to go now," she said, leading the way as they left the dance floor.

"If you must."

"I must. And really, there's no reason for you to walk me to my car."

"A promise is a promise."

The man was persistent. If the cops handling Cornell's missing-person case had been half as determined, they likely would have located him by now.

"No reason for you to leave the reception," she said. "I'm sure I can find my way to my car on my own."

"But what kind of gentleman would I be if I let you?"

"A sensible one."

"Not my strong suit."

"I got here late and had to park in the pasture across the road. You'll get those gorgeous boots of yours dirty," she said.

"I'll risk it."

Further protests would sound ungrateful or just plain pigheaded. Besides, it would be a lot darker once they left the twinkling lights. Her car could be difficult to locate among all the other vehicles. Travis might just come in handy.

Reaching into the petite jeweled evening bag that swung from her shoulder, she took out the keys to her aging Honda and started walking. Their shoulders brushed. A zing of awareness shot through her.

Disgusted with herself for letting Travis affect her, she picked up her pace. Bad call. Maneuvering the grass and uneven ground in her six-inch stilettos proved to be a dangerous balancing act.

The second time she almost tripped, she was forced to accept the arm Travis offered for support. A traitorous flutter appeared in her stomach.

It had to be just her nerves, or the fact that Travis was several cuts above the perverts she'd been spending her time with. Not every night the way she had in the beginning, but every weekend.

A breeze stirred. Faith looked up and was struck by the brilliance of the stars now that they'd left the artificial illumination.

"Amazing, aren't they?" Travis said, apparently noticing her fascination with the heavens.

"Yes. Hard to believe those are the same stars that appear over Dallas. They look so much closer here."

"Nothing like getting out in the wide-open spaces to appreciate the splendor of nature," Travis agreed.

"Do you spend much time out here?"

"At the Dry Gulch? No way."

"I guess that will change now that Leif will be living out here."

"It won't change anytime soon."

"Because of your relationship with your father?"

"You got it. And you apparently know a lot more about me, Faith Ashburn, than I do about you."

"Joni told me a bit about why you and Leif have issues with R.J. But Leif changed his mind about his father. Perhaps you will, too."

"Sure, and Texas might vote to outlaw beef."

"Stranger things have happened."

"Not in my lifetime," Travis countered. "But it was a beautiful wedding."

"I've never seen Joni so radiant."

"Have you and Joni been friends long?"

"Eight years. We met in a psychology class at Oklahoma University. We clicked immediately and became fast friends even though I was divorced and had a young son."

They made small talk until she spotted her car and unlocked it with her remote device. The lights blinked. "That's my Honda," she said, grateful for an excuse to end the conversation before he started asking personal questions again.

She let go of Travis's arm and hurried toward her car.

Travis kept pace, then stepped in front of her at the last minute, blocking the driver's side door. "You know, Faith, you look a lot better without all that makeup you were wearing the first time we met."

Her mouth grew dry, her chest tight. "I don't know what you're talking about. I've never seen you before tonight."

"Actually, we met a few months ago. You're not the kind of woman a man could forget."

Faith wondered at what point during the night he'd figured that out. She shrugged. "Sorry. You must have me confused with someone else."

"Not a chance." He propped his left hand against the car roof and leaned in closer. "Let me refresh your memory. The Passion Pit. Four months ago. You were cruising the bar when one of your admirers got out of hand."

She rolled her eyes. "Cruising the bar?"

"Don't go all naive on me, Faith. A lady doesn't just drop into the Passion Pit unescorted because she's thirsty.

You were wearing a black dress that left little to the imagination and a pair of nosebleed heels that screamed to be noticed. We talked. I asked you to wait so that I could see you safely home. You didn't."

"You definitely have me confused with someone else."

"Not unless you have an identical twin. I asked Joni. She assured me you don't."

And Faith was a terrible liar. That left truth or some version of it as her only feasible choice if she wanted to get the detective off her back.

"You're right." She cast her eyes downward, to the tips of Travis's cowboy boots. "I'm embarrassed to admit it, but I was in that disgusting place once. A detective came to my rescue when a rowdy drunk got out of hand. That must have been you."

"Yep. Apparently, I am easy to forget. So why the denials?" Travis asked. "As far as I know, you didn't break any laws that night."

"I absolutely didn't. Not that night or any other. I'd just rather Joni not know I did something so stupid."

"Not only stupid, but dangerous," Travis corrected. "Why were you there?"

"I was writing an article for a magazine on the increase of gentlemen's clubs in the Dallas area. I decided I should at least visit one of them for firsthand research."

"Dressed like that?"

"I thought I'd be less conspicuous that way."

"There was no way you'd ever go unnoticed, looking the way you did that night. Those red shoes alone were enough to guarantee you'd get hit on."

So he'd noticed more than that she'd needed help. At least she'd had an effect on him. Not that she cared.

"I'd love to read that article," Travis said. "Which magazine was that in?"

"It doesn't matter. It was a busy month and they decided not to run the story, after all."

"So all that work for nothing."

"That's freelance," she quipped. Even to her ears the attempt at nonchalance fell flat. She was too nervous. And she'd never written a magazine article in her life. The closest she'd come was a letter to the editor they had actually printed in the newspaper.

"I thought Joni said you worked in the personnel department of a department-store chain."

"Benefits manager, but I occasionally freelance."

"You're a lousy liar."

And always had been. She was going to have to come nearer to the truth if she expected Travis to buy her story.

"Okay, I wasn't there to write an article. A good friend of mine was worried about her daughter. She'd heard a rumor that she was dancing at the Passion Pit. I offered to go there and find out for certain."

"Just helping out a friend."

"Yes. Look, Travis, I know your cop instincts are running wild. But this time they're way off base. I went to a strip club one night. I wasn't looking for a job or trying to pick up tricks. I'm thirty-five years old, for heaven's sake. Way too old to peddle flesh even if I was interested. End of conversation."

"Not quite. If I ever find out that you've exposed my niece to drugs, alcohol or any other sordid behaviors, I'll tell Joni everything and see that you never come around Effie again."

Travis Dalton was not only arrogant, but overbearing. That would have turned her off in a second, except that he was being that way to protect his niece. That was the kind of dogmatism she'd craved from the cops investigating Cornell's disappearance.

The temptation to tell him the truth flared inside her. It passed just as quickly. There was no reason to think he'd be any different than the other officers she'd talked to.

No. She'd made her decision. She had to go higher than the cops if she was to find Cornell. She'd done that. Now she was just waiting to hear back from a man she knew only as Georgio.

"You don't have to worry about Effie," Faith assured him. "I would *never* corrupt a child."

"Good." He opened the door.

She slid past him and climbed behind the wheel. "Good night, Travis."

"One last thing."

She looked up just as he leaned forward. Their faces were mere inches apart. The musky scent of soap, aftershave and sheer manliness attacked her senses, and a riotous surge of attraction made her go weak.

His hand touched her shoulder. "If you ever need to ask me about your friend's problems—if you ever need to talk about anything at all—call me." He reached into his pocket, pulled out a business card and pressed it into her hand.

His voice had lost its threatening edge. His tone was compelling. "I'll do what I can to help, Faith. You can trust me."

Finally, he closed her door. She jerked the car into Reverse, backed from the parking space and then sped away. Her insides were shaking. Tears of frustration burned the back of her eyelids.

Trust him. She'd love nothing more than to believe that. Desperation urged her to turn back. Put Travis Dalton to the test. Avoid getting involved with Georgio, a man whose power frightened her and whose dark and forbidden world made her sick to her stomach.

But she'd tried working with the cops first, lost months doing things their way, wasted precious time not knowing if Cornell was sick, in pain, held captive or even…

No. Cornell was alive. She'd find him. She was on the right track now. Trusting Travis would accomplish nothing except to drag Joni into this nightmare.

Far better if she never saw Travis Dalton again, never gave him another chance to mess with her mind or her resolve.

TRAVIS TOOK A few steps, escaping the cloud of dust Faith left behind in her haste to get away from him. He was one of the best interrogators in the whole homicide department. He could recognize a liar as easily as some people could recognize a guy was bald or a woman was wearing a wig.

And that was with a good liar. Faith Ashburn wasn't. But he still couldn't buy that she was a hooker or an addict looking for a way to feed her demon. So what had she been doing at the Passion Pit that night and what really haunted those captivating deep brown eyes?

Travis started back to the party. He'd lost the mood for celebrating, but he couldn't haul ass without letting Leif know he was leaving. His boots stirred up loose gravel as he neared the sprawling ranch house. Music from the band wafted through the night, competing with the cacophony of thousands of tree frogs, crickets and the occasional howl of a coyote.

Welcoming lights spilled out from every window of the old ranch house. The glow did nothing to make Travis feel more at home, but oddly, he didn't experience any rancor toward the house or the ranch.

Even more surprising, he didn't hate R.J., not the way Leif had at first or the way Travis had expected to before he'd met the man. Hard to hate a dying man, even a father who hadn't bothered to find out if you were dead or alive or being daily abused after your mother died of cancer.

Not hating R.J. didn't mean Travis gave a damn about him or wanted anything to do with him or the bait R.J. was casting out to lure his estranged family home.

Bottom line: if home was where the heart was, the Dry Gulch Ranch didn't make the cut for Travis.

He spotted R.J. rounding the side of the house. The old man hesitated, then swayed as if he was losing his balance. Travis rushed over and caught him just as he started to crumple to the hard earth.

R.J. looked up at him, but his expression was blank and he looked pasty and dazed.

Travis kept a steadying arm around his waist. "Do you need an ambulance?"

R.J. raked his fingers through his thinning gray hair and looked up at Travis. "An ambulance?"

"You almost passed out there."

"Where's Gwen?"

It was the first Travis had heard of a Gwen. "Why don't I get you back inside and I'll see if I can find her?"

R.J. muttered a string of curses. "Just get Gwen. And tell everyone else to go home. Don't know what the hell all these people are doing here, anyway."

His words were slurred, difficult to understand. There was no smell of alcohol on his breath, so Travis figured this had to be related to the tumor.

Leif said R.J. had occasional moments when he wasn't fully lucid, but he hadn't indicated R.J. totally lost it like this. Could be the tumor had shifted or increased in size.

Travis looked around, hoping to see someone who knew more about R.J. than he did heading back to the house or to their car. No such luck. Everyone was obviously still in the party tent.

"Let's go inside," Travis said again. "Maybe Gwen's in there."

He began leading the old man toward the back porch. "Just a few yards to go," Travis said. He walked slowly, supporting most of R.J's weight. When they reached the steps, R.J. grabbed hold of the railing.

"Take a second to catch your breath," Travis told him.

R.J. shook his head, then straightened, still a bit shaky. He looked back toward the area where the reception was going full blast and then up at Travis, as if trying to figure out what the devil was going on.

"Did I drag you away from the party?" he asked.

"Nope," Travis said. "I walked someone to their car and ran into you a few yards from the house. You looked like you could use some help."

R.J. scratched his chin. "Damned tumor. Can't make up its mind if it wants to kill me or drive me crazy. Gets me so mixed-up I don't know if I'm shucking or shelling."

"Do you want me to drive you to the emergency room?"

"Hell no. Nothing they can do. I'll just go inside and sit down awhile. Tell Leif that if you see him. I don't want him worrying about what happened to me while he should be celebrating."

"Shouldn't I get someone to come stay with you? You probably shouldn't be alone."

"Nope. Tumor's going to kill me and that's a fact, but it ain't gonna rule me. I'm okay now. You go back to the party afore that looker friend of Joni's you were dancing with hooks up with some other guy."

So the old man didn't miss much when he was lucid. "If you're talking about Faith Ashburn, she's already left."

Probably to hook up with another guy. Hopefully not one picked up anywhere near the Passion Pit.

"C'mon. I'll walk inside with you—not that I think you need help," he added before R.J. could rebuke him. "I could use a glass of water. Then I'll let Leif know where you are and see if I can find Gwen for you."

"Gwen?"

"You mentioned her a minute ago."

"Did I?"

"You did."

"Don't that just stitch your britches? Far as I know, there ain't no Gwen around these parts."

But there had been one wherever R.J. had gone in his mind. By the time they were inside the house, the old man seemed as alert as he had at the start of the evening. He walked on his own to the kitchen, opened the fridge and took out a bottle of milk. Travis reached into the cabinet, took out a glass and set it on the counter for him.

"Join me in a drink?" R.J. asked. "There's beer or whiskey around here somewhere or you can just get water out of the faucet. We don't drink that fancy bottled designer H_2O around here."

Sitting around drinking like old friends with R.J. had about as much appeal as being invited to shovel manure out of the horse barn.

"Another time," Travis said. "If you're okay, I need to be going."

"Sure. I'm good. You head on back to the party. You know your being here tonight meant a lot to your brother."

"I wouldn't have missed it. Leif's family." All the family he had. Meeting R.J. hadn't changed that. "You take care," Travis said. Eager to clear out before the man started talking family or brought up his bizarre will, he turned and started back to the party.

"Thanks, son," R.J. called after him.

Travis didn't stop or turn around. But the word *son* clattered in his head, knocking loose some bad memories as he pulled the front door shut behind him. Memories he'd banished to the deepest, darkest abyss of his mind years ago and wasn't about to let R.J. rekindle.

But Travis had accomplished one thing tonight other than doing his duty by Leif. He now knew the mystery woman from the Passion Pit's name.

First thing tomorrow, he'd start his own investigation of Faith Ashburn—which might plunge him into a new set of problems.

If he discovered that she wasn't as innocent as his hunch indicated and she was involved in some kind of criminal behavior, he'd have no choice but to arrest her.

News that your brother had just arrested your wife's maid of honor would no doubt ensure a dynamic beginning to the honeymoon. Leif would love him for that.

FAITH PULLED ON the cotton T-shirt, drew her bare feet onto the bed and slipped between the crisp sheets. The once-cozy home felt even lonelier than usual tonight.

Perhaps it was the contrast between the glorious future filled with love and happiness stretching in front of Joni and Leif, and the heartbreak that filled these walls that made the desperation almost too much to endure.

Whatever the reason, the fear for Cornell pressed against her chest with such force she could barely breathe. Tales of past real-life abduction horrors roamed her mind like bands of deadly marauders. Victims kept against their will, sometimes for years. Abused. Tortured. Killed.

She shuddered and beat a fist into the pillow. Knowing she'd never find a shred of peace on her own, she finally gave up and retrieved the bottle of antianxiety medication the doctor had prescribed.

She shook two pills from the bottle and swallowed them with a few sips from the glass of water she'd placed on her nightstand earlier. She switched off the lamp and lay in the muted moonlight that filtered through her window. The branches of the oak outside creaked in the wind and sent eerie shadows creeping across her ceiling.

Counting backward, she tried to force her mind to dull and welcome sleep. Instead, her thoughts shifted to Travis. The instant attraction she'd felt in his arms was difficult to figure. Not that his rugged good looks wouldn't have been enough to grab almost any woman's attention, especially one who hadn't been with a man in over two years.

Only it was more what she sensed with him than what she saw. Strength. Determination. Protectiveness toward his niece.

And a promise that she could trust him. She'd wanted to believe that, wanted it so badly that she'd almost turned around and driven back to the ranch after fifteen minutes on the road.

But she'd tried the police. They saw things in black-and-white. Her son had left home. His friends had suggested he was on drugs. He'd been seen in the seedy area of town and inside a strip club where he'd appeared to be enjoying himself.

Their deduction: no foul play suspected.

The police might be right to a point, but she knew her son. He might have caved in to peer pressure and smoked a joint, but he was not an addict. He might even have gone along with friends for a night of carousing, but unless something terrible had happened, he would have come home.

The black of night had eased into the gray of dawn before sleep finally claimed her.

She woke to the jarring ring of the phone. Anticipation stabbed her heart the way it did at every unexpected call, and she grabbed the receiver, knocking over the glass of water. The liquid splattered her arm and the side of her bed as she clutched the phone and put it to her ear.

"Hello."

"Mom."

Chapter Three

Faith's heart pounded against her chest. Her breath caught. She jerked to a sitting position and forced her words through a choking knot at the back of her throat.

"Cornell. Is that you? Is it really you?"

"It's me."

"Where are you? Are you okay?"

"I'm okay. Only…"

"Tell me where you are, Cornell. I'll come get you. Just tell me where you are?"

"I can't, Mom."

"Are you having seizures? Have you been taking your meds?"

"I have a new prescription. No seizures in months." His voice shook. "I'm so sorry. So sor—"

His voice grew silent. Curses railed in the background. The phone went dead.

"Cornell! Cornell!" She kept calling, but she was yelling his name into a lifeless phone. Her insides rolled sickeningly.

"Please call me back. Please, Cornell, call me back," she whispered. The phone stayed silent.

There had to be a way to reach him. A hard metal taste filled the back of her throat as she punched in *69.

A brief sputter of interference was the only response to her attempt to reach the number Cornell had called from.

Her head felt as if someone had turned on strobe lights inside it. A pulsing at the temples tightened like a Vise-Grip. She buried her head in her hands in an attempt to stop the dizzying sensation.

Was this just another nightmare or had she actually heard her son's voice?

No, even trapped in the shock, she was certain the call had been real. Tears burned in the corners of her eyes and then escaped to stream down her face.

Cornell was alive. Finally, the truth of that rolled over her in waves. Her son was alive.

But where was he and what could he possibly be sorry for? For taking drugs? For drinking? Was he staying away because he thought she was mad at him? But if that was all there was, who had yelled the curses in the background that had frightened Cornell into breaking off the call midsentence?

He was not alone and whoever was with had him under their control.

Possibilities exploded in her mind, all of them too frightening to bear.

There had to be a way to find out where that call had originated. If she knew where Cornell was, she could rescue him. She could bring him home.

His interrupted call was proof he was being held or at least intimidated by someone. Even the Dallas Police Department couldn't deny that.

Call me. You can trust me.

Travis's words echoed in her mind. But was it Travis Dalton she should put her faith in or a man she knew only as Georgio?

OFFICIALLY, IT WAS Travis's day off. Unofficially, he strolled into the precinct about 7:00 a.m. No one in the front office seemed surprised to see him. Homicide detectives never kept normal hours.

Neither did crime.

Jewel Sayer raised one eyebrow as he passed her desk. "I thought you were partying in Oak Grove this weekend?"

"Just stayed long enough to get my brother married."

"What? No hot chicks at the wedding reception?"

"None as hot as you, Jewel."

"Can't go comparing the rest of the mere mortals to me, Travis. You've got to learn to settle for someone in your league."

"So you keep telling me."

Jewel was in her mid-thirties and a far cry from the beauty-pageant types who filled the Dallas hot spots six nights a week. She had a boxlike face hemmed in by dark, straight hair cropped an inch from her scalp. Her breasts were lost beneath boxy, plain cotton shirts. Her trousers bagged. Her face was a makeup-free zone.

Jewel was, however, a wildcat of a homicide detective. She could tear more much meat out of a seemingly useless clue than most of the men who'd had years more experience. And she had great instincts. She also had a husband who adored her.

Her phone rang. She lifted her coffee mug as a sign of dismissal before answering it.

Travis stopped at the coffeepot, filled a mug with the strong brew and took it to his office. He dropped to the seat behind his cluttered desk and typed *Faith Ashburn* into the DPD search system.

A few sips of coffee later, her name came up as having filed a missing-person report a few days under ten months ago, on June 25. That would have been approximately six months before he ran into her at the Passion Pit.

He pulled up the report she'd filled out. The missing person was her eighteen-year-old son, Cornell Keating Ashburn, a high-school student about to start his senior year.

According to the report, Cornell struggled with academics and received special help with his classes in a mainstream setting. He made friends easily but he was easily influenced by his peers. He was also on medication for seizures and reportedly needed daily meds to prevent them.

According to the report, Faith Ashburn had gone in to work early the day he'd gone missing, leaving before Cornell got out of bed. She'd come home from work to find a note from him saying he was hanging out with some friends from the neighborhood. He might spend the night at his friend Jason's, but he'd call later and let her know.

He'd never called. He'd never come home. He'd never showed up at Jason's.

That explained the torment that haunted her mesmerizing eyes.

Now that Travis thought about it, Leif had questioned him a couple months ago about how effective the police were with following up on missing-persons cases. Travis had assured him that they were thorough and professional.

No doubt Joni had told him about Faith's missing son and that had prompted the questions.

Travis printed the original report and a series of follow-up notes by the investigating detective, Mark Ethridge. Mark headed up the missing-persons division and reportedly had handled Cornell's disappearance himself. Ethridge was one of the best in the business at tracking missing or runaway teens.

Travis skimmed for the most pertinent details. Faith and Cornell's father were divorced. He'd died two years ago in a work-related accident, so that eliminated any chance he'd run away to live with him. His maternal grandmother lived in Seattle. His maternal grandfather lived in Waco. Neither had seen Cornell in years. Nor had his paternal grandparents. Ethridge had checked that out thoroughly.

Faith had called everyone Cornell ever hung out with. No one had seen him that day.

His clothes were still in the closet except for the jeans, shirt and sneakers he'd obviously been wearing when he went missing. His iPad and computer were still in his room. Only his phone was missing. She'd called it repeatedly. There had been no answer.

Easy to see why she feared foul play.

Of course, it was also possible the young man had decided to chuck it all and run away from home. At eighteen, he wouldn't technically be a runaway. In the eyes of the law, he was an adult with the right to live wherever he chose.

Travis finished off his coffee and then moved on to the notes Ethridge had provided. There was no final report, as the investigation was ongoing.

Not good, Travis decided as he delved into the investigation discoveries. Although Faith had insisted that her son had no issues that would cause him to run away, his friends from school painted a different story.

Several of his classmates, including Jason, had said he'd started acting strange in the days before he'd disappeared. They said he'd stopped hanging out with them after school, always said he was busy.

Ethridge had checked out the local drug and prostitute scene. Two strippers from the Passion Pit had recognized him from his picture, said they'd seen him in the club a couple times over the past few weeks, but not since his disappearance. One claimed he was hot for one of the dancers.

Even Georgio admitted to having seen him. Said he'd caught Cornell trying to touch one of his dancers inappropriately, and kicked him out. Claimed he realized then the kid was underage, and had told him to go home before he got into trouble.

After that, the clues ran dry.

Ethridge would have told Faith what he'd discovered. That explained her hanging out in the city's scummiest dive. She'd been looking for her son or someone who could tell her where to find him.

The only good news was that Cornell's body had not turned up at the local morgue.

That was the reality Travis lived with every day. He and his partner were the lead detectives in five unsolved murder cases of male victims between the ages of sixteen and eighteen who'd been killed over the past nineteen months. All had been shot twice in the back of the head, gangster-style, their bodies either left in an alley or dumped into the Trinity River.

At first people had paid little attention to the murders, attributing them to gangs or drug deals gone bad. But the last victim had been from a prominent family.

Now the media had jumped on board and were suddenly clamoring for information about the murders and pushing the idea that a serial killer was stalking Dallas.

Nothing got the citizens more riled and afraid than the possibility of a serial killer who chose his victims randomly.

Neither Travis nor his partner, Reno Vargas, believed the murders were random. In fact, they were convinced Georgio was behind them. What they didn't have was proof of his involvement.

Any way you looked at it, Faith Ashburn had plenty of reason to be worried.

Travis was about to go for more coffee when his cell phone vibrated. He yanked it from his pocket and checked the caller ID. Faith Ashburn's name lit up the display.

He glanced at his watch. Only seven thirty-five and on a Sunday morning. He'd hoped he might hear from her, but he definitely hadn't expected her to call this soon. He doubted it was personal, which meant she was calling about Cornell.

"Detective Travis Dalton," he answered. "What can I do for you?"

"Travis, this is Faith."

He liked the way she said his name. He didn't like the tremor of apprehension in her voice. "Hi, Faith. Nice to hear from you."

"It's…" She paused. "I need to talk to you, as a detective. It's about my son."

"Cornell?"

"You know about his disappearance?"

"I didn't until a few minutes ago. I just finished reading the missing-person report."

"There's a new development," she said.

"Since last night?"

"Yes."

"What kind of development?"

"I'd rather not talk about it over the phone. Actually, I suppose I should call Mark Ethridge, but I'm not even sure he's kept the investigation open, and you did offer to help."

"Don't worry about the chain of command. I'll handle that. I was going to talk to Ethridge about the case, anyway. When do you want to get together?"

"As soon as possible."

"Right now works for me. How about breakfast?"

"That would be great. I can meet you anywhere you say."

"I'm almost finished up here, so how about I pick you up at your place?"

"What time?"

He reached for the form she'd filled out, and checked her home address. It was probably a twenty-minute drive in light Sunday-morning traffic. "Is a half hour from now too soon?"

"That would be perfect, but, Travis…" She paused again. Unsure of him or facing new fears? He couldn't tell which.

"Go on," he urged.

"Don't mention to Joni or Leif that I called you."

"Joni surely knows your son is missing."

"Yes. They both do. Leif even offered to hire a private detective to help find him."

"You turned him down?"

"I'd already hired one."

That, Travis hadn't known. "Your decision," he said. "You don't have to admit to anyone you called me, if that's how you want it."

"It's just that I don't want to spoil Joni and Leif's honeymoon, and there's nothing either of them can do.

Besides, Joni has spent enough time holding my hand and crying with me over the last ten months."

"Then this is our secret," he said. "See you in half an hour. I'll try to offer more than a hand or a shoulder to cry on—though I have both if they're needed."

"Just help me find Cornell and bring him home."

Travis couldn't promise to bring him home. Cornell would have a say in that. But he would find him. Hopefully, alive.

He left the precinct and headed to her house. She lived in a neighborhood of small brick homes built close together, with well-tended yards. No gated access. Few trees. Driveways sported basketball hoops.

A young man pushed a baby stroller down the narrow sidewalk. An attractive woman in white shorts and a knit shirt walked behind them, keeping a close watch on a toddler who was pedaling furiously on her bright red trike.

It looked to be a good middle-class neighborhood to grow up in. Much nicer than the one Travis had lived in for the first few years after his mother's death.

Then, most of the houses had been in need of repair and drive-by shootings were as commonplace as his foster father's drunken binges.

Travis figured if it hadn't been for his mother's influence during the early years and Leif's efforts to rescue him from the ghetto, he might have grown up as troubled and in trouble as the young punks who committed most of the crimes in Dallas.

He turned at the corner and started checking addresses. Faith's house was in the middle of the block, a redbrick with white trim. The hedges were neatly groomed. Colorful pansies and snapdragons overflowed from pots by her door. In spite of her grief, she was keeping up appearances. Probably wanted home to be welcoming if or when Cornell showed up again.

Travis pulled into the driveway and took the walk to her covered entry. She opened the door seconds after he pushed the bell, handbag in hand, clearly ready to go.

"You're prompt," she said, stepping out the door without inviting him in.

"Also loyal, and I floss after every meal."

A quick smile played on her lips but didn't penetrate the veil of apprehension that covered her eyes.

She walked in front of him to his car. The white jean shorts she wore were cuffed at mid-thigh. Not too tight, but fitted enough to accentuate the sway of her hips. A teal blouse tied at the waist. The morning sun painted golden highlights in her dark hair.

He had to hurry to reach the door and open it for her before she climbed in on her own. He got a whiff of her flowery perfume as she slid past him. Crazy urges bucked around inside him. Not the time or the place, he reminded himself. Business only—at least until Cornell was found.

"There's a breakfast spot in a strip center just a few blocks from here," Faith said. "I hear they have good pancakes."

"Do you like pancakes?" he asked.

"I used to, when I was a kid. I usually just have toast and coffee for breakfast now. I doubt my stomach will even tolerate that this morning."

"No appetite, huh? Is that because of the new development you're going to tell me about?"

She nodded, and he thought again how youthful she looked to be the mother of a teenager. She'd said she was thirty-five, which meant she'd given birth to him at seventeen. There must be a story there, as well.

"Tell me where to go," he said.

He followed her directions. The restaurant was small, noisy and crowded. Not the best spot for a serious conversation."

"Any chance we can get a seat on the patio?" he asked the young blonde hostess.

"How many in your party?"

"Two."

"I think I can manage that."

She smiled and led them to a table in the middle of the patio.

"How about that table in the back?" he asked.

"Okay with me, but it doesn't have an umbrella, so you're going to be in the sun."

But it would give them a lot more privacy. He looked to Faith.

"The sun is fine with me," she said.

Once they were seated, the hostess set two menus in front of them and announced that the waitress would be with them shortly.

"I didn't realize the place would be so noisy," Faith said. "I just need to talk and this was the closest café I could think of."

Her apprehension seemed to be growing. He scooted his menu aside. "Let's hear it. I can't do anything about solving the problem until I know what it is."

She clasped her hands in front of her. "I got a phone call from Cornell just before daybreak this morning."

Travis hadn't seen that coming. Even if he had, he would have expected it to be good news. Hearing the kid was alive made him feel a hell of a lot better, and he didn't even know him.

"What did he say?"

"That he was sorry."

"That's a good start. Sorry for what?"

"He didn't say."

"Where is he?"

"I asked, but he didn't answer that, either."

"He must have said something more than 'I'm sorry' to have you this upset."

"It's what he didn't say that has me so afraid, Travis. The call was a cry for help. I have to find out where he was when he made that call. That's why I came to you."

The waitress appeared at their elbow. "Are you ready to order?"

"Just coffee for now," Travis said. "Black."

"Same for me," Faith said, "except I'll need cream and an artificial sweetener."

"Something got lost in translation," Travis said as the waitress walked away. "The dots between 'I'm sorry' and the call being a cry for help don't connect for me. Start at the beginning and tell me exactly what was said."

The waitress returned with their coffee. Faith stirred in the cream and sweetener slowly, as if she was trying to get her thoughts together. Finally, she looked up and locked her gaze with his.

"'Mom,'" she murmured. "I answered the phone and heard 'Mom.'" She picked up her napkin and used it to dab a tear from the corner of her right eye. More moisture gathered. "At that point I think I went into momentary shock."

In Travis's mind she wasn't far from shock now, just having to relive the moment.

"After ten months of silence, I can see why that jolted you," Travis said.

"So much so that I asked if it was really him."

"You weren't sure from the sound of his voice?"

"Only for a few seconds. My heart was beating so fast

I couldn't think. I thought I might be dreaming. But it was Cornell. I know it was. I'd know his voice anywhere."

"And after he said 'Mom'?"

"I asked him about his seizure meds. He said he'd gotten a prescription and that he was taking them. Then he just said he was sorry."

"For leaving home?"

"He didn't *leave* home." Frustration laced her voice. "At least not of his own accord. He would never do that. I told Detective Ethridge and the private detective I hired that he had no reason to leave home. I don't think either of them ever believed me, but a mother knows her son. At least I know Cornell."

Travis reached across the table and laid his hands on top of hers. "I believe you, Faith. I'm just trying to see the whole picture here so I can get a handle on the situation. It would help if he'd said what he was sorry for."

"He never got the chance to tell me. Someone started yelling curses in the background. Before he could say more, the connection was broken, either by Cornell or by the person who was yelling at him."

"Was the voice in the background male or female?"

"Male. I pushed *69 and tried to redial the number, but it wouldn't come up. I called the phone company. They were no help, either. But you're a homicide detective. You must have ways to get that number."

"Did he call your cell phone or landline?"

"The house phone. I can give you my number."

"I'll need that for starters, but I'd like to take a look around Cornell's room and also check out his computer."

"Arsenio checked the computer thoroughly."

"Arsenio?"

"Arsenio Gomez, the P.I. I hired. He said there was nothing there to lead him to Cornell."

"I'd like to look for myself."

"Of course. Do anything that you think might help us find my son. Please, just do it quickly, before the lead grows cold again."

"I'll do everything I can to help you find Cornell, Faith. But first we need to set a few ground rules."

Faith met his gaze head-on, suspicion arching her brows. "What kind of ground rules?"

"I expect the truth from you, the total truth."

"I have no reason to lie."

"No, but sometimes it's difficult for parents to face up to the truth about their child. If there's any indication that Cornell was on drugs or mixed up with a gang, I need to know that up front. Not to judge him. But it might change the way I go about the investigation."

Faith yanked her hands away from his. Her lips grew taut, her eyes fiery. "I know what you read in his missing-person file, Travis. I know what his friends said about him and that he was seen at the Passion Pit, but Cornell was only eighteen. He may have made some bad decisions. But he wasn't a thug or an addict. He didn't leave home by choice, and wherever he is, he's being held against his will. I'm as sure of that as I am that my name is Faith Ashburn or that today is Sunday."

Travis wasn't convinced, but he did understand her desperation. It was a dangerous world out there. No one knew that better than him.

Which brought up another issue. "There's one other ground rule," Travis said.

"Do you always have so many rules?"

"All depends on the game I find myself in."

"So what's the rule?"

"You leave the investigating to me. No more trips to the Passion Pit or any other questionable location."

"I'm smart enough to know how to avoid trouble."

"I'm questioning your judgment, not your intelligence. I saw you in action, remember? Besides, I have a lot more experience and muscle than you, and I wouldn't go near that dive if I wasn't carrying a weapon."

"If it's that dangerous, why don't the police shut the club down and put Georgio out of business?"

Georgio. Merely hearing his name from her lips made Travis sick. "What do you know about Georgio?"

"Just that he's the owner of the Passion Pit."

"And an offspring of the devil. Stay away from him, Faith. That's an order."

The waitress returned with refills. This time Travis ordered two eggs, over easy, with sausage, grits, biscuits and gravy, without bothering to look at the menu. Faith ordered a slice of wheat toast.

"If you'll give me your home phone number now, I'll make a call and get the ball rolling," Travis said.

She took a pen from her purse and scribbled the number down on a paper napkin. "How long will it take to track the call?"

"Depends on where the call was made from. If luck's on our side, we could have the phone number by the time we finish breakfast."

"In minutes." She sounded almost breathless. "Cornell could be home in time for dinner."

Damn. He should never have gotten her hopes up like that. "Don't count on instant gratification," he cautioned. "Have to take things one step at a time, but if we discover where that call was made from, we'll be one huge leap ahead of where you were when you went to bed last night."

"I'll take that," she said. "But if we find out where he called from, we should be able to find him."

They would have to play this smart. No rushing in without knowing for certain what they were up against. If Cornell was really being held against his will, making a foolish mistake could get him killed.

At this point, the best they could hope for was that Cornell Ashburn had just developed a sudden taste for independence, women and drugs, and taken a leave of absence from home to satisfy his cravings.

He definitely wouldn't be the first eighteen-year-old to sow his wild oats. Travis knew that firsthand.

He put the search for the phone number in motion and then his focus returned to Faith Ashburn. She wasn't beautiful, but she was attractive and natural. Her smile, her eyes, her intensity—it all got to him.

And it was meshing with an overwhelming need to protect her and get to know her better. Maybe it was the wedding thing. Seeing Leif so happy to settle down with one woman could be addling Travis's brain.

If he was smart, he'd turn this back over to Mark Ethridge and run for the hills. But even if he wanted to, he couldn't do that. Not with the possibility that her son's disappearance could in any way be connected to the four others who had gone missing over the past nineteen months and turned up dead. The pressure was on to solve the case before another young man lost his life.

A young man like Cornell.

In spite of his concerns, when the waitress arrived with the food, Travis dived in like a starving man. If he let worry or even murder interfere with his eating, he'd have to go on life support.

He didn't hear back about the origins of Faith's early-morning call during breakfast or on the drive back to her house. Once there, he went straight to Cornell's room and began searching with the same intensity he'd use for a fresh crime scene.

Travis pulled several boxes from the back of the closet. One held a half-dozen pairs of tennis shoes, two jackets that were too heavy for Dallas winters and a pair of hiking boots.

"Cornell loved outdoor activities," Faith said by way of explanation. "Skiing, hiking, white-water rafting, horseback riding. His dad's brother used to own a condo in the Colorado Rockies, and Cornell visited him with his dad several times. He loved it out there, even talked about moving there one day."

"Have you checked with his uncle to see if he was with him?"

"His uncle died in a snowmobile accident three years ago, just a year before Cornell's father was killed while working on an oil rig in the Gulf of Mexico. My son has never fully gotten over those deaths."

"That would be hard on anyone." And it definitely gave Cornell a reason to be troubled. "How old was Cornell when you got divorced?"

"Ten. That's when I met Joni. I needed some job skills, so I went back for an associate degree."

Faith's house phone rang. She gasped and grabbed her chest as she ran to answer it. Travis followed, listening in on the conversation until he was certain Cornell wasn't the caller.

He went back to the boy's room alone to continue the search. All he found was typical teenage stuff. A worn baseball glove. Video games. Old comic books. Some swimming trophies from when he was in grade school.

Nothing that provided even a hint or a clue of where Cornell might have gone or why. Travis had started to put them back in place when he noticed a smaller box pushed to the back of the shelf. He took it down, opened it and peered inside.

A porn magazine stared back at him. He lifted it to find eight more, all with pictures of naked women, nothing sadistic or particularly kinky.

All well hidden from his mother.

No surprise. Guys of eighteen seldom confided those kinds of thoughts and activities to their mothers. But if Travis and Faith were going to find Cornell, they would have to go into this with their eyes wide open.

He stuck his head out the bedroom door. "Faith, want to come in here a minute?"

She arrived a few seconds later, breathless from racing up the stairs. The look on her face was expectant, downright hopeful.

He hated that what he had to show her would replace it with a kick in the gut. He tried to think of something to make this easier on her, but he'd never been great at dancing around the truth.

He set the box on the table. "This might explain why Cornell was spotted at the Passion Pit."

Faith pushed back the cover of the top magazine with one finger, as if was too disgusting to touch. Tough on a mother to find out her baby wasn't one.

Travis's cell phone vibrated. Caller ID indicated it was from the precinct. "I need to take this," he said.

Faith nodded.

His focus quickly switched to the call and the information relayed to him by one of the younger officers recently appointed to serve under him in the homicide division.

The news was not good.

Chapter Four

Travis's find made Faith sick to her stomach. She steadied herself against the bedpost while she tried to put the magazines into perspective.

So he wasn't as innocent and naive as she'd believed. It was only natural he'd have the same physical urges as other boys his age. That still didn't explain his disappearance.

Or the interrupted phone call. Or why he hadn't called back.

But she hated that it had taken ten months to find out that her son had porn hidden in his room. That probably wouldn't have helped her or the police find him. But what else had been going on in his life that she didn't suspect?

Had he grown from a kid to a man without her realizing it? When had she lost touch with him?

Faith looked up, suddenly aware of the gravity in Travis's low, deep-toned voice as he talked on the phone, and wondered if he was talking about Cornell or one of his homicide cases.

She studied the lines and planes of his profile. His face was tanned, his brows as dark as his hair, his face narrowing into a prominent chin and jawline.

He wasn't pretty-boy handsome, but he was definitely the kind of man who'd stand out in a crowd. The archetype of strength and masculinity. His looks and manner instilled confidence. If anyone could find Cornell, it would be Travis Dalton.

Or was it her own desperation that made her read those qualities into him? If so, it was a mistake she couldn't afford to make.

"Disturbing news?" she asked once he'd broken the connection and returned the phone to his pocket.

"Could have been better."

"Does it have to do with Cornell?"

"Afraid so."

A new wave of apprehension flooded though her. "Were they able to trace the call?"

"Yes and no."

"What does that mean?"

"We have a general location, but not a specific one."

"But a general location is better than nothing," she insisted. "It gives us an area to start searching for him."

"A very large and undefined area. The call was made from Texas, somewhere near the Mexican border south of San Antonio. But the phone used to make the call was purchased in Mexico. That places Cornell either north or south of the border."

"Doesn't the phone-service company have an address for the subscriber?"

"It's not registered to a subscriber."

"So it's like one of those phones you can buy at a convenience store with a certain number of minutes included."

"Exactly."

"So all we really know is that Cornell is somewhere near the Mexican border." Terror rumbled inside her. The border towns were known for their violent drug cartels, especially on the Mexico side.

Murders had risen to the point that few Americans ventured into them. Most of the police were rumored to be corrupt or so afraid of the cartels they couldn't do their job. She and Cornell had watched a special about that on TV just last year. He'd been disgusted with the whole idea of criminals running over honest citizens.

"Cornell would never have gone to Mexico on his own," Faith said. She dropped to the side of the bed. "He's been abducted, Travis. I'm more certain of that than ever now. I have to find him, even if it means going into Mexico." Her voice rose with her growing hysteria.

Travis shoved the magazines aside, dropped to the bed beside her. "I know how frightened you are, Faith, but believe me, going down there won't help, and it could put you in danger."

"Then what will help, Travis? Sitting here doing nothing? Endless talking and promises from Mark Ethridge and now you? Waiting to hear that my son has been…"

A shudder ripped through her. Tears burned her eyes and then began to roll down her cheeks.

Travis snaked an arm around her shoulder. She started to push away from him, but the pain overpowered her stubbornness. Impulsively, she dropped her head to his shoulder and submitted to the ragged sobs.

Travis didn't say a word until she'd cried herself out and pulled herself together. Even then, he didn't move his arm from around her shoulder.

She pulled away. Talk. For ten months all the police had given her was talk. Why had she ever thought Travis would be different?

"I have connections in the towns on both sides of the border, Faith. Let me speak with them and put them on alert," Travis pleaded. "They know how to handle this, who to talk to, where to look."

"Then why haven't the police already done that?"

"I'm sure they have, but I'll put on the pressure. Give me forty-eight hours. If we don't have a lead by then, I'll make a trip to the area."

Faith walked to the other side of the room before turning back to him. "Anything could happen in forty-eight hours."

"Anything could have happened in the last ten months," Travis said. "But you heard Cornell's voice. You know he's alive, and he didn't actually tell you he was in danger when he called."

"If he wasn't being held against his will, he'd be home. I don't know why I can't make anyone understand that."

"I'm trying, Faith. Believe me, I'm looking at this from all angles. I'd like to take Cornell's computer with me to see what additional information I can glean from it."

"It's a waste of time. Officer Ethridge and the private investigator I hired have both already checked the computer out and found nothing. Nothing suspicious on his email or any of his social-media pages. And nothing in the websites he'd visited offered so much as one decent lead."

"I'd like to take that a step further," Travis said. "The DPD has one of the best computer forensics experts in the country. He can discover ambient data that the average Joe has no idea exists on the hard drive. He's found critical information to help me solve a murder case more times than I can count."

"What kind of data do you expect to find?"

"It's the unexpected that usually produces the best evidence. I'll see if I can get a rush on this."

Travis's dedication seemed genuine, and if she could believe his rhetoric, he was ready to make finding Cornell a priority. But why? He was a homicide detective. This was way outside his line of duty.

"Why are you taking this on with such fervor, Travis? This isn't your job. It isn't you responsibility."

"Let's just say any friend of my new sister-in-law's is a friend of mine. And from what I hear, you're her best friend, practically family."

"And from what I hear, you don't even claim kin to your own father."

"There is that," Travis admitted. "So I guess we'll have to go with that I'm one of the good guys."

Strangely, she believed him. Yet she wasn't convinced he understood the urgency. All her instincts stressed that the call from Cornell had been a sign that his fear was growing. He'd taken a risk to call her, and someone else had heard him on the phone. They were running out of time.

"You'll let me know immediately if you hear anything at all?" she insisted as they went back downstairs.

"I promise. You do the same. If you hear from Cornell, call me at once."

"I will, and I pray that's tonight."

"Keep that thought." Travis stopped at the foot of the stairs. "I have a few more questions, but I need to get started with what I have, talk to my contacts, call in some favors."

All things that should have been done months before. Instead, Cornell had simply fallen through the cracks. She really wanted to believe it would be different this time, that Travis was as good as his word.

But did she trust him enough to cancel her appointment with Georgio tomorrow? A man like that didn't play by the rules, but he got things done. At least that was the impression she'd gotten anytime his name had come up while she was hanging out in his territory, searching for Cornell.

Travis stepped out the front door. Then, propping his hand against the doorframe, he leaned in close.

Awareness zinged through her. Her response to his nearness was unwelcome, almost frightening. She was thirty-five years old. She'd been married and divorced. Her son was missing and likely in danger. She didn't fall for men she'd just met.

It was just that her nerves were so rattled her emotions couldn't be trusted.

"Remember the ground rules," he warned. "No putting yourself in danger. Leave the investigation up to me."

"Then find my son."

She took a backward step, willing her mind to focus only on Cornell. Still, as she watched Travis turn and saunter down the walk, she couldn't help wondering what it would be like to have his arms around her for something more than to offer comfort.

A DROP OF MAYONNAISE dripped from Faith's cheese sandwich onto the granite countertop. Grabbing a napkin, she dabbed her mouth and then wiped up the spill. Eating dinner while standing at the counter had become a habit since Cornell's disappearance, a way of avoiding the empty feeling of sitting at the table without him.

Faith took another bite of the tasteless sandwich and then crushed it into the napkin and tossed it into the trash. Before Cornell had gone missing, Sunday nights had been her favorite time of the week. She and Cornell had initiated it as family night right after the divorce, and with few exceptions, they always spent it together.

They'd order in a pepperoni pizza—Cornell's favorite—and wash it down with icy glasses of root beer as they watched a movie in the family room. Most of the time Cornell picked the flick, so in recent years there had been no shortage of car chases, explosions, villains and heroes. Not Faith's genre of choice, but relaxing with Cornell had been worth enduring the gore.

Her phone rang. Hope sent a jolt to her heart, making it bounce off the walls of her chest. She grabbed the phone.

"Hello."

"Hi. It's me, Joni."

Faith swallowed the disappointment and tried to keep her tone light. "You're on your honeymoon. What are you doing wasting your time calling me?"

"I just wanted to say thanks again for being my maid of honor last night."

"You're welcome. It was a beautiful wedding."

"It was. I feel so lucky to be part of the Dalton clan. As soon as we get our house finished, you'll have to come out and stay a few days."

"Sure. I'd like that. But you didn't have to call and tell me that from your honeymoon, not with that gorgeous hunk you're married to."

"Actually, that's not the only reason I called. I wanted to make sure you're all right."

"Why wouldn't I…?" Her mind answered the question before she finished asking it. "You must have talked to Travis."

"He called Leif. He said he was going to help you find Cornell."

"Is that all he told him?"

"Is there more?"

Joni was already worried about her. There was no point in lying. "I had a phone call from Cornell this morning."

"That's great news. You must be so relieved to know he's alive and safe."

"I know he's alive. I don't' know that he's safe. If he wasn't being held against his will, he wouldn't have just called and said nothing. He'd be home."

"Travis said you took the call as a cry for help."

"How else can I take it? You know Cornell, Joni. You know how close we were."

"I do know, Faith. That's why I called. I was hoping to reassure you."

"How can you, unless Travis told Leif something he hasn't told me?"

"I only know what Leif told me. He said Travis is committed to finding Cornell. And according to Leif, once Travis makes up his mind to do something, you can consider it done. I thought it might help if you heard that."

"Thanks."

"So trust him, Faith. Get some sleep tonight and try not to worry."

"I'll try."

Leif's confidence in his brother was reassuring, but even as she finished the conversation with Joni and broke the connection, Faith knew she'd never have a moment's peace until she was face-to-face with her missing son and could see that he was unharmed.

That was why at noon tomorrow, she'd make her way to the Passion Pit. She'd ignore Travis's ground rules and keep her appointment with a mysterious man from the dangerous underbelly of the city.

She'd do whatever she had to do to find her son—inside or outside the law.

Chapter Five

Cornell turned the water as hot as it would go, picked up the bar of soap and rubbed his hands vigorously. Staring at the drain as the bubbles spun into the pipes, he felt the memories hit again.

The liquid instantly changed from clear to a bright crimson. His hands were sticky. His throat was so dry he couldn't swallow. He took deep breaths, trying to keep from throwing up into the sink and having the vomit mix with the blood. Sickeningly, the way it had done that first morning after the murder.

The room began to spin and he closed his eyes and clutched the edge of the stained sink to keep from falling. Finally, the horrifying sensations passed.

When Cornell opened his eyes again, it was only water spraying over his fingers to disappear down the drain. He turned off the faucet, grabbed the worn, faded towel and dried his hands.

"You okay?" Tom Snyder asked as Cornell walked out of the bathroom. "You're not about to have one of those seizures, are you?"

He shrugged. "What if I do?"

"I don't like 'em. They freak me out."

"*You* don't like them?" Cornell muttered a few curse words that he'd never have uttered around his mother.

Not that he got any thrill out of cussing. When it was all you ever heard, it got to be habit. "What the hell do you think they do for me?"

"Obviously make you insane."

"Well, they never did before. Anyway, I'm not having a seizure."

"Good. But no more stupid stunts like calling your mother. Georgio would throw you to the wolves if he knew about that."

"Don't worry. I won't make that mistake again." But not for the reasons Tom was talking about. Hearing his mother's voice had done strange things to Cornell's thinking. Made him so homesick that it was all he could do not to cry. Made him ache to open up and tell his mother everything.

But what would that do except destroy her? She'd try to love him the way she always had, but how could she once she knew what he'd done? And in the end, there was nothing she could do to change any of it.

"Want to go out and get a margarita?" Tom asked. "Looks like we're gonna be stuck here for another night. Might even get a little action, if you know what I mean."

Cornell knew what he meant. "You go ahead. I think I'm going to hit the sack early tonight."

"Man, if you get any more boring, even the cockroaches are going to quit hanging around."

"I can live with that."

"Suit yourself."

Cornell could live without the cockroaches, but he wasn't sure how much longer he could live with Tom and having no control over his life. He couldn't go home, but that didn't mean he had to do slave duty for Georgio for the rest of his days.

Not if things worked out the way he planned.

Chapter Six

Faith parked her car at approximately a quarter hour before her noon appointment with Georgio. This time she was dressed comfortably in black slacks and a white blouse. The turquoise cardigan she had thrown over her shoulders was not for the weather, which had turned quite warm, but because people in Dallas tended to keep their air-conditioning blasting from the first sign of spring well into October.

She looked around as she got out of the car. It was a fairly safe area in spite of the bars and clubs that were on almost every corner. Someone had told her once that it was because Georgio was the law around here and trouble was bad for business. All she knew was that he was a hard man to get to talk to—unless he decided he wanted to deal with you.

It was an old section of town, a mix of decaying residential structures and businesses that were struggling or out of business. Many of those had boarded-up windows and were decorated with fading graffiti.

Two elderly ladies were checking out baskets of fresh produce set just outside the front door of a mom-and-pop grocery store. A few adolescent boys were recklessly darting through traffic on their skateboards. One man shook his fist out his car window and yelled at them to get out of the way. They laughed and kept going.

Three elderly men sat on a bench in front of the barbershop, chatting. An overweight woman with frizzled brown hair was sweeping the walk in front of a hair and nail salon. She looked up and smiled, the lines around her eyes crinkling as Faith hurried past.

Faith hesitated at the double doors to the Passion Pit and then pushed through them, head high. No more pretending she had any business in this establishment except finding her son.

An attractive blonde in tight-fitting black shorts and a scrap of top that covered little more than her nipples greeted her.

"I'm here to see Georgio," Faith said.

The hostess barely glanced at her before tossing her hair and studying the glittery red polish on her long nails as if she was totally bored. "If you're looking for a job, you'll have to talk to Laney. He does all the hiring, but he won't be here until after four."

"I'm not looking for work. My name is Faith Ashburn. I have an appointment with Georgio," she said firmly.

"In that case, wait here and I'll see if he's available."

He'd better be available. If he wasn't, Faith would stage a sit-in at his office door until he was. No way was she going to be given the runaround today, the way she had been for the past ten months.

The first time she'd tried to talk to Georgio—before she knew anything about him except that he was the owner of the club where Cornell had been spotted before his disappearance—she'd just walked up to him one night and started asking questions.

Okay, accosted him and accused him of luring underage kids into his depraved establishment. She'd stuck

Cornell's picture in his face and demanded to know if he'd seen her son.

His bulging-muscled bodyguards took over from there, appearing like attack dogs called to defend. They'd escorted her to the door and forbade her to return, with threats of arrest and prosecution.

Another reason she'd started dressing in full slut regalia whenever she went searching for Cornell.

But that hadn't stopped her from trying to get in touch with Georgio. She'd called at least a dozen times to request the opportunity to talk to him about her son. She'd never gotten past his assistant, Laney, who'd been no help at all.

But today was different. This time Georgio had initiated their visit. Apparently, he'd finally noticed the flyers she was continuously posting around the neighborhood, and had mentally paired Cornell's last name with that of the woman whose calls he'd been ignoring for months.

Hopefully, some of her hard work was finally going to pay off.

Faith followed the hostess down a narrow hallway with a multitude of doors, mostly closed. At the end of it, the seductive young woman tapped on one and announced that Faith was here.

"Show her in."

The voice was deep. The broad-shouldered, well-dressed man who looked her up and down as she entered his office was younger than she'd remembered—early fifties or thereabouts. He was no less intimidating, even without his bodyguards.

She took a deep breath and stared him down. Cornell's life was at stake. She wouldn't be bullied into not going through with this.

"Have a seat, Ms. Ashburn." Georgio motioned to the

leather chair near his desk. She sat, crossing her legs and taking in the expensive furnishings. There was no doubt about his financial success. The hostess left them alone, closing the door behind her.

Georgio continued to stand for a few seconds, towering above the massive desk. He was several inches over six feet tall, with thick salt-and-pepper hair, neatly coiffed. He wasn't bad looking, but his square face and dominating jawline gave him a tough ruffian look in spite of his impressive suit and tie.

When he finally sat down, he leaned back in his chair and smiled. "What can I help you with, Ms. Ashburn?"

She had an idea that he knew exactly why she was here. He didn't seem like a man who liked surprises.

"My son, Cornell Ashburn, is missing," she said, the tremble returning to her voice the way it always did when she was forced to say the dreaded words out loud.

"So you must be responsible for the many flyers I've noticed in the area."

"Yes. I'm glad someone's seen them. They seem to disappear as soon as I put them up. I'm offering a twenty-five-thousand-dollar reward for information leading me to him." The total amount left in her savings account.

Georgio propped his fingertips together and let his penetrating stare lock with hers. "Then I'd be surprised to learn you're not getting a few calls."

"Not even one."

"I'm sorry to hear that. Have the police had better luck?"

"Not much. Nor did the private detective I hired. You're my last hope."

His brows arched. "Exactly how is it you think I can be of service?"

"The Passion Pit is one of the last places my son was seen before he disappeared."

"Really? Was he here with friends?"

"No. Apparently he was here alone."

"And you say he came in here before he went missing?"

"Yes, but only a few nights before."

"Do you know that for a fact?"

"The police questioned you and showed you his picture. You told them that you'd seen him in here yourself on at least two different occasions. One of your dancers also recognized him, only she said he'd been a regular over the last few months."

"How long ago was that?"

"Ten months."

Georgio's face registered surprise. "No wonder I don't remember. I own not only the Passion Pit but two other gentlemen's clubs as well, both busier and more impressive than this one. A lot of young men have walked through my doors since then."

"But surely not all of them went missing."

"Why did you wait so long to come talk to me?" Georgio asked.

"I didn't." She tried unsuccessfully to hide her irritation. "I've called countless times. You either ignored the messages I left or decided not to see me."

Faith pulled Cornell's picture from the side pocket of her handbag and handed it to him. "This is my son's yearbook picture from last year. It was taken several months before he disappeared. It's the same picture the police showed you."

Georgio studied the photo. "Nice clean-cut young man, but if he was in high school, he was too young to be hanging out at the Passion Pit. He would never have gotten past the front door."

"He shouldn't have, but he did. You told Detective Ethridge you realized he was underage and kicked him out."

"We follow policy." He dropped the picture to the desk. "I wish I could help you, Ms. Ashburn, but I haven't seen your son around the club. But if I do, I'll definitely give you a call. How old is he?"

"Eighteen. I know what you're thinking. But he didn't just choose to move out. Cornell's not like that. He's..."

The words caught in her throat. When she tried to tell people about Cornell, she made him sound weak and nerdy. But that wasn't it.

She took a deep breath. "I know my son. He would never have just left and shut me out of his life."

"So you think he met with foul play?"

"Yes. I'm convinced of it, more than ever since the phone call."

Georgio leaned forward, showing the first traces of concern. "Cornell called you?"

She fed him the details as succinctly as possible.

"I can certainly understand your worry, Faith. May I call you Faith?"

"Please do." Especially if that meant he was warming up to her and considering offering his help.

Georgio stood and walked to the front of the desk, leaning back against it so that he was looking directly at her. "I can see how upset you are, but what makes you think I can do more than the police have done?"

"You don't have to keep to the strictures of the law."

A satisfied smile crossed his lips, as if she'd paid him a compliment. If it took flattery to bring him around, she could dish it out.

"I know you're a rich and powerful man with many

contacts," she said, feeding his ego. "If anyone can help me find Cornell and bring him home safely, I think it's you."

"I'm not sure how you reached that conclusion, but I'll tell you what, Faith. I like you and I can tell you're worried sick. I can't make any promises, but I'll see what I can find out."

Her pulse began to race. All these months of searching with little real progress, and now both Travis and Georgio were offering their help. That had to be a good sign.

"Time is of the essence," she urged.

"Okay, but don't go expecting miracles, Faith."

"I have to. If I didn't, I'd never be able to keep going."

Georgio nodded. "Then we'll see what we can do. But there is one thing you should know."

"What's that?"

"I run an honest business here and in my other Dallas nightclubs as well, but I don't work with the police."

"Why is that?"

"Let's just say they don't appreciate some of the finer points of my business. If I'm going to help you find your son, let's keep them off the radar. Don't mention to anyone with the Dallas Police Department that you've even talked to me."

"If that's the way you want it."

"It's the way I insist it be."

That should be easy enough, since Travis had warned her to stay away from Georgio.

"This is between you and me," she promised. "When can you start?"

He smiled. "You do get down to business. I like that. I'll make some calls today, see what I can dig up."

"Is there anything else you'll need from me?"

"Perhaps. But not yet." He picked up the photo again. "May I keep this?"

"Absolutely."

His desk phone rang. "Excuse me for a minute." He punched a button on the receiver and took the call. From his end of the conversation she could tell that he didn't like what he was hearing.

"Something's come up that requires my immediate attention," he told her when he'd finished. "But I have your number and I'll get back with you soon."

"I'll be waiting for your call." That was the understatement of the century. She let herself out and started down the long hallway.

She couldn't deny the relief that his promise of help had stirred, but her nerves were still on edge. Travis had been specific. She was to stay away from Georgio and the Passion Pit and let him handle this.

If it came down to which of the two men she trusted more, it was definitely Travis. But he was a cop. Georgio was an inside man. She needed them both and couldn't afford to turn down any offer of help. Travis should understand that.

She picked up her pace, eager to get back into the sunshine and grab a cup of coffee before going to her office. Her boss had been extremely understanding over the past months, but they were shorthanded this week and she had to carry her load.

She rummaged in her handbag for her keys as she walked. She could hear the music coming from the club now, and footfalls and low voices.

Travis's voice. Her heart pounded. She stopped dead still and listened. What would he be doing here in the middle of the day on a Monday?

But it was him, apparently just around the corner and

walking toward her. She so did not need this. At the last second, she ducked into an open doorway and pulled the door closed behind her.

She barely breathed until she heard him pass. From the sound of the footsteps and voices, she guessed he was with another detective.

Were they here to question Georgio about Cornell or as part of a homicide investigation? Was Georgio in some kind of trouble? Was that why he wanted nothing to do with the police? Whatever the reason, he had clearly been irritated at their arrival.

She waited until the voices and footsteps had faded into the distance before cracking the door enough to peek out and see into the hall. There was no sign of Travis. Her insides rolled as she slipped out of the room and walked as fast as she could to her car.

A sudden and frightening premonition sent cold chills up her spine as she climbed behind the wheel. Involving Georgio in her search might turn out to be the worst mistake of her life.

THE REST OF the day passed at a slow crawl. When she heard the cleaning crew outside her door, she glanced up at the clock. It was 7:00 p.m. No wonder the office had grown so quiet.

One of the maids stuck her head inside Faith's office. "You're so quiet I didn't realize you were still here."

"I'm wrapping up. I'll be out of your way in about ten minutes."

"Don't hurry for me. I got all night in this building. I can always come back and catch your office."

"I need to get of here, anyway." Not that she had anywhere to go but her empty house.

She used to love her job. Loved the challenges it presented and the office camaraderie. She hadn't loved anything for the past ten months, but the routine kept her occupied and the work kept her sane.

Thunder was rumbling in the distance by the time she reached home, and bolts of lightning created a fiery display as a storm rolled in. Huge drops began to splatter on her windshield as she pulled into the driveway.

She wondered if Cornell was watching the same storm blow in. When he was little he'd come running to her bed at the first clap of thunder. That had been so long ago.

She'd hoped to hear from Travis this afternoon with news of helpful information he'd gained from the analysis of Cornell's computer. He hadn't called. Neither had Georgio.

New pangs of guilt hit as she closed the garage door and then stepped into the mudroom. She hated lying to Travis about Georgio. Hated it so much she'd almost called him a couple times this afternoon. Once she'd actually started punching in his number before she broke the connection and put her phone away.

Even now she was tempted to call him. She could invite him over for dinner. Stupid idea. He was a busy cop. He'd call when he had news. He wouldn't be interested in spending the evening with a desperate mother who did nothing but whine and wallow in missing her almost-grown son.

If only she knew Cornell was safe.

Thunder hit again, this time so loud it rattled the windows. She made herself a sandwich, poured a glass of white wine and settled in front of the TV.

She was just in time to catch the hook for the evening news.

"Tonight at ten, Lieutenant Marilyn Sylvester of the Dallas Police Department will give further details about the murder of Scott Mitchell, the seventeen-year-old Dallas high-school student whose body was found floating in the Trinity River last week."

The bite of sandwich in Faith's mouth suddenly tasted like cardboard. This was the reason she'd practically quit watching TV altogether. News of murders or abductions gnawed at her stomach and her control like rabid rats. She turned off the set and picked up a magazine.

She thumbed through the pages. Beautiful women dressed in the latest fashion. Probably the kind of women Travis dated. Women who were fun and made him laugh, with no problems more significant than what color to paint their nails that week.

Or he might have a special woman in his life, maybe even a live-in. Only if he did, he hadn't brought her to the wedding. But that didn't mean he wasn't making out with her right now.

"Jeez!"

Faith tossed the magazine back to the coffee table. What was wrong with her that she was having these bizarre and unwanted thoughts about Travis? It had to be the apprehension. Or maybe just a crazy need to have a man to hold on to.

Only no other man affected her the way Travis did. Certainly Georgio hadn't.

Determined to push any sensual thoughts about Travis from her mind, she tossed the sandwich and went to do a load of laundry.

As she did she said a silent prayer that Cornell was safe and would call again tonight. And this time he'd tell her where to find him.

The phone rang two hours later, just as Faith was climbing into bed. Her heart jumped to her throat. She grabbed the phone with both hands and held it to her ear.

"Cornell."

"No."

The voice was soft and feminine. Her next words were icy, fearful, yet threatening.

Chapter Seven

"Stay away from Georgio."

Faith steadied the phone in her hand and kicked off the light blanket. Still reconciling herself to disappointment that the caller wasn't Cornell, she let the woman's words sink in.

"Who is this?" she demanded.

"Someone who knows what you're up to. I'm warning you, back off before you make things a hundred times worse."

"Worse for who? You? Georgio?"

"Yes. And for your son."

The words sent shock waves of dread rushing through Faith. She struggled to breathe. "If you know where my son is, please tell me. I beg you. Just tell me where he is."

"If he wanted you to know, he'd call you himself. Just back off and leave him be."

"I can help him. I will help him. He needs me."

But there was no one to hear the last of her words. The connection had gone dead.

Faith tried to call the number back. Not surprisingly, there was no answer. She was being jerked around. But by whom? Who would know she'd seen Georgio today?

The answer was obvious: anyone who happened to see

her in the Passion Pit today. Maybe even Travis, though he hadn't seen her. The only way he'd know she'd been there was if someone had told him.

It wouldn't have been Georgio. He'd made it clear he didn't want the cops to know he was involved in the search. But that left the hostess, perhaps a bartender or any number of employees that she hadn't noticed but who might have seen her.

And one of them did not want Faith anywhere near Georgio. Which meant the woman had to know what had happened to Cornell. She might even be behind his disappearance.

Faith needed to talk to Travis. He was a cop. He should be able to get a handle on the threat. Only discussing this with him would mean she'd have to level with him about seeing Georgio.

She rolled over and pounded her fists into her pillow, so hard that a few feathers started poking through the case. Why hadn't she given him at least a few days before defying all his stupid rules?

When her need to pummel something passed, she got up and went to the kitchen. God, she hated this empty house. It creaked and echoed, and tonight it even spit accusations at her.

Well, actually, it was rain pelting the windows and not spit she heard, but it had the same bewildering effect. She poured herself a glass of cold buttermilk, a habit she'd picked up from her granddad when she was just a kid.

He'd insisted that the clabbered cream had a soothing effect on his stomach and his mind when he couldn't sleep. It didn't work for her, but weirdly, she'd developed a taste for it. A curse of being Southern, her Yankee grandma had teased. Thanks to her mother's rebellious nature, Faith had spent far too little time with her grand-parents before they and their small car had been crushed by an eighteen-wheeler. They'd died two days before Faith's twelfth birthday. To this day, she missed them.

Faith took the milk and walked out to the covered deck, which took up about half the backyard. She dropped to a rocker and sat in the dark, watching and listening to the steady rainfall as it puddled on the lawn and rushed through the downspout.

Thoughts of her own parents filled her mind. She'd never really known her father. He and her mother had never married and he'd never been part of her life.

But there had been plenty of men around. Her mother had been involved with a series of boyfriends, marrying three of them.

She'd been going through her third divorce when Faith had met Melvin Ashburn, a surprise guest at her seven-teenth birthday party. He'd introduced her to marijuana, alcohol and sex.

And pregnancy.

But she'd never expected to face that kind of rebellion with Cornell.

Faith set the empty glass on the deck beside her, leaned back and closed her eyes. Going over the past wouldn't help. She had to deal with the here and now. Things were no longer at a standstill.

The buttermilk was useless. She should have had a whiskey.

She got up, stretched and started to walk back inside. As she did, she had the creepy feeling that someone was watching her.

Add paranoia to the mix of anguished emotions at-tacking her soul.

"I KNOW THE MEDIA is clamoring for a juicy ratings booster, Chief, but we're not dealing with a serial killer out randomly targeting innocent teenage boys."

"We have four unsolved murders in eighteen months, Travis. All boys aged eighteen or under. No suspects."

"Three of those were known gang members and drug dealers. Get rid of drug smugglers like Georgio and you might stop some of those senseless murders."

"Then get the goods on Georgio."

"I'm getting closer," Travis assured him.

"But this last victim wasn't a drug dealer or a gang member," the chief said.

"We don't know that for certain yet."

"That's the problem. We don't know much. I need a suspect on this last murder before the mayor has my ass on the line."

"We're working on it."

"So, do you and Reno have any evidence, or is this just a guessing game?"

"I have a hunch." That was it, and not much of a hunch at that.

"Trying to tie this one to Georgio, too?"

"Not to the man himself," Travis admitted. "He'd never get his own hands bloody. But the victim had been seen in the Passion Pit a few times before he was killed."

The chief scratched his whiskered chin. "Damn. I thought sexting was supposed to be taking the place of strippers." He threw up his hands. "That remark was not for citizen consumption."

"Gotcha."

"Good. Now go out and find me a suspect before I get a Mothers March on the precinct. And before someone else's son comes up dead."

Travis knew the chief. The last statement was his real

concern. It was Travis' as well. That was why he had to find Cornell Ashburn fast. He had to make sure he wasn't their next victim.

He pushed up his sleeve and checked his watch. Almost five o'clock and still no word on Cornell's computer analysis. If Travis didn't hear something soon, he'd give Clark a call.

He went back to his office and back to work. He was still hard at it when one of the clerks came in and dropped a fax on his desk.

"This just came. I figured you might be waiting around for it."

"Thanks."

Travis started to read. Clark had come through for him again. The surprises started on page two of the printout. Either Faith Ashburn had been lying to him or she had no idea what her son had been into.

It was time to get down and dirty. The fairy tales were officially off the table.

FAITH SET THE round iron table on the deck with plates, silverware, napkins and two tall glasses of water. She considered adding wineglasses and a bottle of merlot, but had no doubt that even though Travis had suggested bringing Chinese, tonight's meeting was business.

There had been no missing his avoidance when she'd asked about the findings from Cornell's computer. She was almost sure she wouldn't like what he had to tell her.

Table set and with a few minutes to spare, she went back to her bedroom to freshen up. Instead, she stood in the doorway, staring at the phone and feeling fresh pangs of guilt. Would she ever make it through the night without blurting out the truth about Georgio and the latest phone call?

She forced her eyes from the phone and her feet to her dressing table. She never wore much makeup, but even that was long gone today. Her hair was slightly tousled, but she left it like that and brushed a smidgen of color onto her cheeks and lips.

Unzipping her black pencil skirt, a staple of her work wardrobe, she stepped out of it. White shorts, she decided. Casual but chic with the black-and-white pullover she was already wearing.

Not that her appearance mattered. This wasn't a date. She didn't even remember dating. Well, she did, but only because her last one had been a disaster. It had ended with her throwing up on the man's shoes.

She'd go easy on the Chinese tonight. As rattled as her nerves were, there was definitely the possibility of an encore performance.

The doorbell rang. She yanked up the zipper on her shorts and hurried to the entry. *Please just let there be good news about Cornell.*

"HOPE YOU'RE HUNGRY," Travis said when she opened the door. Both his arms were busy juggling cartons of food. A bottle of red wine was tucked precariously under his right elbow.

"Oops. I should have told you I've already eaten this year."

He grinned. "I may have gotten a little carried away while I was ordering, but it all looked so good. And I missed lunch. Maybe breakfast, too. It's hard to remember on an empty stomach."

She took a few of the cartons from him before he dropped them and sent noodles and sauce splattering across her floor. "Do you mind eating on the deck?"

"Would love it. I've been cooped up inside all day with

cops, criminals, the chief and other undesirables. What can I help you with?"

"You can open the wine. The corkscrew is in the top drawer next to the fridge."

"I can handle that. Not sure if the vino's decent, but the salesman at the liquor store said it goes well with Chinese. I'm usually a beer man myself, pop a top and drink it straight from a longneck."

"So what's the occasion?"

"I fake a little sophistication from time to time."

He was trying too hard to keep things light. That could only mean bad news. She made a couple trips outside with the food and wineglasses. When she opened the cartons, sweet and spicy odors escaped and her stomach began to roll.

Travis joined her as she dropped into a chair. He filled the wineglasses and then took the seat opposite hers. He held up his glass for a toast. "To a quick and successful search for Cornell."

A surge of hope swept through Faith as she clinked her glass with his. "Does this mean you found something helpful on his computer?"

"We definitely have new information to work with. It could be helpful." Travis passed her a container. "Shrimp fried rice. Hope you're not allergic to seafood."

"No." She put a spoonful on her plate and passed it back to him. He piled his plate high and took a bite before reaching for the next container.

He might be hungry, but he wasn't starving, not the way she was for news. "What new information?"

Travis forked up another bite of fried rice. "Why don't we eat and then get down to business?"

"I can't eat until I know."

He nodded while he chewed and finally swallowed. "What do you know about Angela Pointer?"

"I've never heard of her."

Travis wiped his mouth on his napkin and took a sip of wine. "Evidently, she and your son were an item."

"When?"

"Just before his disappearance. Are you sure he never mentioned her?"

"Not only did he never mention her, but neither did any of his friends when I questioned them. Was she a student in his high school?"

"He didn't know her from school. Angela's officially an exotic dancer, or at least she was when she and Cornell were exchanging hot and heavy emails."

"There must be some mistake. If Cornell had been serious about someone, he'd have told me about her. He's always told me about his crushes."

"This appeared to be more than a crush. The two of them were apparently spending a lot of time together."

"He was home most nights—except when he was studying with friends." And he had done that a lot just before his disappearance.

Even as Faith protested, her doubts were growing. Involvement with an exotic dancer would explain his being at the Passion Pit. She'd never been able to buy that he'd inappropriately touched a stripper. Being aggressive was against his very nature.

But if he and the young woman were sexually involved, their touching might have been seen as inappropriate by other employees or by Georgio.

Faith could even buy that he'd kept the relationship a secret from her, knowing she would have disapproved. But where was he now? Where was Angela?

More confused and disturbed than ever, Faith opened

her wooden chopsticks and used them to push her food around on the plate. When she looked up, she realized that Travis had stopped eating and was watching her.

She met his penetrating gaze and knew the worst might be yet to come. "There's more, isn't there?"

"A little."

"You may as well hit me with all of it," she said.

"Angela was pregnant."

"Pregnant?" Faith's spirits took another plunge. This girlfriend she'd never even heard of had been pregnant ten months ago. The baby would have been born by now. An ache swelled inside her, but still her mind refused to wrap itself around the obvious implications.

"That doesn't mean Cornell was the father," she insisted. "I can't believe he would have kept my own grandchild a secret from me—not for months."

I'm sorry. I'm so sorry...

Cornell's words echoed in her head, haunting, tearing at her soul. Was this what he was sorry for? Getting a woman pregnant and running away with her? Putting Faith through hell for the past ten months?

But why? Why wouldn't he come to her? And where would he have gone with no money? The woman could hardly have worked at that profession while she was pregnant.

She looked away, hating for Travis to see the tears burning in her eyes. She didn't see him reach across the table, but felt his hands close around hers.

Big hands. Rough skin, yet the touch was gentle. Comforting. Protective.

"I'm sorry I had to tell you like this, but I couldn't think of an easy way to break it to you."

"It's not your fault. I asked for the truth. It's just hard to swallow."

"Look on the bright side," Travis said. "This makes it a lot more likely your son left of his own free will and that there was no foul play involved."

Travis was right, of course, yet her heart felt incredibly heavy. For Cornell to have done something so irresponsible, for him to have disregarded her fears and feelings this way, would mean she didn't know her son at all.

Travis's thumbs stroked the back of her hands, but she wasn't sure he was even aware of the soothing motions. His brow was furrowed, his lips stretched into a tight line. She could envision theories whirring in his mind, none of them giving her the answers she craved.

Finally, she pulled her hands away and wrapped one around the stem of her wineglass. She tipped it up, stared into the swirling liquid and then took a large sip. She couldn't avoid reality just because it didn't suit her.

"Looks like I wasn't the mother I thought I was."

"Don't go judging yourself. Teenagers are famous for making bad decisions. Besides, I have an idea we've just scratched the surface in this investigation."

"It was a deep scratch."

"It opened lots of possibilities, but we can't be certain that Cornell was the baby's father or that the girlfriend was even pregnant. It could have been a trap to get money out of him."

"He had no money."

"She might not have known that."

"That doesn't explain his dropping off the face of the earth for ten months."

"Until the phone call the other night," Travis reminded her—as if she could forget. "He's made the first step toward reaching out to you, and even though it sent you into panic mode, I have to think it's a good sign."

She couldn't argue the point in light of all she'd learned tonight. It didn't lessen her desperation to find him.

"We have to locate this Angela person," Faith said. "Have you checked to see if she's still working at the Passion Pit or if anyone there knows how to get in touch with her?"

"Not yet. I wanted to talk to you first."

Faith considered her options. She could talk to Georgio herself now that he'd agreed to help find Cornell. There was no reason to think he wouldn't level with her.

Pangs of guilt attacked again. She felt as if she was two-timing Travis, creating a lovers' triangle. How crazy was that?

Nonetheless, she had to tell Travis she'd talked to Georgio. If not tonight, then soon. She'd never been able to stomach lies and deceit, and this was proving to be no exception.

She forced down a few bites of food while Travis ate ravenously. He ate like a man with an appetite and appreciation for the tastes and smells and textures. She'd be willing to bet he jumped into life with that same gusto.

No holds barred. No limits. Daring the odds to play against him.

"Have you ever been afraid of anything or anyone, Travis?"

He stopped eating and looked up, his dark eyes meeting hers. "Sure. Probably wouldn't be alive today if I didn't have a healthy fear of thugs and addicts with guns."

"That's wisdom and caution. I'm talking about real fear."

He put down his fork and wiped his mouth with the napkin. "I was scared to death when I was little, sure the monster that my foster mother told me would get me was waiting for dark to come, and me to close my eyes, before it snapped me up and ate me."

Faith shuddered. "Your foster mother frightened you like that?"

"One of them did. She was a real sweetheart."

"I'm sorry."

"Don't be. I got over it. What doesn't kill you makes you stronger and a hell of a lot smarter."

"So monsters, that's it?"

"There was this two-ton bull a few years back. Wanted to show me who was boss after he threw me off his back and into the dirt. When I saw that hoof coming at my head, I knew a moment or two of panic."

"Ouch." She cringed at the image. "You could have been killed."

"Yep. That's the night I gave up bull riding for keeps. Figured I could do more good as a cop than a corpse, so here I am."

Here he was, on her deck, chatting as easily as if they'd known each other for years. A knight in cowboy boots and carrying a badge. He'd found out more about her son in two days than the DPD missing-persons division, the P.I. she'd hired and she with all her questions had discovered in ten long months.

"So the Western boots you wear are not just for show. You really are a cowboy."

"Every chance I get." He scooted back from the table, stretching his long legs in front of him. "I know I hit you with a lot tonight, Faith. I know how worried you are about Cornell. But give me a little more time. I promise I'll find him. If he's in any kind of trouble, I'll go in and even the odds. Trust me on that."

Strangely, she did. She owed him big-time. But she couldn't deny that it was more than gratitude he inspired.

She liked his being here, liked his touch when he'd held her hands across the small table. Even liked watching him eat.

If she wasn't very careful, she might start liking him so much that she forgot he was here only as a cop and as a favor to his brother's bride.

When they finished eating, Travis gathered the nearly empty food containers and carried them to the trash while Faith cleared the dishes from the table. "Leave the wine and glasses," he suggested. "I have a few more questions and it's too nice outdoors to go inside yet."

"Questions about Cornell?"

"Yeah, though feel free to wow me with your personal exploits if you like. You've heard my tales of horror and stupid acts of daring."

"You were in attendance during my most stupid act of daring," she said.

"Fighting off the drunk at the Passion Pit?"

"In full hooker garb."

"Do you still have that outfit?" He grinned devilishly.

"No," she lied.

"Yet it lives forever in my mind."

She made a face. "Now, that's scary."

But not nearly as scary as the zany pulses of sensuality she felt at his teasing. "I'll finish in here," she said, before the sudden flushes of heat inside her grew any hotter. "I'll meet you back on the patio in a few minutes."

"Sounds good."

"But no more wine for me," she said. "I'm a light-weight drinker." And not used to sexual temptation in any shape or form, certainly not the shape and form of a rugged cowboy cop on a night when, thanks to Cornell's secrets, her vulnerability was at an all-time high.

TRAVIS RETURNED TO the deck, worrying that the questions he needed to ask were only going to upset Faith more. But Cornell was clearly not the innocent schoolboy Faith had portrayed him as. He was a man, albeit young and probably inexperienced.

Messing around with one of Georgio's dancers could have led him into real trouble. Travis only hoped that actually had been Cornell and not an imposter who'd made that phone call in the wee hours of the morning. His being alive was the best news they could have hoped for.

It was Cornell's connection to Georgio through Angela Pointer that worried Travis the most. Georgio ruled his world like a third-world dictator. No one crossed him. No one ratted on him. He made sure they were too scared to do that.

Travis poured himself a half glass of wine and walked to the edge of the deck, his thoughts wandering back to Faith. Her heart was literally breaking with worry over Cornell.

His mother must have felt that same kind of love for him and Leif. She'd left R.J., her sorry, alcoholic, womanizing husband, and raised them by herself.

Only instead of losing him or Leif, she'd lost her own battle with cancer, knowing she was leaving two young sons to make it without her.

Travis wished he remembered more, but most of what he knew of her came from Leif. She had loved them more than anything. Leif had assured him of that. Travis figured that if she were alive today, she'd like Faith.

He liked her, too. More than *liked*. He didn't understand it himself, but some weird chemistry had come into play the first night he met her. She'd stayed on his mind, haunted his dreams, fueled more than a few fantasies.

But then she'd been more image than person. Now

she was real. She was a key component of an investigation that might link to a lot more than Cornell's running off with a stripper.

No two ways about it. Faith ignited urges and feelings in him that had no place in a police investigation. Reactions like those made lawmen weak and all too frequently stupid. The brain tended to check out when emotions checked in.

He looked up as Faith rejoined him on the porch. The sun had set and the moonlight filtering through the branches of a stately oak tree painted silver streaks in her silky brown hair.

The crazy need to take her in his arms and hold her close hit again. Damn. Why did this have to be so hard? She was attractive, but she was just a woman. He worked with them all the time. None had ever gotten to him like this.

"What else do you want to know?" she asked.

"Anything that might help me to get inside Cornell's head, figure out what and how he'd react to stressful situations."

"After what you told me tonight, I'm not sure how well I even knew him."

"Let's start with the seizures," Travis said, needing her to focus on specifics. "Was this something new or had he dealt with them for a long time?"

"They started when he was fourteen. Cornell's father was working for a Central American oil company at the time. Cornell went for a two-week visit. A few days after he came home, he started running a high fever. The seizures started soon after."

And that had surely scared her to death. "How long was he sick?"

"Two weeks. He was finally diagnosed with some rare

strain of flu. Twice we were told he might not make it through the night."

Faith's voice broke. She swayed and then leaned against a corner post for support. Travis could fight it no longer. He walked over and put an arm around her shoulders.

She leaned into him, her head nestled against his chest. His thumb rode the tight veins in her neck.

"I'm sorry," she finally whispered between sniffles. "I've relived this often enough that I should be able to talk about it without falling to pieces. It's just that everything is so stressful right now."

"No apology needed." He'd always figured he'd had a tough life growing up, but Faith's hadn't been a picnic. A divorce. Raising a son alone. And now this. "You've earned the right to a little meltdown," he said.

"But it doesn't change anything."

She stepped from his arms. They felt incredibly empty without her.

Travis's cell phone vibrated. He was tempted to ignore it, but was too much a cop to do that. He checked the caller ID. It was his partner, Reno.

He took the call. "What's up?"

"You know that dancer you asked me to run through the system?"

"Yeah."

"No rap sheet, but she's a runaway. Lived with her mother and stepfather in West Texas before she left home at sixteen."

"And since then?"

"Worked at a convenience store in Austin before ending up in Dallas and going to work as an exotic dancer at the Passion Pit. But get this, she made a 911 call a couple of weeks before Cornell disappeared. Said her boyfriend had beat her up and she needed an ambulance.

Spent two days in the hospital, then dropped charges against the guy."

"Do you have an ID on him?"

"Walt Marshall. Also one of Georgio's employees."

"Subject ever been married?"

"I take it you're not free to talk right now?"

"Not really, but go on. Where is Marshall now?"

"Missing in action, at least from the Dallas area. Never reported as missing, but I can't find anything on him for the last ten months."

"Anything else on the subject?"

"According to her landlady, Angela Pointer left about the same time Cornell disappeared, without paying her rent. That's all I've got so far. So you want to tell me what this is all about?"

"Yeah. I'll call you back in about ten minutes."

He wasn't going to get into this with Faith until he had more facts. But it was turning into one hell of a mess.

Travis didn't even want to speculate what kind of trouble Cornell had gotten himself into if he was messing around with the pregnant girlfriend of a lunatic.

"An emergency?" Faith asked when he broke the connection.

"Appears that way. I hate to rush off, but my partner has some new evidence on one of our cases and I need to go over it with him."

"No problem. I understand completely. I can't thank you enough for what you've already done."

"I'll check out Angela Pointer tomorrow," he promised. In truth, he planned to do a little snooping tonight. "I'll get back to you as soon as I find out anything further. In the meantime, call me if you hear from Cornell again."

"I will."

She walked him back through the house and to the

front door. When she looked up at him, he got hit with that crazy rush of emotions again. He had to make the goodbye short and not too sweet before he did something really foolish—like kiss her.

"Lock your door," he cautioned. "You can't be too careful in the big city."

"I always do."

He took one of her hands, squeezed it tightly and then turned and walked away while he still could.

With any luck he'd find Angela Pointer alive and well and swinging from a pole at the Passion Pit tonight. He had an ugly hunch that wouldn't be the case.

Chapter Eight

"They were lying," Reno said as they walked back to Travis's pickup truck.

"The two dancers who actually admitted knowing Angela?"

"Yeah. Their spiel sounded rehearsed."

"Right," Travis agreed. "I don't figure I'll do any better talking to Georgio when he gets back in town—if he's actually out of town."

Reno opened the door and swung into the passenger side. "Easy to see how Ethridge hit a brick wall."

"We've already gotten a few steps further than he did," Travis said as he slid behind the wheel. "At least we know about Angela Pointer."

"But not her whereabouts," his partner said emphatically. "Nor are you any closer to locating Cornell. And lest you forget, we are in the middle of a very high-profile murder investigation."

"All true. But I promised Faith Ashburn I'd find her son, and I never walk on a promise. Besides, I'm not totally convinced Scott's murder and Cornell's disappearance are exclusive."

"Now you're pushing it. Eighteen-year-old runs off with his sexy girlfriend—not the kind you take home to Mama—then calls his mother months later and says

'I'm sorry.' Doesn't sound like foul play to me," Reno said. "Sounds like a teenager whose hormones are calling all the shots."

"Normally, I'd agree with you, but Faith is so sure he wouldn't have left home."

"The same Faith who didn't even know her son was boinking a stripper?"

"I know. It doesn't all add up, but having Georgio involved in this in any way makes me naturally suspicious. Add the abusive boyfriend to that mix and there's plenty of reason to worry."

"I still don't see a connection with Scott Mitchell."

"I know. Just call it one of my wild hunches." Travis started the engine, shifted into gear and pulled into traffic. It was light even for a Tuesday night.

"So tell me again. Exactly how are you connected to Cornell's mother?"

"She's a good friend of Leif's new wife, maid of honor at the wedding."

"So no kin to you?"

"None."

"Good-looking?" Reno asked.

Easy to see where this was going. "What does that have to do with anything?"

"Just curious."

"She's attractive."

"And unattached."

"It appears that way, but I'm not doing this just so I can jump her bones, if that's what you're insinuating."

"Actually, that would make a lot more sense than any other reason you've given for jumping headfirst into Ethridge's case. About damn time you jumped somebody's bones. Might make you a lot less irritable."

"Well, it won't be Faith Ashburn's, not until her son is found, and probably not then."

"Why not? Too old for you?"

"Nope."

"Too hot for you?"

"Too complicated." And too damned irresistible. The kind who'd make you think of forever. Travis was not a forever guy.

"Complicated? What the hell is that supposed to mean? She smarter than you are?"

"Probably. Most women I date are. But the complicated part is if we date and she gets serious."

"Break up like you always do when a girlfriend gets serious."

"Only with Faith, that wouldn't be the end of it. I'd have my brother's wife mad at me. Would make those family gatherings real chummy. Plus I'd have to worry about running into her if I showed up at the Dry Gulch to visit Leif."

"That's all a bunch of B.S. Face it, partner. You're falling for her and it's scaring you to death."

"Not a chance. Cops and marriage are a lousy mix. You're the only one in Homicide not divorced or cheating on your wife."

Reno laughed and gave him a friendly punch to the arm. "Yep, already thinking about marriage. You're all but roped and tied. Can't wait until I meet Faith. She must be a hell of a woman."

"She is. But this is about finding her son, and that's the only place our relationship is going."

But in spite of his denial, Travis was having a devil of a time keeping Faith off his mind.

He wondered what Leif would say about that. But then Leif was probably the wrong one to ask. He'd fallen madly in love with Joni in a matter of days. And now he was living at the Dry Gulch Ranch with a father he'd always claimed to hate.

Must be something in the water. Travis would stick to beer.

FAITH LOOKED UP from the notes she was going over, and punched the buzzer to retrieve the message from her secretary. "You have a caller on line one, a man, says it's personal."

"Did he give a name?"

"No, but he said this was about Cornell."

Her heart lurched. "Thanks. I'll take the call."

"Good morning, Faith. Hope I didn't catch you at a bad time."

"Georgio." She hadn't expected to hear from him this soon—or at this number. "The timing is fine. I'm busy, but I always am. I just didn't remember mentioning to you where I work."

"You didn't, but information like that is easy to find. I tried your cell-phone number first. There was no answer."

"I just got out of a meeting and I'd turned it off." She pulled the cell from her desk drawer and checked it as she talked. Sure enough, one missed call.

Cautious anticipation surged. "This must be important for you to call me at work."

"Something I find worrisome, but I'd rather not talk about it on the phone. I was hoping you could meet me for lunch."

She checked her watch. Eleven-thirty, and she had a meeting at one. But anxiety had replaced anticipation now and she wouldn't be able to concentrate on anything until she heard what Georgio had to say.

"I can get away for a little while, but I need to be back here a few minutes before one."

"Perfect. I'm on my way to the airport, but I built in a little time in case you were available. I can pick you up in front of your office in about ten minutes."

"I'll be there." Hopefully, Georgio's worrisome news was the same information she'd already gotten from Travis and not something else to complicate matters. No use speculating. She'd know in a matter of minutes.

As far as she was concerned, they could bypass lunch and talk in the car. In fact, she'd suggest it. That way she wouldn't have to wait to hear what he had to say, and he could go straight to the airport.

She filed the reports from the morning, took a quick bathroom break and then rode the elevator down to the first floor. She walked out the double glass doors right on time.

A black luxury car was stopped in front of the building. A chauffeur stepped out and opened the back door for her. Georgio leaned over and waved a welcome.

So much for talking in the car. She climbed into the backseat, straightening and tugging her skirt down to cover most of her thighs when she noticed Georgio ogling them. As if he didn't see enough flesh in his nightclubs.

"There's a small bistro around the corner," he said. "The menu is limited, but Chef François is creative and the food exquisite. I took the liberty of making reservations there. I trust that's agreeable."

"Anyplace is fine with me as long as we can talk."

"We'll have a private room."

Her apprehension burgeoned. Was what he had to tell her so alarming that he couldn't chance it being over-heard? Or was she afraid of her reaction when she heard what he had to say?

The short ride to the bistro seemed endless.

Once they were inside, the maître d's welcome was officious as he showed them to a private room and a white-linen-covered table. A bottle of wine was open, two crystal stems already filled with the rich purple liquid.

"I never drink when I'm working," she said.

"Not a problem," Georgio assured her as he held out her chair. "It's just that our time is so limited, I ordered ahead. François has prepared a few special treats."

"I'm sure they will be delicious, but right now food is the least of my concerns," she said, cutting short his irrelevant verbiage. "I'm too nervous to wait any longer to hear what you learned about Cornell."

"Yes, of course," he said. "I hate to upset you, but I think you should be aware of what's going on."

"Which is?"

"Two of my dancers at the Passion Pit called me this morning, both of them very upset over being informally questioned by two homicide detectives last night."

The tightness in Faith's chest relaxed a bit. One of the detectives was no doubt Travis, following up on what he'd learned about Angela Pointer.

"Exactly what about the visit upset them?"

"From the questions they were asked, they think Angela Pointer, one of my former employees, may have been murdered."

"Did the detectives say that?"

"Not directly."

"Then why would they assume she's been murdered?"

"All I know is that both of my employees got that same impression."

Dread vibrated through Faith. Travis had definitely not insinuated that with her. "Was there any mention of Cornell?"

Georgio looked down before making eye contact. Concern was etched into every line of his face.

"I'm afraid so. I hate telling you this, Faith. And remember, we're just going on the assumptions made by two ladies who were questioned. But it sounds to me as if the police are looking to pin Angela's murder on your son."

Fear and anger collided inside Faith with such sickening force she was afraid she might pass out. Georgio was wrong. He had to be wrong. Travis was trying to find Cornell, not convict him.

François interrupted the damning conversation to greet Georgio and personally serve an appetizer of champagne-truffle mousse pâté and a promise of more culinary delights to follow.

Faith struggled to pull herself together. She had to stay focused, had to concentrate on the facts.

"What was said to make them reach such a bizarre conclusion?"

"It was pretty clear from the leading questions the detectives asked, and I'm afraid the answers the ladies gave them didn't help Cornell's case."

"What did they say?"

"The truth, so you can't blame them."

"What truth?"

"That Angela was being stalked by someone she described as being just a kid with overactive hormones. She said he'd followed her home on several occasions and had somehow gotten her email address. He was sending her notes saying he loved her and that they were meant to be together, that sort of thing."

"That doesn't sound like Cornell," Faith said. And it was definitely not the way Travis had described the email communication. "Did Angela mention Cornell's name to them?"

"If she did, they didn't remember."

"If that's the case, why didn't they go to the police with that information when Angela went missing?"

"Because Angela called me and told me there was a family emergency and she was moving back to West Texas. I told the others, and none of us suspected anything different."

"Cornell would never stalk anyone, much less harm them. I know that. I know my son." Faith would not use the word *murder*, could not let herself think it.

This couldn't be happening. Travis had come to her at the reception and offered to help find Cornell. He'd told her she could trust him. Had it all been a ruse to get her to help him find her son, only to put him behind bars?

She'd played right into his hands. Given him Cornell's computer for a forensic analysis. For all she knew, he'd even lied to her about what he'd found on it.

She pushed back from the table. "Is there anything else I should know?"

"Only that I want to help you find your son and clear his name."

"Why? You don't know him. You don't know me."

"But what I do know of you, I like. You're a sensitive woman concerned about your son. I respect that. And I don't trust the cops. Never have. That's why I insisted you not tell them that you've talked to me. Believe me, they'll discredit me and all my intentions. And they'll make my work in locating Cornell even more difficult. You can trust me."

Trust. She wasn't sure she'd trust anyone ever again. Not if Cornell was a suspect in a young woman's murder.

Could it be possible that he knew that? Was that the reason he was afraid to come home?

Alone. Afraid. And innocent. Cornell would never hurt anyone. Never. She'd stake her life on that.

The waiter walked in and set a bowl of lobster bisque in front of each of them.

Faith pushed hers away and stood. She couldn't sit here another minute without going mad. She grabbed her handbag from the back of her chair. "I have to go."

"You should try to eat something."

"I can't eat. Really, I have to go. I need to be alone to think."

"Whatever you say. I'll call for my driver."

"No. I don't want a driver. I'll walk back. It's not far and I need the fresh air."

"If you insist. I'll call you when I get back to town in a few days, but in the meantime, don't talk to the cops, and if you hear from Cornell, phone me at once."

All she could manage was a nod. She bumped into the maître d' as she rushed from the private room, mumbled an apology and kept going.

Barely aware of the traffic or the warmth from the sun seeping through her blouse, she almost ran the few blocks back to her office. Once there, she stared at the doors, but couldn't make herself go inside. She kept walking, not stopping until she reached a nearby coffee shop.

She ordered an espresso, took it to a back table and put the cup to her lips and sipped. The burn of heat and bitterness washed into her empty stomach.

She'd finished the coffee before her mind cleared enough that she knew what she had to do. Still, her hands shook as she punched Travis's cell number into her phone.

She would not be used as a pawn by Detective Travis Dalton. She'd demand he tell her the truth.

And to think she'd been worried she was falling hard for the traitorous cowboy cop.

DAZED TO THE POINT she could barely function, Faith managed to stumble through the one-o'clock meeting before she gave up and took the rest of the day off. She'd thought she'd been through a lot, with concerns for Cornell's health and then the terror of his sudden disappearance.

Nothing had prepared her for this. Cornell, a suspect in a murder case. On top of it all, she felt betrayed. A fool for taking a homicide detective at his word.

Please come home, Cornell. We can get through this together the way we always have.

Why hadn't she said that in the few seconds he'd been on the phone?

Faith closed the garage door and stepped into her mudroom. She hesitated by the back door as a disturbing sensation swept through her.

Something was different than when she'd left this morning. Nothing obvious, just a feeling. No. A faint but unfamiliar odor. She looked around. Everything was in place. Nothing appeared to be touched.

She definitely had to add paranoia to her growing list of problems.

Still, she scanned the area cautiously as she walked back to her bedroom and kicked off her shoes. She checked her landline phone for messages. There were none, meaning not only that Travis hadn't called back on that number, but that her prayers for a call from Cornell had not been answered.

She changed into a pair of cropped jeans and a bright pink T-shirt, then walked barefoot to the kitchen for a glass of cold water. She stopped in her tracks when the soles of her feet felt something gritty.

Her shattered nerves reacted with a new wave of apprehension. She was certain she hadn't spilled anything this morning.

Impulsively, she walked over and pulled a sharp chef's knife from the wooden block on the countertop. Not that she'd ever used a knife as a weapon before. Not that she'd ever used a weapon, for that matter.

She dropped to her knees for a closer look. The few grains of gritty substance were easier to feel than to see. She'd probably tracked in whatever it was herself when she'd stepped outside for the morning newspaper.

Her cell phone rang, jolting her back to reality from paranoiaville. She grabbed the phone from her pocket and checked the caller ID. Joni. Never had she needed to hear the voice of an old friend more. An old friend who didn't need to be saddled with Faith's problems on her honeymoon.

Faith took a deep breath and faked a normalcy to her tone. "Hello, honeymooner. Don't you have better things to do than call me?"

"Have to come up for air occasionally. What are you doing home this time of day?"

"What makes you think I'm home? You called me on my cell phone."

"I know, but I called your office first. Melanie said you'd left work early. That's not like you."

Faith swallowed hard. "I had a headache." Even a white lie didn't come easy, especially to Joni.

"Leif just got off the phone with Travis," her friend said.

The statement sounded like an indictment. Joni clearly knew more than Faith had anticipated. "Good. Nice that brothers keep in touch."

"Travis is worried about you, Faith."

So worried he hadn't bothered to call her back. "Did he call Leif just to tell him that?"

"No. Leif called him. He thinks Travis should visit the Dry Gulch Ranch and at least have a conversation with R.J. while he's still lucid."

"How did I get into that conversation?"

"Travis just said you were dealing with a lot right now and he thought it might be a good idea if I called you."

"He told you about Angela Pointer, didn't he?"

"A little," Joni admitted. "I know it was hard to face that Cornell had a life he kept secret from you, but I'm sure there are lots of teenage guys who don't tell their mothers everything."

"I know, but Cornell... I mean, we were so close. He was a good kid, always."

"I know. Travis is going to find him and get to the bottom of things. When he does, you and Cornell will be close again. Whatever went wrong, you can work through it."

Travis, the hero. Faith could take it no longer. "Travis's interest in Cornell goes a lot deeper than just bringing him home safely."

"What are you talking about?"

The accusations against the callous detective spilled straight from Faith's heart. Once she started, she couldn't stop. She left nothing out, from the computer analysis to her talk with Georgio.

By the time Faith stopped for breath, her voice was as shaky as her insides.

"Are you telling me that you'd believe what that flesh-and drug-peddling rat Georgio had to tell you over what Travis says?"

"It's not that I trust Georgio," Faith admitted. "But how would he know that Travis was even at the Passion

Pit last night unless he'd talked to the dancers who were questioned? His information came from them. Angela was their friend. They'd have no reason to lie."

"None that you know of. I don't know who knows what, Faith. Neither do you at this point. But I know my husband, and he knows his brother. If he says you can trust Travis to help you find Cornell, you can."

"And I know my son," Faith argued. "He didn't kill anyone. He couldn't."

"Then you don't have anything to worry about on that score. Tell Travis exactly what you told me, including Georgio's part in all of this. Travis will have a reasonable explanation. Give him a chance."

"Travis doesn't even want me talking to Georgio."

"Because he's a dangerous snake in the grass. Already he's poisoning your mind. You can't play Travis and Georgio against each other. Think this through, Faith. Trust Travis completely. He wants to help and he can help, the same way Leif saved my life."

She wanted to. More than anything, Faith wanted to trust Travis, but she would not throw her son to the lions. "I don't think I can do that, Joni."

"Then I'm coming home tonight to talk some sense into you."

"Don't you dare. A honeymoon is a onetime thing."

"Not for Leif and me. Our love grows deeper by the day."

The doorbell rang. "Someone's at the door," Faith said. "I need to go, but promise me you won't come rushing back to Texas."

"Then give Travis a chance to explain everything. Trust him."

"I'll listen to what he has to say." That was all she could promise.

She broke the connection as she padded though the house to the door.

She peeked through the peephole.

Travis stood there, a few feet away so that she saw his full six-feet-plus, imposing frame. A six-pack of beer dangled from his right hand as if he was expecting this to be a social call. The dark lock of hair that fell over his forehead made him look almost boyish.

But the jeans, the cowboy boots, a light blue shirt opened at the neck and an unbuttoned rust-colored sport coat swinging from his shoulder left no doubt that he was all man.

Her stomach fluttered, but this time she wouldn't be influenced by the traitorous sizzle of awareness he ignited in spite of everything she'd heard.

She swung open the door. "Come in, Travis."

"Sorry I missed your call. I was in a meeting with the chief of police and the mayor."

"I realize you're a very dedicated *homicide* detective."

"Busy, anyway. I tried to reach you at the office, but they said you'd left, so I took a chance on finding you here."

"Fine. We need to talk."

And this time she'd be asking the questions.

Chapter Nine

Travis had no idea what had set Faith off, but she was definitely in dragon-lady mode. Hopefully, it was something to do with work and not with Cornell.

He held up the six-pack. "Join me in a beer?"

"No, thank you, but you go ahead."

"Mind if I put the rest in your fridge?"

"Help yourself. I'll be on the deck."

He joined her a few minutes later, cold beer in hand. She was sitting in one of the outdoor chairs, legs crossed, her right one kicking like crazy. Her toenails were painted hot-pink. The cropped jeans showed off her terrific calves.

Travis took a sip of beer and then leaned his backside against the deck railing next to a pot of blooming pansies.

She stopped swinging her leg and shot him an accusing stare. "When did you decide to go after Cornell as a murder suspect?"

The bitter accusation caught him off guard. He set the beer down on the railing. "What the devil are you talking about?"

"No pretense, Travis. Just answer the question. Was it before Joni's wedding? Was that why you pretended to be so interested in helping me?"

He picked up his beer and drained at least a third of

the bottle while he tried to figure out was this sudden outbreak was all about. "I didn't pretend anything that night. It's not like I forced you to dance with me." Though he had coaxed.

"Then why trick me into turning over Cornell's computer so you could search for evidence to connect him to Angela Pointer?"

"Trick you?" He finished the beer and stepped in closer. "You wanted your son found. You were eager for me to see what was on his computer. And for the record, Angela was never even reported as missing and there's no indication she's dead. I don't know how you came up with the wild idea I was investigating her murder."

Faith's mouth drew so tight her luscious lips practically disappeared. "It makes sense. You're an overworked homicide detective, yet you take on a missing-person case the Dallas P.D. already said didn't indicate foul play. Why would you take on a missing-person case?"

Damn good question.

He let the truth rumble around in his head. Because he hadn't been able to get her off his mind after seeing her the very first time in the Passion Pit.

Because she'd turned him on like a brick oven when they danced to a belly-rubbing ballad at Leif's wedding.

All of which he was seriously starting to regret. He struggled for an answer that stayed close to the truth.

"You seemed convinced that your son didn't leave of his own accord, Faith. I'm a good judge of character. I believed you, which is more than you're giving me credit for right now. So let's get a few things straight."

"I just want the truth."

"And you're going to get it. I'm a cop, a damn good one. I don't pin murders on people. I discover evidence, not manufacture it, and I don't like comments that suggest otherwise.

"I didn't even know that Angela Pointer existed until I read the computer analysis. No one had ever reported her as missing, so there was no investigation into her whereabouts. If I find out she was murdered here in Dallas, you can bet that I or one of the other homicide detectives will do everything we can to find out who killed her.

"But you're right on one count. I have plenty to keep me busy and I don't push my help on women who don't want it. If you don't trust me, we need to break ties right now."

She stared at him without saying a word, which was pretty much answer enough.

"I'm going to the kitchen for another beer," he said. "You decide if you want me to hang around long enough to finish it."

Travis cursed himself under his breath as he walked to the kitchen. He hadn't reacted like a cop. He'd reacted like a man. Police investigations and lust were a mix guaranteed to create chaos. Every cop knew that. The smart ones stayed clear of it.

Normally, Travis was one of them.

He opened the fridge, took out one beer and then reached back in for another. A time-out might help both of them get the burrs out of their saddle blankets.

As angry as she'd made him, he didn't want to just walk away and leave things like this. Even if she kicked him out, he couldn't stop looking for Cornell.

He wasn't sure where Angela Pointer fit into the scheme of things, but whatever had sent Cornell on the run was most likely connected to Georgio Trosclair.

And if Travis's theory about Georgio was right, he ordered a person's murder as easily as most people ordered a pizza. Travis had spent the past year trying to prove that. He wouldn't stop until he did.

FAITH WALKED TO the railing and watched a bluebird swoop from the branches of a redbud tree to the tiny box where its babies waited to be fed. A protective, nurturing mom. Doing what came naturally, acting on instinct.

Faith wondered if she was doing the same. Acting on instinct where Cornell was concerned, jumping to conclusions, attacking Travis without even hearing his side of the story. But she couldn't just blindly trust him or let her attraction for him affect her in any way. Nor could she afford to turn away from him if he was actually trying to help her find Cornell.

Travis stepped out the back door, an open bottle of beer in each hand. He held one out to her. "I thought you might need this," he said.

She never drank beer. Bad for the waistline. This time she took it. She sipped it slowly and then walked over and sat down on the wide, wooden steps that led down to the lawn and her neatly planted butterfly garden. The blue phlox were already in bloom.

Travis dropped to the step beside her, not too close, but near enough she caught the light, woodsy fragrance of his aftershave. He leaned against the railing post, his long legs stretched in front of him, as he watched a honeybee flying among the blossoms sampling the nectar.

Faith studied his profile and then looked away quickly when she felt her resolve not to be affected by his heady masculinity begin to dissolve.

"Sorry for the explosion," she said, determined to keep everything in perspective. "I had a rough day."

"So I gathered. Is that why you left early?"

She nodded.

He didn't push for more. She drank a few more sips of beer, rehearsing in her mind what she had to say. Finally, she took a deep breath and dived in.

"The information about Angela Pointer preyed on my mind all day and I guess I let my imagination get out of hand."

His expression indicated he wasn't buying it, and the lies were starting to ferment and turn to acid in the pit of her stomach.

"I was so upset I became paranoid," she added.

He turned to face her. "And decided I couldn't be trusted. You sure jumped to that conclusion fast."

"Worse. I was paranoid about everything. When I came home from the office I thought someone had been in my house while I was away. I even picked up a knife to fight off the intruder who didn't exist."

"Does that happen often?"

"Never."

He leaned in closer. "What made you think there had been an intruder? Was something out of place?"

She shrugged, hating to admit what a wreck she'd become. "No. I detected an unfamiliar piney scent that reminded me of a man's aftershave, probably the smells of spring that came in with me when I'd opened the door."

Travis's expression darkened. "Anything else?"

"I was barefoot when I went into the kitchen and I stepped on what felt like spilled salt on the floor under the ceiling light fixture. When I looked closer, it was more like a chalky sand, no doubt something I tracked in myself."

"Makes sense. I wouldn't worry."

The grimace on his face didn't match his tone. He stood and studied the roof of the deck as intensely as if he were looking for killer spiders.

He put his finger to his lips to shush her even though she wasn't talking, and shot her a warning look she didn't understand. "I gotta be going," he said. "We can talk later if you want, but if you don't trust me, you should find someone else to look for your son."

Still holding his finger to his lips, he took her hand, tugged her to a standing position, and led her off the deck and onto the cushiony carpet of grass. He didn't speak until they reached the back gate of the fenced yard.

"Do you have a stepladder handy?" he said, his voice barely more than a whisper.

"What's going on, Travis?"

"Probably nothing, but I want to make sure that's the case."

"Do you think there actually might have been an intruder?"

"Yes, but I'm a cop. We tend to suspect the worst."

"Why the stepladder?"

"Playing a hunch, but just a hunch, so don't get upset yet. Just tell where to find the ladder."

"It's in the garage. I'll get it for you."

"No, I want you to stay in the yard until I get back. Don't even walk back to the deck."

If this was some trick to scare her into doing everything he said, it wasn't going to work. Yet her heart was pounding as she watched him walk away.

She grew more nervous by the second. By the time he returned twenty minutes later, her emotions were vacillating between fear and doubt. Without saying a word, he opened his hand so that she could see what he was holding. It was no bigger than a penlight battery.

"What is that?"

"A microphone. Turns out you're not paranoid. Your house has been bugged."

"Bugged. Who would do such a thing? What would they expect to learn from me?"

"I'm not sure, but I intend to find out. In the meantime, you can't stay here."

"How many spy boxes are there?"

"I found four. I don't think there's one on the deck, but there could be."

"Can't you just remove all of them?"

"I'd rather they stay in place while I find out who had reason to bug you. That way we can feed them false info if we need to. I'll put this one back in its original position."

"I'll be careful what I say, Travis. I'm here alone every night. It's not like I do a lot of talking. But I can't leave home. Cornell may try to call me again. If he does, I have to be here."

"Your landline is likely wiretapped, as well. Even if it isn't, they would be able to hear your conversation with Cornell. That might give them exactly what they're after."

This made no sense. Who would need to listen in to a conversation with Cornell? Not Travis, looking to arrest her son, or he'd never be telling her to move out. But if someone was this desperate to find Cornell, that might be why he was on the run. If she stayed, she might lead him into danger.

But danger from whom? This had to be linked to Angela Pointer. "Do you think Cornell and Angela ran away together because they were afraid of what her abusive boyfriend would do to them?"

"That's a possibility."

She was convinced Travis knew more than he was saying.

"Who knows about the phone call you got from Cornell?" he asked.

"You. Joni. Probably your brother. Joni tells Leif everything."

"Who else?"

Joni's words pounded in her head and in her heart like beating drums. *Trust Travis. Trust Travis. Trust Travis.*

Faith couldn't keep playing both ends against the middle. The situation had grown too dangerous. Forced to choose between Travis Dalton and the mysterious Georgio, she decided there was only one way to go.

"Georgio knows."

"Georgio Trosclair of the Passion Pit?"

She nodded.

"How would he?"

"I told him."

ANGER ERUPTED INSIDE TRAVIS. He slammed his right fist into his other palm while he tried to turn on his brain and turn off the fury and frustration.

"I told you to stay clear of him."

"He saw one of the flyers I put up. He called me and offered his help in finding Cornell. I couldn't turn that down."

"So he's the one who poisoned your mind against me. What part of *evil* and *dangerous* do you not understand, Faith? The bastard's the biggest drug smuggler in Texas, and nobody crosses him and lives to tell about it."

"Then why isn't he in jail?"

"Because no one lives to testify against him, either."

"Are you accusing him of murder?"

"Not directly. He has others do his dirty work for him."

Travis raked the hair back from his forehead. He hadn't expected things to heat up this fast, though he'd figured Georgio would find out that Travis was working with Faith to find Cornell. But even before that, Georgio had contacted Faith, so something else had changed.

"Let's take a walk," he said.

He let everything roll around in his mind as they walked side by side, but not touching. No more illusions of romance or lusty fantasies where Faith was concerned. He had to be all cop while he figured out a way to keep her and Cornell safe.

They took a walking trail that ran through her neighborhood, stopping at a bench in the shade of a gnarled oak tree.

He'd expected resistance, but Faith started talking the second they were seated. Her voice was unsteady, so the words spilled from her like water over a rocky creek bed.

The more she told him about her two meetings with Georgio, the madder Travis got. The man was definitely playing her, trying to discover exactly what she knew.

She finally took a deep breath, leaned against the back of the bench and stared into space. "None of this makes sense. Why would the dancers think Angela was murdered? And why is Georgio pretending to be helping me now when he'd refused to talk to me before?"

"I don't know, but right now we have to get you out of your house. How difficult would it be to take a few days off work?"

"I have some vacation time coming. I've been saving it so that I could spend it with Cornell when he comes home."

"Take it. You're going under unofficial protective custody."

"Is there such a thing?"

"There is now."

"Where will I stay?"

"Someplace where you'll be safe and near enough to the city that I can keep an eye on you."

Only one spot like that came to mind. A location where

his nightmares and resentments of the past would collide with the fears and pressures of the present. The last place he'd ever expected to spend even one night.

"I'll walk you back to your house, and I want you to go in and turn your TV or music up loud so that the sophisticated bugs won't pick up the packing sounds."

"What should I pack?"

"Jeans, shorts, T-shirts, boots if you have them, nothing fancy. Whatever you think you need on a ranch."

"What ranch?"

"The Dry Gulch."

CORNELL HELPED LOAD the last horse into the carrier, then wiped the sweat from his brow with his sleeve. He didn't understand half of what the Mexicans who were helping him said, but he understood enough to know they thought he was crazy for heading to the border with this load of smuggled goods.

More money for Georgio. More risk of arrest for Cornell. How long could this go on before one of the border patrol recognized him? How long before an agent figured out that the horses were not the only thing he was transporting into the U.S.?

Five trips. That was what Georgio had promised. The man lied as easily and with the same careless disregard as he manipulated lives. But no one crossed him. No one dared.

Cornell might.

What did he have to lose? Spend the rest of his life on the run or spend it behind bars? Killed by one of Georgio's thugs or facing a death sentence?

At least if he escaped Georgio's clutches he had a chance of staying alive. But never back in the U.S. Never would he return home. Never see his mother's face again.

He couldn't go running back to her, couldn't bear to see the pain in her eyes if she knew what he'd done.

He was eighteen, a man. Men fought wars at that age. Only Cornell didn't really feel like a man.

This time when he brushed away the sweat, his sleeve caught a couple salty tears. Showing that kind of nervous weakness would get him arrested for sure.

He pushed the Stetson back on his head and pretended to be the tough, long-haired, bearded cowboy that looked at him every morning in the mirror.

"Secure that door," he ordered. "Time to roll."

Maybe for the last time, if he could get his nerve up to make a run for it.

Chapter Ten

R.J. sat in the worn front-porch rocker, grateful for his neighbor's company. There was no one quite like Carolina Lambert to help him sort out a few things in his mind. Prettiest grandma he'd ever seen. Smart, too.

Carolina fitted one of the small flowered throw pillows behind her back as she settled in the creaky porch swing. "Do you have any idea why this change of heart with Travis?"

"Nope. I'm as confused as a golf ball on Astroturf."

"But he did say that he and Joni's friend Faith would be staying with you for a few days?"

"He asked me if I had room. Knows darn well I do. Got nothing but room in this rambling old house now that Leif and Joni moved into their own cottage."

"But you're never really alone these days. Your family is coming home."

"Some of them are taking their own good time about it. If they don't get a move on, it'll be too late to be any good. I've already outlived my oncologist's prognosis. Brain tumor's as stubborn as a mule in clover."

"But not as stubborn as you. And your methods for getting your family to move back to the ranch were a bit underhanded."

"Nothing underhanded about it. They want my money,

they dance to my fiddle playing, at least as long as I'm this side of the red Texas clay. 'Sides, I got the idea from you."

"I suggested you leave them the ranch. I never mentioned letting them think you were dead and then showing up at the reading of your own will."

R.J. chuckled. "Sure was worth it seeing the looks on their faces when I walked in. Thought my oldest son, Jake, was going to swallow his tongue."

"Speaking of Jake, have you heard from him lately?"

"Yep. Still complaining about the terms of the will. Thinks I'm a conniving son of a bitch."

Carolina smiled. "Wonder where he'd get an idea like that."

"Don't you start on me, too."

"Wouldn't dream of it."

"More likely he's been listening to his mother. Pretty as a red heifer in a flower bed, that one. Stole my heart the second I met her."

Never gave the dad-blasted thing back, either. Not even when she'd left him.

Not that he hadn't loved all his wives in his own way. Just something about the first time... Now he was getting sentimental. Never did that when he was younger and healthy.

"I remember Joni saying that the best man and the maid of honor had never met before the wedding," Carolina said. "They must have hit it off fast if they're taking a mini vacation together."

"I got the feeling this is more business than pleasure," R.J. said.

"Police business."

He nodded. "I talked to Leif last night. He says Travis

is helping Faith find her teenage son, who went missing months ago. Never a dull moment around the Dry Gulch."

"I'm so sorry to hear that. Faith's heart must be breaking. I'll be praying that Travis finds him safe and alive."

"You pray about everything."

"Everything that matters, including you. And whatever brings Travis here, at least you'll get the opportunity to connect with him."

"I'll see him. Not so sure about connecting. He sounded more guarded than friendly."

"He can't be any more reluctant to have a relationship with you than Adam and Leif were, and look how well that worked out."

"You're right. Reckon two out of six adult kids forgiving me for being a lousy dad is better than I deserve."

"Forgiving is not related to deserving. And call me an optimist, R. J. Dalton, but I have this sneaking suspicion that all six of your children will at least make a visit within the next few months. If not, it's their loss."

"I won't be holding my breath for Jake to show up. If he does, it will be to harangue me." R.J. scratched his jaw, thinking that even his face felt unfamiliar now. He'd lost thirty pounds since the doc had handed him the death sentence.

The only real pleasure he had was having Adam and his family and Leif and Joni around. Those two adorable twin girls of Leif's were a pure joy.

"I'd best be going," Carolina said. "I'm on my way to my Bible-study class and just wanted to drop off some of the vegetable-beef soup I made this morning."

"Appreciate that. You know how I love that soup. Rich, beautiful and you cook. Don't know how you keep the men from breaking down your door."

"I keep my shotgun loaded."

R.J. hooted and slapped his hand against his knee. "That'll keep out the riffraff."

"You know that Hugh was the love of my life, R.J. There's not a man in Texas who can fill his shoes."

But Hugh was dead and Carolina was much too young to crawl into bed alone every night. "No need to fill Hugh's shoes," R.J. said. "Get a man who's got his own boots."

"It would never be the same."

"No," he agreed. "But that don't mean it can't be good. Growing old alone can get mighty lonely."

Carolina rose from the porch swing, walked over and laid one of her graceful hands over his ruddy, wrinkled one. "Don't you worry about me, R.J. I'll never be alone as long as I have my family and my memories. You're not alone, either. And now you have another son on his way home."

"Yeah. Stay tuned. I'll let you know how that goes."

"You do that." She bent over and kissed him on his cheek.

He resisted the urge to give her a harmless pinch on her shapely bottom. She was too much a lady for his antics. So he merely watched and appreciated the view as she walked down the front steps and to her car.

He was courting the grim reaper, but he wasn't dead yet.

"Are you sure this is necessary, Travis? I feel awkward staying in your father's house with him suffering from a brain tumor, especially since he barely knows me."

"Too late to have second thoughts now. We're less than five miles from the ranch and I already told him we were on our way."

Besides, Travis was having enough second thoughts for both of them. He'd fought to push his resentment toward R.J. aside years ago. You took what life handed you and you ran with it. It was called survival.

But with every mile, the memories he'd stashed away became more vivid. He'd left the hell behind him, but the images would never disappear entirely.

Faith tugged on the restraining band of her seat belt and turned toward him. "I thought you and R.J. barely spoke."

"Hopefully, that won't change much in the next few days."

"I can see why you'd feel some residual bitterness," she said. "I can't imagine being farmed out to foster homes when your own father didn't take you in after your mother's death."

So his past was common knowledge. "Did Leif tell you that?"

"Joni. She says relations between Leif and R.J. were so strained at first, she feared Leif would never feel any kind of connection with him. And now he and Joni are building a house on Dry Gulch land."

"I'm not Leif."

"I've noticed," Faith said. "Cop versus attorney. Big difference, but you look like a man who'd be at home on a ranch. You have that natural cowboy swagger."

"Is that bad?"

"You wear the attitude well." She smiled in spite of the situation.

Unfortunately, Faith didn't leave it at that and let the subject of R.J. die.

"Joni says R.J. has lots of regrets about the way he lived his life."

"Dying reprobates usually do, or so I've heard."

"Joni didn't know the old R.J., but she really likes the man he is now. She's thrilled that he and Leif are finally working things out between them."

Time to change the subject, Travis decided as he turned onto the narrow county road that led to the ranch.

"Let's go over again what I need you to do and not do while you're staying at the ranch."

Faith rolled her eyes. "Isn't that overkill? You drilled it into me before we ever left Dallas."

"I thought I'd drilled it into your head to stay away from Georgio, too, and look how that turned out."

"Point made. I'm not supposed to tell anyone that I'm staying at the Dry Gulch Ranch. But do you really think that whoever bugged my house is going to try to track me down?"

"Yep. I do. Georgio is not one to be deterred by a small inconvenience like you not coming home after work."

"You really are convinced that he's the one who had the house bugged, aren't you?"

"Unless you've got a stalker or jealous lover you're keeping secret."

"No stalkers. No lovers, jealous or otherwise."

The no-lovers assurance was the only thing about this he liked. The one thing that shouldn't matter to him at all.

"Georgio feeds you a line of bull, says he'll take over the search for Cornell and warns you not to talk to the cops. Then your house is bugged while he makes sure you're not at home to get in the way. Doesn't take a detective to figure that one out."

She shifted and stared out the window. "I don't doubt you, but it's still hard to digest all of this. Georgio seemed so sincere."

"He's sincerely evil and manipulative and used to having things go his way. Take my word for that and don't say anything to give him a clue where you are or that you're with me."

"I'm sure he'll never guess that I'm at your father's ranch."

Travis found that hard to believe himself. The closer he got to the ranch, the stronger the temptation to turn around and find somewhere else to take Faith.

But he couldn't be with her every second, and she'd never be alone at the ranch. Adam, R.J., a wrangler named Corky and a couple of young wranglers from Canada Adam had hired on to work for the summer would all be there. They could handle trouble if it popped up, not that Travis expected it to. Georgio limited his witnesses.

Adam's wife and twin daughters would be on the Dry Gulch as well, so Faith would have female company to hopefully keep her spirits from bottoming out.

He slowed and turned off the county road onto the ranch blacktop. The metal gate was closed. He stopped and shifted into Park.

"I'll get it," Faith said, opening her door and jumping out before he could beat her to the task. She was graceful as a doe, her dark hair dancing about her slender shoulders, her hips swaying as she walked to the gate and then unlatched it.

Travis's mind battled with his libido. There was no doubt which was winning as she swung open the gate and waited for him on the other side.

Worst part of it all was that his infatuation with her went far deeper than just physical attraction. It was her vulnerability, her toughness when she looked as soft as spring hay, her commitment to her son. Hell, it was everything about her.

Five minutes later they arrived at the old ranch house. The structure looked years older in the glaring sun than it had in the glittering lights that had illuminated the area on Leif's wedding night. The shutters needed replacing. The paint was fading.

Yet somehow the pots of blooming flowers, the worn rockers and the colorful pillows tossed onto the wooden porch swing gave the place a homey feel.

But it wasn't Travis's home.

Hadn't been since he was much too young to remember it, and would never be again. Leif, Adam and the others could do as they chose, but Travis wasn't about to grovel for a share of the inheritance that should have come automatically to him.

Even if it had, he wasn't sure he'd have accepted it. R.J. hadn't been there when Travis was all alone and desperately needed a father. As far as he was concerned, R.J. was no kin to him.

Travis got out of the truck and rounded the front of it on his way to open Faith's door. The sound of horse hooves slapping against the dry earth caught his attention. He turned and watched R.J approach on a beautiful filly.

Atop the magnificent animal, R.J. looked much more virile than the frail, confused man Travis had helped into the house after the reception Saturday night. Leif had said he had his good days and his bad days. Apparently, this was the former.

Faith got out of the car and walked over to where he was dismounting.

"Sorry I wasn't here when you arrived," R.J. said. "Be a shame to waste a day like this inside, so I took Miss Dazzler for a ride. Left the door unlocked, though. Always do."

"No problem," Faith said. "We just arrived."

"I'll hitch Miss Dazzler to the porch railing and then call Corky to come ride her to the barn and get her un-saddled."

"I can do that for you," Travis offered. Might as well make an attempt at friendliness, since they were going to be sharing a roof for a few days.

"Appreciate the offer," R.J. said. "But Corky can handle Miss Dazzler while you two fill me in on what brought you here. Not that you're not welcome, whatever it is. Lord knows I got the room. Place is so empty and lonesome at night, even ghosts avoid it."

Faith took R.J.'s arm as they climbed the steps. Travis lingered behind for a few seconds, attempting to come to grips with the fact that no matter why he was here, he was about to reopen a cask full of old wounds.

His cell phone vibrated before he reached the top step. John Patterson. An old friend who had worked for the DPD before taking a position with Border Patrol.

Travis took the call. "What's up, John?"

"You know that missing son of a friend you asked me to check out? Cornell Ashburn?"

"Yeah. Did you locate him?"

"Yes and no."

"What does that mean?"

"He's in the area, but he managed to get away from my agents. It's a long story, and I'd rather not go into it on the phone. But I can tell you this. Cornell Ashburn is not just some innocent runaway. There will be a warrant out for his arrest by morning."

Chapter Eleven

Travis swallowed the curses that flew to his throat. The news from John Patterson hadn't shocked him, but it meant he'd have to destroy Faith's trust in her son—the only thing getting her through this.

"I'll try to be there before that happens," Travis said.

There was a short period of silence. "Don't come to the office. Just give me a call," John said. "I'll meet you someplace where we can talk—off the record. Officially, you and I haven't spoken."

"Got it."

When Travis broke the connection, he realized that both R.J. and Faith were staring at him expectantly.

Faith's expression was grim and her smooth hands were knotted into tight fists, the strain mirrored in her dark, expressive eyes. "Was that phone call about Cornell?"

Travis hesitated, determining how to handle this. If he lied to her, she'd find out eventually, anyway. The lie would break their fragile bonds of trust. It might even backfire completely and send her running back to Georgio for help.

"It was, wasn't it?" she repeated.

Travis nodded, dreading the questions that would follow.

"Has someone located him?" Her voice trembled.

"No, but there appears to be a credible lead."

She exhaled slowly. "Finally. Is he in Texas?"

"Laredo, or at least that's where I have to go to meet my source and follow up on the lead."

"Sounds vague," R.J. interjected. "Who is this source of yours, anyway? Is he in law enforcement?"

Travis stopped himself from blurting out that this was none of R.J.'s business. In a way it was his business now. Bringing Faith here for protection had changed the rules.

"He's a friend," Travis said, not giving anything else away.

"I don't care who he is," Faith said, "as long as he can help me find my son."

"Nothing's guaranteed," Travis reminded her, knowing that if John was right, finding Cornell would dump a whole new set of worries and heartbreak on Faith.

"How far is it to Laredo?" she asked.

"Somewhere around five hundred miles, give or take a detour or two," R.J. answered.

"Then just a short flight," she declared, excitement building in her voice. "Planes fly out of Dallas every few minutes. Surely there's one to Laredo tonight. All we have to do is call and see which ones have seats available."

"Seats?"

"I'm going with you," she said. "I'd go crazy just sitting around here waiting."

How the devil had he bungled this up so bad? "Not a good idea," Travis said.

"Why not?" Faith demanded.

Because she wouldn't like what she'd learn. Because they might find her son behind bars.

"All I have is a lead, Faith. It may take days to track it fully. You'll be a lot more comfortable waiting here."

"I'm going with you," she said firmly.

R.J. scratched his chin. "Might wind up no more than chasing a hawk's shadow, Faith. If I were you, I'd let Travis do the legwork. He's used to it."

At least this time R.J. was interfering in Travis's favor.

Faith shook her head. "It's been ten months. Ten months of tears and heartbreak and fear that never lets go. If there's even a chance this will lead to finding Cornell, I deserve to be there."

Travis gave up the argument, but he still had no intention of taking her with him.

"I'll check with the airlines," he said.

"If we can't get a flight, we can drive," Faith urged.

"Take you half the night to get there in a car," R.J. stated.

"But we'd be there. I'd rather be driving than just waiting," Faith insisted. "You said yourself the clue is credible, Travis. We shouldn't waste time. We can take turns driving while the other sleeps. We'd be in Laredo by morning."

"You'd be plumb tuckered out," R.J. said, still doing the arguing for Travis. Not that there was any way he'd wait until morning.

Travis moved to the front door. "Let's talk inside."

"Good idea," R.J. agreed. "Matilda was making a fresh pot of coffee when I left for my short ride. She does that every afternoon. Has her a cup and then heads home. Once you get settled, that just might hit the spot." He opened the door and led the way.

"I hope I'm not putting you out too much," Faith said. "If we'd had any idea we'd be catching a plane tonight, we wouldn't have had to bother you at all."

"Never a bother having a pretty woman around. And God knows I've got the room, what with Adam and

Hadley and the girls in their own place, and Leif and Joni off honeymooning. This house is as lonely as a church pew on Saturday night."

He should have thought of that before running off on all his wives. Travis stopped behind Faith as R.J. flung open a door off the hallway.

"Plenty more guest rooms upstairs," R.J. said, "but this is the best of the bunch. Bought a new mattress for the old four-poster. Joni and my other daughter-in-law, Hadley, did the rest of the sprucing up."

Faith stepped inside. "It's lovely," she said, though it was obvious her thoughts were still on getting to Laredo and the prospect of finding her son.

Their only hope was that John Patterson had the wrong man. John never did.

Faith turned to R.J. "Do you have a computer we can use to check flights?"

"There's a laptop on the desk in the family room. We've even got wireless in the house now. Adam's bringing the Dry Gulch up to snuff with all that tech stuff. I swear he can tell you how many bulls got lucky last night with just a couple of double clicks."

Travis seriously doubted that and didn't want to even think about getting lucky, since he was certain he wouldn't be.

"I have my laptop with me," he said. "I'll check for flights."

"Good idea," R.J. said. "Password is *NOTLAD,* all caps. That's *Dalton* spelled backward. Had to find something I can remember. My memory being what it is these days, I can't always recall something as simple as that."

Travis turned on the computer and began to scan for available flights. As he suspected, the last direct flight out tonight left in forty-five minutes. No way could he make that. There were a few later flights, but they went around the moon to get there and didn't make it until tomorrow morning, anyway.

Faith was hanging over his shoulder, so he didn't have to explain the situation to her. What he needed was to get her out of the room while he made a call and booked a charter flight. One that would cost him a small fortune and get him to Laredo as quickly as possible.

He pushed back from the antique mahogany desk where he'd been working. "We need to talk, Faith."

TRAVIS LOOKED EVERY bit the classic hero, from the rugged planes of his face to the piercing stare that seemed to see right through her. But tonight there was no smile to add that mischievous flair to his lips. No swagger to his step once he'd taken that phone call on the porch.

Yet even with tension so thick it seemed to squeeze the air from the room, she was drawn to him in a way she'd never been drawn to any man. More than sensual. Far more than physical. A mysterious bond that made her ache to trust him.

In spite of that, she knew he was holding back, keeping things from her. Protecting—or manipulating? Either way, she wouldn't be humored and kept in the dark.

She walked over and sat on the edge of the bed, the new mattress barely giving beneath her weight. "We do need to talk, Travis, but honestly. I admit I'm naive, especially where Cornell is concerned. But I'm not stupid."

"I never thought for a second that you were."

"But you're treating me like I am."

He stood and began to pace the room, avoiding eye contact. "How do you mean?"

"You said there was a credible lead, but I didn't hear any relief in your voice—not when you were talking to the caller or to me and R.J. Your words say one thing, your body language something completely opposite."

"Good thing the suspects I interrogate don't read me the way you do."

"What did the caller really tell you, Travis?"

"You're not totally off base," he admitted. "But I didn't lie to you, Faith. There is a good chance that Cornell is in or near Laredo, perhaps on the Mexican side of the border."

"What else did he say?"

"You're not going to give up until I level with you, are you?"

"No, but I can handle this. I'm tougher than I look."

"I'm figuring that out." He started to sit down beside her, but then walked over to the desk chair and pulled it over instead. He sat facing her, inches away, a pained look glazing his dark eyes.

"John, that's the caller's first name. I'd like to leave the rest anonymous for now. Anyway, he says there will be a warrant out for Cornell's arrest before morning."

Her temper erupted. "What are the charges?"

"John didn't say. He didn't want to talk over the phone, but my guess is that they have to do with smuggling drugs across the border."

"Why would you guess that?"

"Because of Georgio's involvement in this. If he's using your son to run drugs, then it would explain why he bugged your house once he found out Cornell was trying to get in touch with you."

"You're wrong," she said. "Cornell would never get involved in smuggling—unless…"

"Go on," Travis encouraged.

"Unless he's being blackmailed by Georgio. Only I

can't imagine what he could have done that would give Georgio grounds for blackmail."

Faith knew what Travis was thinking, the same thing she'd be thinking if this was someone else taking about her son. That she was a mother who refused to think her boy capable of committing a crime, even though he'd clearly had a life he'd kept secret from her. A lover who was an erotic dancer. That he was possibly the father of a child, a grandson or granddaughter she'd never seen or rocked to sleep or sung a lullaby to.

A suffocating ache swelled in Faith's chest. In her mind, Cornell was still a child. Had she clung too tightly? Had she needed him to need her so badly that she'd blinded herself to what was going on with him? Had he turned to Georgio instead of her?

And now...

"The young men whose murders you've been investigating, Travis. Do you think it's possible Georgio had them killed for crossing him?"

Travis reached over and took her hands in his. He massaged her palms with his thumbs. "I don't think there's anything Georgio is not capable of, Faith."

"Then if he thinks Cornell is about to be arrested, he might go after my son himself, to keep him from implicating him under interrogation."

It had taken her a few minutes to come to this conclusion, but Travis would have thought it the second he took that call. "And to think I almost played right into Georgio's hands."

"But you didn't," Travis said.

"We have to find Cornell before Georgio does," Faith said, a new sense of urgency making her more determined than ever. "We have to get to Laredo at once. Charter a plane. I'll find a way to pay for it."

"I can take care of the flight, Faith. But you just heard me explain how dangerous this could be. I can't take you with me. Surely you understand that now."

"I only understand one thing. We have to find my son and there is no time to waste. And I will be going either with you, Travis, or on my own."

"You make it hard for a man to protect you, Faith Ashburn."

"But it means a lot that you want to," she admitted.

She wanted to say more. Tell him that when this was over, how much she'd love to be held in his strong, protective arms and taste his tempting, heroic lips.

But first they had to find Cornell. She had the needs of a woman, but the heart of a mother.

THE JARRING RING of the doorbell interrupted the fourth phone call Travis had made in search of a charter service that could get the two of them to Laredo tonight without swallowing his meager checking account. He heard deep male voices in the house mingling with R.J.'s weaker one.

Hopefully, the company would leave before Travis was forced to interact with them. He had too much on his mind for small talk.

"No plane available before morning," he said, reiterating what the woman on the other end of the phone had just told him.

"I'm sorry, but there's a major international energy conference in town and people have been jetting in and out all week," she added.

"What about your turboprop planes?"

"Have one that might be available about 1:00 a.m., but I'll have to see if I can locate a pilot. Regulations won't let the guy piloting it now clock any more hours without a significant break."

"Okay. I may get back to you."

But first Travis would get back to John Patterson and ask to be informed immediately if and when Cornell was arrested. If he was behind bars, not getting there before tomorrow would pose no problems, though Travis was certain Faith wouldn't see it that way.

Travis massaged the back of his neck, a futile effort to relieve the ever-building tension.

Faith put a hand on his shoulder. "No luck?"

"Not yet."

"Cornell, about to be arrested. I can't bear the thought of him behind bars and yet I wish he would be. Then I could at least talk to him, know he's safe. We could get this horrible misunderstanding straightened out and I could take him home."

As always the desperation in her voice turned Travis inside out. He longed to hold her close and whisper that everything would be all right, but it would be an empty promise. And once she was in his arms, with her soft body pressed into his, comfort wouldn't be the only thing on his mind.

He wanted to kiss her, had wanted to since the night he first laid eyes on her in the Passion Pit, though he hadn't admitted that to himself then. Now the desire was entangled with his need to keep her safe and help her find her son.

The urgency should have cooled his sensual cravings. Instead, it was making them worse.

He heard R.J.'s scuffling footfalls outside the guest room, followed by taps on the door.

Travis walked over and flung it open.

"I got a couple of guys in the kitchen I'd like you to meet, Travis."

Not the best of times for being sociable, but Travis

could use a cup of coffee and a break from the lustful urges that were starting to pummel his senses.

R.J. leaned against the doorframe. "You're welcome to join us, too, Faith. I think you'll be interested in what the Lamberts have to say."

Reluctantly, Travis closed his computer and followed Faith and R.J. to the kitchen.

One of the men was refilling his coffee cup. The other was sitting at the table, his elbows resting on an unfolded map of Texas. Both looked the part of real ranchers. Tanned. Lean and muscular. Dressed in jeans and Western shirts and wearing work-worn cowboy boots.

R.J. took care of the introductions. Tague and Damien Lambert. The names sounded familiar. Perhaps Leif had mentioned them.

"I don't mean to pry into your business, but I hear you're in a hurry to get to Laredo," Damien said once Faith and Travis had coffees in hand.

"We were hoping to get there tonight," Travis said. "Not having much luck with that, though." He let it go at that, not willing to get into details with a couple of strangers.

"We have a new four-seater Piper we use mostly for ranch business," Damien said. "It's not as comfortable as the corporate jets owned by Lambert Oil, but it'll get you to Laredo with no problems and it's available. All we'd have to do is fill it with fuel."

The Lamberts, one of the richest oil and ranching families in Texas. No wonder the names had sounded familiar. "Do you have a pilot?" Travis asked, suddenly fully engaged.

Tague grinned. "Me. And it just so happens I have a few hours to kill."

"Are you offering to fly Faith and me to Laredo tonight?" Travis asked.

"Yeah, if you're interested. Only problem is I'll have to fly straight from Laredo to A&M in the morning for a seminar I'm leading on innovative breeding ideas."

"No problem there," Travis said. "We can find a commercial flight back. It's just getting there that's urgent."

"Then I guess it's settled." Tague lifted and tipped his cup as if it were a crystal flute and they were making toasts.

Problem solved almost too easily, Travis decided. Easy always made him suspicious. "What's the charge?"

"No charge. Just call it a neighborly gesture."

"A very thoughtful gesture," Travis said, shocked that R.J., a womanizing boozer who hadn't bothered to keep in touch with any of his own children for most of his life, was such good friends with a family as socially elite as the Lamberts.

"R.J. says you're looking at some real trouble that needs immediate attention," Damien said. "If we can help, it would be a downright sin not to."

"Plus, we've all been there," Tague said. "When trouble hits, you need family and friends. No questions asked, by the way. No explanations required. It's the cowboy way of doing business."

Travis knew the cowboy way. It wasn't so different from the cop code. But none of his cop friends owned prop planes.

"If you're sure you don't mind, Faith and I will definitely take you up on your offer."

"We're sure," Tague said.

They worked out the details over a second cup of coffee. Two hours later they had taken off and were headed toward Laredo.

GEORGIO STARED AT the traffic ahead, cursing the other drivers, seething with anger. Things were going south at the speed of light. Somehow Faith Ashburn was behind all this. He should have given the word to have Cornell killed the second he'd heard that the mixed-up kid had called his mother.

No, he should have had him killed the first night Faith had showed up at the Passion Pit. The woman had always been trouble. Too gutsy. Too determined. A pit bull without a leash.

Instead he'd stupidly found her amusing, been impressed by all that motherly concern. A quality his own mother had sadly lacked.

Georgio had figured that after a few months, Faith would grow weary and leave the search for her son to the police. Cops, or any other law-enforcement officials for that matter, had never been much of a challenge for Georgio. Either they were too tied up by rules and regulation to be effective, or they could be bought.

Travis Dalton was the exception. He and his latest partner, Reno Vargas, had dogged Georgio constantly for the past eighteen months, had been in and out of his clubs more often than any of his paying clientele. Asking questions. Making Georgio's customers and employees nervous.

And now Cornell had screwed up royally. There was a warrant out for his arrest. He was on the run—not only from the hapless border agents, but apparently from Georgio, as well. There had been no contact.

The kid couldn't possibly think Georgio wouldn't know about the incident. Or maybe he could. Cornell was naive enough to buy into everything Georgio had told him to this point. Naive and desperate.

In spite of that, Georgio had started to like Cornell. He'd even anticipated a few romps with Faith.

Too bad that both Cornell and his mother would have to die. Georgio liked his problems wrapped up neatly, and there was one thing you could always count on with corpses. They never squealed or testified.

Chapter Twelve

Faith stared straight ahead at the string of red taillights that stretched out in front of their rented sedan. Her muscles were stiff from the constant tension. The lining of her stomach felt as if it had been smeared with acid.

She stretched and pulled one foot onto the seat with her. "How much farther to the truck stop where we're supposed to meet John?"

"Ten more miles."

"Did you ever tell him that I'd be with you?"

"No, but there's something else I should tell you. John is not just a friend. He's a border-patrol agent."

"Why didn't you tell me that originally?"

"He's talking to me unofficially. That's why we're meeting at the truck stop. I'm not sure he'll be as open if I show up with you."

Her frustrations swelled yet again. "Cornell is my son. I have every right to know why he's being arrested."

"I'd still like to talk to John alone first."

"So I just sit in the car?"

"No. I'm not comfortable with that."

"So what's the plan?"

"You go in first," Travis said. "Take a seat and order from the menu, even if it's just coffee. I'll come in a few minutes later and go sit by John. After that, I'll just have to play this by ear."

"I don't see why you get to call all the shots, Travis."

"Because I'm a cop and you—"

The ringing of her phone interrupted his answer. She checked the caller ID.

Unavailable.

Faith's breath caught. Her heart pounded. "It must be Cornell," she whispered. "Hello?"

She heard breathing on the line, but no voice.

"Cornell. Cornell."

"Mrs. Ashburn."

A woman's voice. Low. Shaky. Faith took a deep breath and bit back tears as dashed hope churned in her stomach.

"Yes," she said. "Who's calling?"

"You don't know me, but my name is Angela."

Faith's heart skipped a beat. "Angela Pointer?"

"Yes, ma'am. How do you know about me?"

"From emails found on Cornell's computer. Have you talked to Cornell? Do you know where he is?"

"I don't know where he is. He wouldn't say, but I did hear from him. He's in trouble, Mrs. Ashburn. Bad trouble."

"What kind of trouble?" If she pretended not to know anything, perhaps Angela would tell her the full truth.

"I can't say. But he wants you to know that no matter what you hear, he loves you. And he's sorry for all he's done."

"What has he done, Angela? What has he done that he would need to apologize to me for?"

"He's broken the law. He wants you to know that it's all his doing, and he doesn't want you to get involved. Don't try to find him."

"If Cornell broke the law, he had to have a very good reason. I can help him, Angela. I'm with a cop right now who's on his side. I just have to know where to find him."

"He doesn't want you to look for him, Mrs. Ashburn. He loves you. Just know that."

"I do, but I have to find—"

Angela broke the connection. Faith held tight to the phone, willing her to pick up again, but the phone stayed silent. Her one link to Cornell had vaporized into thin air.

"I take it that was Angela Pointer," Travis said.

"Yes. She refused to tell me, but I'm sure she knows where Cornell is. We have to track down that number."

"I'll call the precinct and have someone trace the call. What did Angela tell you?"

Faith shared the gist of the message, new fears forming as she did. "I think Angela is turning against Cornell, if she was ever with him. She worked for Georgio. It makes sense that they were both involved in Cornell's disappearance."

"Anything's possible," Travis agreed.

The possibilities made Faith nauseated. If she was right, this conniving, lying woman might be the mother of her grandchild—a child that might never be part of Faith's life.

Memories flooded her, of the first time she'd held Cornell in her arms. She'd worried that she wouldn't know what to do, feared that she might not even like the baby who would soon take over her life.

But then he'd wrapped his tiny fingers around one of hers and wrapped himself around her heart. That the tiny infant could be a living, breathing being, part of her, part of his father, had seemed like a miracle almost beyond comprehension.

At that moment, she'd become a real mother.

She remembered his first seizure. Faith had walked into his room and found him writhing on the floor, his eyes rolled back in his head. And then there was the night she and Melvin had stayed at his bedside all night, crying, praying, afraid he wouldn't make it until morning. Each breath had been a struggle—for Cornell and for them.

That same sick panic that she was about to lose him was taking over again.

She looked up as Travis slowed and then pulled into the parking lot of a truck stop. The big rigs were parked in the back. A few cars, two pickup trucks and a cluster of motorcycles lined the front.

Travis parked near the front door. "I'll call my partner while you go inside," he said. "I want to get someone tracing that phone number pronto."

"What does your friend look like?"

"Mid-fifties, receding hairline, salt-and-pepper hair. Wearing a red plaid shirt."

She realized then that he'd already spotted the man through the wide, dirt-smeared windows. She nodded, then opened the door and stepped out onto the pavement.

A few seconds later, she walked right by the secretive border-patrol agent. There was a gun at his hip. No doubt loaded and ready to fire.

A gun that he would undoubtedly use to kill her son if it came to that.

"FIND ANGELA POINTER," Travis said once he'd filled Reno in on the latest phone call from her. "If we do, I'm almost positive she could lead us to Cornell."

"I'm working on it," Reno said. "I've also put a tail 24/7 on Georgio. If Cornell screwed up smuggling a cache of drugs for him, Georgio will do his best to keep Cornell from being arrested and interrogated."

"Exactly," Travis agreed. "And we both know what he's willing to do to make sure no one involves him in his own dirty work. I figure he's already been in touch with Cornell and is calling all the shots."

"Like a possible execution, gangster-style. Do you need me in Laredo?"

"Not at the present. I'd rather have you on top of things in Dallas. Finding Cornell is getting more critical by the second."

"Right. Give me a call once you talk to Patterson."

"Will do. Later."

Travis pocketed his phone, got out of the car and went inside. He glanced at Faith and then sidled into a chair opposite John.

John pushed an empty plate away. "Fast trip."

"Friend with a plane."

"Ah. Moving up in the world. I heard you were in for a big inheritance."

"Where did you hear that?"

"Word gets around. Money and part interest in a ranch was the way I heard it."

"Don't believe everything you hear."

The waitress came over and refilled John's cup. "What can I get you?"

"Hamburger's good," John said. "Onion rings are even better." He wiped his mouth on a paper napkin.

"I've eaten," Travis said. "Just coffee for me."

John waited until the waitress was out of earshot. "Exactly what is your connection to Cornell Ashburn?"

"His mother is best friends with my new sister-in-law." That was a fact, though it barely scratched the surface of the truth.

"This news is not going to make her happy."

"No doubt about that, but she's so desperate to find him that an arrest might be a relief."

"I can understand that. I've got a sixteen-year-old son myself. A good kid but a bit of a rebel. I worry about him all the time."

"I'd worry he wasn't your son if he didn't have a bit of a rebel in him."

John grinned and then went right back to business.

"The warrant for Cornell's arrest has been issued and the case is officially open, so I can fully level with you now."

"Hit me with it."

"Cornell has been towing a horse trailer across the border every few weeks for months. He picks up two to three horses and brings them into America."

"Are the horses stolen?"

"No. He's been stopped more than once in the past. Paperwork is always in order. They are legitimate sales and animals have passed inspection. But you know how it is. We're always suspicious that a young man crossing the border at frequent intervals may be into drug smuggling."

"You must have found proof that he was."

"No. Even the dogs never found a trace of drugs in that horse trailer or the pickup truck he was driving."

"Until today?"

John shook his head and waited as the waitress set a white mug of steaming coffee in front of Travis.

She leaned over, revealing a seductive glimpse of cleavage. "We have some great apple pie. Sure you don't want a piece to go with that java?"

Travis waved her off. "Not tonight, thanks.... So why the warrant?" he asked when the waitress had left.

"We were anonymously tipped off today that there was a hidden compartment built into the floor of the horse trailer. I ordered in some extra agents to check out the tip."

"If not drugs, what did you find?"

"Solid-gold religious icons and other statues and jeweled relics believed stolen from a church in Peru over the last few years. The stolen goods were estimated to be worth billions."

"Son of a bitch. Georgio Trosclair has apparently branched out into new, even more lucrative endeavors."

John's eyebrows arched. "I never mentioned Georgio."

"Then I should tell you the rest of the story. But first, if you found stolen relics in the horse trailer, why didn't you take Cornell into custody then?"

"A question I've asked everybody at the scene. He slipped away even before they found the contraband. It was as if he knew they'd been tipped off that it was there."

"Maybe he was the one who supplied the tip."

"I considered that," John said.

Travis filled him in on the details of Cornell's disappearance, his connection with Angela Pointer and Georgio's recent attempt to reach out to Faith, culminating with her house being bugged.

"That explains a lot," John said. "I figured there was no way Cornell Ashburn had masterminded and carried this out on his own. I wish I had known that sooner, but we didn't even know Cornell's real name until we realized the ID he carried today was fake. It still might have taken days to identify him if you hadn't sent that picture to me personally."

And by that time, Georgio would likely have found Cornell first. He still might. The gory reality of that pushed a new wave of adrenaline through Travis's veins.

"We need every available resource dedicated to finding Cornell," he urged. "Rangers, state police, border patrol and local cops. You know what it means if Georgio gets to him first."

"I'm on it the second we leave here," John said. "And I need to talk to Cornell's mother. What's the best way to reach her?"

"Through me." Travis turned, caught Faith's eye and motioned her over.

"Just a friend of your sister-in-law," John said, clearly not believing him. "You failed to mention she was a knockout."

"Is she? I never noticed."

"Right."

The kidding around stopped the second Travis introduced Faith to John. The situation was dead serious.

AN HOUR AFTER meeting Travis's friend, Faith was practically numb, still fighting off shock at the ludicrous accusations against Cornell. She dropped her handbag to the sofa, barely noticing the roomy suite in the recently renovated motel John Patterson had recommended.

Patterson had spoken of a man. Cornell was just a kid, a teen beginning his senior year in high school when he'd disappeared. Listening to the accusations Patterson had spouted so coldly had been difficult. Believing them was impossible.

Yet John Patterson believed them. She suspected Travis did, as well.

"It's been a long day," Travis said.

"Only a day. It seems weeks since I met Georgio for lunch."

"You should probably get some sleep. You take the bed. I'll take the sofa."

"Or we could toss a coin for it," she suggested.

"No. The couch is fine with me. I never sleep much when I'm working on a case."

"Aren't you always working on a case?"

"Yep. Sleep is overrated."

"I'm pretty sure I won't sleep tonight, either," she said.

Travis dropped to the sofa and propped his feet on the wooden coffee table. "Want to talk?"

"I may not make sense. I'm bewildered, unable to relate to the person John Patterson says is my son."

"I can understand that. Talking about it might help."

"I don't see how." She sank to the sofa beside him. "I know it's hard to understand if you don't have a son of your own, but I know this is not what it seems. If Cornell was driving that horse trailer, he either didn't know about the contraband or was somehow forced to do it."

"Tell me about the Cornell you know, Faith."

"You think I'm just a prejudiced mother, don't you?"

"I think you're an amazing woman who loves her son very much. I had a mother like that—or so I've been told. I don't remember much about her. You've probably heard that she died of cancer about the time I started school."

"She'd be proud of you," Faith said. How could she not? He was tough, a man's man. Yet he was also protective and gentle and…

And she was falling hard for him. Crazy to feel this when her life was in chaos and her heart was breaking. But she'd love nothing more than to find refuge in the protective warmth of his strong arms.

"I don't know where to start talking about Cornell," she said.

"Start wherever you like."

She closed her eyes for a few seconds, letting the thoughts of happier times creep into her consciousness. "I was seventeen and pregnant when I married Melvin

Ashburn. He was two years older, out of high school and working for his dad in the construction business."

"Awful young to start a family. Of course, I'm almost thirty-nine and have never even gotten married. But that's a topic for another time."

She wondered if that was his way of warning her not to get any romantic ideas where he was concerned. It was a warning her heart should heed.

"We were young," she agreed, "so I guess it wasn't so surprising that once Cornell was born, Melvin felt trapped. He hung out with his friends, drinking and carousing."

"And you stayed home with Cornell?"

"I did. He was my life. I marveled at each new thing he did. The first words. The first steps. And somehow the marriage survived far longer than the teenage hormone-induced lust we'd been sure was the real thing."

"How did Cornell react to the divorce?"

"He took it hard, the way any kid does when his father walks out. He felt as if his dad had abandoned him instead of me."

"What kind of father was Melvin after the divorce?"

"The kind who was seldom around, the same as before the divorce. But he did breeze in on occasion and take Cornell on exciting trips. And he was there with me when Cornell almost died from his mysterious illness."

Travis pulled his feet from the coffee table and turned to face her. "A divorce, an illness that almost killed him, a seizure disorder and the death of his father. Cornell had a tough few years, more than most grown men could have handled without it breaking them."

The comment hit a nerve. She was opening her heart to Travis and he was using her words to find reasons for her son to become a criminal.

"We've talked enough," she said, her voice shaky. She walked to the kitchen area, found a glass and filled it with ice and water.

"I didn't mean to upset you, Faith."

"It doesn't matter, Travis. Nothing you say can change my mind about Cornell. He's a good kid. None of the hardships he went through changed that."

Tears came to her eyes and this time she didn't try to fight them back. She propped her elbows on the counter, buried her face in her hands and began to sob.

She heard Travis's footfalls and then felt his arms close around her. He held her tight until the sobs that racked her body grew still.

Then he tugged her around to face him. His thumb fitted under her chin and he nudged it up until she was staring into the depths of his dark eyes.

"I believe you, Faith. I don't see how anyone could have a mother like you and not be a loving, decent human. Now you have to believe me. I'll do everything in my power to help you find your son and clear his name."

"He's my world."

"I know."

In the same breath, Travis's lips found hers. She dissolved in the kiss, letting his heat and sweet reassurance wash over her and steal her breath away.

She didn't understand how passion could come in the midst of heartbreaking turmoil. All she knew was that it felt right to be in Travis's arms.

Finally, he pushed away. "I think we better stop," he said. "Unless…"

Unless she didn't want to. She didn't. She ached to fit herself in his arms and have him carry her to the bed. But would they both be sorry in the morning?

"I want you," she whispered. "But not tonight. Not until Cornell is safe and we have nothing between us but each other."

THE PAIN IN Cornell's side was growing worse. He'd pulled a muscle jumping across a fence and landing on a small ranch a few miles north of Laredo.

It was dark now, and there was light coming from just one room in the family home. Upstairs, a bedroom, he suspected. As long as he didn't do anything to upset the four horses in their stalls, he should be safe until morning.

Hunger pangs growled in his stomach. He'd drunk from the hose at the back of the barn, but he hadn't eaten since morning. He should have planned more thoroughly, but the idea had crystalized all at once. A plan to keep the artifacts out of Georgio's hands without openly double-crossing him.

Cornell had figured he could get away while they searched the horse trailer. He'd thought of it before, wondered if he'd have the nerve to make a run for it if he was caught in the act of smuggling. He'd seen others do so. Only once had he seen a man shot for trying to escape.

Cornell sat on a pile of hay and removed his boots—nice shoes, the kind a rancher's son would wear. That was what Georgio had said when he'd given them to him, along with the clothes he was to wear when he crossed the border with a shipment.

Just a few shipments. Not drugs. Not arms. Georgio had promised him that. Not that his promises meant much. He'd also promised that he'd set Cornell up with a job and a new identity on the West Coast.

The alternative was a prison cell for the rest of his

life or a cell on death row. At the time, it had seemed the only way out.

But Cornell was tired of living a lie. Sick at not being able to see anyone he cared about. Starting to hate himself for not standing up like a man and taking the punishment he deserved.

He was ready to turn himself in. The hardest part would be seeing the pain and heartbreak on his mother's face when he admitted the truth.

He had killed an unarmed man.

Chapter Thirteen

Travis spent another restless night, this one on a couch so short that his feet hung over the end. He could have pulled it out into a bed, but comfort was the least of his concerns.

A far bigger one was the fact that he could hear the sound of Faith's gentle breathing and imagine her lying between the sheets, her hair spread across the pillow, her soft breasts free.

The kiss had been his undoing. Any arguments he'd had for why he shouldn't fall for her were moot points now. He'd fallen and fallen hard.

He'd been with lots of other women. None had ever affected him the way Faith did. He couldn't explain it. Didn't understand it. Had no reference point for how love should make a man feel.

All he knew was that he would be there for her no matter what happened next, no matter what crime her son had or hadn't committed. Travis couldn't fathom not wanting to be with her every day for the rest of his life.

But if something happened to Cornell, would she ever be able to love anyone again?

When the first glow of dawn finally peeked around the edges of the drapes, he kicked off the sheet and padded to the kitchen to start a pot of coffee. He drank it in the morning quiet as he considered his next move.

Every law-enforcement agency in the state was looking for Cornell, especially now that they knew Georgio Trosclair might be the mastermind behind the smuggling. Georgio's sins were legend. He'd been getting away with drug trafficking and murder for years. There wasn't a cop worth the badge he wore who didn't want to have a hand in getting Georgio off the street and behind bars.

The bedroom door creaked just as Travis was about to start a fresh pot of coffee. He looked up. Faith stood in the doorway, her long brown hair rumpled from sleep, her face makeup-free, her eyes wide and haunted.

Desire hit so hard and fast he grew dizzy. But this was no time for weakness. He managed to pull it together.

"Good morning."

"What time is it?" she asked.

"Almost seven."

"I'm sorry. I never dreamed I'd sleep so late, but I was awake until after two."

"Then you needed the rest."

He flipped the switch on the coffeemaker. His cell phone rang. He grabbed it from the lamp table near the sofa and checked the caller ID. Reno.

"It's my partner," Travis said. He hated to talk in front of Faith in case it was bad news. "I'll be right outside."

He answered the phone as he closed the door behind him. "What's up?"

"Price of gas and a trace on the number that Angela Pointer used to call Faith."

"Good work. What's the location of origin?"

"About twenty miles north of Laredo. Phone is registered to Dolores Guiterrez."

"Any info on her?"

"She's married, has five kids, works as a cook at the Jackrabbit Chase Ranch."

"So I can probably find her there?"

"If not, I have an address for her, but here's the interesting part. Several calls were also made yesterday not from Dolores's cell phone but from Jackrabbit Chase Ranch to Georgio's encrypted cell phone, the first within a half hour after the contraband was confiscated."

"Suggesting the rancher might be the fence who was waiting for delivery."

"That's my take on it," Reno agreed. "So it's anyone's guess how Angela Pointer fits into this."

"Do we have a name for the rancher?"

"Alex Salinger, age sixty-three, well known in the community as an upright man—at least that's what I deducted from what I could find on him. He's connected to Georgio, so I'm sure there's more to the story."

"No doubt."

"All of this is out of our jurisdiction," Reno said, "so don't even think about going to the ranch."

"Is that your official position?"

"Yep. That said, give me a few hours and I'll be in Laredo to go there with you. We can't question Alex about the smuggling, but we can damn sure pretend to be looking for an old friend named Angela Pointer."

"Thanks for the offer, but you know I don't have a few hours. It's a race now to see who finds Cornell Ashburn first—law enforcement or one of Georgio's hit men."

"Either way, the kid is screwed," Reno said.

"But one way, he lives to tell about it."

"I'M NOT STAYING with some Department of Public Safety babysitter, Travis. I'm the one Angela called. She's a lot more likely to talk to me than to you."

"We don't even know that we'll find her there."

"I'm going with you."

"It could be dangerous."

"You'll protect me. And we don't have time to sit around arguing about protocol. I'll be showered and ready to go in ten minutes."

Travis threw up his hands in frustration. "Once we get to the ranch, you do exactly as I say. No wandering off by yourself and no taking over the conversation. I call the shots."

"I wouldn't want it any other way."

Faith let her hands drop from her hips, knowing she'd won. She had to talk to Angela. If she looked her in the eye, she'd know if the woman was lying.

And on the off chance that Angela really did have feelings for Cornell, surely she'd do everything she could to help Faith find Cornell. It wasn't just the best opportunity they had of finding her son quickly; it was the only option.

TRAVIS PULLED UP to the gate at Jackrabbit Chase at exactly 8:48 a.m. The time was displayed on a digitalized keypad. This was a much more sophisticated operation than he'd anticipated.

The metal gate was locked and required a code to open it. He punched the call button, sporting a friendly smile for the surveillance camera as he did.

"Can I help you?" The voice was male, a bit gruff and scratchy.

"Sure hope so. If not, this is another of my wife's wild-goose chases," he said, sticking to the lies they'd rehearsed on the drive out. "She's looking for a friend of hers named Angela Pointer. We heard she was living here at Jackrabbit Chase Ranch."

"You heard wrong."

"You sure? We got it on good authority she was here."

"Someone gave you a bum steer. But hold on a minute. I'll check with the boss and make sure I'm giving you the straight of it. Can I have your names?"

"Sure. Calvin and Eloise Hartford. Eloise and Angela go way back, all the way to sixth grade. If we don't find her here, we'll just have to visit every ranch in the area until we find her."

The silence lasted about two minutes before the voice came back online. "Mr. Salinger said he can spare a few minutes. Just follow the main road for a quarter of a mile and you'll see the house on the right."

"Sure do appreciate that."

The gate opened. So far, so good.

Faith shifted restlessly and rearranged the visor to block the glare from the sun. "She's here. I know it. But we'll never see her. They're all in this together. Cornell is only a pawn. Whatever he did wrong was against his will."

"Just remember the rules," Travis cautioned again. "I do the talking. And there will be no mention of Cornell. Not by us. John Patterson's team will have a warrant when they come out, and they can search the premises."

"And by that time, my son may be dead."

"TALK ABOUT THE LIVES of the rich, famous and corrupt," Faith said as they approached the house.

The place looked more like a plantation house than a South Texas dwelling. It was white and three stories, with a wide staircase that led to the main entrance on the second level. Giant white columns supported a covered veranda.

Tall flagpoles bearing Texas and U.S. flags flanked

the circular drive. Perfectly manicured plots of green shrubs and blooming plants ran across the front of the massive house.

Travis parked and he and Faith climbed the outdoor stairs to the heavy wooden door on the second floor, where a man met them.

"I'm Alex Salinger. Welcome to my ranch."

"Damn nice house," Travis said. "I had no idea raising cattle made this much money."

Alex chuckled and clapped him on the back. "It helps if you have a rich pappy."

Or crooked friends.

Alex led them into a huge room with two chunky leather sofas and a stone fireplace. It was a man's room, as rugged as Salinger looked with his weathered face, whiskered chin and an eagle tattoo on his left biceps.

"My security man tells me you're looking for a woman named Angela Pointer," he said.

"Yeah. My wife's on a quest to find the daughter of her best friend who died years ago. You know how it is when a woman gets something in her mind. Can't be deterred."

"I sure wish I could help, but I've never heard of an Angela Pointer. Lots of people around here I've never heard of, though, so can't go by me. Have you tried the local sheriff?"

"That's next on our list," Travis said. "Do you have anyone working for you who might know her?"

"Not likely, but I'll ask around. Tell you what," Alex said, as if what he was about to say was an afterthought. "I'll have my cook bring you some coffee and you can ask her about your friend's daughter. Dolores knows everybody around these parts."

Dolores. That sealed the deal as far as Travis was concerned. Angela had called from the ranch using Dolores Guiterrez's phone, most likely at Alex's direction. He was fishing to find out if Travis and Faith knew where Cornell was hiding.

He knew the police would trace the call but he had no qualms about letting them talk to his cook because Dolores and everyone else who worked for him knew to keep their mouths shut.

Even if Travis searched the premises, there would be no sign of Angela. Alex Salinger, like Georgio, wouldn't make mistakes.

Only they had made one. Cornell had gotten caught smuggling their stolen goods.

Alex left and returned a minute later. He settled in an oversize dark brown recliner and propped a foot over his knee as if they were there for a friendly chat.

"Ever worked as a wrangler?" the rancher asked.

"Naw. I'm a mud logger. Started out as a worm years ago out in West Texas and moved up the ladder." Travis threw out the oil-field terms most Texans were familiar with.

"Really? You wear a Stetson and boots like the real McCoy."

Dolores appeared a minute later with a tray of filled coffee mugs and a platter of warm cinnamon buns that smelled too tempting to refuse. Travis took one of each.

Faith took a cup of coffee from the tray. It tipped in her hand and drops of the hot beverage spilled over the rim and into her lap.

She yelped and jumped up, brushing coffee from her pale gray slacks. Travis hurried to her aid, but Dolores got to her first. The woman started wiping at the spill with her apron.

"I'm so sorry," she said. "I shouldn't have filled the cups so full."

"It's okay," Faith assured her. "And it was my fault, not yours. I could use a wet cloth to wipe it off, though, before it stains."

"Of course."

Dolores hurried away, with Faith a step behind her. Travis realized almost immediately what was going on. Faith had spilled the coffee deliberately for a chance to talk to the woman in private.

So much for her promise to let him handle this. He started to go after her, but on second thought changed his mind. If anyone could get information out of Dolores, it was probably Faith. Woman to woman.

Faith returned a minute later, wet cloth in hand. Dolores wasn't with her.

Alex's phone rang. He excused himself to take the call. When he returned, he was clearly irritated. "I'd like to stay and talk, but I have to get back to work. I'll see you to the door."

Just as well, Travis thought. They were wasting their time here, though he'd love to know if the phone call Alex had received concerned Cornell.

The only way to prove Salinger was lying about Angela's having been there was for the local-law enforcement team to get a search warrant, and right now Angela was not their first priority.

Thankfully, apprehending Cornell was. But it had been hours since he'd disappeared. He could be hiding out in Mexico by now.

Or lying dead in a ditch or floating in the Rio Grande, the work of Georgio's hit men.

And that would tear the heart out of the woman Travis loved.

FURY BURNED INSIDE FAITH. Dolores was a mother. She of all people should have empathized with her. And she might have if she hadn't been so scared she'd turned a ghostly shade of white.

"Dolores didn't lie when I questioned her in the kitchen," Faith said, continuing the rant she'd started the second they'd left the ranch. "She was too scared to open her mouth. She just kept shaking her head and looking over her shoulder, as if she expected Alex to walk in on us. How can someone hold that much power over another individual in this day and age?"

"It happens more than you'd guess. From school-yard bullying to adult threats of intimidation. Some people thrive on control."

"Psychos without a conscience."

"Even if we'd located Angela and you'd been able to talk to her, I don't think she could have told you where to find Cornell."

"But you don't know that."

"No, but if Georgio and Salinger knew where to find Cornell, the phone call to you would have been pointless."

"So you think Dolores was charged with finding out if I'd talked to Cornell?"

"That's a definite possibility."

"I wish Cornell would call. If I could just hear his voice…"

"My guess is he doesn't want to drag you into this."

"Or maybe he fears my phone is bugged. Can we be sure it's not?"

"Yep."

"How?"

"It's being monitored. Any attempt to bug it will automatically send a signal to the precinct and to me and Reno."

"I never knew you could do that."

"Marvels of modern technology. The trick is staying one step ahead of the criminals."

"And we're not."

"Not yet," Travis said. "We have an all-points bulletin out for Cornell's arrest. He could be apprehended at any time. So just trust your gut feelings. You've said time and time again that once we find him, there will be an explanation for all of this."

"I'm sure of it." She had to hold on to that conviction with all the strength she had left.

"We need fuel," Travis said. "And I could use some breakfast. One cinnamon roll doesn't cut it for me."

"Fine," she said. "Stop anywhere. Toast and coffee are all I can handle."

Five minutes later, Travis pulled into a service station. Faith got out of the car to go to the restroom. She stretched, then stopped and looked around to see where the annoying knocking sound was coming from.

Instead of pumping gas, Travis was standing at the back of the car.

She hurried to join him. "What is that?"

"Step away, Faith." His tone was tense. His right hand was inside his lightweight wind jacket, no doubt resting on the butt of the small pistol he carried in a shoulder holster.

Her already edgy nerves reacted with a new wave of apprehension. The knocking sounded again—three taps, as if something were signaling them.

"Step away," he repeated.

This time she did as he said.

He looked around as if to make sure no one was standing too near before pushing the trunk release button on the car key.

The trunk opened slowly. The knocking stopped, re-placed by a soft cry, similar to the mew of an injured cat. Two bare feet and one thin arm poked out.

"What the hell?" Travis reached in and offered a hand to the young woman who emerged. She tried to stand, but winced in pain and leaned against the back fender for support.

"Who are you and how did you get in my trunk?" Travis asked.

She looked around nervously and then turned to Faith. "I'm Angela Pointer. We talked last night and also a few nights before, when I warned you to stay away from Georgio."

"Both phone calls were from you?"

She nodded."

The young woman was nothing like the seductive, heartless cougar Faith had pictured. She was pretty but incredibly thin and probably not much over Cornell's age. Her hair was dishwater blond, straight and long. Her eyes revealed a troubled innocence that touched Faith in spite of the circumstances.

"Who locked you in the trunk?" Faith asked.

"No one. Sending me with you is the last thing Alex Salinger would do. He'd have killed me before he'd let me talk to you. He locked me in an upstairs bedroom and ordered me to keep quiet after his bodyguard announced you were at the ranch gate."

Faith exhaled slowly as the new and ever-changing reality sank in. "So Alex knew who we were all along."

"He's known who you were ever since you first showed up at the Passion Pitt," Angela said. "And Georgio made sure he knew who Detective Dalton is."

"How did you get out of a locked room?" Travis asked, his voice tinged with suspicion.

"I climbed out the window, crawled over the veranda railing and dropped to the ground." She reached down and massaged her swollen ankle. "That's how I got hurt."

"You could have gotten a lot more than a sprained or broken ankle," Travis said.

"And if I hadn't escaped, I would have been killed— not today, but eventually. I know too much for them to let me live. Besides, they have no reason to keep me around now that they don't need me to help keep Cornell in line."

"I don't understand," Faith said.

"I'll explain everything, but not here. We're too close to the ranch, and Alex and his so-called security staff are no doubt searching for me."

"I have enough fuel to get us a few miles farther and off the main highway," Travis said. "I'll help you into the backseat. But before we do anything, I need you to answer one question for me. Not lies. Not games."

"If I can," Angela said.

"Do you know where we can find Cornell?"

"No. All I know is what he told me when he called, just before dumping his phone into the Rio Grande."

"Which was?"

"He's on the run from Georgio and the law. He just wants to stay alive."

"How did he contact you?"

"Through Dolores Guiterrez. She's a good woman, but she's scared of Alex. Really scared. We all are."

"Okay," Travis said. "But I'd best not find out you're lying to me. If I do, I can promise you a jail cell."

"I'm through with the lies," Angela said.

"Then we'll talk. After that, you need to see a doctor about that ankle. It might be broken."

"No doctors," she declared. "No hospitals. Not in Laredo. It's too risky."

"We can argue medical care later," Faith said. "Let's just get out of here." The young woman's fear was contagious and Faith was desperate to hear what she had to say about Cornell before Alex showed up and chaos ensued.

But first she needed the answer to one important question of her own. Faith waited until they were in the car and the engine was running.

"Where's the baby, Angela? Where's my grandchild?"

Chapter Fourteen

Angela leaned forward, her gaze locked with Faith's. "How did you know about that?"

"The same way I heard that my son was involved with you—from a forensic analysis of his computer. Were you pregnant?"

"I was, but I miscarried in the first trimester. The baby wasn't Cornell's. My ex-boyfriend convinced me to give our relationship one last chance. It was a mistake. I knew that within the week, but though I wasn't aware of the fact, I was pregnant when I called everything off again.

"I know it's hard for you to believe, considering all the trouble I brought on your family, but I never had sex with your son."

That twisted the situation even more. If there was nothing between Angela and Cornell but a crush on his part, it was incredible that this had gone so far astray.

"Are you denying that you encouraged Cornell to leave home and run away with you?"

"I begged him to stay away from me and the Passion Pit. He didn't listen."

"Because he was so infatuated with you."

"No, because he has a heart of gold and he wouldn't walk away when he knew I was in trouble."

"I saw the notes he wrote you, Angela. He fancied himself in love with you."

"I'm not denying there was a strong attraction between us. I've never known anyone as honest and giving as your son. But I didn't fool myself. I've always known he deserved better than me."

Honest. Giving. A heart of gold. Those were all the things Faith knew to be true about Cornell. And yet… "All I know is that one day I had a son who was happy, who came home every night. A son who confided in me and laughed with me. Then he met you and vanished into thin air. Now there's a warrant out for his arrest."

"I know. His life is ruined."

"How did it happen? I have to know, Angela. What made Cornell turn to a man like Georgio?"

The young woman started to cry softly. Faith felt sorry for her. She truly did. But Angela was here and safe, at least for now. Cornell was on the run from the law and a man who'd see him dead before he'd let him confess his crimes.

"I think we should table this conversation until we get back to the motel," Travis urged. "And then we need to discuss it as calmly as possible—without accusations and recriminations. There will be plenty of time for those later."

"I can't go to a motel with you." Panic bled into Angela's voice. "That's the first place Alex and his men will look for me."

"I can't dump you on the street," Travis said. "Either you trust me to protect you or we go directly to the police, and you can tell your story to them. You might be able to persuade them to put you in protective custody. It's your decision."

"I can't go to the police. If I tell the truth, it will harm Cornell. I'd rather be dead than cause him more trouble."

"Then I guess you're stuck with me for a while."

Travis stopped for fuel and then at a fast-food chain with a drive-through lane. He ordered breakfast sandwiches and coffee for all of them. He also got a cup of ice for Angela to hold against her swollen ankle.

Faith tried to eat, but one bite into the sandwich she grew nauseated. Angela had promised to explain everything, but in the end it would just be more talk. She couldn't tell them where to find Cornell, and nothing else mattered at this point.

Faith reached into her pocket and touched her phone, willing it to ring. If she could only hear from Cornell, they could go to him. He surely knew that no matter what he'd done, she would never turn her back on him.

She closed her eyes and then opened them quickly as a deadly premonition wrapped strangling fingers around her heart. She might never see her son again.

As if reading her pain, Travis reached for her hand and squeezed it.

But even Detective Travis Dalton, as amazing as he was, couldn't win all the time.

By the time they reached the motel, Angela's ankle was turning a weird shade of purple. Travis picked her up and carried her inside. They used a side door that opened into a courtyard to avoid questions from the attendant at the front desk.

Unfortunately, the cleaning lady was just finishing with their suite. She moved out of the way as Travis situated Angela on the sofa and Faith retrieved pillows from the bedroom to elevate her leg.

"What happened? Did you fall?"

"It's just a sprain," Angela answered quickly. "I wasn't looking and twisted it stepping off the curb."

"I'll get you some ice."

"Thanks."

The cleaning lady rolled the vacuum cleaner out into the hall as she went for the ice.

"I NEED TO MAKE one quick call to Reno," Travis said. "I'd appreciate it if you save the explanations until I'm through. No use having to repeat everything for my benefit."

"We'll wait," Faith agreed.

An awkward silence filled the room when he stepped out. Now that the moment of truth had arrived, she wasn't sure she wanted to hear it.

If Angela's talking to the police would harm Cornell, then the facts might not set him free. Still, better a jail cell for a little while than living on the run.

"Any news?" Faith asked when Travis rejoined them.

"Nothing. Hopefully, you can shed some light on what's going on, Angela. How did Cornell get mixed up in a smuggling operation?"

She had the look of a prisoner facing a firing squad. Faith sucked in her breath and waited for an explanation that might destroy her world.

"I guess I should start at the beginning."

"Please do," Faith said. "Don't sugarcoat anything. I can't fight for Cornell unless I know exactly how he got into this situation."

Angela curled her long blond hair around her fingertips, twisting it first one way and then the other. Her eyes remained downcast, her long lashes shielding them from view.

"Cornell came into the Passion Pit one night with a bunch of his high-school friends."

"How did they get in if they were all underage?"

"They had fake IDs. All the teenagers carry them these days. Old enough to go to war at eighteen, old enough to drink and go to see a scantily clothed woman dance around a pole. That's how most of them see it."

"Is that the night you met him?"

"Yes. My ex-boyfriend showed up and started trouble. Georgio had warned him never to come inside the club when he was high, but there was no reasoning with him in that condition."

"What kind of trouble?" Faith asked.

"He cornered me as I was leaving the stage to work the tables. I tried to fight him off, but he was touching me, you know, sliding his hand inside my G-string and trying to kiss my nipples, that sort of thing."

Faith's stomach rolled as the image seared into her brain.

"Where was the bouncer?" Travis asked.

"Dealing with a rowdy customer. Before he realized what was going on and could get to me, Cornell caught Walt off guard. He threw a punch that sent Walt's head slamming into the wall.

"Blood poured from his nose, and his eyes rolled back into his head. He literally passed out for a few seconds. When he came to, he pulled himself to his feet and staggered toward Cornell, fists up for a fight.

"The men in the room started yelling to Cornell to finish him off. Fortunately, the bouncer reached them before another punch was thrown.

"He would have tossed them both out, but I intervened. I was scared that if they left together the fight would continue on the street and Cornell would get roughed up bad.

Walt was crazy when he was high, and a street fighter. Knives, blades, broken beer bottles, metal pipes. He was skilled in all of them."

Angela's voice grew shaky. She stopped talking, but finally looked up and faced Faith. "If Cornell would have left with his friends, it would have all been over. They'd have had a laugh over the fight and then forgotten about it."

Faith shared Angela's regrets. But all the ifs in the world wouldn't change things now. "What did happen?"

"I had a drink with Cornell. We connected. I'd never met anyone like Cornell. He didn't come on to me sexually or start bragging about what a big shot he was. We just talked, like old friends."

"He was a very special kid," Faith murmured.

"Almost a man," Angela reminded her. "He came back to the club a couple of times that week. On each occasion we had a chance to talk. It was two weeks before he kissed me. From that moment on our relationship changed."

That, Faith could identify with. But Cornell was so young. As she had been when she'd hooked up with Cornell's father. But the relationship had given her Cornell, and she would never be sorry for that.

"Cornell didn't want to lie to you, Mrs. Ashburn. He loves you very much. After he kissed me, he wanted me to come home with him and meet you."

"Why didn't you?"

"I knew you wouldn't be blinded like Cornell. You'd see right through me and realize how wrong I was for him."

"Yet you didn't break up with him?"

"I couldn't. He made me feel decent and special. He saw me as more than an exotic dancer. When he found out I was pregnant, he begged me to leave my job and let him take care of me. He wanted to quit school and get a job. For a few days, even I got wrapped up in the fantasy."

"He wanted to take care of you even though you were pregnant with another man's child?"

"He did. How could I not love him for that?" Angela moved her ankle and rearranged the hand towel and ice, wincing as she did so.

"Is that when Cornell went to work for Georgio?" Travis asked.

"No. Cornell would never have willingly had anything to do with Georgio. He hadn't even met him at that point, though evidently Georgio knew about us. I'm sure Walt told him."

The story seemed to be going in circles. Faith was no closer to understanding how a teenage infatuation had led Cornell into smuggling stolen religious artifacts across the border. "So your ex-boyfriend and Georgio were friends," she said in an effort to keep the order of events straight.

"Walt worked for him."

"Doing what?" Travis asked.

"Keeping the customers happy. He sold them crack cocaine, marijuana, ecstasy—anything they wanted, except when the narcs were around. Sniffing out narcs was Walt's specialty."

"I still don't understand," Faith said. "If Cornell didn't go to work for Georgio, how did he become a smuggler?"

"Walt decided he wanted me back. Apparently, he started a fight with Cornell one night when I was in the backstage dressing room. The bouncer threw them out. That's when I heard the shots."

Travis leaned forward. "Gunshots?"

Angela nodded. "I ran out of the dressing room and into the bouncer, who had come after me."

"Does this bouncer have a name?"

"Brad. That's all I ever heard him called. Anyway, he said Georgio wanted to see me. When I got to his office, Cornell was sitting in a chair, the front of his shirt covered in blood. I thought he was the one who'd been shot. I ran to him, but he pushed me away. He wouldn't look at me. Wouldn't talk to me."

The dread swelled in Faith's chest until every beat of her heart felt as if it were knocking against cement. She listened, stunned, as Angela told how Georgio had found Cornell standing over Walt's dead body, the murder weapon in Cornell's hand.

He'd shot Walt in the back of the head. He'd killed in cold blood an unarmed man walking away from him.

"No. Cornell would never do that. He couldn't." For a second Faith didn't even realize that her anguished cries had come from her lips instead of just echoing through her entire being.

Travis pulled her to her feet and into his arms. He held her against him, so close she could feel his own heart beating against her chest.

When she finally stopped shaking, she pulled away. "Finish what you have to say, Angela." She'd hear the words, but she would never believe her boy was a murderer.

"Cornell didn't deny that he'd killed Walt. He was ready to call the cops and confess. Georgio convinced him that he shouldn't."

"Did he also convince him not to call me?" Faith asked. "I'm his mother. I should have been with him, helping him make the decisions that would follow him forever."

"Cornell didn't want to hurt you, Mrs. Ashburn. He was worried more about you than he was about himself."

Worried, but he'd shut her out. He still was shutting her out. Somehow she'd failed him. A mother's love hadn't been enough.

The rest of the explanation began to blur in Faith's mind. Georgio had offered Cornell a way out. He'd make sure no one connected him to a crime that might send him to the electric chair. All Cornell had to do was go into hiding until the investigation blew over.

Georgio had insisted Angela leave town as well, since the cops would surely question her about the murder. That way she wouldn't have to lie to them.

Angela had encouraged Cornell to accept Georgio's offer. She'd gone to the Jackrabbit Chase Ranch and lived in isolation, warned that the cops were looking for her and that she had to lie low. Cornell had gone to live with one of Georgio's contacts living in Mexico, an American named Tom.

She'd talked to Cornell only on rare occasions after that. At first he'd told her that he was transporting horses across the border. It wasn't until a couple weeks ago, when she'd overheard a conversation between Alex and Georgio, that she realized Cornell was smuggling contraband. That was when she'd become a prisoner instead of a guest.

"Alex had me call you a few nights ago. He made me tell you to stop searching for Cornell."

"You also said to stay away from Georgio."

"That was only to throw you off. You must hate me for the role I played in this," Angela said.

"I'm not sure how I feel about you," Faith said.

"I understand and I don't blame you if you hate me. Just drive me to the border. I'll get out of your life forever."

But it was too late for that now. The damage was done.

"No. You're coming back to Dallas with us," Faith said. "The lies, the blackmail, the fear—it has to end. Besides, you've already confessed everything to the best homicide detective in Dallas. There's no point in running."

A homicide detective who'd be instrumental in sending her son to prison for the rest of his life, if not the electric chair.

If she'd had any hope of a future with Travis, it had just come to an end, along with all her dreams for Cornell's future.

"If I go back to Dallas, Georgio will track me down and have me killed," Angela said. "Maybe that's what I deserve."

"It's Georgio and Alex who need to get what they deserve," Travis said. "I plan to make sure they do. In the meantime, I'll get you full-time police protection."

"Where will I live? I have no money. No job. No friends I can trust."

"You'll live at the Dry Gulch Ranch with Faith and me for now. R.J. wants family, and he's about to get some, with all the complications that go with it. That won't begin to make up for the pain and suffering he put me through when he left me to be raised by foster parents who hated and abused me."

"I'm not family," Angela said.

"Nor am I," Faith added.

"That's okay. He'll like you both better than he ever liked me," Travis said.

CORNELL JERKED AWAKE. Something furry was inside his pants, climbing up his thigh. He unzipped his jeans and shimmied out of them. The tarantula skimming his briefs was unperturbed.

He knocked the big creature away and leaned against the trunk of the tree he'd been sleeping under, trying to catch his breath and get his bearings.

The dregs of sleep disappeared and reality set in again. It was far more frightening than dealing with the wicked-looking spider.

The air was chilly. He'd lost his jacket, probably left it back at that horse barn he'd tried to sleep in last night.

He remembered sneaking out of the building before daylight when one of the mares began to neigh and stamp, protesting the nearness of the stranger who'd invaded her space. With only moonlight to illuminate his path, he'd stumbled upon a fence line and then followed the strings of barbwire until he'd reached the creek, where he'd stopped to rest and evidently fallen asleep.

He reached for his phone to check the time, then remembered he'd hurled it into the Rio Grande after making that last call to Dolores. He'd wanted Angela and his mother to know he was safe.

Safe. Georgio had promised him that once. What a joke. A man nobody crossed unless he had a suicide wish, though Cornell hadn't figured that out until long after he'd sold his soul to the devil.

Now he had crossed the devil. Georgio wouldn't know at first that it was Cornell who'd tipped off the border patrol that the horse trailer would be carrying more than steeds. But it wouldn't matter.

He had screwed up. Georgio had no patience for people who screwed up, especially when they knew as much about his business as Cornell did.

But Cornell didn't care anymore. They'd made a prisoner of Angela. Even if Cornell had continued to play by the rules, it was only a matter of time until Georgio came to the conclusion that he and Angela were dispensable.

It was past time for someone to take the monster down. All Cornell had to do was get to the police and tell all before Georgio found and killed him. Then both of them could rot in prison. A man should pay for his crimes.

Cornell pulled on his jeans and started walking again. By the time he reached a country road, the sun indicated it was midmorning. He walked along the shoulder, stopping to put up a thumb when a car passed.

He figured he'd walked a good two miles before someone finally slowed down. A black sedan with a man in the passenger seat.

"Need a lift?"

"If you're going into Laredo."

"Sure. Get in."

Cornell took one step toward the car before he saw the gun. He started to run. Shots cracked through the still air. Blood splattered the ground around him like red rain.

He pushed on, staggering toward the fence. He grabbed for a fence post. He missed and the earth rose to meet him. The world went black.

But he could hear his mother's voice calling to him, pleading with him to come home.

"I love you, Mother. I'm so sorry I let you down."

Chapter Fifteen

"Sounds awful fishy to me," Reno said. "Did Cornell even own a gun?"

"Not according to Faith. And I don't remember a body showing up outside the Passion Pit ten months ago."

"Had there been, we would definitely have remembered, since we were already knocking ourselves out trying to find some solid evidence against Georgio."

"We had evidence," Travis corrected. "An eyewitness who conveniently fell from a ladder and died before he could testify."

"And now we have Cornell, who could possibly testify that Georgio had him kill Walt, except that his testimony would also send Cornell to prison, so why confess? Georgio always manages to stay ahead of the game."

"Only why would Cornell go along with that?" Travis questioned. "Supposedly, he wasn't an addict, so that counts out his doing it to get drugs. He had no police record, no juvenile infractions. No history of violence of any kind. I checked his school records just before I called you. He was never even suspended for fighting."

"There's always a first time, and women can bring out the worst in a guy."

"So I've heard."

"But then we have Walt Marshall," Reno continued.

"I also talked with his high-school counselor. He was expelled in the eleventh grade for bringing a gun to school. Before that he had a number of suspensions for fighting, including one for threatening a teacher."

"Have you talked to that teacher?"

"No, but I left a message for her to call me once she's out of class for the day. In the meantime, I'll check out the national database and see what kind of rap sheet he's accumulated."

"And see if he ever showed up in the Dallas morgue," Travis said. "But for now, the first order of business is making sure Cornell stays alive."

"I guess that means no arrests have been made yet."

"Not that I've heard," Travis said grimly. "I have a call in to Patterson so I can fill him in on Angela's story and see if there's been any progress in locating Cornell. John should be calling me back any minute."

"How's Faith taking this?"

"She's hanging in there, still holding out hope that this is all some huge mistake."

"Ever met a mother who didn't think her son was innocent?"

"Only one. Gloria Keating. Called 911 and reported he'd stolen her heroin."

Reno laughed. "I remember. She was a jewel of a mom."

The difference was that Faith was a loving mother and this was pure agony for her. Before meeting Faith, Travis had been obsessed with putting Georgio behind bars. He still wanted that, but it was killing him that accomplishing that goal might send Faith's son to prison, as well.

For the first time in his life, he wished he wasn't a cop.

His phone clicked. "I've got another call, probably

Patterson. I need to talk to him while he's available, but phone me once you get the lowdown on Walt."

"I'm on it," Reno said. "I'll keep you posted and you do the same."

Travis switched the call to John. "Any news?"

"Yeah. Is Faith Ashburn still with you?"

"Yep. A few feet away, but out of hearing."

"Then I hope you're good at delivering devastating news."

Travis's muscles tensed. He swallowed a curse, afraid to even speculate about what was coming next.

"Cornell was found by a rancher out checking his fence line for breaks about an hour ago," Patterson said. "He was covered in blood and lying facedown in the grass. The rancher took him for dead at first, but then found a weak pulse and called for an ambulance."

"Gunshot wounds?"

"Two of them. Shot at close range, once in the shoulder, once in the back of the head. Whoever shot him probably believed they'd killed him, or they would have finished him off."

"The shooter will have holy hell to pay when Georgio finds out Cornell isn't dead."

"I hope Cornell rallies enough to talk before he dies," Patterson said.

"Any idea where Salinger was at the time of the shooting?" Travis asked.

"Sitting on the deck of his ranch house, drinking coffee and talking to me. I paid a friendly visit to Jackrabbit Chase this morning."

"Did he admit to you that Angela Pointer had been living on his ranch for the past ten months?"

"To the contrary, he swore he'd never heard of her. His word against Angela's. Take that to a jury and guess who they'll believe? The generous, well-respected rancher or the Big D stripper?"

"I picked her up at his ranch," Travis reminded him.

"No, you found her in your trunk at a gas station. A good defense attorney will twist that every which way but straight."

That still left Dolores Guiterrez, but Travis knew she'd be too afraid to testify against Salinger. Even if she risked it, she'd never live to take the stand. She'd have some kind of freak accident.

A fall. An accidental drowning. A house fire. Georgio's methods were effective if not particularly creative.

Here they went again.

"Exactly where is the ranch where Cornell was found?"

"About twenty-five miles north of here. Reports from the scene of the crime indicate the shooting took place just off the narrow shoulder of a little-used county road. He apparently stayed conscious long enough to stagger into a clump of tall grass along the fence line."

"Where is he now?"

"Doctor's Hospital, in surgery. His condition is listed as critical."

"Georgio didn't waste any time."

"No," John agreed. "Pisses me off that his thugs were more effective at finding him than we were, but it is what it is."

"They had to get tipped off from somebody," Travis said. "I'm sure Salinger has his own web of informants in these parts." But right now, Travis could think only about Faith and how she'd take the news. "Can Cornell's mom see him?"

"As far as I'm concerned, as long as the surgeon doesn't object. The kid is under arrest and there's a guard stationed at the door, but I'll see that the two of you are allowed in to see him."

"I appreciate that. I'll need someone to stay with Angela Pointer. She's scared to death that Salinger is going to track her down and kill her."

"Drop her off here. It's safe enough. But no questioning Cornell about the smuggling, Travis. I don't want anything to come back and bite me when this case goes to trial."

"No questions," he agreed. The smuggling charge was the least of Travis's concerns now. It was the murder charge that worried him.

That and the fact that there would be no way he could protect Faith from this new bombshell.

Travis thanked John for keeping him on the inside track and broke the connection.

Now came the hard part.

FAITH'S EYES OVERFLOWED with tears as she stepped into the intensive-care unit and got her first look at her wounded son. His eyes were closed. His skin ghostly pale. His breathing erratic in spite of the numerous tubes attached to his body. The monitors measuring his vital signs clicked ominously in the background.

She reached over and caressed his hand with her fingers and then brushed her lips across his cheek. "I'm here, Cornell," she whispered. "I'm here beside you. You're safe."

He didn't open his eyes or twitch or show any sign that he knew she was there.

She turned to the nurse, who was only steps away. "Can he hear me?"

"I'm not sure, but it never hurts to reassure him. He

may recognize your voice and get comfort from that even though he's not conscious."

"Has he regained consciousness at all since the shooting?"

"Not since arriving at the hospital, but the doctors don't want him to just yet. He's being kept in a medically induced semi-coma to avoid unwanted stress. It's not uncommon to do that after a traumatic brain injury."

A traumatic brain injury. The words conjured up new horrifying possibilities. She grabbed hold of the bed rail to support her watery muscles. "How serious is the injury?"

"I think it's best to discuss that with the surgeon. We've alerted him that you're here and he said he'll see you momentarily."

She couldn't blame the nurse for not wanting to be the bearer of bad news. Faith finally had her son back, but the nightmare had acquired new monsters.

Painful memories returned in a rush of sickening anxiety. She'd been through this before during the worst of the virus. Sat at Cornell's bedside, praying, crying, afraid to close her eyes for fear he wouldn't be alive when she opened them again.

How could life do this to Cornell and to her all over again?

She took a deep breath when she felt Travis's hand on her arm. Amazingly, his strength seemed to transfuse from his veins to hers. Sometime over the past few days he'd changed from cop to protector.

She didn't fully understand their new relationship, but he was the one person in the world she wanted with her right now. The one person she could lean on.

The feeling of being protected was only an illusion.

Travis was a cop. He would come down on the side of the law no matter what that meant for Cornell.

Even knowing that, she needed his touch. She let her head fall to his shoulder. He raked a hand through her hair, smoothing it and brushing it back from her cheeks.

"Thanks for being here," she whispered.

"I'll be here as long as you let me, Faith."

The doctor walked into the room. He introduced himself, then checked out his patient and the chart before turning back to Faith.

"I'm sure you have lots of questions," he said. "There's a small conference space off the waiting room where we can have some privacy."

They followed him past the guard and out of ICU.

"I realize my patient is under arrest," the doctor said once they'd reached the conference room. "Let me assure you, Mrs. Ashburn, that will not affect my treatment. Nor will it keep me from being as honest with you as possible."

"Thank you."

"There's no necessity for you to have Detective Dalton in the room with us now unless you want him here."

"He's also a friend. I'd like him to stay."

"Very well." The surgeon motioned for her and Travis to take a seat at the small round table, and he sat down, as well.

"How serious are the injuries?" she asked.

"Critical."

The doctor pulled two X-rays from Cornell's chart and showed her where the bullets had entered his body. He followed that with a string of medical jargon that was difficult to follow.

Faith studied the X-rays and then pushed them back

across the table. "Exactly what does that mean in layman's terms?"

"We removed the bullet from the shoulder, and barring any complications from infection, there should be no lasting impairment of the muscles."

"And the bullet to the head?"

"Brain injuries are never totally predictable, but I was able to remove the bullet without any further damage and stop the bleeding. There is temporary swelling that's pressing against the skull and extensive trauma to the tissue at the entry point.

"However, your son was extremely lucky, Mrs. Ashburn. If the bullet had hit an inch to the right or at a more direct angle, I doubt Cornell would be alive right now."

Faith trembled, hearing how close her son had come to death. But he was alive. God had been with him this morning, the same way He'd been with him during his illness.

"What are his chances for a complete recovery?" she asked.

"Right now I'd say good, assuming he makes it through the next twenty-four hours. This is the most critical period for him. But recovery will take time and most likely require rehabilitation."

"How much time?"

"That's impossible to predict. He could be fully functioning in as little as a few months or he might never regain all his facilities for memory and movement. Right now I think the former is more likely, but I can't promise that."

The odds were in his favor. That was enough for now. Only what chance for recovery would he have in prison?

"I'd like to stay with him tonight," Faith murmured.

"I understand," the doctor said. "I'll see that you're allowed to. But that brings up our next concern."

"Which is?"

"If all goes well tonight, I'd like to transfer your son to a trauma unit in Dallas either tomorrow or the following day. It's one of the best facilities in the country for this type of injury."

Faith considered the tubes and monitors he was hooked up to. She'd love to have him in Dallas, but… "Do you think it's wise to move him so soon?"

"Not by ambulance, but we'll arrange for an emergency medical air transport. A trauma nurse will travel with him. Do you have any problems with that?"

"Not if you're sure it's safe."

"I wouldn't recommend it if I wasn't convinced it was not only safe but a sound medical intervention for Cornell."

Back to Dallas, as soon as tomorrow. They would be going home. But that also meant they'd be closer to Georgio Trosclair, the monster who'd ruined Cornell's life and surely had a role in trying to kill him.

"Will Cornell still have a guard at his door when he's moved to Dallas?"

"You'll have to discuss that with John Patterson."

"He'll have a guard," Travis assured her. "I guarantee you that neither Georgio nor any of his thugs will get near Cornell while he's in the hospital."

She breathed easier, determined to see the positive side of this. Cornell was not only alive, but was getting the best medical treatment available. And he'd be in Dallas, where she could see him every day. That was miracle enough for now.

As long as he made it through the night.

ANGELA, FAITH AND TRAVIS drove through the gate at the Dry Gulf Ranch at 4:30 p.m. two days later.

Fortunately, Cornell had come through the first night at the hospital in Laredo without any serious complications and had made steady progress since then. Faith had left his bedside only once, long enough to go back to the motel for a quick shower and change of clothes.

She was clearly exhausted. Even the surgeon had noticed. He'd urged her to stay home and get a good night's rest tonight while the Dallas trauma team completed their evaluation.

While she'd been at the hospital, Travis had spent his time at the local police department, using their resources to dig up every speck of information he could on Walt Marshall. There was plenty to be found.

Walt had a history of arrests for everything from possession, distribution and trafficking of controlled substances to road rage and assault with a deadly weapon.

He'd served three years in a Georgia prison for the last charge. Shortly after his release he'd moved to Dallas. No surprise that he and Georgio had found each other.

Travis spotted Leif's car as they drove up to the house, though Faith was so preoccupied with her own concerns she didn't appear to notice. Just as well; she could use a pleasant surprise.

"It's a big house," Angela said as she climbed from the backseat of Travis's double-cab truck, which they'd picked up at the Lamberts' after Tague had flown them home from Laredo. "Your father must get lonesome living in it all by himself."

My father. The expression always threw him. Planting his seed in Travis's mother did not make R.J. a father any more that sowing hayseed made a man a rancher.

"I still don't feel right about imposing all my problems on him," Faith said. "His brain tumor is more than enough for him to deal with."

Angela stopped in her tracks. "He has a brain tumor? You didn't mention that. Is he bedridden?"

"He still gets around," Faith said, "just not like he used to. He gets dizzy and confused occasionally, but most of the time he's lucid. He goes horseback riding down to his favorite fishing hole every day. At least that's what his new daughter-in-law, my friend Joni, told me."

"I love horses," Angela said. "I used to ride when my father was alive."

The front door opened before they reached it. Joni flew out and came running to meet them. The signs of fatigue vanished from Faith's face. Her smile was radiant. Travis had never been as grateful to anyone as he was to Joni at that moment.

The two friends collapsed into each other's arms and the tears started to flow down both their faces.

R.J. and Leif were waiting at the door.

Leif gave Travis a manly clap on the back, but then pulled him into a half hug. "Welcome back, bro. Tough week?"

"*Tough* is not the word I'd use for it," Travis said, "but you're on the right track."

"Mighty glad to have you back," R.J. said. "Who's the young woman?"

Travis introduced Angela as a friend of Cornell's. He'd save the details for later, when he had a chance to talk to Leif alone.

R.J. flashed a big grin for Angela and escorted her inside.

"I want to hear everything," Leif said. "Adam and

Hadley are bringing dinner down here around six, so we need to find some alone time before that."

"Good idea. R.J. can show Angela to a bedroom, and Faith and Joni won't even notice that we're not around."

Travis had no qualms about leveling with Leif. He'd give him the inside scoop on everything. Well, almost everything. He'd leave out the part about falling so hard for Faith that he couldn't think straight where she was concerned.

That didn't change the fact that he might have to be instrumental in sending her son to prison.

Talk about a dead-end relationship.

"WHY DON'T YOU LADIES take a break and we men will clean up the kitchen?" Adam suggested.

"I agree," Leif said. "But I may finish off that blackberry cobbler first. I don't normally like cobbler or blackberries, but that is one scrumptious dessert."

Hadley passed him the remaining cobbler. "It's Caroline Lambert's recipe. She taught me how to make the crust, too. That's the real secret to good cobbler."

"Caroline as in Taguc's mother?" Travis asked.

"Yes, she's an amazing cook. In fact, she's pretty amazing at everything she does."

"I can't believe some man hasn't grabbed her up and married her," R.J. said. "'Course, old Hugh will be a hard man to replace."

"He must be," Hadley said. "Caroline speaks of him often. I'm sure she still misses him."

Faith stood and started clearing the dishes from dining-room table.

Adam took them from her. "Seriously, get out of the kitchen. The men have KP duty tonight."

Leif and Travis added their agreement.

"You don't have to tell me twice, lover boy." Hadley handed Adam an apron and kissed him on the cheek. "Besides, I'd best check on Angela and make sure Lacy and Lila haven't worn her out."

"It was thoughtful of her to take them outside to catch fireflies while we visited over dessert."

"I think the girls with their energy and giggles are just what Angela needs," Faith said.

"I'd love to hear her life story," Joni interjected, "but no rush. I know everything is still part of an ongoing investigation." She put her arm around Faith's waist. "I'm just glad you're both here on the ranch with friends and family. One of the things I've learned from my brilliant, marvelous husband is that everything is easier to face when you're with people who love you."

Faith wasn't actually family, but she had to admit she felt more at home here tonight than she had anywhere since Cornell's disappearance.

But then anywhere with Travis might feel like that.

R.J. STAYED AT the table nursing a cup of decaf coffee that had grown cold. He looked surprised when the men rejoined him, each with a cold beer in hand.

He pushed his cup away. "Where's Gwen?"

"Do you mean Mattie Mae or Hadley?" Adam asked.

"If I'd meant 'em I would have said 'em. What did you do with Gwen?"

It was the same name he'd asked about the night of the wedding reception, when Travis had found him disoriented and confused.

"Gwen don't like beer in the house. If she sees you guys with those beers, she's gonna throw you out."

"It's okay," Adam said, trying to calm him. "She's

probably already gone to bed. Why don't I walk you to your bedroom and then we'll throw out the beers?"

"You better. She gets so mad she's like a cranky mule. No reasoning with that woman."

"You got that right," Adam agreed. "Let her sleep. I'll take care of things in here." He helped R.J. from his chair and then led him out of the dining room.

"What's with all the Gwen stuff?" Travis asked when Adam returned.

"Time travel, we think. Gwen was the middle name of his first wife, though who knows if that's the Gwen he's looking for. His doctor said it's not unusual for a brain-tumor patient to confuse the past with the present. It also happens with a lot of healthy elderly folks."

"Does he get confused like that often?"

"Usually once or twice a week, but it never lasts long. It usually occurs when he's excited or upset about something. He's been worried about you and Faith ever since you flew to Laredo."

"How much does he know about that?"

"Just what I told him on the phone yesterday," Leif said. "That you found her missing son and he's in the hospital. I didn't mention the shooting or the arrest, so he thinks Cornell is sick."

"I don't know much more than that," Adam admitted. "Not that it's any of my business."

"Actually, it is," Travis said. "Leif and I talked just before dinner, but I won't make any decisions about having Faith and Angela stay here unless you okay my plan. After all, this is your home. I'm the outsider."

"Then let's hear it."

"Better get another beer first," Travis said. "This gets complicated."

An hour later, they'd agreed on a plan that they could

all live with. Hadley and the girls would spend a few days with her mother, a visit they'd already been talking about.

Joni would have the option of staying with the Lamberts for a few days or at the big house anytime she was at the ranch when Leif wasn't around. That wouldn't be often, since most of the day she was making her rounds as a large-animal vet.

Angela, Faith and R.J. would have two police officers on duty at the ranch house anytime Travis couldn't be there to protect them. That way, if any of them left the house to go horseback riding or just to get outdoors for a walk, they could have an armed bodyguard with them.

"How do you think R.J. will react to having guards around?" Travis asked.

"I'll tell him they're some of your cop friends, just here on vacation to do some riding and get in some target practice," Leif said.

Adam nodded. "R.J. will buy that and talk their ears off. I'm a former marine, you know. Getting in some target practice of my own against a man like Georgio would be downright fun. But do you really think he'd be crazy enough to try to get to Angela or Faith out here at the Dry Gulch Ranch, where any one of us might see him?"

"No," Travis admitted. "Georgio normally plays it smart. No witnesses. No obvious risks. But if he thinks Cornell told Faith something that implicates Georgio in the smuggling or Walt's murder, he'll be desperate to shut her up. And Angela definitely knows too much, so he might be just as desperate to silence her."

"Time to take him down," Adam muttered. "And would I love to be the one who did it!"

Travis lifted his empty beer bottle in a toast. "Get in line, podner."

"Hate to break up a good battle-strategy session,"

Adam said a few minutes later, "but I've got two little girls who are hopefully ready for bed."

They all walked him to his truck. Travis, Faith and Angela waved goodbye to the others from the driveway.

The moon came out from behind a cloud and frosted the world in silver as they climbed the stairs to the porch. Faith waited for Travis to catch up with her, and he wondered if she had any idea of the sensual upheaval she caused him.

He should hate being here at the ranch. But how could he hate anyplace that included Faith? Unwanted urges surged, making his mind soft and his need rock hard.

Angela reached the door before them. "You have a really nice family, Detective Travis. You're lucky."

Thankfully, her interruption of his lustful thoughts cooled his desire enough that the bulge in his jeans didn't give him away.

"My family life growing up was far from normal," he answered truthfully. "But I am lucky that I didn't let my rotten childhood poison me on life."

"I wish I'd been that smart."

"You're young, Angela," Faith reminded her. "You still have time to turn your life around."

"Not if Cornell goes to prison for killing Walt. I won't deserve to be happy if that happens. It was my fault, even though if Cornell hadn't killed him Georgio would have."

"What makes you think that?" Travis asked.

"I heard Georgio tell him that one more screwup and there would be hell to pay."

"When did he say that?"

"Two days before Walt was killed."

That added a lot of weight to Travis's hunch that Georgio had been behind the murder all along.

"How did you ever get mixed up with a man like Walt?" Faith asked.

"He was big and tough and he looked out for me. I'd never had anyone want to protect me before. But then he started roughing me up and I knew he was just like my stepfather. Mean to the bone."

Kind of like Travis's early foster parents. Thanks to R.J. never coming for him and Leif after their mother died.

Angela opened the door and stepped inside. "I'm going to bed now, but thanks for everything, Detective and Mrs. Ashburn. I'll be praying for Cornell."

"Me, too," Faith said. She reached over and gave Angela a hug.

A nice gesture, Travis thought, a hug for the young woman who'd been the root of all Cornell's misfortunes. Faith was far more forgiving than he had ever been.

He walked Faith to the guest room. She lingered at the door, looking up at him in the dim glow of moonlight filtering through the window at the end of the hall.

A ravenous hunger that mere food would never satisfy rocked through him.

"I don't know what I would have done without you," she whispered.

"I'm glad we didn't have to find out." He trailed his fingers down her right cheek and the smooth column of her neck. He ached to kiss her, had to keep reminding himself that she was vulnerable, under his protection, nowhere near ready to deal with all that he was feeling.

And then she kissed him. One long, wet, sweet, tantalizing kiss that delivered a jolt clear to his toes—and elsewhere. He was on fire when she pulled away.

"Good night, Detective."

"That's it?"

"For now."

She backed away, closed the door and left him standing there. He walked away, still trying to get a handle on what had just happened. All he was sure of was that he needed a very cold shower tonight.

And tomorrow he'd need to find a way to prove that Cornell Ashburn was as innocent as his mother believed.

Without that, Travis might never get to see where that kiss could lead.

FAITH SLEPT LATER than she had in days. She woke to bright rectangles of sunlight pouring through the slats in the blinds and to the taste of the heart-stopping kiss still on her lips.

She kicked the sheet away and threw her feet over the side of the bed. The thrill of the kiss continued to titillate her senses as she padded to the bathroom.

Looking back on last night, she wasn't sure why she'd pulled away. She could have slept in his arms. Could have made love to him and woken up to his naked body stretched between her sheets.

But it wouldn't have been right. Not yet. Not with Cornell in a coma, not even aware that he was safe and home again.

When she made love to Detective Travis Dalton, she wanted everything to be perfect.

She splashed cold water on her face and smoothed her hair. She'd have breakfast and then see if Travis would drive her to the hospital.

Her cell phone rang and she hurried back to get it from her bedside table. She checked the caller ID. It was the trauma center. Calling this early had to mean something was wrong.

Her blood ran cold.

"Hello?"

"I'm calling for Faith Ashburn."

"This is she."

"I have good news, Mrs. Ashburn. Cornell has come out of the coma and he's asking for you."

Chapter Sixteen

Travis drove Faith to the hospital. They took the elevator to the trauma unit and went directly to the nurses' station, as she'd been instructed, and asked for Betty Norton, the head nurse.

The nurse was smiling when she greeted them. "You must be Cornell's mother."

"Yes. I'm Faith and this is Detective Dalton."

"You got here quicker than expected."

"I may have exceeded the speed limit a few times," Travis admitted.

"Are you a relative of the patient?"

"No, ma'am. I'm a friend of the family's, but I am with the Dallas Police Department."

"But you're not here as an officer?"

"Not this morning."

"I have to ask, because no one with law enforcement has clearance to talk with the patient yet—doctor's orders."

"He's only here as a friend," Faith assured her. "Is there anything else I should know before I see my son?"

"Only that the doctor does not want the patient to become stressed. Keep things on a light note. If he starts to get upset, I'll have to ask you to leave."

"I understand. May I see him now?"

"Yes. Just don't be upset when he exhibits confusion. That's to be expected. Even though he asked for you, he may not recognize you at once."

Faith hadn't thought of that possibility.

"Visiting times will be limited until his lead doctor indicates otherwise," the nurse continued. "You can have thirty minutes with him, but then he'll need to rest."

"How often can I return?"

"Every two hours, unless the visits unduly upset him."

As badly as Faith wanted to see Cornell, the warnings were making her increasingly anxious. She didn't want to do anything to cause him to suffer a setback.

Ten months without knowing where he was or if he was dead or alive. Ten months of longing to hear his voice. Now he might not even recognize her.

Travis took her hand, as always seeming to read her fears. "It's going to be fine. Just don't expect too much too soon. Give him time to open up to you."

"I'll try."

The nurse led them to his room and the cop standing guard gave them clearance to enter.

A lump formed in Faith's throat. She couldn't swallow. Her hands were clammy. Her stomach was churning.

Travis opened the door and silently nudged her inside with a hand to the small of her back. The nurse followed them.

Cornell's eyes were closed. The tube had been removed from his throat, but there was an IV needle in his arm. The monitors were on, clicking rhythmically.

"Say his name softly," the nurse urged.

"Cornell."

His eyes opened a slit. He closed them and then opened them again, wider this time. He looked from Faith to Travis but showed no sign of recognition.

"I'm your mother, Cornell. It's me."

He ran the tip of his swollen tongue across his chapped lips. The nurse dipped a cloth in a bowl of water and handed it to Faith. "His lips are dry. Why don't you wet them for him?"

She took the cloth and gingerly dabbed his mouth. "I love you, Cornell. I've missed you so much. I'm glad you're home."

"Mom?"

Her heart sang. "Yes, son."

"What happened to me?"

"You were in an accident, but you're in the hospital and the doctors and nurses are taking very good care of you."

The nurse smiled, patted Faith's arm approvingly and tiptoed out of the room.

"What kind of accident?" Cornell asked.

She looked to Travis. He nodded for her to tell Cornell the truth.

"You were shot."

"Why?"

"I don't know, but we're going to find out."

"Did you call the school?"

"The school?"

"To tell them I won't be there today?"

He was more confused than she'd guessed. It was as if he'd never left home.

"The school knows you're out," she said. "They said to take as long as you need to recover."

He looked at Travis. "Who are you?"

"A friend of your mother's."

"I've never seen you before."

"No, but I hope we're going to become good friends."

Faith had to smile at that. Her anxiety began to dissipate. Cornell might have been forced into a life of smuggling, but deep down he was the same as he'd always been. A good kid. With a good heart. He couldn't have possibly killed Walt Marshall or anyone else in cold blood.

When his memory returned, he'd tell them that. He'd explain everything.

"Do you think I could have a Coke?"

"I'll see."

"If not, just get me some water. My mouth feels like I've been eating sand."

"I'll bet it does."

"I'm sorry, Mom…."

"You don't have to be sorry, Cornell. Whatever happened…"

"Yeah, I know, not my fault. But if you have to take your sick days to take care of me, you won't ever get to go on that cruise to Bermuda you've been saving for."

"You take care of getting well, and I'll make sure she goes on that cruise," Travis offered. "Is that a deal?"

"Yeah. Deal." Cornell closed his eyes and drifted off to sleep.

Tears filled Faith's eyes as she wiped his mouth again with the damp cloth.

"He didn't kill anyone, Travis. We can't let him go to prison. You have to find a way to prove he's innocent."

"I'm working on it. All I need is proof of his innocence."

"You'll get it. As soon as Cornell can explain everything."

He was glad one of them believed in miracles.

"ARE YOU SURE you're not so hung up on this woman you barely know that you're feeding into her delusions?

"I told you, I'm following a hunch."

Reno shook his head. "If Cornell didn't commit the murder, what did Georgio use to blackmail him into smuggling the artifacts into the country?"

Travis pushed a stack of folders aside and propped his feet on his cluttered metal desk. "That's the little detail I haven't quite figured out."

"If that's a little detail, the Gulf of Mexico is a nice little fishing pond."

"My hunch isn't that far-fetched. Look at the facts I've put together." Travis pointed to a chart he'd hung on his office wall. "Up until the time he met Angela Pointer, Cornell had no criminal record. No juvenile charges. No school offenses. He's never even been suspended."

"Right. Good kid. I get that part of it. Kids can change."

"Walt Marshall is a hothead with a rap sheet long enough to paper your bathroom wall. Lots of people would probably have loved to put a bullet in him, including Georgio Trosclair."

"You don't have proof of that."

"I have no reason not to believe Angela."

"Except for her statement that Cornell killed Walt."

"She wasn't there when Walt was shot."

"Even if Georgio paid or persuaded Cornell to kill Walt, that's still murder."

"But what if he didn't kill him?" Travis argued. "What if Georgio or one of his paid thugs actually pulled the trigger and made Cornell believe he did it?"

"How?" Reno insisted. "By hypnotizing him?"

"I don't know how yet. I'm working on that, but it makes more sense than Cornell shooting some guy who was walking away. He wasn't one to look for trouble. He'd done a good job all his life of avoiding it."

"Like you said, until Angela Pointer came on the scene. Hot exotic dancer wanting him to protect her from big, bad Walt. Women can screw with your psyche. Like the way Cornell's mom is screwing with yours."

"I'm not getting screwed. Neither is my psyche. But I still say there's a knot in this rope the way it's hanging now. Cornell is a very unlikely murderer. Georgio is our chief suspect behind a string of murders."

"Show me the proof, Travis. You know I'd like nothing better than to put Georgio behind bars, but all we have to even link him to the smuggling at this point is Angela's statement. You know as well as I do that the prosecutor would tear her story to shreds in court. Not to mention that her version also includes the chapter where Cornell kills Walt."

"I haven't taken an official statement from her yet, nor read her her rights."

"Eventually, one of us has to."

"I know."

"To semi change the subject, how is Faith holding up?"

"Better than I expected, though I haven't seen much of her for the past two days. She's been at the trauma center, hoping for a memory breakthrough for Cornell. I've been working sixteen hours a day on this case."

"Maybe you should both take some time off."

Not a bad idea, and Faith was at the Dry Gulch Ranch this afternoon.

Travis dropped his feet back to the floor. "It's officially my day off and I've been on the job since six this morning. I think I'll take your advice and call it quits."

Reno grinned. "Don't blame you. Nothing like afternoon delight."

"I wouldn't know."

And unfortunately, he had no expectations of finding

out today. But if he hurried he might get home in time
to go horseback riding with Faith. She had to be tired of
staying inside the house and under guard anytime she
was at the ranch.

More reason to find evidence to prove Georgio was
responsible for Walt's murder. Putting him behind bars
might be the only way to keep Faith safe.

THEY STOPPED AT the edge of the river, though it seemed
far more like a creek to Faith. Travis took her reins and
helped her dismount. She walked over, took off her shoes
and waded into the water. The icy temperature made her
catch her breath.

Or maybe it was just being with Travis that had that
effect on her. In barely a week, he'd changed her life. He'd
found her son. He'd brought her to Dry Gulch to keep
her safe. He'd been there every time she'd needed him.

The sound of his voice made her pulse quicken. His
touch stole her breath. His kiss had completely undone
her.

Faith knew it was too soon to be sure the relationship
would last, but nothing had ever seemed so right.

Travis let the horses drink and then knotted their reins
to the low-hanging branches of an oak tree. He bent down
and picked up a fishing pole that had been left lying in
the grass.

"This must be R.J.'s. The hook and cork are ready to
go. All it needs is bait."

"He catches minnows in that net over by the tree trunk
for that," she answered.

"Have you been fishing with him?"

"Today. One of the guards rode out with us."

"Catch anything?" Travis asked.

"Snagged a soft-drink can."

"That would have been tasty."

"I went wading. The water is nice." She stepped farther into the water that lapped the bank. "Take off your shoes and socks and join me."

"I'd rather watch."

Faith bent over and splashed water in his direction.

"I like R.J.," she said. "I know the two of you have issues, but he admits he's made lots of mistakes in his life. He's so excited to have Adam and Leif living at the Dry Gulch. He hasn't given up hope on the rest of you, either."

"Not going to happen, at least not with me."

"I don't see why not. You look, talk and ride like a cowboy. I could live here."

"In that case I bequeath my part of the ranch to you."

"I accept."

She waded back to the bank and dropped to a grassy spot in the shade of a gnarly oak. She stretched out on her back and made a pillow of her hands.

Travis kept his distance, though he couldn't take his eyes off her. He was mesmerized by Faith, from the perky rise of her breasts beneath the cotton shirt to the way her hair swirled around her narrow shoulders.

If he lay down beside her, he'd never be able to fight the unbridled desire ripping though him. If he didn't go to her, he was going to go crazy with wanting her.

He walked over and stretched out alongside, propping himself up with his elbow so he could look into the depths of her dark eyes.

This time he didn't wait for her to initiate the kiss.

Chapter Seventeen

Travis's lips touched Faith's, softly at first, their breaths mingling in a delicious blend of salty sweetness. Desire erupted in her blood, shooting her senses to dizzying heights.

The musky smell of him, the exciting taste of him, the intoxicating feel of his body pressing into hers... She closed her eyes and gave in to the thrill of him.

The kiss deepened until his lips had a ravenous hold on hers. His fingers slipped beneath her shirt and splayed across her bare back. His right leg worked its way between her thighs. Her body arched toward his, aching for more.

When his lips left hers, they seared a path down her neck. She turned and began to fumble with the buttons on his shirt, loosening them one by one until his gorgeous, golden chest was bare.

Travis returned the favor, kissing his way down her chest and abdomen until her shirt fell open. His thumbs slipped beneath her bra, finding and massaging her nipples until they were pebbled and erect.

She pressed against him and felt the hard length of his need pushing to escape his jeans. He reached down and unzipped them.

"I can stop if you say the word, Faith. It will half kill me, but I can stop if you want me to."

"No," she whispered, her voice hoarse with a driving need that wouldn't let go. "Nothing will change because we make love, but I need this. I need you. I need you so very much."

He kissed her again, but this time there was no holding back. He wiggled out of his jeans and then helped her out of hers. His hand found the inside of her thighs and his fingertips reached into her most intimate area, stroking the wet desire that had pooled there.

Then he lifted himself on top of her and thrust deep inside her.

She squealed in pleasure and then whispered his name with a moan.

His breath came in quick gulps. The thrusting grew faster and deeper and then he exploded inside her, taking her with him over the crest.

The sun beat down on their naked bodies as they lay in each other's arms, melting in the afterglow.

Nothing had changed on the outside. All the problems that had been there before were still present. Her fears for Cornell hadn't lessened.

But something had changed inside Faith. No matter what the future held for her and Travis, the moment had been golden and she would never be sorry for having lived it.

Love, however fragile and tentative it might prove to be, had found a place in her heart, and her world would never be the same.

"ARE YOU SURE you're calling me from a phone that can't be traced?"

"You know I wouldn't make a mistake about something that important."

"I never thought you'd shoot Cornell and leave him alive, either, but you did."

"It wasn't as if I didn't check. I was certain he was dead. The second bullet hit him in the back of the head. He went down. His eyes were rolled back in his head. I couldn't find a pulse."

"But someone did."

"And I'm doing all I can to make up for my mistake. I had someone hack into Cornell's online medical records. He's brain damaged. Even if he can talk, nothing he says will ever hold up in court."

"That doesn't make up for your mistake."

"I did some things right and you know it. We never would have found Cornell before the law did if I hadn't spread the word to all the ranchers in the county that I was looking for one of my wranglers who took off with an expensive saddle. Otherwise Billy Lewes would have called the police, not me, when he found that strange jacket in his horse barn."

Georgio couldn't deny that. But even if Cornell was as good as dead, Faith Ashburn wasn't, and she was as unrelenting as a Texas drought. She'd never give up on finding the man who had lured her son into a life of crime that almost cost him his life.

She'd fight the murder charge until she had the full truth.

"Did you get the information I asked for?"

"I did. Faith Ashburn is staying at the Dry Gulch Ranch with Travis and his dying father."

"And?"

"The old man rides his horse to his favorite fishing hole every morning after breakfast, occasionally alone, but usually accompanied by one of the wranglers."

Even as Georgio listened to the details Alex spouted, a plan formed in his mind.

He'd take care of Faith and then lie low for a few months, perhaps take a trip to Europe and let his new drug czar run his clubs.

Too bad Faith had to die. They could have had some fun together if she hadn't gone running to Travis.

On second thought, it wasn't too late to have some fun with her. The old guy might even get his jollies from watching them get it on.

FAITH WALKED TO the kitchen for morning coffee with a sweet ache between her thighs and a spring to her step that hadn't been there yesterday. She and Travis had shared the bed in the first-floor guest room last night.

They'd made love again—and again. They might have made it a third time except that Travis was called out on a homicide at the crack of dawn. It would be difficult to get used to hours like that. Not that she could afford to sleep this late every morning. It was after eight.

The coffeepot was nearly full, obviously not the first brew of the day. She filled a mug and went looking for R.J. Instead she found Angela in the front-porch swing.

"You slept late," the young woman said. "Five more minutes and I was going to knock on your door and see if you were okay."

"I was just tired, I guess. Where is everybody?"

"Joni's at work. R.J.'s gone fishing."

"This early?"

"He said it was going to rain later."

"There's not a cloud in the sky."

"I mentioned that. He told me his arthritis was a better predictor of the weather than clouds were."

"Then I better carry an umbrella to the hospital with me this afternoon."

"Where's Detective Travis?"

"On his way back to the ranch."

"Did he work all night again?"

"No, just from daylight on. Apparently, homicide detectives don't keep regular office hours. He's coming home to clean up, pick me up, deliver me to the hospital and then go back to work."

"I wish I had somewhere to go today. I love the ranch, but it gets boring. Do you think Detective Travis would mind if I tagged along with Joni tomorrow? She said it was okay with her."

"You'd best ask him that."

Faith's cell phone was ringing when she got back to the bedroom. She grabbed it from the dresser. "Hello?"

All she picked up was static. "Hello. Who is this?"

"Dizzy… Can't… Horse."

She could make out only half the words. "Is this R.J.?"

"Hurry."

The connection went dead. She kicked off her slippers and tossed her robe to the bed. In seconds, she'd pulled on a pair of jeans, a T-shirt and boots. She went tearing back to the porch.

"R.J. just called. I think he's disoriented. I'm going to find him."

"Not without me."

She turned to see Ray, the friendliest of the guards Travis had hired, standing at the foot of the steps.

"Okay, but we have to hurry."

"Do you want me to go with you?" Angela asked.

"No. You stay here in case Travis shows up and wonders where I am."

"Carl's checking the immediate premises," Ray said. "Holler if you need him."

Faith took off running toward the horse barn, with Ray right behind her. They saddled up two of the horses, mounted them and pushed the strong animals to a gallop.

Faith didn't slow down until she reached the spot where Travis had found the fishing pole yesterday.

A shot rang out. A cry of pain came from behind her. She pulled on the reins, bringing her horse to a stop. When she turned around, Ray was sliding off his saddle, blood soaking his chest.

Behind him, she saw R.J. tied and gagged and strapped to the trunk of a towering pine tree.

Georgio stood next to him smiling, gun in hand and pointed at her head.

"So nice to see you again, my dear. Here, let me help you off your mount."

She ignored his offered hand and dismounted on her own. "How did you get here?"

"By horseback, same as you. I just took a shortcut across a neighbor's pasture. I gave up on you calling me back, so I had no choice but to come to you. So here we are, together again, and with your omnipresent detective nowhere in sight."

Another rider appeared from behind a cluster of short, stubby cedars. He rode over to Ray, dismounted and tied the unmoving guard's hands and feet behind him.

"You want me dead, Georgio," Faith said. "Fine. Shoot me, but let Ray and R.J. go."

"Haven't you heard? I hate leaving witnesses around to clutter up a crime scene. But I won't kill them yet. They should stay around for the party."

"Is that why you killed Walt? Because you didn't want him to testify against you?"

"No, I killed Walt because he was a stupid jerk who didn't know when to keep his mouth shut."

"But you did kill him?"

"You surely don't think that prissy son of yours shot him."

"How did you convince Cornell that he was a murderer?"

"I hadn't planned to. It was serendipity. I walked out the back door of the club to see what the ruckus was about and found Cornell in the alley writhing, his eyes rolled back in his head. Having one of those seizures you kept talking about. And there was Walt, walking away, the perfect target."

"So you killed Walt, smeared his blood on Cornell and planted the murder weapon on him."

"Yes, and the beauty of it was that Cornell saw me as a hero. I got rid of the body for him and saved him from a death sentence. It took him months to figure out he was moving more than horses across the border. He was the perfect smuggler. He passed for innocent because he believed he was innocent.

"But enough about him. Let's get back to you. Take off your shirt first and then the bra. I love it when a woman's breasts fall free."

She slipped her hands beneath her T-shirt and slowly peeled it over her head. She couldn't die like this. She had to find a way to save herself and R.J. and Ray.

"Now the bra," Georgio said.

He was going to rape her while the others were forced to watch. Rape her here, near the same spot where she'd made love to Travis.

She couldn't stop him, but she wouldn't help him.

"The bra," he repeated. "Take if off and throw it to me."

"Go to hell, Georgio Trosclair. I'd rather have sex with

a snake than have you touch me." She straightened her spine and spit in his direction.

She was going to die at his hands. Finally, she knew her son was innocent of murder and smuggling charges, though it was too late to help him.

But Travis would discover the truth. Somehow, she knew that he would. She was glad they'd made love. Her only regret was that she hadn't told him how much she loved him.

Now she never would.

Chapter Eighteen

Angela met Travis as he started up the walk.

"Something's happened to R.J."

"Did you call for an ambulance?"

"No. He wasn't here. He said he was going fishing, and then he called Faith for help."

"Had he fallen?"

"I don't know. She just said he was disoriented, and she and Ray jumped on horses and went to find him."

"So Ray did go with her?"

"Yes, but I thought they'd be back by now."

"Okay, settle down, Angela. You know R.J. gets disoriented at times. Adam and Leif have told him not to go riding by himself. He does it anyway."

"I guess you're right."

"I'll call Faith and see what's going on."

"I tried that. She doesn't answer. Neither does Ray or R.J."

Apprehension set in. Travis punched in Faith's number as he walked to the kitchen and poured himself a mug of coffee. No answer.

And then he saw R.J.'s phone, plugged into the charger, half-hidden by the toaster. R.J. had not called Faith.

Travis shot out the back door and raced to the horse

barn. No time to waste on saddling, so he stopped at the corral, jumped on the back of a palomino and pushed it to the limit.

The neighing of a horse led him straight to Faith. He spotted Georgio and saw the glint of the sun bounce off his pistol. And then he saw Faith, on the ground, face-down.

The drug lord's right foot was crushing her shoulders into the hard Texas clay. The gun was pointed at her head. A young thug, also armed, was standing next to Georgio.

R.J. and Ray were tied and gagged.

Travis brought his horse to an abrupt stop that almost sent him flying over its head. One wrong move on his part and Georgio would pull that trigger. Faith would be dead.

How could Travis have let this happen?

"Welcome to the party, Detective. You almost missed the fun."

"You'll never get away with this, Georgio. This time you've gone too far."

"And what are you going to do about it when you'll be as dead as Faith? I've always been able to outsmart you and the other cops on the DPD. You know that."

"And you think no one will suspect you after Cornell links you with the smuggling and Walt's murder?"

"Cornell has a brain injury. You can't believe a word he says. And Angela. She's a stripper who was breaking up with Walt to get it on with Cornell. You'd expect her to lie.

"This all comes down to your poor old pappy and his deteriorating condition," the drug lord continued. "He lost it. It happens with those pesky inoperable tumors. He lured you out here, killed you one by one and then turned his gun on himself."

A guttural noise sputtered in R.J.'s throat. His face was bloodred. It was easy to see he was fighting mad.

"Keep your gun pointed at the detective, but take the gag from the old man's mouth," Georgio ordered his henchman.

The young man jumped to do as he was told.

The gag fell from his hands to the grass. R.J. let out a war cry that would have made Geronimo proud.

Miss Dazzler went wild. She stamped and reared up on her hind legs. Georgio dived away from her, trying to get out of her reach. The horse's front hooves came down on the drug lord's back and knocked him to the ground.

Georgio fired once. So did Travis, but his shot was the one that hit its target. It burrowed into Georgio's chest. He fell to the ground face-first.

The young thug tried to make a run for it, but somehow Ray rolled over in the grass and managed to trip him.

Faith grabbed Georgio's fallen pistol and pointed it at Georgio's accomplice. "Move and I shoot to kill."

"Good work, partner," Travis called.

"I'm learning from the best."

And hating every second of it. But if this was what it took to save her son, she'd fight the devil himself. Maybe she just had.

Travis tied up the accomplice while Faith freed R.J. Then she rushed to Ray and checked his pulse. He opened his eyes and tried to talk. Instead he only gurgled blood.

He was still breathing, but he was losing blood. She grabbed her shirt and used it as a bandage, pressing it lightly against the gunshot wound.

"I'm calling for an ambulance," she said. "Lie still and don't try to move."

R.J. shuffled over and checked Georgio's pulse. "You'll need a hearse for this one."

Once the accomplice was secured, Travis walked over and slipped an arm around Faith's shoulders. "Are you all right?"

"Not yet, but I will be."

"Good. Please don't ever scare me like that again. I was afraid I'd get here and find you dead, and then when I saw Georgio…" His voice broke. "Love can kill a man."

"Or save him," she whispered. "Especially when the woman loves you right back."

Epilogue

Two months later

The kitchen in the big house at Dry Gulch Ranch was overflowing with food of every description. Ham, smoked brisket, fried chicken, potato salad, purple hull peas, butter beans, corn pudding and enough desserts to fill a bakery.

"Where shall I put this banana pudding?" a neighbor whose name Faith had forgotten asked.

"There's room in the refrigerator in the mudroom," Joni said.

Someone else came in and added a plate of cupcakes to the mix.

A boy who looked to be about eight years old grabbed one of them and kept walking.

"Is it like this every Fourth of July?" Faith asked.

"Not according to Caroline Lambert. She says the local Cattlemen's Association's annual Labor Day celebration is normally held at the Oak Grove Civic Center."

"Why the change in venue?"

"There was a fire last month that destroyed the center's kitchen. Apparently R.J. not only offered to have the fire damage repaired, but volunteered the Dry Gulch for the celebration."

"That man never ceases to surprise me," Faith said.

"He's hoping you and Travis will surprise him soon with a wedding and a move to the Dry Gulch Ranch. He thinks ranch life would be good for Cornell."

"Did he say that?"

"He did. He's disappointed his other three children haven't come around yet."

"They still may," Faith said.

"They'd best hurry if they expect to get to know him while he's still healthy enough to interact with them. His bad days are becoming more and more frequent. Yet, weirdly, he seems more at peace every day."

"I think so, too. I like him a lot and so does Cornell."

A group of teenage girls wandered through the kitchen and asked where to find the soft drinks. Joni pointed them to a huge cooler on the back porch. "Let's get out of here and find a place where we can talk without constant interruption," she suggested to Faith. "I don't get to see nearly enough of you lately."

They moved to an upstairs sitting room.

"So tell me about Cornell. Has he regained all his memory yet?"

"For the most part. He's still hazy on a few things that happened while he was living in Mexico. The doctor has given him permission to start school next week and I've hired a tutor to help him with his studies."

"And Angela. Do they still see each other?"

"They stay in touch, mostly through social media. They both wisely decided they need to get their individual lives on track before they start making long-term commitments. She's living with an aunt in Kentwood, Louisiana, and is working to earn her GED. When she does, she hopes to enroll at LSU, thanks to a scholarship R.J. provided."

"And I heard on the news last week that Alex Salinger is cooperating with the police now that he's facing the possibility of life in prison."

"Travis said he's spilling his guts about the crimes he and Georgio committed, even the murders Georgio ordered to keep his drug-lord status secure. Walt made murder number six. His body was discovered last week."

"Travis must feel good about that."

"I think so," Faith said. "I haven't really seen that much of him lately. I never realized that homicide cops keep such long and irregular hours."

"He could probably take a desk job," Joni mused. "Leif says he has lots of seniority."

"He'd be miserable. He has the life he loves." There was just no indication it was going to include marriage to her.

And yet when they were together, he rocked her world.

"We better go back and join the party," Joni said. "It's about time for the president of the Cattlemen's Association to give his speech."

"That, I could miss," Faith admitted.

She ran into Travis on her way downstairs.

"I should have known you two were cooking up something," he said. "I've been looking all over for you."

"Am I missing something?"

"Yeah. Take a walk with me. I have something to show you."

"We'll miss the speeches."

"How's that for perfect timing?"

He grasped her hand and led her outside and down the path to the horse barn.

"Don't say no until you hear me out," he cautioned.

"You're talking in riddles."

"I get that way when I'm nervous."

They stopped at the door to the barn. "Close your eyes and hold my hand," he instructed.

"Wait a minute," she said. "If you're going to give me that abandoned black Lab puppy you found wandering around the ranch last week, the answer is no. My landlady forbids pets."

"No puppies," he promised. "Though you have to admit he's really cute and cuddly."

Faith closed her eyes and let him lead her inside. When he told her to open them, she was standing in front of a stall. A scrawny colt stood next to its mother.

"What do you think?" Travis asked.

"My landlady definitely wouldn't allow a colt in the house."

"It's not for you. It's for Cornell. I think raising a horse of his own would be good for him."

"If we lived on a ranch."

"Yeah, about that. I'm thinking of building a cabin here at the Dry Gulch. I know it'll mean long drives, sometimes in the middle of the night, but I can keep a small condo near the precinct for those times I can't make it back to the ranch."

"What does that have to do with giving Cornell a colt?" Her heart jumped ahead. Anticipation made her giddy. "Is this a proposal?"

"No. No way. Not yet."

Faith's spirits plummeted.

Travis dropped to one knee and pulled a ring from his pocket. "Now it's a proposal. But first the warning label."

"Okay."

"Homicide detectives make lousy husbands. They work weird hours. They get too caught up in their cases. They usually see more of their partners than they do their spouses. But if you'll have me, I'll work on being the best husband to you and the best stepfather to Cornell I can be.

"I love you, Faith, more than I ever dreamed I could love anyone. I can't imagine living without you. Will you marry me?"

"Yes. Yes! Oh, God, yes. I love you so much. I thought you'd never ask."

He slipped an amethyst ring on her finger. "I know this isn't the typical engagement ring, but it was my mother's. She gave it to me before she died. I'd love for you to wear it. Unless you hate it."

"How could I hate it? It's beautiful. And it's from you. I'll wear it forever."

Travis stood, pulled her into his arms and kissed her. Her heart sang.

"It's been a long, hard ride for me," he said, "but I feel like I'm finally home. Home to Dry Gulch and home to you."

"Home to love," she whispered. "And, okay, home to a newborn colt and a black Lab puppy, too."

One more Dalton son back in the saddle again and he wanted her at his side. She couldn't wait to start the ride.

* * * * *

"You know, Mack, I'd have made you as a player. What's the matter? Got some kind of lawyer rule against kissing a client?"

He swallowed, unsure how to answer her. The thing was, he *was* a player—when the game was being played by his rules, which this game was not.

He allowed himself a small smile at her brazen challenge.

Watch out, Miss Martin, he said to himself. *This game's about to change.*

"Well?" she taunted.

"You don't know what you're doing," he said softly, the smile still in place.

"What do you mean?" she asked, feigning innocence.

"Oh, it's not your fault. You've only had boys to play with. It's understandable that you don't know what you're getting into by flirting with a man. I'd advise you to stop now."

"Stop?" she said as a flush rose all the way to her cheeks. "I don't want to stop."

SANCTUARY IN CHEF VOLEUR

BY
MALLORY KANE

Published in Great Britain 2014
by Mills & Boon, an imprint of Harlequin (UK) Limited,
Eton House, 18-24 Paradise Road, Richmond, Surrey, TW9 1SR

© 2014 Rickey R. Mallory

ISBN: 978-0-263-91365-1

46-0714

Harlequin (UK) Limited's policy is to use papers that are natural, renewable and recyclable products and made from wood grown in sustainable forests. The logging and manufacturing processes conform to the legal environmental regulations of the country of origin.

Printed and bound in Spain
by Blackprint CPI, Barcelona

Mallory Kane has two very good reasons for loving reading and writing. Her mother was a librarian, and taught her to love and respect books as a precious resource. Her father could hold listeners spellbound for hours with his stories. He was always her biggest fan.

She loves romantic suspense with dangerous heroes and dauntless heroines, and enjoys tossing in a bit of her medical knowledge for an extra dose of intrigue. After twenty-five books published, Mallory is still amazed and thrilled that she actually gets to make up stories for a living.

Mallory lives in Tennessee with her computer-genius husband and three exceptionally intelligent cats. She enjoys hearing from readers. You can write her at mallory@mallorykane.com.

For Anna, who has been so supportive.
Thanks for understanding how it can be.

Chapter One

Hannah Martin's heart leaped into her throat as she waved at Mr. Jones, their neighbor, whose house was a mile away from theirs. He was watering his window boxes as she drove past.

Billy Joe had told her to be friendly with the neighbors but not to talk to them. "If you say one word to anyone, you'll never see Stephanie alive," he'd told her more than a few times in the past twenty-four hours.

Her mom, Stephanie Clemens, had gone into liver failure from cirrhosis a couple of weeks ago and was receiving hemodialysis while waiting for a donor liver. Then two days ago, Hannah had overheard Billy Joe, her mother's boyfriend, talking on his cell phone. He was arranging some kind of delivery to Tulsa, Oklahoma. And from his side of the conversation, it was obvious to Hannah that the goods were illegal and very valuable. It had to be drugs.

She'd confronted him and kicked him out of her mother's house, saying if he showed back up, she'd go to the sheriff. He'd left.

Then, yesterday, when she'd returned from a short run to the drugstore, her mother was gone and Billy Joe was back. He'd abducted her mom and was holding her somewhere.

Hannah growled in frustration and desperation as she pulled into the driveway of her mother's house. Popping the trunk lid, she grabbed one heavy case of beer, leaving the other case for a second trip.

"Billy Joe?" she called as she hooked her index finger around the handle of the screen door and then toed it open enough to catch it with her elbow. "Billy Joe? I'm back. My car's battery died again. That's why I took the Toyota."

She set the beer on the kitchen counter and listened. Nothing. The house felt empty. Where was he? He was always waiting at the door to make sure she got back from the grocery store not one minute later than he'd told her to be—with his cigarettes and beer.

An ominous thought occurred to her. Had something happened to her mother? She went through the house, but as she'd known, it was empty. Billy Joe wasn't there. Nearly panicked, she ran back outside. The setting sun reflected on the tin roof of the garage, but she thought she could see a light on inside it. Billy Joe never left a room without turning off the light, just like he never left the house without checking the locks three times. And woe to anyone who didn't put a tool or a book or even a ballpoint pen back exactly where they got it, down to the millimeter. So if the lights were on in the garage, then Billy Joe was in there.

From the first moment her mother had let him move in a few months ago, he'd taken over the garage. He'd kept it locked and never let her or Hannah near it. His reasoning was because he was working on his prized vintage Mustang Cobra and the engine had to stay free of dust. He was as obsessive about his cars as everything else.

Hannah walked across the driveway to the garage,

her shoulders stiff, her heart thudding so hard it physically hurt. Maybe her mother was in there? It wasn't the first time she'd thought that, but she was genuinely afraid of Billy Joe. After all, he'd pushed and slapped her mother a couple of times.

She wasn't sure what she thought—or hoped—to find when she looked through the glass panes of the side door, but she couldn't continue to sit by and do nothing while her mother was missing. Luckily, she'd just had her dialysis and wouldn't need it again until the end of the week. But Hannah didn't trust Billy Joe to take care of her. So although her stomach was already churning with nausea and a painful headache was making her light-headed, she was determined to see the inside of the garage.

Then she heard Billy Joe's voice. She nearly jumped out of her skin. In the first instant, she thought he was yelling at her. But by the time she'd heard three or four unintelligible words, she realized that his tone wasn't angry, it was afraid. Then she heard another voice. It was low and menacing, and she didn't recognize it.

With horrible visions swirling in her head of her mother dying while Billy Joe and some buddy of his drank beer, she approached the door cautiously. She slid sideways along the outside wall until she was close enough to see through the glass panes, her heart beating so loudly in her ears that she was positive the people inside could hear it.

When she peeked through the dusty glass panes, Billy Joe's back was to her, so she couldn't see his face. He was standing in front of his workbench, arms spread plaintively, talking in an oddly meek voice.

Her gaze slid to the man standing in front of him. He was twice the size of Billy Joe. Not quite as tall but *much* larger. He had on a dark, dull-colored T-shirt that fit his weightlifter's torso and beefy biceps like a glove. On the back of his right wrist was a tattoo. It was red and heart-shaped with what looked like letters in the center. Hannah blinked and squinted. Did it say MOM? She thought so, although the *O* wasn't exactly an *O*. It was a dark circle. Before she could focus on it, the man reached behind his back and pulled a gun. The fluorescent light glinted off the steel barrel. Hannah stared at it, her pulse hammering in her throat.

Billy Joe froze in place. His voice took on an edge of shrill panic and he stepped backward and turned his palms out. "Hey, man, watch out with that thing. It could go off." He laughed nervously. "I swear! You know everything I know. I'd never cheat the boss. I ain't that stupid."

Hannah saw a quick smirk flash across the other man's face and knew he was thinking the same thing she was. Billy Joe *was* pretty stupid.

"So what happened to the drugs and the money?" the man said, not raising his voice. "Because our customer says he was shorted, and the last payment you sent to Mr. Ficone was short, as well. Mr. Ficone depends on his distributors to pay him so he can pay his suppliers. Now his suppliers are expecting to be paid everything they're owed when Mr. Ficone meets with them in three days. So you've got three days to get that money to him."

"I don't know what happened to them, man. I had to use a new courier because my regular guy got picked up for not paying child support. Maybe he took it. I swear it was all there when I sealed the envelope. Or, hey, it coulda been the girl. Hannah Martin. My girlfriend's daughter. Smart-mouthed bitch." Billy Joe was sweating, literally. "She's always snooping around. She probably stole the money out of the envelope. That new guy coulda left it lying around."

The man with the red tattoo looked bored and disgusted. "I don't think Mr. Ficone's going to be satisfied with *somebody else must have done it.* He doesn't like people that can't control their people. That delivery was short almost twenty grand."

"Twenty? That's im-impossible," Billy Joe stammered.

Beneath the fear, Hannah heard something in his voice she'd heard before. Billy Joe was lying.

He took another step backward, toward the door. "I'm telling you, it had to be Hannah Martin. She's as sneaky as a fox. She musta got into it. I wouldn't be surprised. But I swear, when I sealed that envelope, it was all there. I counted it."

Hannah felt a heavy dread settle onto her chest, making it hard for her to breathe. He was throwing her to the wolves. She'd known he was trouble the minute she'd first laid eyes on him, and she'd tried to tell her mother, but Stephanie had never been smart when it came to men.

The man with the red tattoo shook his head. "Money doesn't disappear from a sealed envelope," he said. "I've got better things to do than stand here and listen to you lie. Mr. Ficone needs his money and he needs the drugs that were missing from your last delivery to our customer in Tulsa."

"But, man, I swear—"

"Shut up with your whining," the man yelled. "Where's the money?"

Hannah jumped at the man's suddenly raised voice.

She shrank back against the wall by the door, terrified. He was holding a very big gun and his voice told her he was sick of Billy Joe's rambling excuses.

What if he shot him? Everything inside her screamed "no!" Billy Joe was the only person in the world who knew where her mother was. She wanted to burst into the garage and beg the man to make Billy Joe tell her where her mother was, but the man looked ruthless and he was already sick of Billy Joe's whining. If she called attention to herself, he was liable to shoot her, too.

"All right, punk. Mr. Ficone has no use for you if you're not going to talk about where the money and the drugs are. That's all he wants."

Hannah shifted until she could see through the door again. She saw the man lift the barrel of the gun slightly, aiming it at Billy Joe.

"What he doesn't want is screwups like you working for him. He hates people who can't control their women. He hates thieves and he sure as hell hates loose ends."

"Listen. I'll get the money back. I've got a plan," Billy Joe said, his hands doubling into fists. "My girlfriend's sick. Real sick. And I kidnapped her. I've got her hidden away."

Hannah gasped. *Where? Tell him where,* she begged silently.

"I told Hannah she'll never see her mom again if she doesn't do what I tell her. She'll give me back the money."

The larger man frowned and brandished the huge gun. "You kidnapped your sick girlfriend? You're a real piece of work."

"Okay, listen, man." Sweat was running down Billy Joe's face and soaking the neck of his T-shirt. "Here's the deal. The drugs are hidden in the Toyota. But that bitch Hannah took it to town. She's got strict orders not to touch my damn car, but she took it anyway. Bet you can't guess where I put 'em. The drugs." Despite the gun pointed at him, Billy Joe's voice took on the bragging tone he used when he was sure he'd done something brilliant. "They're hidden in the trunk lining."

The man rolled his eyes and raised his gun.

"No, wait," Billy Joe begged. "I was trying something new. A better way to hide them for transport. I swear man, that's all. As soon as I made sure it worked, I was going to ask to show it to Mr. Ficone." Billy Joe took a nervous breath. "Or you. Maybe you'd want to see it first. You could take the credit for thinking it up if you want."

The man with the tattoo flexed his fingers around the handle of the handgun.

"Okay, listen. Hannah will be back any minute. She'd better be." He turned his hands palms out and continued babbling. "Wait till you see the car. It's brilliant, the way I hid the drugs. It's all fixed up, ready to go."

Fear and desperation twisted Hannah's heart. Billy Joe was off on his favorite subject. Cars. The moment when he might have revealed where her mother was had passed.

"It's a blue Toyota. Oh, I said that already. Anyhow, I painted it and boosted the engine. Th-the passenger-side mirror is broken and there's a crack in the windshield. It looks like any old family car on the outside, but under the hood is a screaming turbo-charged V-8. It's perfect for transport." Billy Joe had turned his body slightly to the right and was gesturing with his left hand to emphasize what he was saying, but Hannah saw him slowly reaching behind him to the waistband of his jeans.

"What about the money? I don't buy that your new guy or the girl—Hannah?—stole it."

"No, no. Listen. I swear. I'm giving you the real deal." Billy Joe's words tumbled over each other. "It's Hannah. That bitch is the key." He giggled. "The key. You'd better believe me. She's the one you want." He got his fingers wrapped around the handle of the gun that was stuck in his waistband and covered with his untucked shirt.

The man with the red tattoo stiffened and gripped his weapon tightly. "Don't move, slimeball!" the big man shouted.

"Look, I swear on my mama's life. Okay, so I kept those few drugs that are hid in the Toyota. But Hannah's the one who took the money. Not me. Make her talk. She's holding the key to everything," Billy Joe stammered.

Then, as Hannah watched in horror, he pulled out the gun. *No! Don't!* She covered her mouth with her hand to keep from screaming.

Billy Joe fired. The gun bucked in his hand and the bullet struck the garage wall at least three feet above the other man's head.

Without changing his position or his expression, the big man's finger squeezed the trigger. Billy Joe bucked once, then the back of his shirt blossomed with red, like ink in water. He made a strangled sound, then collapsed to the floor, right where he stood. The small gun he was holding dropped to the concrete with a metallic clatter.

Hannah tried to scream, but her voice was trapped behind her closed throat. The last thing she saw before she turned and ran toward Billy Joe's car was the big man's dark eyes on her and the gaping barrel of the gun pointed directly at her.

A LONG TIME later, Hannah wrapped her hands around the thick white mug, savoring its warmth. It was almost midnight—four hours since she'd watched a man shoot Billy Joe in the heart. In one sense it seemed as though it had happened to someone else. But then she would close her eyes and she was there, watching the blood spread across the back of his shirt like a rose blooming in fast-forward on a nature show.

He was dead. Billy Joe was dead, and the secret of where he'd taken her mother had died with him. A spasm of panic shot through her and her hand jerked, spilling the coffee. She grabbed a napkin from a chrome dispenser and laid it on top of the spilled liquid.

Ever since her mother had disappeared, Hannah had been imagining things. She knew her mother was not literally dead yet—not from her disease. But nightmarish images of where she was being held swirled continuously in Hannah's mind.

She could be lying in a bed or on a pallet on a cold floor, her breathing labored, her paper-thin skin turning more and more sallow as the time since her last dialysis treatment grew longer. Without the life-giving procedure, the toxins that her diseased liver couldn't metabolize would kill her within days, if Billy Joe hadn't killed her already.

Her once-beautiful mother, still young at forty-two, was an alcoholic. She'd been as good a mother as she could be, given her addiction, while the liquor had systematically destroyed her liver. By the time Hannah was sixteen, she had become her mom's caregiver.

Right now, sitting in the bright diner with the mug of hot coffee in her hands, she couldn't even remember how she'd gotten into Billy Joe's car, peeled out of the driveway or gotten on the interstate. Her only thought had been to run as if the hounds of hell were behind her. All she remembered was that desperate need to stay alive so she could find her mother.

A few minutes ago, four hours and almost two hundred miles later, she'd been forced to stop because she was about out of gas. She took a swallow of hot, strong coffee. What was she going to do? Go back to Dowdie, Texas, where Sheriff Harlan King was already suspicious of her and her mother? He'd been called twice in the past few months, once by neighbors and once by Hannah herself, complaining about her mom's and Billy Joe's screaming fights. Two years ago, he'd nearly busted her mom for possession of marijuana.

She thought about what he and his deputies would find this time. Her brain too easily conjured up a picture of Billy Joe, lying in a puddle of his own blood on the floor of the garage, her mother, missing with no explanation, Hannah herself gone, with brand-new tire skid marks on the concrete driveway, and who knew what kind of evidence of illegal drugs in the garage, on Billy Joe's body, even in her mom's house.

She couldn't go back.

The sheriff would never believe her. He'd arrest her and send her to prison and one day they'd find her mother's body in a ditch or a remote cabin or an abandoned car, and people in Dowdie would talk about Hannah Martin, who'd killed her mother and her mother's boyfriend, and how quiet and friendly she'd always seemed.

It was a catch-22. If she went back, all the sheriff's emphasis would be on her, and they probably wouldn't find her mother until it was too late. But if she didn't go back, then it might be days before anyone knew her mother was missing. Either way, she was terrified that her mom's fate was sealed.

She put her palms over her eyes, blocking out the restaurant's harsh fluorescent lights. She'd spent the past twenty-four hours begging Billy Joe to bring her mother back home. She'd sworn on her mother's life and her own that she wouldn't tell a soul, that she would do anything, *anything* he wanted her to, if he would only bring her mother back home so Hannah could take care of her.

But Billy Joe had been cold and cruel. He'd pushed her up against the wall of her bedroom and told her in explicit detail what he would do to her if she didn't *shut up*.

At that moment, Hannah had begun to devise a plan to follow Billy Joe to where he was holding her mother. But now, Billy Joe was dead.

Hannah's eyes burned and her insides felt more hollow and scorched than they'd ever felt before. Her mother was her only family, and she had no way to find her. Pressing her hand to her chest, Hannah felt the loneliness and grief like a palpable thing.

She picked up the mug and drained the last drops of coffee, then slid out of the booth and went to the cash register. A girl with straight black hair and black eye shadow that didn't mask the purplish skin under her eyes gave Hannah a hard look along with her change. "You want a place to sleep for a couple hours?" she asked.

Hannah shook her head.

"No charge. There ain't a lot of traffic tonight. I'll give you the room closest to here. You don't have to worry about anybody bothering you."

"Thanks," Hannah said, "but I've got to get to—" Where? For the first time, she realized she had no idea where she was going. Or where she was. "Where am— I mean, what town is this?"

The girl frowned. "Really? You don't know? Girl, you need some rest. You're about ten miles from Shreveport."

"Louisiana?" Hannah said.

The girl angled her head. "Yeah.... You sure you don't want to sleep awhile?" She paused for a second, studying Hannah. "You can park your car in the back. Nobody'll see it back there."

Hannah shook her head as she took her change. "Thanks," she said, giving the girl a tired smile. "That's awfully nice of you, but I'd better get going."

"Where you headed?"

Hannah stopped at the door and looked out at the interstate that ran past the truck stop, then back at the girl. She'd driven east, but she had no idea where she was going or what she was going to do when she got there. She had to have a plan before she went back to Dowdie. Otherwise all she'd accomplish would be to get herself arrested.

Shreveport, Louisiana. She wasn't quite sure where in the state Shreveport was, but there was one place in Louisiana she did know. Chef Voleur, on the north shore of Lake Pontchartrain.

She recalled a photo her mother had given her a long time ago. It was a picture of two young women, arm in arm, laughing. Her mother had always talked about Chef Voleur and her best friend. *We loved that place, Kathleen and me. That whole area around Lake Pontchartrain, from New Orleans to the north shore, is a magical place. She stayed, and I wish I had. Living there was like living in a movie.*

She made a vague gesture toward the road. "This is I-20, right?"

The girl nodded.

"I'm going to a town called Chef Voleur," she said. "To visit a friend of my mother's."

"You know you're going to get there around three o'clock in the morning, right?" the girl said dubiously.

Hannah waved a hand. "My mom's friend won't care."

Hannah prayed that her mother was right about the place being magical. Maybe things would be better there. They certainly couldn't get much worse. Could they?

As she walked back to Billy Joe's car, Hannah scanned the nearly empty parking lot, looking for the large maroon sedan that must have belonged to the man with the red tattoo, but she didn't see any sign of it.

Chapter Two

Just like the girl at the truck stop had predicted, Hannah wound up in Metairie at 3:00 a.m., unable to hold her eyes open any longer. She found a small, seedy motel that she figured wouldn't push the limit of her credit card, checked in and managed to sleep a little—in fits and starts, interrupted by nightmares of finding her mother just as she was breathing her last breath, or worse, leading the killer to her.

Around eight, she got up, showered and dressed, then sat down on the bed and dumped the contents of her purse. Like her mother, Hannah carried everything essential, valuable or meaningful in her purse. And like her mother, she wasn't sentimental, so most of the bag's contents were practical, except for two items. One was a photo her mother had given her years ago. The second was a sealed envelope.

Hannah picked up the envelope. With the traumatic events of the past couple of days, Hannah had totally forgotten about it. Looking at the words scrawled across the front made her want to break down and cry, but she didn't have time for that. So she carefully placed the envelope back in her purse and picked up her wallet.

She pulled the fragile, dog-eared photo out of a hidden pocket. It had to be thirty years old and was of her mother and Kathleen Griffin, her best friend. On the back it read, "Kath and me at her house." In a different hand was written "sisters forever," and an address in Chef Voleur, Louisiana.

Hannah looked up the address and took note of the directions. She was about to head out when her cell phone rang.

When she looked at the display, her heart skipped a beat. It was the Dowdie, Texas, sheriff's office. Hannah's already queasy stomach did a nauseating flip, the result of too little sleep, too much coffee and the image of Billy Joe's blood in her head.

She stared at the display, not moving, until the phone stopped ringing, then she dropped the phone back into her purse. There was no doubt in her mind why they were calling. They'd found Billy Joe's body. But how could she talk to them? What would she say? How would she explain to the authorities why she had run away to South Louisiana after witnessing a murder if she couldn't explain it to herself?

It took her about half an hour to drive to the address written on the back of the photo. It was across the street from a pizza place. With the photo in her hand she walked up to the building, hope clogging her throat.

A small voice deep inside her asked why she thought that talking to her mother's old friend would help her find and rescue her mother back in Texas.

She had no idea. Except that her only other choice was to trust Sheriff King to believe her, and she'd been taught at her mother's knee that authorities couldn't be trusted. Sheriffs. Police. Lawyers. They were the people who took children away from their mothers and placed them in foster care. They threatened sick people with prison for using marijuana to relieve the debilitating nausea associated with cancer and other diseases.

SHE KNOCKED ON the heavy wood door, then realized immediately that her tentative rapping probably couldn't be heard by anyone inside. So she rapped a second time, harder.

For a long moment that probably spanned no more than eight or ten seconds, she stood there listening and heard nothing. As she lifted her hand to rap again, she heard soft thuds on the other side of the door, as if someone was walking on a hardwood floor in socks or barefoot.

Standing stiffly, not quite ready to believe that she'd actually found her mother's best friend, Kathleen, she waited for the door to open.

When it did, it was not a pretty, dark-haired woman with even, striking features and a beautiful smile who stood there. It was a man. He was tall and lean and he had the same even, striking features but they were distorted in a scowl. And he had a cell phone to his ear.

After a brief, dismissive glance at her, he scanned the hallway behind her. Once he'd assured himself that she was the only one there, he said, "Hang on a minute," into the phone. "I've got to deal with somebody at the door." His tone was irritated and impatient.

Private investigator MacEllis Griffin kept his expression neutral as he eyed the young woman from the top of her streaked blond hair to the toes of her clunky sandals.

"What is it?" he growled. She stood there looking at him with all the apprehension of a kid called to the principal's office. Only she was no kid and he was no schoolteacher.

She could have been a kid. Her hair was pulled back

into a single messy braid that looked like she'd slept in it. The skinny jeans were slightly loose on her slender frame and the shirt looked more slept in than her hair.

"Hmm? Oh, nope. It's pretty slow here," Mack said into the phone as he tried to guess her age. Twenty-five? Twenty-six? Under twenty-five? Hard to tell. She had that heart-shaped face that always looked young. But faint blue circles under her eyes that matched the color of her jeans told him she was much older than her hair or clothes might indicate. She opened her mouth but he held up a finger. "Buono's working a missing person case," he said. "A seventeen-year-old. Probably ran away with her boyfriend."

"Well, get to the office and do something useful," Dawson Delancey, his boss, replied. "You could file your past three months' expenses if you're bored."

Mack didn't take his eyes off the young woman as he laughed. "I'll never be that bored," he said. "In fact, I might be real interested in something real soon." He smiled when the woman's gaze dropped from his and her cheeks turned pink.

"In what?" Dawson asked. "Was that the mailman delivering your latest issue of *Playboy?*"

"Right. He just got here from 2002," Mack responded. "Nope. Looks like I'm about to be hit up for Girl Scout cookies or a donation to a religious cause. I'd better go."

"I hope it's the donation. You don't need the cookies," Dawson said.

"Bite me," Mack said conversationally. "You're the one getting fat on your wife's Italian cooking."

"You're just jealous. Juliana and I will be back in Biloxi in a few days. I'll give you a call when we know for sure."

"Okay. Later. 'Bye."

As Mack hung up the phone, the young woman met his gaze and gave him a sad, self-conscious smile. The smile didn't reach her eyes and the only thing it accomplished was to make her look older and sadder.

A familiar sinking feeling gnawed at his stomach. He knew that smile. He'd never met this woman before, but he knew her type way too well. Standing there with that sadness in her eyes, that furrow between her brows. She was the embodiment of a lot of things he'd worked very hard to forget. She was exactly the type of person— the type of woman—he'd spent his adult life avoiding.

He upped his scowl by about a hundred watts and aimed it directly at her. With any luck, she'd turn and run. Her type was easily intimidated.

But her gaze didn't waver. She lifted her chin and to his surprise, he recognized a staunch determination in her green eyes, along with a spark of stubbornness. Interesting. But the small furrow between her brows didn't smooth out and the corners of her mouth were still pinched and tight.

He put his hand on the doorknob, preparing to close the door and get back to his coffee. "Can I help you?" he asked grudgingly.

"I'm looking for Kathleen Griffin," she said quietly.

The name hit him like a blow to the solar plexus. "Who?" he said, an automatic response designed to give him a second to think. But his brain seemed suddenly to be caught in a loop. *Kathleen Griffin, Kathleen. Kathleen.*

"K-Kathleen Griffin. The mailbox said Griffin." She gestured vaguely toward the front door.

It had been twenty years since his mother had died. This young woman wouldn't have been more than five or six at the time. Why would she be looking for his mother? "What's this about?"

"It's…personal," she said, glancing behind him into his foyer.

"I doubt that," he said flatly. "Go peddle whatever you're selling somewhere else. Kathleen Griffin doesn't live here." He started to close the door, but she held out a small, dog-eared photo. The paper was old and faded, but one of the two women in the picture looked familiar.

"Please," she said. Her hand was trembling, making the paper flutter.

"What's that?" he asked, knowing he was going to regret having asked that question. He held the door in its half-shut position.

The young woman's throat quivered as she swallowed. "It's a picture of my mother and Kathleen Griffin," she said, lifting her chin. "I really need to see her. It's a—" she bit her lower lip briefly and her gaze faltered "—it's a matter of life and death."

He gave a short laugh, but cut it off when she winced. "Life and death," he said dubiously. "Who are you?"

"Hannah Martin," she responded. "My mother is Stephanie Clemens."

She waited, watching him. But he didn't recognize the name. He gave a quick shake of his head, took a small step backward and started to close the door.

"You're her son, aren't you?"

Her words sent his stomach diving straight down to his toes. He shook his head, not in denial—in resignation. She had him and he knew it. He also knew that if he didn't do whatever he had to do in order to get rid of her this minute, he was going to regret it for a long time. "I'm sorry, but Kathleen Griffin is dead. So…" He put his hand on the door, preparing to close it.

"Oh. Oh, no," Hannah Martin said, her eyes filling with tears and her face losing its color. "I'm so sorry—" she started, but at that instant, her phone rang. She jerked at the sound, then reached into her purse and pulled it out.

As Mack watched, she looked at the screen as if she was afraid it might reach out and bite her. When she checked the display, her face lost what little color it had. She made a quiet sound, like a small animal cornered by a hungry predator. Her fingers tightened on the phone until the knuckles turned white, and all the time, the phone kept ringing, a loud, strident peal.

Whoever was on the other end of that call frightened her. In fact, she looked as if she'd seen a ghost. When the ringing finally stopped, Hannah dropped the phone back into her purse as if it were made of molten lava.

Mack had missed his best opportunity. He should have closed the door as soon as her phone rang. It was the perfect opportunity to escape. But he hadn't taken it. He wasn't sure why.

"I'm sorry about your mother," she said in a trembling voice. "I don't know what I was thinking, coming here. I apologize for bothering you." She closed her eyes briefly.

She'd let him off the hook. He took a step backward, preparing to close the door, because of course, she was about to turn and walk away.

But she didn't move. Her ghostly white face took on a faint greenish hue. She swayed like a slender tree in a punishing wind. Then she fainted.

Mack dived, catching her in time to keep her head from hitting the floor. She was fairly short, compared to his six-foot-one-inch height and he'd already noticed that she wasn't a lightweight. Her body was compact and firm. Lowering her gently to the floor, he grabbed a pillow off the couch and placed it under her head, making the decision to leave her on the floor rather than try to move her to the couch or a bed.

By the time he'd gotten the pillow under her head, she'd woken up. He recalled a paramedic telling him once that if someone passed out and woke up immediately, they were probably in no immediate danger.

Her face still had that greenish hue, although surprisingly, it didn't detract from its loveliness. He retrieved the photo she'd dropped when she'd passed out. He looked at the two young women—girls, really. They were both pretty and pleasant-faced. They were laughing at whoever was taking the picture, and behind them, Mack recognized the furniture. Most of it was still here. He knew one of the girls. It was his mother. He smiled sadly, seeing how young and happy and innocent she looked.

He'd never seen the other girl before, but the young woman lying just outside his door bore a strong resemblance to her. He turned the photo over. On the back was written "Kath and me at her house" in an unfamiliar hand. The other handwriting he knew. It was his mother's flowery script. She'd written "sisters forever" and his address.

Hannah stirred and tried to sit up. "What happened?" she asked, looking around in confusion.

"You fainted," he said.

She stared at him. "No, I didn't," she said, frowning at him suspiciously. "I never faint. Did you do something—?" But then her hand went to her head. "I feel dizzy."

"Just sit there a minute. I'll get you some water," he said grudgingly. He rose and drew her a glass of tap water. When he handed her the glass, she drank about half of it.

Then she shook her head as if trying to shake off a haze. "I guess I must have fainted."

"I guess," he said, a faint wryness in his voice.

She rose onto her haunches and stood, then grabbed on to his forearm for a second, to steady herself. "I never faint," she said again.

Mack smiled. "So I've heard," he said, thinking she was stubborn. He assessed her. Her color was still not good. "Do you want to sit down?" he asked, then felt irritated at himself for asking. Hell, she'd stood up on her own. So it was the perfect time for her to leave. And again, he'd missed his chance. And right there was one of the primary reasons why he didn't get involved with her type. She was obviously on some personal mission that would consume her life until she accomplished it. A certain clue—she'd driven all night without stopping except to get coffee and gasoline.

"Thanks," she said, and turned and headed, a little unsteadily, for the small dining table. He followed her.

She started to sit, then looked around.

"Here," Mack said, handing her the photo. "This what you're looking for?"

She took it. "Was this what we were talking about when I—" she gestured toward the front door.

"When you didn't faint?" He nodded, deciding for the moment not to remind her that she'd received a phone call that had scared her.

She held the photo in one hand and touched the faces of the two girls with a fingertip. "According to my mother, she and Kathleen Griffin swore they'd always be there for one another. *Sisters forever.*"

"And?" Mack said, working to sound disinterested,

even though he was becoming more and more fascinated by this pretty, determined young woman who had driven all night to find her mother's best friend.

"And—" She stopped, looking confused. Then she shrugged. "And, I don't know. I'm not really sure why I'm here. I just remember my mother talking about how much she and Kathleen loved Chef Voleur and how they had made that promise to each other."

She picked up her purse from the dining room table and stood, gripping the back of the chair to steady herself. "I'm truly sorry about your mother." She paused.

He nodded. "She died a long time ago," he said dismissively.

That was another reason he didn't like to be around women like her. Although Hannah was obviously in need of help and had pushed herself beyond her limits, right this minute her concern was for him and he didn't like that one bit.

She looked down at the photo, then up at him. "You look just like her," she said. "You have to be her son."

"MacEllis Griffin," he said, offering neither his hand nor any further explanation. "Call me Mack."

"Mack," she said, "I apologize for bothering you." She started to stand.

"Wait," he said. "What's this life-and-death emergency?" He bit his tongue, literally. But it was too late.

To his dismay, hope flared in her eyes. "I'm—not sure I should—"

"Why don't you tell me what's wrong." What the hell was happening to him? When had his mouth cut itself off from his brain? He was just digging himself in deeper and deeper. And why? Because a pretty woman had fainted in his doorway? No. It was because he had the very definite feeling that when she'd said *life and death,* she wasn't overstating the issue at all.

She sank back into the chair and casually picked up a business card from a small stack on the table. "MacEllis Griffin," she said. "D&D Security?"

"It's a private firm that takes on certain security issues," he said, watching her.

"Security—like night guards at office buildings?"

Mack sent her an ironic look. "No."

She frowned for a second, then eyebrows rose. "You're a private investigator?"

"You could use that term, although we don't take the usual divorce or spouse-tailing cases."

"What do you take?"

The faint hope he'd seen in her eyes grew, although she was still stiff as a board and tension radiated from her like heat.

"We've handled our share of *life-and-death* cases," he said.

Her eyes went as opaque as turquoise.

"Sorry," he said. "I can be a sarcastic SOB at times. Here's a quick rundown of me. I'm thirty-one years old. I've been with D&D Security for three years. I'm licensed as an investigator with the state of Louisiana. Now, will you tell me why you drove all night to find my mother?"

"How do you know I drove all night?" she asked.

"Your eyes are twitching and the lids are drooping. Headache and exhaustion, I'd guess. You're trembling, probably from too much coffee. You haven't combed your hair and your clothes smell faintly of gasoline. You must have spilled a little while you were filling up. How far have you driven?"

She shifted in her chair. "What are you, some kind

of Sherlock Holmes?" she asked drily. "Maybe you can tell me what I had for dinner last night."

He smiled. "You didn't eat dinner. You didn't stop until you were out of gas. You had a cup of coffee and nothing else. Then you didn't stop again until you got a motel room. You slept in your clothes, although you didn't sleep much. You couldn't stop thinking about whatever happened that frightened you so much that you took off without packing."

"How—?"

"If you'd packed, you'd have changed clothes." He stopped. "My question is, what or who are you running from?"

She opened her mouth to speak and then closed it again. He saw tears start in her eyes, but she blinked to keep them from falling. When she spoke, there was no trace of the tears in her voice. "I'm not running from anyone," she said, straightening her spine.

Mack knew from her voice that she was lying, and from her determined glare that she'd decided something. Probably to unload her woes upon him. He braced himself.

She stared at him for so long he was beginning to wonder if she'd fallen asleep with her eyes wide-open. But about the time he'd decided to snap his fingers in front of her face, she sat back with a sigh. "I drove here from Dowdie, Texas. Eight hours. And I've got to start back today. As soon as I can. My mother is—" She stopped as tears welled in her eyes. She wiped a hand down her face, then swiped at the dampness on her cheeks with her fingers.

"Your mother?" Mack said encouragingly.

"She's very ill. She has to have dialysis or she'll die." Mack waited, but she didn't say anything else. She pressed her lips together and clenched her jaw, doing her best not to cry.

"Do you need money?" he asked gently. "To pay for the treatments?"

"What? No! I don't need money. My mother has insurance."

"So why did you drive all this way just to turn around and go back?"

"It's complicated," she said.

"Most things are, especially if they involve running."

Tears welled again, and she pulled a tissue out of her purse and wiped her eyes. "I've kept that photo in my purse for years. Mom always told me that if I needed anything and she wasn't—wasn't—" She took a quick breath. "I should find Kathleen."

Mack's brows rose when she'd stumbled over her words. He pushed his chair back and stood. "Okay. Well, I'm Kathleen's son, so if you'll tell me what you need, I'll take care of it for you."

She played with the water glass, tracing a droplet of water up one side and down the other. "I can't tell you. It's too dangerous."

"Dangerous to who?" Mack asked.

"To my mother."

"Look," he said. "You need to start at the beginning. I can't figure out what you're talking about and I haven't heard anything that sounds dangerous yet, except your mother's illness. And you said she's getting dialysis."

"That's just it. She's not."

"Why not?"

"Because—" She sobbed, then banged her open palm on the table. "I can't stop crying."

Mack got up and refilled her water. He set it in front

of her and watched her as she drank it, hiccuped, then drank some more.

"Now. Why isn't she getting dialysis?"

"Because she's been kidnapped."

Mack flopped down in the chair. "Kidnapped? Is this some kind of joke?"

She stared at him, anger burning away the tears. "A joke? That's what you think?"

He opened his mouth then shook his head. He wasn't sure what he thought at the moment. He'd figured she *had* come to ask for money and it was just taking her a while to work up the nerve.

He studied her. Her skin was still colorless. She looked exhausted and terrified and so far she wasn't making a lot of sense.

"Okay. Your mother's been kidnapped. By who? Have they contacted you? Do they want a ransom? And have you talked to the police?"

"No! No. It's not that kind of kidnapping. And I can't go to—" She stopped talking.

Mack sighed. "Of course you can't. Why not?"

"They can't help. Nobody can help. I don't even know why I came here. I had to run. He was going to shoot me." She looked at the water glass. "I should have stayed," she said, her voice a mutter now. "I should have confronted him."

Well, she wasn't talking to him any longer.

"But there was all that blood," she continued. "And Billy Joe just collapsed and died. So I ran. I thought I had to save myself so I could find my mother before she died. But now she's going to die anyway. Oh, I don't know what to do."

"Whoa, damn it! Slow down." Mack did his best to put everything she'd said into logical order. If she wasn't just crazy, then she'd been through some kind of horrible trauma. "Hannah. Let's start over and take this slow. Who was going to shoot you? Whose blood did you see and who is Billy Joe?"

She stared at him for a moment, as if trying to figure out what he was doing there, in her reality. Then she blinked. "Oh." She shot up out of the chair and slung her purse strap over her shoulder. "I apologize," she said. "I think I've made a mistake." She looked at the business card in her hand, then stuffed it into her jeans pocket and ran out the front door.

"Hannah, wait!" he called. He started to run after her, but his protective instincts kicked in.

Good riddance, he thought when he heard the outside door slam. She had to have come here for money, then lost her nerve and tried to make up some kind of story. She'd never make it as a grifter. Her heart-shaped face gave too much away. He'd watched the kaleidoscope of expressions that flitted across her features as she'd listened to her cell phone ring. Bewilderment, fear, anger, resignation, each taking its turn, then the cycle had started all over again.

He felt sorry for her. *Whoa.* That was the kind of thinking that could get him into deep trouble, if he let himself get drawn in. He was lucky she'd run out when she did. Good riddance, indeed.

While his brain was congratulating him for dodging that bullet, he found himself rushing out the front door. She'd made it down his long sidewalk to her car, digging a large ring of keys out of her purse and unlocking a dark blue Toyota.

Mack used his phone to snap a shot of the rear of her car just as she climbed in. The license plate was from Texas. And even from half a block away, he could see two bullet holes in the bumper near the plate. Recent ones.

Maybe she hadn't been making it all up.

Although he had the snapshot, he jotted the license plate number down on a small notepad that he always carried. When he put the pad back into his shirt pocket, it seemed to burn his skin. He sighed. He was going to regret this.

No. That wasn't accurate. He already did. But even as he thought that, his mind had already latched on to the mystery of Hannah Martin. Kidnapping, murder, blood, pursuit, death.

"Who are you, Hannah Martin?" he muttered. "And why did you come to me?"

Chapter Three

Hannah drove straight from St. Charles Avenue to her motel in Metairie in an exhausted haze. But now, sitting in her parked car, her brain was whirling, replaying every second of the past hour.

What had possessed her to place all her hopes of saving her mother on an old photo of a friendship from more than thirty years before? All she'd done was exhaust herself driving and waste over twelve of the precious hours her mother had left before her body went into toxic liver failure. All she'd gained for her trouble was the not-so-sympathetic ear of Kathleen Griffin's handsome if grouchy son.

She turned off the engine and got out of the car. As soon as she put weight on her knees, they gave way. She barely managed to grab at the door frame to keep from falling. Her heart raced, her head felt weird—light and heavy at the same time—and the edges of her vision were turning black. It had to be exhaustion and hunger.

After a few seconds, she gingerly let go of the hot metal door frame and tested her ability to walk. Not too bad. But her hands trembled so much that it took her three tries to insert her key card into the motel's door.

Once she was inside with the door closed, the tears she'd been holding back ever since she'd watched Billy

Joe collapse and die came, as if floodgates had opened. She flopped down onto the bed and grabbed one of the pillows to hug as she cried. But within a couple of moments, she clenched her jaw and wiped her face.

That was enough of that. She didn't have time to cry. She had to figure out what she was going to do. Here she was, eight hours away from her home, and if someone asked her why she'd driven all that way, she wouldn't have been able tell them. In fact, she'd run away again as soon as Mack had started questioning her. He'd made her realize just how little she'd thought about what she was going to do.

What if she drove back to Dowdie and did what she should have done—gone to Sheriff King? For that matter, what if she'd gone to him about Billy Joe's obvious involvement in something illegal? Would things be completely different now? Would Billy Joe be in jail instead of dead and would her mother be safe and sound at home, preparing to go for dialysis later in the week?

Or would she and her mother be sitting in an interrogation room trying to explain to the sheriff that they knew nothing about what Billy Joe was or was not doing?

When she'd raced to the Toyota and taken off with Billy Joe's killer on her heels, she had actually considered going to the sheriff—for about ten seconds. Until she reminded herself that in her world, authorities like the police or Children's Services had the power to destroy her life.

From long ago when she'd been barely old enough to understand, her mother's admonitions were ingrained in her. *If you tell the police Mommy fell asleep with a cigarette and started a fire, they'll take you away from me and put you in an orphanage. You can put the fire*

out, can't you, sweetie? Just put it out and don't tell any-
body. Then we'll be safe. We'll take care of each other.

And they had. Her mother had raised her alone. It
had been just the two of them against the world. Then,
when the roles had become reversed as her mother's
cirrhosis worsened, Hannah had taken care of her without regret—until the moment she'd witnessed a murder
and run away.

Suddenly, Hannah remembered the phone call she'd
gotten while she'd been standing outside Kathleen Griffin's apartment. She blotted her cheeks on her shirtsleeve then fished inside her purse for her phone. Her
fingers touched the smooth paper of the envelope, but
she pushed it aside. Whatever was inside it wasn't going
to help her right now. In fact, it might make things
worse.

She found her phone and sat there holding it, not
wanting to look at the display. Maybe she'd misread
the caller ID. Maybe her exhausted mind had merely
overlaid Billy Joe's name over whoever had really been
calling her. But when she looked, the display definitely
read "B.J." Her heart jumped, just as it had earlier.

Someone was calling her from Billy Joe's phone.
There were only two possibilities. The man with the red
tattoo, who'd shot Billy Joe in cold blood, or the sheriff.

As she'd peeled out of her mother's driveway in her
haste to escape Billy Joe's killer, she'd prayed that the
man would keep shooting at the Toyota until he'd emp-
tied his gun. She'd prayed that one of their unconcerned
neighbors would hear the shots and call the sheriff, and
that the sheriff would catch him red-handed and charge
him with Billy Joe's murder. And she'd prayed that everybody in town would become so wrapped up in the
murder that they'd forget about Hannah Martin.

She accessed new voice mails. There were two. If it was the killer who had called her, had he really been dumb enough to leave a message? She skipped the message from the sheriff's office without listening to it and played the second incoming message.

"Where'd you go, Hannah?" She cringed and swallowed against a sick dread that settled in her stomach. That wasn't the sheriff. It was the man with the red tattoo on his hand. She'd never forget that awful voice as long as she lived.

"I know you don't want to talk to me, but I need to see you, talk to you. I need to make sure you're all right. Call me as soon as possible and let me know where you are. I'm worried about you. Bye-bye, Hannah."

Numbly, Hannah pressed the off button. She sat there, trying to will away the nausea that was getting worse with every passing second. Then, unable to stave it off any longer, she jumped up and ran into the bathroom, where she heaved drily. After a moment the heaves slowed, then stopped. She splashed water on her face over and over, trying to cool her heated skin and soothe her burning eyes.

At last the nausea dissipated, but there wasn't enough water in the world to wash away the sight of what that man had done to Billy Joe.

Had her mother's boyfriend deserved to die in such a horrible way? Maybe. Maybe not. But she wondered—if she'd gotten the chance to kill him, would she? She couldn't honestly deny it. Of course, she'd have tortured him first to find out where he was holding her mother.

When she'd come home from the drugstore with her mother's prescriptions only to find her missing, she'd threatened Billy Joe with going to the sheriff, but he'd quickly and effectively reminded her of his earlier warning.

She should have made good on her threat and gone to the sheriff then. She should have realized that of the two, Billy Joe or the sheriff, the sheriff was the more trustworthy. He'd have arrested Billy Joe and Hannah and her mother would be at home now, safe and healthy.

But instead she'd done the cowardly thing. She'd kept her mouth shut. She'd pretended nothing was wrong. It was what she'd always done. Long, harsh experience had ingrained the habit into her, as deeply as drinking was ingrained in her mother. It was what alcoholics did. It was what the children of alcoholics did. They pretended and lied and never told their secrets.

But now, doing what she'd always done was going to get her mother killed.

Hannah stood, grabbing the back of a chair when she felt light-headed. She needed to head back to Dowdie, but a lifetime of taking care of her mother and herself had taught her to pay attention to her body. There was no way she could drive eight hours tonight, no matter how desperate she was to get back home and find her mother. She'd fall asleep at the wheel.

Digging into her purse, she pushed aside the sealed envelope and her wallet, searching for the two high-energy protein bars she'd seen earlier. They were a little misshapen and the worse for wear, but still sealed. When she opened the first one, it was practically all crumbs, but she ate it anyhow, then ate the second one as well, washing them down with water from the tap in the bathroom, hoping that they'd be enough to satisfy her hunger and keep her from feeling so faint.

Then she took a shower, which made her feel a little

better, if she didn't count the exhaustion and her still queasy stomach.

Dressed in the only clothes she had, she lay down on the bed and turned on the TV, hoping to relax by watching a mindless sitcom for a while. It was five o'clock in the afternoon, according to the bedside clock. She groaned. It had been twenty-two hours since she'd witnessed Billy Joe's murder and run for her life. During that time, she hadn't closed her eyes, except for that fitful nap she'd taken early that morning.

She flipped channels until she recognized an episode of *Friends*. She leaned back against the pillows and tried to concentrate on the jokes Chandler was making. Four episodes later, she groaned and shifted position. She scrolled through the other channels on the old TV, but there was nothing interesting on. She reached for her paper cup of water, but it was empty, so she dragged herself up from the bed and went into the tiny bathroom to refill it. The next thing she knew, she'd dropped the cup and splashed water all over her legs and the floor. She'd fallen asleep standing up and dropped the cup.

She tossed a towel down and dried the water, but when she straightened, she started feeling queasy again. And now the edges of her vision were turning black and sparkly, which told her she'd faint if she didn't lie down.

She lay down on the bed. Was all this caused by her exhaustion and hunger? She'd eaten and rested— a little. She didn't have to consider for long to figure out that the nausea and light-headedness were the result of all the stress she'd been under added to hunger and weariness. Within the past forty-eight hours, her mother had been abducted from her house, her life and her mother's had been threatened and she'd witnessed the kidnapper—the only person who knew where her mother was—murdered in cold blood.

Then, panicked and thinking only of staying alive, Hannah had fled.

Breathing shallowly, Hannah waited for the nausea and light-headedness to pass. She closed her eyes and tried her best to relax and clear her mind. But Mack Griffin's slow, knowing smile rose before her closed lids.

During those first few seconds after he'd opened the door, she'd had the odd notion that her mother had sent her to Kathleen Griffin's home for this very reason. Because her own personal knight in shining armor had opened the door, ready and waiting to charge into battle for her, to rescue her mother and sweep them both away from harsh reality, pain and heartache.

But as soon as he'd fixed those hazel eyes on her, it had been immediately obvious that he had no idea who she was, nor did he care.

She should have turned and run sooner than she had, but at the time, she hadn't realized that with each passing second she'd become more mesmerized by his greenish-gold eyes and his large, capable hands and more dismayed that she was so affected by a perfect stranger. Still, in that first fairy-tale moment, something in his eyes behind the cynical smile and the worldly attitude had made her think he really could rescue her, even though she knew nothing about him except that he apparently was Kathleen Griffin's son.

He might look honorable and trustworthy and knight-like, but Hannah reminded herself of what she had learned at her mother's knee—men were *never* trustworthy. As big and strong and protective as they seemed, the reality was that men were always liars, bullies and cheaters.

But somewhere along the line her mother had gotten it wrong, because Stephanie also believed that women were weak. All they could do to protect themselves was pretend there was nothing wrong, lie when questioned and trust the untrustworthy men, since they had no other choice.

Well, not Hannah. She'd decided a long time ago that she would only trust herself. She hadn't met a man yet who could take care of her as well as she took care of herself and her mother. She lay down and tried to relax. She'd sleep for a couple of hours, then check out and get the car filled up so she could—

The car.

Her eyes flew open. *Oh, dear Lord, the car.* How had she forgotten about the car? Billy Joe's voice, filled with naive pride, came back to her. *My car. That's where the drugs are. They're hidden in the trunk lining.*

She sat up, her heart thumping wildly. She'd driven for eight hours in a car filled with drugs. A *stolen* car, as she'd discovered when she'd gone through the glove box and found that it was registered to a Nelson Vance, of Paris, Texas.

She couldn't drive the Toyota back to Dowdie. She couldn't drive it one more foot. She needed to abandon it and leave the motel. Now.

She closed her aching eyes as tears of exhaustion, frustration and hopelessness welled up. That meant she had to wipe down the car, inside and out, to get rid of her fingerprints, and take a cab to another depressing motel, then make arrangements to find another car or ride the bus back to Dowdie. And she had to start right now. She couldn't afford to sleep until she'd put miles between her and the Toyota.

She pressed her palms against her eyes, wishing she dared to set her phone's alarm and sleep—if only for a half hour.

As if prompted by her thoughts, her phone rang. Hannah's heart jumped into her throat and every muscle in her body went on full fight-or-flight alert. It was him again. The man with the red tattoo. The man who'd killed Billy Joe. She sat up straight, wringing her hands. Her chest tightened until she could barely breathe. She was afraid to answer and afraid not to. Cringing with dread, she pressed the answer button and put the phone to her ear.

"Hey, Hannah Martin," the dreadful menacing voice said.

Terror arrowed through her. She wanted to drop the phone and smash it, but her fingers clutched it tightly and she pressed her other hand against her chest as she waited to hear what he said. She shouldn't have answered. She should have let it go to voice mail so she'd have a record of what he said.

"Not talking? That's okay," the voice said conversationally. "I just wanted to let you know I'll be seeing you soon. Very soon. You've got something that Billy Joe promised us."

She didn't speak, wasn't sure she could. She pulled the phone away from her ear. She needed to record him if she could just find the record button.

"Wh-what are you talking about?" she rasped, hoping to keep him talking. Where was the stupid button? She pressed Menu, Settings, every button she could think of. Then finally, there it was. Memo Record. She jabbed it.

"You know what I'm talking about," the man was saying. "You ran off with Billy Joe's car and we need to get it. Why don't we meet and I'll trade you my brand-new car for that beat-up Toyota. Oh, and I can pick up that other little item, too, that Billy Joe gave you. I've got to say, Hannah, it'll be good to see you." The voice was barely audible, but Hannah heard every word. There was no mistaking the implied threat. "Now, remind me where you're staying."

"I don't know who you are and I don't have anything. Billy Joe didn't give me anything!" she cried. "Leave me alone!"

"Don't act all innocent, Hannah. Billy Joe was fighting for his life. Why would he lie? But you were there. You know what he said. He said you stole Mr. Ficone's money. He said you're the key to the missing money." He paused, but she didn't take the bait. She didn't answer.

"Hey, that's okay. I'll call you back once I get closer to you. I'm driving right now and I really shouldn't be on the phone. So I'll be talking to you later, once I get to that town. Watch yourself, Hannah. Don't make the mistake of lying. You'll end up like Billy Joe."

She gasped. "You killed him. I know you did. I saw you."

"Oh, Hannah, you really should try to control that imagination of yours." he said, his voice as gentle and sweet as a new father's. "Oh, by the way, your mom says hi. Bye-bye, now."

"Wait!" she cried. "You know where my mother is—?"

The line went dead. "Wait—please. No, no, no." She stared at the display. The icon indicated that the computer was recording. With a shaking finger, she stopped it.

Your mother says hi. That couldn't be true, could it? The man with the red tattoo couldn't know where her mother was. Only Billy Joe knew and the man had killed him.

She held her finger over the play button, but after a few seconds, she shuddered and dropped the phone into her purse. She couldn't listen to it again. Besides, he was lying about her mother. When Billy Joe told him he'd kidnapped her, the man had sounded surprised and shocked. Then Billy Joe had died right in front of him. No. He didn't know where her mother was. He couldn't.

Could he?

MACK DRUMMED HIS fingers on his kitchen table as he waited for the search results to show up on his tablet. He'd input "Stephanie Clemens, Texas." There were eleven Stephanie Clemenses in the state, apparently, not to mention all the Clemenses that weren't Stephanies and all the Stephanies that weren't Clemenses.

He'd found one whose age was about right in a town called Dowdie. She was listed as forty-two years old and living with Hannah Martin, age twenty-five. Mack sat back in his chair, staring at the screen. So Stephanie Clemens was his odd visitor's mother. She was forty-two, which meant she'd been seventeen when her daughter was born. Mack shook his head. *Children having children.*

There was a telephone number listed beside Stephanie Clemens's name. He entered the number into his cell phone under the name Hannah Martin. Then he dialed it. There was no answer. Probably a landline.

He input Stephanie Ann Martin Clemens, Dowdie,

Texas, into a search engine, and three police reports popped up. The first, dated two years previously, was a call regarding drug activity at her home address. Mack skimmed the short paragraph. No arrests. Clemens claimed she used marijuana to alleviate nausea from an illness. Although she couldn't produce a doctor's order or even a note confirming that, the police hadn't placed her under arrest.

The second and third calls were for domestic disturbances. The location was the same address, but were four and five months before. They involved Clemens and Billy Joe Campbell, age thirty-eight. One of the calls had been made by Hannah Martin.

Mack typed in Hannah Martin, Dowdie, Texas, but found no other references to her. He sat, staring out through the French doors that opened onto the small patio behind his house. St. Charles Avenue, but what he saw wasn't a big concrete fountain and fish pool, it was Hannah. He should have known the instant he'd laid eyes on her that she'd be trouble. He should have recognized the signs.

"Two domestic disturbances involving your mother and her boyfriend," he said aloud. "That's been your life, hasn't it, Hannah? Watching your mother get beat up by thugs that didn't deserve her. She's the only role model you've ever had, isn't she? That's all you've ever known!" His voice gained in volume as anger built inside him.

Suddenly, the house was too small and hot for him. He vaulted up out of his desk chair, sending it crashing into the kitchen counter behind him. Then he threw open the French doors and stepped outside, gulping deep breaths of the cool breeze that had blown in with an afternoon thunderstorm. It was unusual for a summer storm to cool the air, but he wasn't complaining. After a few moments, the pressure in his chest and the heat along his scalp dissipated.

Mack knew too much about women like Stephanie Clemens and Hannah Martin. And he knew *way* too much about abusive boyfriends. He'd been six years old the first time he'd seen blood dripping from his mother's nose. Her boyfriend had slammed her face against one of the tall columns of the four-poster bed. Mack had flung himself at the guy, trying to break *his* nose, but at six, he wasn't strong enough or tall enough.

The jerk had swatted him away like a bothersome fly, then bent down to whisper in his ear, "If you try that again, your mom will hurt worse. Understand?"

Mack's hands cramped and he looked down to find that he'd clenched his fists. Carefully, he relaxed them, shaking them a little to ease the cramping. He took a few more breaths of chilly air, letting it flow through him, cooling the frustrated anger.

He found himself once again wishing Billy Joe Campbell were alive, because he'd like to have a few minutes with him, just long enough to give him a taste of his own medicine. But Mack had more sense than that, and more self-control—and Billy Joe was dead. He took one more deep breath, filling his lungs with the scent of damp earth and fresh rain, then went back inside.

As he was retrieving his chair and rolling it back up to the table, his phone rang. He looked at the display and sighed. It was Sadie, the woman he'd been seeing. "Hello," he said, making sure his voice was bland.

"Hey," Sadie said. "What happened to 'hi, doll,' or 'sexy Sadie'?"

"Busy," he said impatiently, not really trying to mask

the frustration in his voice. He looked at the clock in the corner of the screen.

"Well, business can wait until tomorrow. I'm back in town and I want to see you," Sadie said in her low, sexy voice. "Come over."

Mack arched his neck. It was easy to get too big a dose of Sadie. And he'd gotten a nearly lethal overdose about the time she'd gone out of town. Her absence had convinced him that he'd had enough of her to last a lifetime. He'd told her from the beginning that he wasn't interested in anything long-term, and she'd responded that she wasn't, either. As he rubbed his eyes, he wondered if she'd been telling the truth.

"Can't," he said. "I'm working on a new case and I'm pretty sure I'm going to be tied up for quite a while."

"Oh, come on," Sadie said. "You have to eat. Let's grab dinner and—"

"Sadie," he interrupted, gently but firmly. "No."

"Fine," she said. "Tell me about this big case you can't tear yourself away from."

"It's not just the case," he said. "It's a lot of things. It's been fun, but…"

"But?" she echoed.

"You know. We talked about this. We were never in it for the long haul. We both agreed."

There was a slight pause. "That's true."

He didn't speak. He really didn't like this. He wasn't quite sure why he'd chosen tonight as the night to break up with her.

"Okay, then," she said. "I enjoyed—everything."

"Me, too," he replied. He took a breath to say something else, but she hung up. He winced. That abrupt hang up was the only indication that she might have been upset.

Maybe he should have handled that in person, but unfortunately, Sadie could be quite persuasive in person. Or at least she had been once, he amended, as his brain compared Sadie and Hannah. Hannah, with her unmade-up face and flyaway hair and no lipstick, won by a mile.

Mack shook his head and resisted the urge to pound on his temples with his fists. He didn't want Hannah Martin in there. She was nothing but trouble. Mack had always loved women, but he'd learned very young that relationships were not for him. Whenever he met someone he was attracted to, he made his position clear from the first moment. If the woman protested at all, then she was not the woman for him. Most women he asked out were happy with the arrangement, because Mack was very careful to pick like-minded women. Usually he picked well. After a while, by mutual agreement, he and the woman parted ways and eventually he met another like-minded woman.

He sat down to send an email to Dusty Graves, Dawson's computer wizard, to ask how much longer until she had information back on the license plate of the car Hannah had been driving. As he did, his phone rang. Surely it wasn't Sadie again. *Give it up, doll.*

But when he looked, the display name was Dust007. "Hey, Dusty, what you got for me?"

"Finally got the info on that plate you wanted me to run," Dusty said, "but you're not going to like it."

"Why not?"

"It's registered to a Nelson Vance, of Paris, Texas. He reported it stolen about a week ago. The license and registration also report the vehicle as sky blue, not dark blue."

Mack's stomach sank. Stolen *and* repainted? Ten to

one, whoever stole it was either reselling cars or running drugs. Either way, this wasn't good. "A witness? Any sightings by highway patrol? Anything?"

"The Tyler, Texas, police have a BOLO out on the car. The DEA has been watching a small-time narcotics distribution ring operating around the area. The perps apparently steal a vehicle from a neighboring town or county, use it for one drug delivery, then clean it out and abandon it. This vehicle is suspected to have been stolen by the ring."

Dusty was right. Mack didn't like what he was hearing at all. What was Hannah Martin doing driving a car suspected of being stolen by a narcotics distribution ring?

Chapter Four

"What kind of narcotics do they deal in?" he asked Dusty.

"Mostly Oxy," Dusty said.

Stunned, Mack muttered a curse. *Oxycontin.*

"Yeah," Dusty continued. "Word is, they're bringing it into Galveston from Mexico. Get this. The DEA knows all about a big-time trafficker named Ficone in Galveston, but they've been spending their time watching a suspected small-time operator, until he was murdered yesterday."

"Murdered?" Dread settled heavy as an anvil in Mack's chest. "Yesterday? Who was he?"

"Campbell. Billy Joe Campbell. He was shot once in the chest at close range. A neighbor complained about gunshots." Dusty took a breath. "You know something about this?"

Hannah's jumbled words echoed in Mack's ears. *I had to run. He was going to shoot me.*

"Where did this happen?" he croaked, positive he knew the answer.

"Hang on."

Mack heard computer keys tapping.

"A little town called Dowdie." Dusty paused for a

second. "Mack, tell me you don't have a client who's driving that chopped car. That would not be good."

"Nope. No client. Just checking for a friend." Not a complete lie.

"O-kay," Dusty said, her tone making it obvious that she didn't believe him. "You want me to send you the details from the police report?"

"Yeah. Everything you've got on Billy Joe Campbell. I appreciate it."

"No problem, Mack. You be careful. I'll TTYL. 'Bye."

Mack hung up, remembering the changing expressions on Hannah's face and the terror in her eyes when her telephone rang. He knew that terror, knew it intimately. Had Hannah done what Mack hadn't been able to do when he was twelve? Had she killed the man who had hurt her mother?

He waited impatiently, repeatedly checking for new mail until Dusty's message about the murder came in. He scanned the police report, his heart sinking with every sentence. A neighbor had called the sheriff's office around 7:00 p.m. complaining about gunshots at 1400 Redbud Lane, Dowdie, Texas.

A sheriff's deputy arrived at around seven-thirty to find the house and driveway empty. A quick investigation by the deputy turned up a body of a white male, mid to late thirties, in the garage. Cause of death, a single gunshot wound to the chest. The victim was identified as Billy Joe Campbell of Fort Worth, Texas. The police report indicated that neither the owner of the house, a Ms. Stephanie Clemens, nor her daughter, Ms. Hannah Martin, could be found. Both were being sought for questioning in the matter.

Campbell had been killed around twelve hours before

Hannah had turned up at Mack's door, looking for Kathleen Griffin. She'd also mentioned seeing Billy Joe collapse and die and being shot at. What were the odds that Hannah had witnessed her mother's boyfriend being murdered?

A LOUD CRASH and a harsh male voice startled Hannah out of a restless sleep. Her pulse drummed in her ears and she couldn't catch a full breath. "Mom?" she called, before she came fully awake.

The crashing began again. With a start, she remembered. It couldn't be her mom. Her mom had been kidnapped by Billy Joe and Billy Joe was dead.

Hannah rubbed her eyes as she forced her brain to sort out the noises that were battering her ears. It had to be the man with the red tattoo. He'd found her.

"Police! Open up!"

Police? Surprised and terrified, Hannah jumped out of bed and ran to the door. "What is it? Did you find my—" She stopped herself just as she was about to throw the dead bolt. What if it wasn't the police?

She glanced at the clock on the bedside table. It was almost one o'clock in the morning. She'd slept for a couple of hours. "I need proof you're the police." She made her voice as stern as she could, but it still quavered.

"Hannah Martin, I'm Detective Anthony Teilhard of the Metairie Police Department. I've got the motel's night manager here. He's going to unlock the door and we're coming in. I'd suggest you move back."

She scrambled backward as a key turned in the doorknob and then in the dead bolt. The door swung open and slammed against the wall as three officers burst into the room, guns at the ready. Hannah shrieked as two of them, one male and one female, turned their weapons on her. The third officer quickly checked the bathroom and the tiny closet.

"Clear," he said.

The officer who'd entered first took three steps forward and looked down the barrel of his gun at her. "Hannah Martin?" he said.

Hannah's head jerked in a nod. Her first instinct was to retreat, but she bumped her hip on the corner of the bedside table. She was trapped between the bed and the wall. "Who—wha—?" Nothing but broken, senseless sounds escaped her constricted throat. She clutched at the neck of her shirt with trembling fingers.

"I'm Detective Teilhard. Keep your hands where I can see them. Good. Now, where did you get the car, Hannah?"

"The car?" she parroted. "It's—I don't—" All she could think about was Billy Joe saying, *That's where the drugs are. They're hidden in the trunk lining.*

"Come on, Hannah. Pull yourself together. You're in a lot of trouble. The best thing you can do is answer my questions. Now tell me about the car."

"I don't know anything," she said. It wasn't exactly true.

"Nothing?" Teilhard said wryly. "Okay, Hannah. In that case, looks like we're going to have to do this down at the station. You're under arrest for possession of a stolen vehicle, driving a stolen vehicle and transporting a stolen vehicle across state lines."

She waited, her heart in her throat, but he didn't mention illegal drugs or homicide.

The detective looked at the female officer. "Officer Waller, would you check her for weapons and cuff her, please?"

"Arms straight out at your sides, please," Officer Waller said.

Hannah obeyed, feeling a profound relief that the police were here about the car and not about Billy Joe's murder. When she caught Teilhard gazing at her with a puzzled look, she ducked her head and tried to compose her features. Had he seen the relief on her face?

The female officer started to pat her down. Hannah recoiled. "No, wait," she said quickly. "Please. I didn't know it was stolen. I'll tell you what I know. You don't have to arrest me." She felt a lump growing in her throat. If they arrested her, how was she ever going to get back to Dowdie to find her mother?

She swallowed hard, trying to stop the tears. She was sure Teilhard wasn't the type who could be swayed by a damsel in distress. In fact, his mouth was already thinning in a line of distaste at her hedging.

She needed to figure out what to do and fast, because it wasn't going to take the detective long to find out what she already knew—that the person who had stolen the car was dead, murdered, and that the car was filled with drugs. Then what would he do? He'd put her in jail. No question about it. She'd be charged with grand theft auto and murder. That meant that her mother would surely die.

Officer Waller quickly and efficiently finished patting her down, then pulled her arms behind her back and cuffed her hands.

"Do you really have to do this?" Hannah asked as the cold metal bit into her wrists, desperate to try anything to get out of being arrested. Anything but telling the truth. She was in too deep. If she tried to explain, Teilhard would laugh as he threw her into lockup. "It's got to be a misunderstanding. I apologize for the trouble. I mean, I thought I was borrowing my mom's boyfriend's car. Can't we just give the car back to its owner? I'll pay for any damages." She made her voice sound hopeful.

She could pretend all she wanted, but she knew that there was no way any sheriff's office or police station would send three armed officers to bring in one relatively harmless female driving a stolen car. This had to be about something else. Then a horrible thought occurred to her. Had her mother been found—dead? Were they really here to arrest her for two murders, Billy Joe's and her mother's?

Teilhard laughed. "Yeah. It's a misunderstanding," he said sarcastically. "Why'd you go to the trouble to repaint the car when you didn't bother to change the license plate or replace the broken passenger-side mirror? Kind of amateurish for a car thief. But it certainly narrows the suspect pool." He turned toward the door. "Let's go. I don't have time to stand around all day listening to 'he's my mom's boyfriend' and 'I didn't know.'" The last was said in a tinny falsetto. The other two officers laughed.

Hannah wanted to cry as she felt the last droplets of hope drain from her heart.

They put her in the back of the squad car and drove to the Metairie Police Station. Waller and Teilhard were in the car with her. The third officer had taken her key to drive the Toyota to the impound lot.

After several intensely uncomfortable minutes as she tried to keep her hands from going to sleep and her wrists from being permanently marked by the tight metal cuffs, they arrived. She was pulled out of the car and marched into the police station, handcuffed like a common thief. Officer Waller stood her in front of the booking counter in view of all the other officers, detectives and criminals, with the cuffs hurting more after the ride, while Teilhard got the forms filled out. Then he turned to her.

"I'm placing your purse in this plastic bag to be held until your release or until someone posts bail. Officer Waller?" He turned to the female officer.

"Yes, sir," Waller said, stepping forward.

"Please remove her earrings," Teilhard said, nodding toward Hannah. "Hannah, do you have any other jewelry? Piercings? Any prosthetics like a partial bridge in your mouth?" he asked.

She shook her head.

"Sir?" Waller said to Teilhard. "Do you want a full search?"

Teilhard assessed Hannah, then shook his head. "I don't think that will be necessary." He turned to a cop who'd been waiting at the counter. "Put her in one of the interrogation rooms and get her some coffee if she wants."

Hannah shook her head, but neither one of them paid any attention to her.

The cop took her into a small, stark room. "I'll get that coffee," he said and left.

She stood there next to the wooden table, not wanting to try sitting again with her hands cuffed behind her. As hard as it had been to sit in the police car with its upholstered backseat, a hard-backed chair would be torture.

She tried to take her mind off her aching shoulders and stinging wrists by studying the Formica tabletop. It was old and chipped, and had names and phrases carved into it. Idly, she wondered where Tony or Eddie Jewels or Turk had gotten their hands on something sharp enough to use to carve those deep grooves. She spent a few moments trying to read some other names and phrases, but her eyelids kept drooping.

The young officer came back with a cup of coffee that he set down on the table. He gestured toward it. "Sit," he said as he sat and drank a swallow from his cup.

Hannah tilted her head. "Do you think you could—"

For a moment, he stared back, bewildered, then she saw the light dawn in his eyes and he took a key from his pocket and undid her cuffs.

She sat, rubbing a red streak where the metal of the cuffs had pressed into her skin. Once she was seated again, she took a sip of the lukewarm liquid, which, although it was nearly transparent, still managed to taste burned. She drank the awful stuff, though, because she was thirsty and maybe the caffeine would keep her from giving in to the sleepy haze that was threatening to overtake her. When Detective Teilhard opened the door, she jumped and realized that she'd dozed off.

The officer stood and Teilhard took his place at the table. After nodding toward the two-way mirror and adjusting the position of the microphone, then making a short statement of date, time and individuals present, he spoke directly to Hannah.

"So, Hannah, we talked a little bit earlier about the car you were driving, didn't we?"

"Yes," she said.

"And we established that the car had been stolen and repainted."

"That's what you told me."

"Could you repeat for the record what you told *me* about the car?"

Hannah frowned at him. "All I know is that I thought it belonged to my mom's boyfriend."

He sighed audibly. "Could you be a little more specific?"

"Nobody told me it was stolen. It showed up at the house on—"

"I said, be specific, please," Teilhard said. "Who brought the car to the house and where exactly is the house?"

Hannah recounted what he'd asked her to. She was careful not to say Billy Joe's or her mother's names, but to refer to them as "my mother" and "her boyfriend."

Detective Teilhard drummed his fingers on the Formica table as Hannah talked. As tired and sleepy as she was, Hannah knew what he was doing. He was trying to make her nervous—trying to make her slip up and say something she didn't intend to say.

He continued drumming his fingers after she'd finished. Then he leaned forward. "Who's Billy Joe Campbell, Hannah?"

She started. The detective's silence while she'd talked had lulled her into a false complacency. Judging by the twinkle in Teilhard's eyes, that was exactly what he'd wanted.

"Billy Joe?" she stammered. "That's my mother's boyfriend."

"The one whose car you took?"

She lifted one shoulder.

"What happened to him?"

Hannah didn't have to work very hard to appear confused and worried. "What happened to him? I don't—" She paused but Teilhard didn't jump in. He let the silence stretch out.

Hannah clasped her hands in front of her and looked Teilhard straight in the eye. "It's something bad, isn't it?"

Teilhard assessed her. "You know the answer to that."

She nodded to herself, wondering how long she would have to keep up the pretense. How long she *could*. As tired as she was, she was afraid she might drift off to sleep while talking. If she did, she might mutter the truth. Her palms were clammy and her chest felt as if it were being squeezed in a vise.

"What are you trying to tell me?" she asked as the sight of Billy Joe's shirt blossoming with blood rose in her mind. "He's dead, isn't he? I can tell by the way you're looking at me."

Teilhard's dark eyes sparkled. "That's right, but you already knew that, didn't you? Come on, Hannah. Save us both some time, will you? Just tell me what I need to know."

Hannah started to cry, even though she knew it would alienate Detective Teilhard. She couldn't help it. She shouldn't have been surprised. She'd been fighting tears off and on ever since that instant when the bullet had exploded out of Billy Joe's back and his blood had spattered the panes of glass in the garage door. The tears poured down her face, pushed out because of everything that was bottled up inside her.

"Why'd you kill him, Hannah? Did you get tired of him whaling on your mom?"

"That's what you think?" she said, her voice going shrill. "You think I killed him?" She laughed and brushed tears off her cheeks, doing her best to stop crying. But she couldn't. Teilhard wasn't at all moved, but she was too far gone to stop.

"Well, if you didn't, then who did? Tell me. Was it your mom?"

"No!"

"Where is your mother? I haven't seen any sign of her at the motel or in the car. I understand she's quite ill. Did you leave her there in Dowdie, Texas, to face the music alone?"

"No. Of course not. I'd never leave her. I—"

"You what, Hannah? Tell me. I know you want to. It would make you feel so much better to just tell the truth."

"You don't understand. My mother is—too sick—" Hannah stopped. If she wasn't careful, she'd say too much. She pressed her lips together and tried to calm her throbbing pulse. "You have to believe me. I don't know who killed Billy Joe."

That much was true. She'd seen the man, but she had no idea who he was. For a moment she let herself imagine telling Teilhard the whole truth. The truth about Billy Joe and the drugs. About her mother, grievously ill and missing. And about the man with the red tattoo who shot Billy Joe in the heart, thereby stealing Hannah's only chance to find her mother in time to save her.

But Teilhard was smiling at her. A predatory smile, like the one the crocodile had shown Captain Hook. He was so anxious for her to confess that he was practically rubbing his hands together with glee. Obviously, she couldn't trust him.

After a moment, he spoke again. "Come on, Hannah. Tell me about Billy Joe and I'll put you up in a really nice hotel. I know you're tired. I know you want this to end."

Of course she wanted the interrogation to end. She was tired of crying, tired of lying, tired of listening to the detective's voice. She was just plain tired. Too tired to think straight. Too tired to hold her head up. "I can't tell you anything else," she said dully.

Teilhard narrowed his eyes. "Why did you come here? Were you hoping to establish an alibi here while somebody took care of your problem boyfriend for you?"

She stared at him. "What is wrong with you? I told you, I didn't kill him! And he's not my boyfriend. He's my mom's."

"Then why did you steal his car and run?"

She shrugged, as much to herself as to him. What if she told him? How much worse could it get? All she had to do was describe the killer to the police and tell them what she'd seen. Then they'd go after him and catch him, and she could be free to concentrate on finding her mother.

If they believed her.

But the man who'd shot Billy Joe had looked like a professional, and she'd seen enough television to know that professional killers didn't make mistakes. By the time the police went to her garage, would Billy Joe's body even be there? Or would the big man with the red tattoo have removed it and cleaned up every single bit of evidence, leaving nobody to blame for the murder except her?

She'd also seen the true-life horror stories of people being falsely accused of crimes and spending years in prison trying to prove their innocence. No. The lesson she'd learned from a lifetime of taking care of her alcoholic mother was still her safest bet. *Never tell your secrets. Never trust anybody.*

"Hannah? Why did you run?" Teilhard leaned forward. "I promise you I'll pull in every favor I've got to get you a deal if you'll just tell me what really happened."

"A *deal?* You're going to get me a *deal* for murdering

my mother's boyfriend? I did not kill him." The words scraped her dry throat as exhaustion enveloped her in a sleepy haze. "All I want to do is get out of here. I've got to get back home—to my mother." She stopped. She was saying too much. She waved a hand in a dismissive gesture. "I'm tired. I can't think straight."

"Of course you're tired, Hannah," Teilhard said. "Tired and hungry. Me, too. But I need the truth. That's all. It's simple. Just tell me what happened."

Hannah felt like her body and her mind were shutting down. She hardly understood a word Teilhard had said. Her stomach churned emptily, the protein bars long gone. Her head ached and the sparkly darkness was gathering at the edge of her vision again. She was almost past caring what happened to her.

Teilhard rocked backward in his chair and yawned and stretched.

Hannah tried not to yawn in response to his, but she couldn't suppress it. "I need sleep," she muttered, thinking if she had to sit upright much longer she'd faint.

Teilhard sighed. "Okay, Hannah. I've been patient. I've been helpful. I was hoping you and I could get this all straightened out. But…I'll tell you what. I'm going to give you overnight to think about what you want to tell me."

She roused a bit. "Not in here. I can't stay in here overnight!"

Teilhard perked up. "You won't have to if you talk," he said.

She rubbed her temples, regretting her outburst. She needed sleep. Until she could get some rest, she was incapable of making a decision. Incapable of thinking rationally. Incapable of figuring out how to find her mother. "I can't think. Have to sleep," she muttered.

The detective sighed. "Okay. But tomorrow morning, they're going to call you for arraignment for grand theft auto. At that point, it's probably going to be too late for me to pull any strings to help you. Do you understand what that means?'

Hannah closed her burning eyes.

"It means if you're arraigned for Billy Joe Campbell's murder, you're on your own. You can't depend on me or anyone else to help you."

She shrugged. "That's nothing new," she muttered.

"Fine!" Teilhard snapped and vaulted up, sending the wooden chair scraping across the bare floor.

She jumped and frowned at him in confusion.

"You're on your own. I'll find you a place to sleep and we'll talk again tomorrow."

She almost cried in relief. *A place to sleep.* It sounded like heaven.

Teilhard called for a female officer. When she arrived, he told her, "Please escort Miss Hannah Martin to the tank." He sighed. "I've got to wake up one of the prosecutors."

"The tank?" Hannah echoed as the female officer pulled her to her feet and led her out the door. "What's that?" But no one answered her question.

The officer guided her through the big room filled with desks and computer stations to the back of the building. When she opened the large metal door, Hannah saw the row of barred cells. She led Hannah past an empty cell to one that held two women.

The shorter, younger one wore a crotch-high skirt, over-the-knee boots, silver hair and silver eye shadow. The other woman had been crying. There were black streaks down her face and splotches on her sleeve from her mascara.

The officer opened the cell door. "Get in there," she said, not unkindly.

Hannah looked at the open cell door, then at the officer, then stepped through the door into a world like none she'd ever seen. The room was painted a no-color gray. The floors were tiled in a color that almost matched the walls and a metal bench. An old water fountain hung from the wall.

She took a long drink from the fountain. The water tasted of chlorine, but the chill soothed her burning stomach. She blotted her mouth with her fingers and sat on the end of the bench, as far away from the other women as she could get She moved around, trying to get comfortable as tears began to burn her eyes. She moaned involuntarily. "What's up with you in here, Miss Uptown Girl? I *know* you got somebody to call," the silver-haired woman said.

"Call?" Hannah repeated.

"Didn't you get your phone call?"

She shook her head.

"That ain't right," the woman mumbled. "Everybody s'pose to get a phone call."

Hannah shrugged, too tired and miserable to care about anything but closing her eyes. She looked sidelong at the two women. Silver Hair was peeling silver nail polish off her nails. The crying woman folded her arms and turned sideways on the bench, leaning against the wall.

Hannah copied her and found the position less uncomfortable than trying to sit straight.

"First time, sugar?" Silver Hair asked kindly. "You'll get the hang of it eventually."

"Dear Lord, I hope not," Hannah murmured.

Chapter Five

The next morning, an officer came for her and deposited her in another interrogation room. Desperately tired, she folded her arms on the table and dozed until Detective Teilhard came in, slamming the door behind him.

"Hannah, we need to talk about the vehicle you were driving."

She forced her burning eyes open to stare at him, thinking about what the silver-haired woman had said the night before. "I want my phone call."

"You haven't had your phone call yet?" The detective feigned surprise.

She straightened, wincing at the stiffness in her back. "No, I haven't."

Teilhard's mouth flattened, but he nodded. "Okay. If you say so." He nodded toward the mirrored wall where a phone was mounted next to the mirror.

She stood and stepped over to the phone, lifting the receiver from the cradle. Then she looked back at him. "Privacy, please?"

He got up. "I could use some more coffee."

Hannah lifted her hand, then realized she was about to punch in her mother's number. With a strong arrow of pain piercing her chest, she remembered that her mother wasn't at home. She was somewhere alone and sick and wondering why Hannah hadn't found her.

But there was no one else, unless she called Mack Griffin. Hadn't he handed her a card? Her hand went to the front pocket of her jeans. The female officer who had patted her down hadn't noticed it. She dug it out and looked at it. It was like him, actually. Deceptively simple and starkly elegant, yet completely self-contained. And completely uninterested in her.

She dialed his number, wondering if he would help her.

MACK WAS DRINKING coffee and checking his email when his cell phone rang. He answered distractedly as he scanned Dawson's message inviting him to a dinner party three weeks from the coming Saturday, at the Delancey Mansion in Chef Voleur. He'd probably have to go by himself, since he'd broken up with Sadie.

A tentative voice spoke in his ear. "Mack Griffin?"

Hannah. Mack sat up straight and glanced at the display. The number was a local one, a Metairie exchange. He gave himself a second to decide how to answer. Somehow he'd known he hadn't heard the last of her. He felt a slight loosening of his neck muscles. He realized he was relieved to hear from her.

"Yep," he said, as a frisson of worry took the edge off his relief. "What's going on, Hannah? You don't sound so good."

"It's been a long night," she responded, then, after a pause, "Could you—I mean would you be able to come to the Metairie Police Department? They took my car and kept me here all night and—" Her voice cracked a little.

He wasn't surprised, after what Dusty had told him

about the stolen car, especially since it was suspected to be involved in a drug distribution ring. He was, however, curious. The question still remained whether she'd known about the drugs. He looked at his watch. 8:15 a.m. He never scheduled an appointment before 10:00 a.m. so running over to Metairie for an hour or so wouldn't interfere with his day. Well, except that he'd have to drink his second cup of coffee on the road.

"I'll be there in twenty minutes. In the meantime, don't talk to anybody. Tell them you called your lawyer."

"But I haven't. I don't even know—"

"Hannah? Just tell them. I'll be there soon." Mack hung up and threw on a pair of slacks and a pale yellow dress shirt and headed downstairs to his car. He made it to Metairie in under twenty minutes and into the police station from the parking lot within another three. He told the officer at the desk that he was Ms. Martin's representative and that she was waiting for him.

When Officer Teilhard introduced himself and shook Mack's hand, Mack cut through the Deep South niceties and said, "You're holding my client here. Hannah Martin."

Teilhard gave him a mocking look. "You're Ms. Martin's lawyer? Because I've got to say, you don't look like a lawyer."

"I'm an attorney," Mack said. "But I don't have a regular practice."

Teilhard's face began to take on a ruddy tint. "What the hell does that mean?"

"What are the charges against Ms. Martin?" Mack shot back.

Teilhard yawned. "Not sure yet. I haven't heard back from the prosecutor's office."

"But you know what you're holding her for."

The older detective laughed. "Yep. She is in a lot of trouble."

"And does she know why she's being held here?"

"Right now it's felony, grand theft of a vehicle."

Mack waited, but the detective didn't say anything else. "That's it?"

"For now," Teilhard said with a conspiratorial smile.

Mack had to bite his tongue to keep from asking about the drugs and Billy Joe Campbell's murder. He sure as hell didn't want to tip his hand. It had to be impossible that the detective didn't know both of those things. But Mack wasn't going to tell him.

When they stopped in front of the interrogation room, Mack put his hand on the knob, then paused. "Thanks," he said to Teilhard. "I want to speak to my client in confidence, please. No two-way mirror. No microphones. No recording. Can we do that?"

That earned him a laugh and a deceptively hard pat on the back. "Sure," he said. "Anything for Ms. Martin."

Mack decided he *really* didn't like Teilhard. "Thanks," he said sarcastically, then opened the door and went inside.

Hannah was sitting at an old, scratched, wooden table with a Formica top. She'd taken her hair out of its braid and was finger combing it over her right shoulder; her head was tilted to one side and her eyes were closed. To Mack, she looked like one of the beautiful, graceful and forlorn women Toulouse-Lautrec painted. *Woman Braiding Hair After Arrest.*

Not only did she appear forlorn, she also was even more bedraggled and exhausted than she'd been the morning before. He couldn't take his eyes off her. She was dressed in the same jeans and shirt. The shirt was even more wrinkled and had a small coffee stain on the front. Mack's heart wrenched when her face brightened at the sight of him.

"Hey, there, Hannah," he said. "You look like you slept in the holding tank last night." It was a feeble effort at coaxing a smile, but instead of responding in kind, her wide, sad eyes glimmered with tears. He pulled out a chair, glancing behind him at the mirror before he sat. It wasn't that he didn't trust Teilhard to honor his request for privacy, but there was always the chance that someone might accidentally leave the sound on.

Actually, it *was* that he didn't trust Teilhard.

"Are you okay? Do you need anything?" he asked.

Hannah closed her eyes and took a long breath. "Time travel, so I could go back and change a couple of things?"

To his dismay, he saw a tear leak out from beneath her closed eyelids. "How about some more coffee?" Before he finished the question, she was shaking her head.

"Ugh. No. Coffee you can see through is nothing but dirty water," she said distastefully. "Besides, I'm not sure I can keep anything down right now," she said. She stopped combing her hair with her fingers for a second to wipe her eye. "I'm so tired."

Mack reached into his pocket for a comb to offer her, but before he got his hands on it, she'd thrown her hair back over her shoulder and lifted her arms to braid it. Mack froze, unable to look away. The position of her arms caused her shirt to ride up above the low waistband of the jeans. The skin of her midriff and tummy was pale and smooth. While she was slender, she wasn't skinny. Her body was beautiful and sleek, with curves and muscles in all the right places.

What he wouldn't give to see her dressed like she ought to be—or undressed.

She looked up and caught him staring. To his surprise and chagrin, his face grew warm.

He quickly stood and paced, positioning himself out of her line of sight. What the hell? He'd seen women in all stages of dress and undress. He'd *been* in all stages of dress and undress in front of women. And he'd never blushed in his entire life.

He turned to look at the back of her head. Her fingers were entwined with her shiny, straw-colored hair. She twisted the strands back and forth and, as if by magic, they ended up as a fat, sleek braid. It was fascinating to watch, even though he couldn't keep up with her lightning-fast fingers. By the time she was more than halfway done and had pulled the hair over her shoulder to finish it, he found himself hoping that braid was easier to loosen than it was to braid. He hoped that pushing his fingers through the strands would cause them to unravel until they shimmered around her face and over her shoulders and slid through his fingers like liquid gold.

Then he grimaced and shook his head. He didn't like where his thoughts were headed. He'd already had a talk with himself about not allowing himself to think about her. It seemed that his subconscious mind had not paid attention. Otherwise why would all these thoughts be crowding his brain as soon as he laid eyes on her?

He'd come down here because she'd sounded so tired and so hopeless. That was all. He'd do what he had to in order to help her just enough so that she was able to get back to Dowdie, Texas. He wished he was hard-hearted enough to have refused to come, but that wasn't him. He'd help her. Then he'd forget her. He had to, for his own peace of mind.

He circled back around to his chair and sat down. "Have you been arraigned?" he asked.

She looked at him blankly for a brief moment. "I don't know. But I don't think so. That's in front of a judge, isn't it? They brought me in and questioned me for a long time. Then they locked me in a cell with two other women and left me there all night. Teilhard, the detective, wouldn't even let me make a phone call until this morning."

"What has Detective Teilhard been questioning you about?"

"Last night? He asked me all about the car and what happened to it. Then he wanted to know what happened to Billy Joe." She stopped. "Billy Joe Campbell is my mother's boyfriend."

He nodded. "What about this morning?"

She shook her head. "Nothing yet. He brought me in here but before he could say anything I told him I wanted my phone call. He said okay and left."

Mack rubbed his forehead, right at the hairline, where a small scar sometimes bothered him. So the detective hadn't brought up the connection between Billy Joe and the car and a suspected drug distribution ring operating in and around her hometown. Was that because he hadn't received official word from the prosecutor's office? "So what have you told him?"

"All I've done is answer his questions," she said, looking down at the desk.

"Oh, yeah?" he said, sending her an arch look. She didn't look up, so his expression was wasted. "Listen to me, Hannah. I get that you've got secrets you're not willing to tell. But if you want me to represent you, I've got to know what's going on with you."

She looked bewildered for a second. "Represent? What do you mean?"

"I mean represent. Remember I told you to tell them

you'd called your lawyer?" He gave her a small smile and spread his hands. "Here I am."

"You're a lawyer?" she said, staring at him, then she shook her head. "I don't want a lawyer. I didn't know you were one. I've got to get out of here. So I'm just going to let him arraign me for car theft. I can make bail and be out of here in a couple of hours."

Mack watched her face morph from bewildered and worried to satisfied and guileless. He had to wonder if she was that good, or if she really had no idea how much trouble she was in. "That's what you think? That you're going to waltz out of here in an hour or two with a slap on the wrist for stealing a car?"

She looked up at him, that furrow deepening between her brows.

"What about Billy Joe?"

She pressed her lips together for a second. "What about him?"

"Did Teilhard ask you about him?"

"He told me he was dead and asked me if I'd killed him." She paused. "But I told him I didn't."

"So who did? Did your mother?"

"What?" She looked genuinely stunned.

"You heard me. Did your mother kill Billy Joe Campbell?"

She shook her head. For a couple of seconds, Mack was sure that she was holding her breath. Then she pressed her fingers against her lips, then her palm, then her fist. Tears filled her eyes and spilled over to run down her face.

"What's wrong?"

She shook her head harder, then finally took a deep, gulping breath. "Nothing," she said, swiping at the wetness on her cheeks.

"You didn't answer my question."

"No," she whispered. "My mother didn't kill Billy Joe. But Billy Joe may have killed her."

"Because she needs dialysis," Mack said.

She nodded as more tears fell.

"But you know who did kill him, don't you?"

"No."

Mack studied her for a long time. She clasped her hands together in front of her and stared at them. Twice he saw tears fall onto the backs of her hands. "Are you lying, Hannah?" he asked.

She pressed her fingers against the bridge of her nose, then let out a long sigh. "No. I don't know. Not on purpose."

He leaned forward and placed his elbows on the table and clasped his hands. "Look at me."

She met his gaze, her red-rimmed, bloodshot eyes half-closed.

"You do know. And you are lying. You lied to me and now you're lying to the police, and I need to know why. Otherwise, how can I help you?"

She shook her head, her gaze not meeting his. "I'm not lying—"

Mack cut a hand through the air. "Yes, you are. Listen to me. You're in big trouble. Bigger than you may realize. Now, you've asked me for help. But I don't know a whit more about you or your problem than I did yesterday when you knocked on my door and then ran. Okay, I know a few things more, but that's all. *You* called *me*. But you're not telling me the truth. And as long as you lie to me, all I've got is whatever Teilhard digs up, and trust me when I tell you that I can't use that to help you." He shrugged. "Now one of the things I know is that you saw the man who shot Billy Joe, didn't you?"

She scraped her lower lip with her teeth. Her hands rubbed together nervously. She wouldn't meet his gaze.

Mack's stomach began to turn sour. "If you won't talk to me, I might as well leave, because there's nothing I can do for you. Listen, Hannah, I understand how afraid you are and I know how hard it is for you to trust anyone."

At that instant, the door opened and Teilhard came in, followed by a female officer.

Mack's anger flared. Another three seconds and he might have gotten her to talk. "What the hell? I asked for privacy," Mack demanded. "I'm not done. Not by a long shot."

"Sorry, Mr. Griffin," Teilhard said. "This is an urgent police matter."

Mack's sour stomach flipped upside down. This was it. It was what he'd tried to warn Hannah about. If she couldn't trust him, he couldn't help her.

"Hannah Martin, please stand," Teilhard went on, turning to face Hannah.

Mack scowled at the detective. "What's so all-fired important that you couldn't have waited a few minutes until I was done talking with her?" But Mack knew why Teilhard had barged in. He'd found the drugs. Reluctantly, he nodded at Hannah.

With a bewildered glance at him, she stood.

"Hannah Martin, you're under arrest for possession of Schedule II narcotics, trafficking in drugs and transporting drugs across state lines with the intent to sell."

Hannah swayed and probably would have fallen if the female officer hadn't taken her arm.

"Turn around," the officer said.

Teilhard smiled. "I guess you can see why this couldn't wait. One of our dogs went nuts when we walked him through the impound lot. Turns out the trunk of Ms. Martin's car, as well as some other strategic places, was lined with brand-new bottles of Oxycontin."

"Oxy—?" Hannah's face drained of color.

So she hadn't known about the drugs, or at least not for certain. Mack had seen some women who could lie without blinking an eye, but he'd never seen one who could turn white as a sheet on cue.

The policewoman recited the Miranda warning in a low monotone as Teilhard recounted to Mack all the minute details of the dog's excitement and the discovery of the drugs.

Mack watched Hannah as the policewoman cuffed her hands behind her back. She was still pale, and the desperation was back in her eyes. He knew that the ground he'd gained before Teilhard had burst in was gone. She was avoiding his gaze again. The doubt began to creep back into his mind.

"Mack?" Hannah said as the woman turned her back around.

Mack met her gaze and tried to send her a reassuring look, but in truth he wasn't sure he could get her out of this. He *knew* he should get himself out before he was in too deep. His need to get away from her had nothing to do with her guilt or innocence. That wasn't the issue here. Not for him.

His problem was his tendency to step in as rescuer and protector to any woman who seemed to need him. His own version of a knight in shining armor. He knew if he took Hannah's case, he'd work it until he won or she went to prison, and maybe even longer. And there was a very good chance that while working her case, he'd fall for her.

He supposed it was good that he understood his problem, even if he couldn't cure it. His need to play rescuer was one reason he'd quit his law practice, even though he'd always wanted to be a criminal attorney. He'd always seen himself as a champion against men who abused women. But it hadn't taken long for him to figure out that he wasn't cut out for the job. He was too quixotic to be effective in a courtroom. It required a level of dispassion he didn't possess to be a good defense attorney. He'd finally resigned his law practice and gotten a private investigator license, figuring he'd do better in a more hands-on role where he could put his passion to good use.

As soon as the policewoman was done reciting the Miranda warning, Mack cocked an eyebrow at Teilhard. "Hang on, Detective. You didn't follow the law in Ms. Martin's case. My client requested a telephone call and was not allowed one."

Teilhard's arrogant face froze. "Look, Griffin, she got her phone call. She called you, didn't she?"

"If she'd have been allowed that call last night, she wouldn't have had to spend the night in that holding cell. That was unnecessarily cruel."

"Cruel?" Teilhard laughed. "Are you soft on her or just soft in general? She's a felon. She didn't ask for a phone call last night as far as I know."

Mack let that drop. He'd made his point, and his first mistake. He should have said *punitive* instead of *cruel*. It was a more dispassionate term. Still, he'd given Teilhard notice. The SOB wouldn't get another chance to deny Hannah her rights.

"Well, *counselor*," Teilhard went on. "Do you mind if I ask her a couple of questions?"

"Be my guest," Mack said, sending Hannah a reassuring look that he hoped she could read. "I'll sit right here."

Teilhard ignored him. "Ms. Martin, what were you planning to do with the drugs you transported from Texas into Louisiana?"

"I don't know anything about any drugs," Hannah said.

"You knew about them, all right. In fact, you drove here from Texas to deliver them, didn't you?"

When Hannah didn't answer right away, Teilhard leaned over the table. "Didn't you!" he shouted.

Mack started to intervene, but Hannah lifted her chin and answered. "No."

"But something happened, didn't it? Something that kept you from making that delivery. Did you run into your rivals? Is that how the rear bumper of your car got shot up?"

"I—can't answer that," she muttered, shaking her head. "I can't."

"It's not that you can't, is it?" Teilhard snapped, moving in for the kill. "It's that you—"

"Okay," Mack interrupted, sick of Teilhard's bullying. "That's enough. I don't think you have a case at all, Detective. You have no connection between Ms. Martin and the drugs found in the car." Mack was flying blind now. But he figured his version of what Hannah had done was as plausible as the detective's. "She took the vehicle in question because it was the only working vehicle to which she had access."

Teilhard rolled his eyes. "Tell it to the judge," he said.

"I need some time with my client," Mack said coldly.

Chapter Six

Hannah watched Mack and Detective Teilhard as they faced off, arguing about her rights. She'd been stunned when Mack said he was representing her. So now he was not just a private investigator. He was an *attorney*.

For Hannah, attorneys were another of those authorities whose job had seemed to be to threaten her mother and her. It was the lawyers who set things in motion to take children away from their parents.

But Mack didn't look like any lawyer she ever remembered seeing. Rabb, the lawyer handling her mother's estate, wore baggy suits and looked as though he'd just eaten something sour. The lawyers she remembered from her childhood were always tightly done up in their stiff suits and their striped ties. They all had the same sour expression as Rabb, but her memory of them was of giants towering over her and patting her on the head. And even as a little girl, she'd known that they held infinite power over her in their gnarly hands.

But Mack was dressed in crisply pressed pants and a yellow shirt with the sleeves rolled up. No tie and no coat. He leaned against the wall, one leg casually crossed over the other. He could have been standing at a water cooler discussing last night's scores, his body language was that relaxed.

But not his face. His face wasn't casual or relaxed. But it wasn't sour, either. From the businesslike haircut to the high, sculpted cheekbones to his straight nose and wide mouth all the way down to the small cleft in his chin, Mack's face was a study in control. She didn't miss the slight flexing of the muscle in his jaw or the shadow in his hazel eyes when he glanced in her direction.

She couldn't understand why he was even here. She'd called him because she was desperate and his was the only phone number she had. But she hadn't expected him to come. After all, why would he, a complete stranger, bother with her?

From the first moment she'd seen him, she'd been attracted to him. And she knew he'd been interested in her. That had been obvious from the glint in his eyes as they roamed down and back up her body. But as soon as she'd mentioned his mother's name, he'd withdrawn.

She didn't know what he and Teilhard were arguing about, but she got the dynamic. Whatever it was, the point was to establish the playing field. It was a jockeying for position and a struggle to see who was top dog. An arrow of apprehension lodged in her heart. She'd had enough of arrogant, bullying men who couldn't believe a woman could think for herself. Was Mack one of those? She hadn't thought so, but every so often, he glanced in her direction, his eyes hard and his mouth tight-lipped and disapproving. If there was one thing she knew, it was that Mack Griffin disapproved of her. So why was he here?

Detective Teilhard's cell phone rang, interrupting the two men. Teilhard answered in the middle of something Mack was saying. Hannah saw Mack's jaw flex.

"Detective Teilhard," he said, then listened. "Yeah,

sure." He hung up the phone, sent Mack a glance that could only be described as triumphant and turned to the female officer who stood by the door.

"Get her ready for arraignment, Officer Jeraux," Teilhard said.

"Who was that?" Mack asked. "The D.A.'s office?"

"Wow. Got it in one. You *must* be a lawyer," Teilhard mocked. "They're charging Ms. Martin with grand theft auto, transporting Schedule II narcotics across state lines, possession of a felony amount of narcotics for purposes of transporting across state lines and possession of Schedule II narcotics for the purpose of distribution or sale."

Hannah listened, holding her breath, as Teilhard spewed out the awful, frightening charges. But when he finished, there was one charge missing. Murder. Why were they not charging her with Billy Joe Campbell's murder? And why had no one mentioned her mother? Surely Teilhard had to have talked to Sheriff Harlan King in Dowdie. What if her mother had been found? What if they'd charged her sick mother with Billy Joe's murder?

Suddenly, she felt light-headed and sick to her stomach. She didn't realize that her legs had collapsed until a pair of lean, strong arms caught her and guided her to a chair as if she was weightless. When her eyes fluttered open, she found herself looking into Mack Griffin's greenish-gold ones.

He said something, but there was a loud roaring in her ears, so all she knew was that he was frowning at her and his lips were moving.

"Wha—?" She was trying to say "What?" but all that came out was a small groan.

"—did she last eat?" she heard Mack say over the

roaring in her ears. It was a good question. She certainly didn't remember. The only thing she'd had all night was a couple of swallows of water from the fountain in the cell.

"I don't have time for this, Griffin. We're due in court in fifteen minutes."

"And as soon as we walk in, I'll ask the judge for a delay and accuse you of police brutality and violating Ms. Martin's rights."

Hannah stared at Mack in surprise. He might not look like a lawyer, but he certainly sounded like one.

"Now please get her something to eat."

Teilhard sighed. "Jeraux, get her a sandwich and a Coke, would you?"

The thought of a limp, stale sandwich from a vending machine turned Hannah's stomach, but a Coke sounded good. She hoped it would soothe the burning fear inside her. The fear that she would go to prison and her mother would die.

Just as she'd thought, Hannah couldn't swallow a bite of the droopy ham sandwich, but the Coke—or more specifically its sugar and caffeine—bolstered her energy a little. It didn't erase the fact that she hadn't slept more than a couple of hours the night before, but it did seem to wash away some of the haze from her brain and make her feel a little less like she were carrying around a hundred-pound lead weight. It settled her stomach a little, too.

She was led into the courtroom by a female officer and shown where to sit. She couldn't believe how relieved she was when she saw Mack sitting there waiting for her.

"Mack," she whispered, putting her hand on his arm. She wanted to ask him why Billy Joe's murder hadn't come up in the list of charges levied against her. But he eyed her hand with a frown and shook his head.

"I need to know—" she started, but at that instant, the bailiff appeared in the front of the courtroom and shouted, "All rise. Now entering the courtroom is the Honorable Vivien Gold."

There was a muffled rustle of clothes, a number of sighs and a few grunts as everyone in the courtroom got to their feet. She stood with them and glanced sidelong at Mack, who was studying the judge. From his broad, straight shoulders to the cuffs of his neatly pressed slacks, he was every inch the successful young attorney, one of the authority figures that Hannah had been taught to avoid at all costs. She had seen and talked to him for barely more than one hour, yet of all the people she'd known in her life, including her mother, he was the most stable, the most dependable and, she had a feeling, the strongest.

And she regretted ever knocking on his door or using her one phone call to call him. The trouble with Mack was that she could easily learn to depend on him, and that could not happen. Ever! After watching her alcoholic mother get into one train wreck of a relationship after another, Hannah had vowed that she would never be dependent on another person.

The only person she could trust was herself. Everyone else in her life had proved to be untrustworthy. She might be in for a lonely life, but at least she would be in control of her own destiny, and she'd never be betrayed or abandoned or— She tried to stop the thought, but her brain was already all over it.

Or loved. Still, wasn't that a small price to pay to avoid being hurt? She nodded to herself. Yes. It was.

The sharp, startling rap of wood against wood reminded her that she was *not* in control of her own destiny yet. She was subject to the whim of a stern woman in black robes. As the Honorable Vivien Gold pounded the gavel one last time and frowned at the courtroom, Hannah tried to see behind the severe expression down to the woman beneath.

Judge Gold called the first case up for arraignment. Mack stood and nodded at Hannah, then stepped into the center aisle as the bailiff read her name and the charges against her. The policewoman nudged her. "Stand up," she whispered.

Hannah did.

"How does the defendant plead?" Judge Gold asked, peering over her reading glasses.

Mack glanced at her and inclined his head toward the judge.

"Well?" the judge prodded.

"Not guilty," Mack prompted quietly.

"Not guilty," she said, her voice a raspy whisper.

"Speak up, Ms.—" Judge Gold glanced down at a sheet of paper "—Martin."

"Yes, ma'am," Hannah said, more steadily. "Not guilty."

The judge repeated the charges aloud, then looked up at Hannah. The courtroom was silent and Hannah did her best not to squirm while the judge examined her for a long moment, then looked back at the charges. Finally, she addressed Mack.

"Mr. Griffin, I'm inclined to remand your client until trial, given the nature of the charges against her."

"Your Honor," Mack said, "Ms. Martin knows nothing about any drugs, nor did she know that the vehicle that she borrowed was stolen."

"Your Honor," the prosecutor said. "Mr. Griffin's

statement could be correct. But the defendant has continually refused to answer any questions about why she drove to south Louisiana. She also refuses to answer any questions about her mother's whereabouts. And that, Your Honor, is exactly why she should be remanded. Her mother is a resident in Dowdie, Texas, but she currently seems to be missing. Therefore, there is nothing to keep Ms. Martin here. And then there is the severity of the crimes and the quantity of the drugs found in her possession."

"Objection, Your Honor," Mack said. "The drugs were not in her possession. They were well hidden in a vehicle she *borrowed*."

"Your Honor—" the prosecutor protested, standing.

The gavel rapped again. "Yes, yes, yes, Mr. Simpson," she said to the prosecutor. Then she waved a hand in Mack's direction. "Mr. Griffin, this is an arraignment. You have no right to objection. We merely need a plea, which we have, and a decision on bail, which we are about to have. But first, I want to ask Ms. Martin a few questions."

Hannah looked up, surprised.

"Ms. Martin," Judge Gold said kindly, "where does your mother live?"

"In Dowdie, Texas, Your Honor," she replied, swallowing against a lump that grew in her throat. She was determined not to break down.

"And how is she?"

"She's not well, Your Honor. She has liver disease."

"I'm sorry to hear that. Do you understand that you are being arraigned on some very serious charges and that if you are let out on bail, you may not leave this jurisdiction?"

"Y-yes, Your Honor."

The judge leaned back in her chair again. "Mr. Griffin, Mr. Simpson, I'll hear one more sentence—one sentence—from each of you, but I must tell you, Mr. Griffin, I'm inclined to remand."

Hannah felt her eyes stinging. She was going to have to go back to jail, back to that cold, harsh place, for who knew how long. Terror nearly sheared the air from her lungs. She bit her lip, hard, and concentrated on holding back tears.

"Your Honor, if I may." Mack spoke quickly. "I request that Ms. Martin be released on my recognizance. I will post bail as well, as assurance that Ms. Martin does not leave the jurisdiction."

Hannah gaped at him. "What are you doing?" she whispered, grabbing the sleeve of his jacket.

"Your Honor, I object!" the prosecutor cried.

The gavel rapped. "Quiet, everyone. Mr. Simpson, I shouldn't have to explain again that this is not the place for objections," she said to the prosecutor, then turned to Mack. "Mr. Griffin? You understand the responsibility you're undertaking?"

"Yes, Your Honor, I do."

"Ms. Martin, is this acceptable to you?"

Hannah didn't have a clue what was going on. It sounded to her like Mack was proposing something similar to posting bail for her. She gave a mental shake of her head. Mack Griffin had no idea of the mess he was getting into by taking responsibility for her. She looked at his big, capable hands, his broad shoulders, the taut, determined line of his jaw.

With regret, because by the time all this was over, he was going to hate her for getting him mixed up in her life, she nodded reluctantly. "Yes, Your Honor," she murmured.

"Speak up, Ms. Martin."

"Yes, Your Honor. It's acceptable." She felt her throat close on the word *acceptable*.

The gavel hitting the wooden block rang through the courtroom again and Judge Gold called out, "Thank you." Then she nodded at the bailiff, who stepped forward. "You are dismissed," he said to them. Then he took a breath and spoke loudly. "Next case."

BACK AT THE police station an officer put Hannah and Mack in a cubicle and gave them a stack of forms to sign. Hannah tried to ask Mack what all the forms were for, but she never got the chance because the officer was rushing her through them so fast. Neither Mack nor any of the other officers seemed to be worried about that. Once all the forms were signed, Hannah was told she could leave, as long as she left with Mack. So they walked outside together.

As Hannah stepped outside, she squinted in the noonday sun like a newly released convict. The heat on her head and face caused her to yawn drowsily. She'd never understood the expression bone tired until that moment.

With a sigh, she turned and held out her hand to Mack. "Thank you for posting bail for me. I'll pay you back someday. My mother was right, sending me to Kathleen Griffin's house. I don't know what I'd have done without you. Please bill me for your time."

He frowned at her. "Hang on a minute," he said. "Do you not know what *recognizance* is?"

She sighed and shook her head. "I'm going to guess it's some sort of legal responsibility. I'm responsible for coming back to court when they call me." She held up a hand. "And I'm sure it's expensive, but I promise I'll pay you back. I hope to have part of the payment when I come back here for the first trial date."

"Not a bad definition," he said. "But wrong. It's actually an obligation of record entered into before a court, with a condition to do some act required by law. That act is therein specified. In this case, *I'm* the one who agreed to do the act, said act being take full responsibility for your actions, including keeping you within the law and within the conditions of the recognizance."

Hannah didn't understand most of what he'd said. The words floated past her like dandelion puffs on a breeze, their meaning as scattered as the flower's airborne seeds in the exhausted haze that enveloped her brain.

"In short, you're my responsibility," Mack went on. "So, no. You will not slip out of here like a fox and go back to Texas. You're staying with me. And you're going to explain to me just what's going on with you."

"Nothing's going on with me." She held up a hand. "Look, Mr. Griffin. All I want to do is get back to Dowdie. My mother is there. She's—sick. I've got to take care of her. I'm not going anywhere else." She dug in her purse for her phone and searched for taxicabs.

"What are you doing?" he asked, trying to see the phone's display.

"Looking for a taxi service. I need to get back to my motel."

"Did you hear me?" he said. "You're coming with me."

She used her thumb to flip pages on the phone. "No, I'm not," she said without looking up. "You're not responsible for me. I have to get some sleep."

"Sorry, sweetheart. Lawyer trumps sleepy client. Now, my car is right over there." He held out his hand.

"No," she said, stepping backward. "I'm not going with you. I can't. I have to get back to Dowdie. In case you've forgotten, my mother is missing."

He frowned. "I know, Hannah. And I understand how badly you want to get back there, but Judge Gold issued a court order that says you have to stay here. Now, don't worry. You can tell me everything when we get to the house and—"

"I said *no!*" Hannah was so tired she wanted to cry, but she was so tired of crying. Her eyes burned. Her cheeks stung where the tears had chapped them. And it made her vulnerable, exactly like depending on another person did. Sure, it sounded easy to let Mack take care of her. She knew he could and would. She could tell that just by looking at him.

But during all those hours as she'd driven east from Dowdie, Texas, with no idea where she was going or what she would do once she got there, she'd renewed a vow she'd made years before, when her mother had gotten sick.

Nobody, *nobody,* would control Hannah Martin's life except Hannah Martin. Billy Joe had tried to control her the same way he'd controlled her mother and she'd let him, because she'd hoped he could make her mother happy, but he'd turned out to be a piece of scum, just like most of her other boyfriends. But even if her mother couldn't learn from her mistakes, Hannah could. She'd renewed her vow and she would never break it again.

She realized she was shaking her head and Mack was staring at her.

"Okay," he said, shrugging. "Let's go back inside. I'll need to call the prosecutor and get some paperwork filled out."

"More paperwork?" she sighed. "I can't believe

there's anything we didn't already fill out and sign. Can't you just call me a cab?"

"If you're firing me as your attorney, then yeah. There's going to be a lot more paperwork. And no, I can't just call you a cab. Hannah," he said, "look at me."

She lifted her drooping eyelids to meet his gaze.

"You'll have to go before another judge. This time you *will* be remanded. They'll put you back in jail."

She didn't even bother to answer. He'd defeated her. He knew she wouldn't go back in there. She sighed in exasperation. She was stuck with Mack. Oh, she knew he could keep her safe. She'd known that from the first instant she'd seen him. She also knew she could fight her attraction to him. She didn't have time for that kind of nonsense.

But everything came at a price. Mack's price for taking care of her would be her secrets. He'd want to know everything, and she'd never told *anyone* everything. So why would she tell him?

Chapter Seven

"My car is right there," Mack said.

She followed the nod of his head and saw a large, black Jaguar parked next to an old white BMW 3-series. "The Jag, right?"

It surprised her when he bypassed the Jag to unlock the BMW. She'd have bet money on him being a Jaguar guy. Especially since he was at least six feet two inches tall and the Jag seemed so much larger than the Beemer.

Plus, she'd never ridden in a Jag. Of course, she'd never ridden in a BMW, either. When she got in on the passenger's side, she sank down into a contoured leather seat that felt as though it had been made just for her. To her relief, the car was quiet and elegantly smooth.

As Mack pulled out into traffic, she sank more deeply into the seat, closed her eyes and shaded them from the brightness with her hand. The next thing she knew, Mack's warm hand was on her arm and he was quietly saying her name.

She didn't want to open her eyes, didn't want to be pulled away from the soft, dark haze of sleep back into bright, burning reality. "What?" she muttered irritably.

"We're home. You need to wake up."

The words, delivered in a deep, intriguing rumble,

roused her a bit. She forced one eye open. "Home?" Had he really said *home?*

He opened the driver's-side door. "Come on."

"Mmm," she mumbled without moving. The driver's-side door slammed and there was nothing but peaceful silence. Then the passenger door opened and she nearly tumbled out, saved only by her seat belt and Mack's hand catching her arm.

Not willing to wake up completely, she fumbled with the belt until Mack reached across her to release the belt with the deftness of a magician. When he leaned in close, a subtle scent wafted past her nostrils. She couldn't identify it but it was nice. It was Mack.

"Let's go," he said. "I want to get you up the stairs and into bed before you fall so fast asleep that I can't move you."

He guided her up the front porch steps and through the front door.

"Do you want a soda and a sandwich? I just bought some fresh deli."

The idea of anything in her stomach made her feel queasy. She shook her head as she set her purse down on the kitchen counter. "Just water, please."

He filled a glass from the refrigerator-door water dispenser and handed it to her. She drank gratefully. The water felt cool going down and she knew exactly when it hit her empty stomach. "Where's the bedroom?" she asked hopefully.

"Hannah. We need to talk—just for a few minutes. Teilhard interrupted us before you told me about Billy Joe Campbell's murder. Right now all I know is that he was shot and you saw it and took off in his car. I believe the police know a lot more than that and I *know* you do."

Hannah didn't want to talk about Billy Joe anymore.

What she wanted to do was figure out a way to get back to Dowdie and find her mother. What she had to do first was sleep. "Why are you doing all this?" she asked.

"All what?" he responded, looking puzzled and defensive.

"Helping me. Being my lawyer. Why are you going to all this trouble for a stranger?"

"You're not a stranger," he said, avoiding her gaze. "Your mom and mine were best friends. You came here looking for her to help you and what you got was me."

"But you didn't want to help. You didn't want to have anything to do with me." He still wasn't looking at her. She frowned. "What changed your mind?"

"You called me from the police station. You—needed my help." He gave a little shrug, as if that covered everything.

Something in his voice meshed with something her subconscious mind had been trying to figure out ever since they first met. "But that's just it. I got the definite impression that you don't like being needed."

Mack's gaze darkened for an instant, then he looked away. He gave a short chuckle. "That doesn't make sense. I'm a private investigator. My whole job depends on people needing me."

"No," Hannah said thoughtfully. "Your clients don't need *you*. They need your services."

"Same thing."

"No, it's not." She was much too sleepy to figure out where she was going with that thought, but she knew she was right. Mack had not wanted to help her. So why had he?

"You came to my mother's home seeking help. I didn't help you. If I had, you might not have had to spend the night in the tank. I feel like I let you down. I feel responsible for you."

"Well, trust me, you're not. I can take care of myself, believe me. I've been doing it all my life. I appreciate you coming down there and getting me out of jail..." Hannah interrupted herself by yawning. She rubbed her eyes. "But I've got to get back to Dowdie. My mother can't—" Her breath caught. "She can't last much longer."

Mack nodded solemnly. "I know. But you can't do anything until you've had some rest. You sure can't take off for Dowdie on your own."

"Of course I can. I got here on my own."

"Hannah, you need to think about your situation," Mack said. "First, there was about two hundred thousand dollars' worth of drugs in that car you were driving. The car and the drugs have been impounded and placed into evidence by the police. Do you know anyone by the name Ficone?"

Hannah closed her eyes and shook her head. *Ficone.* She'd heard the name before, but where? She was trying to think, trying to listen to what Mack was saying, but between the sleepy haze in her brain and a growing queasiness in her stomach, she was finding it very hard to concentrate.

"Sal Ficone is a crime boss who operates out of Galveston," Mack said. "He's a very dangerous man in a very dangerous business. If those were his drugs, he's going to be looking for you."

"Looking for me?" she echoed, not quite able to make sense of what Mack was saying. She rubbed her temple, then took a small sip of water, hoping it would stop the queasiness. She knew she needed to eat, but she needed sleep even more.

"That's right. And depending on what's happening with the Dowdie sheriff's investigation of your mother's boyfriend's murder, you may be facing murder or manslaughter charges."

"You think I killed him?" she asked sharply.

Mack pushed his fingers through his hair and sighed. "That's the problem, Hannah. I have no idea."

Hannah put her hands over her face and groaned. "I can't take this. I'm so sleepy I can't think, and I feel sick. I don't care about Billy Joe right now. I just need to sleep for a couple of hours and then get home and find my mom."

Mack didn't say anything. Hannah spread her fingers and peered through them at Mack. His gaze was steady and neutral and for some reason that made her angry.

"I—didn't—kill—him," she said through clenched teeth. She crossed her arms, hugging herself. "When I got back from buying beer for Billy Joe, I heard yelling from the garage. I went out there and peeked in the side door. I saw a big man in a dark T-shirt with a red tattoo on the back of his wrist, holding a gun on Billy Joe. He was accusing Billy Joe of stealing from his boss." She stopped. "Ficone," she said. "I think the man did call his boss Mr. Ficone."

Mack's brows rose and his expression turned grim. "If Billy Joe was stealing from Sal Ficone, I'm surprised he lasted as long as he did. Go on."

"I couldn't believe it. Billy Joe was blubbering, trying to get the guy to put the gun away. Then he threw me under the bus, the coward. The man was accusing Billy Joe of stealing money and drugs from Ficone. Anyhow, Billy Joe told him I was the one who'd stolen the stuff. The man seemed disgusted that Billy Joe would try to blame someone else. But Billy Joe kept telling him that I took the money. That I was the key. The man called him a liar and Billy Joe pulled a gun." She stopped, out of breath because the memory squeezed her chest tight.

"And the man just shot him. Right in the middle of his chest. Blood went everywhere. And his back—the back of his shirt—all of a sudden it blossomed with blood. Billy Joe just fell." Her voice broke. "Now he's dead and he's the only one in the world who knew where my mom is."

"Did the man see you?" Mack asked.

She nodded. "He looked at me—" She stopped. "He shot at me. I don't know why he didn't hit me." She closed her eyes. "I think I turned a ladder over in front of the door."

"I'm not sure how you didn't get shot, either. But I suspect it's because they need you. How did you manage to get away? It sounds like the killer knew the drugs were in the Toyota."

She set the cold glass down on the counter and clasped her hands. "All I could do was run. He was behind me, shooting. I thought I was dead. Then I realized I still had Billy Joe's keys in my hand. So I jumped in the car and took off. All I could think about was that a bullet was going to hit me before I could get into the car and drive away. I don't think I've ever been so scared."

Mack gazed at her, his hazel eyes clouded. "So you drove off in a car that you knew was full of drugs?"

"I was running for my life."

Mack nodded. "If you hadn't, you'd probably be dead, too. It sounds like Billy Joe died before he hit the floor."

Mack's words brought the sight of Billy Joe's blood rushing back to her.

"I think there was so much blood so fast, because the bullet hit his heart."

"I didn't think about that," she said. "The blood just—" She tried to demonstrate by spreading the fingers of both hands to simulate a flower opening, but stopped as an overwhelming nausea began to churn in her stomach. She swallowed acrid saliva. "Oh," she gasped, putting a hand over her mouth.

"What's the matter?" Mack asked.

"I'm— Where's the—bathroom?"

Thank goodness Mack didn't waste any time. He grabbed her arm and guided her quickly to the bathroom. She knelt in front of the toilet just in time. Her stomach heaved, but there was almost nothing in it to come up.

After a moment the spasms eased. She coughed a few times against the acid that burned in her throat, then started to push herself to her feet. To her surprise, Mack's warm hands helped her up and he gave her a cool, wet washcloth. Thankfully, she buried her face in it, breathing the air that was cooled by the damp cloth and letting its coolness take away the last dregs of queasiness.

When she raised her head, she felt dizzy. She grabbed at the edge of the sink, but Mack was watching her closely and caught her. He pulled her close. "Are you going to faint on me again?" he asked with a smile.

"No," she said. "At least I don't think so." She closed her eyes and, just for a moment, let herself be held by him. It was dangerous; it could leave her with a longing and an emptiness that she might never fill, if she got too used to it. But she didn't plan to be around him long enough to get used to it.

Finally, she pushed away, merely leaving one hand

resting on his arm as she tried to stand alone. She waited, wondering if the nausea was going to come back.

"Want to sit for a minute?" he asked, putting the toilet seat cover down.

"No. Can you wait— outside?" she asked, mortified that she'd thrown up in front of him. Even more mortified that her face was sweaty, her eyes were tearing and her breath was undoubtedly awful.

"Sure, if you think you're okay. I don't want you to fall."

"Please," she begged, gripping the edges of the sink like a lifeline.

He frowned at her for a moment, then stepped out of the bathroom and closed the door behind him.

Hannah sluiced her face with cold water for a long time, until her skin was no longer hot. Then she cupped her hands and rinsed her mouth. After carefully swallowing a mouthful or two of water to test her stomach, she looked around for mouthwash. She found some in the cabinet below the sink.

Before she could go back to the bedroom, she had to sit on the closed toilet seat for a moment, until a wave of light-headedness passed. Finally, she opened the door. Mack was waiting right outside.

"Better?" he asked.

"I need to lie down in bed," she said hoarsely.

"Sure," he said as he assessed her. "You're still pale."

"At least I'm not nauseated anymore."

He helped her from the bathroom into the bedroom. When she saw the double bed, Hannah uttered a half moan, half sigh.

Mack's hand touched the small of her back. "Are you going to be sick again?" he asked.

She shook her head, almost ready to cry at the sight of the soft, comfortable-looking bed. "It's a bed," she said, her gaze soothed by the sight of the tan bedspread and a brown afghan folded across the foot.

Mack laughed. "You sound like you haven't seen a bed in months."

"That's how I feel," she replied. "Is this your bedroom?"

"Nope. Mine's across the hall."

Hannah reached for the bedspread to fold it back, but Mack said, "Hannah? I need to get the key to your motel room before you go to sleep."

She sat down on the bed. "Key?" she echoed, then coughed and winced. Her throat was raw from throwing up.

He touched her cheek as if he was brushing an eyelash away. "I know you're sick and exhausted, but I need you to pay attention for a minute. Give me your key card so I can go fetch your stuff. Where's your purse?"

"Kitchen?" she said, ending it as a question, because her exhausted, queasy brain couldn't remember for sure. "Inside pocket, I think. But there's nothing at the motel. Mama always said keep everything important in…purse." She lay down.

She was almost asleep when his voice roused her.

"Never heard of The Metairie Haven Motel."

"Says a lot for your morals," Hannah said, yawning. "And taste." She closed her eyes and let herself relax down into the soft warmth of the bedclothes. She wasn't sure she'd ever felt anything so wonderful.

Several seconds later, she heard a clink near her head. Mack had brought her a glass of water. Then she felt him slipping off her shoes. His hands were warm against her cool skin.

"Hannah?" he said softly. "I'll be back within the hour. I'll lock the door behind me. You try to sleep."

"Good plan," she said. She sighed and stretched, willing every part of her body to relax. There were no words for how good the soft bed felt. Closing her eyes, she tried to wipe her mind clean of all the questions, all the worry, all the fear, and sink into blessed dreamless sleep. A deliciously soft warmth spread over her. It was Mack again, covering her with the bedspread.

"Sleep tight," he said softly, brushing his fingers across her chin. Then she felt something wonderful and warm on her cheek. Mack Griffin kissed her.

That kiss made her feel safer and more sheltered than she'd ever felt in her life. He would keep her safe.

MACK WATCHED HANNAH for a few moments as she slept, just to be sure she was okay, he told himself. But inside his head, his brain was screaming, *What was that all about?* Why had he kissed her? It was only a peck, meant to comfort her. In the short time he'd known her, he'd seen her wary, afraid, angry and pensive, but this was the first time she'd been relaxed and at ease.

Her eyes were softly closed. Her bare eyelids appeared blue from the veins that showed through the nearly translucent skin. Her lips were slightly parted and her breaths were barely audible, even and deep. She was asleep.

After a few seconds, he realized he was staring at her lips. He straightened and arched his neck, then checked his watch. He needed to leave so he could get back before rush-hour traffic. He'd wanted to go by the motel and see what, if anything, she'd left there, but she'd been so exhausted, he'd hated to delay getting her into bed.

That was probably a very good idea, considering that she'd gotten so sick.

She'd be safe in here. He had double-locking dead bolts, ensuring that nobody could get in. She hadn't slept in two days, so he doubted she would stir for hours.

As if to prove him wrong, her breath hitched and she shifted her legs beneath the afghan.

His gaze followed her movements. Her body was barely outlined under the light cover, trim and fit. But as he'd noticed before, she was not fashion-model skinny, like his usual dates. Nothing about Hannah fit his preferences in women. He knew himself and he knew his type and she was not it. He leaned toward tall, lean and leggy. Hannah was small and curvy. She was everything that he didn't want in a woman, not just physically but emotionally, too, everything that made him wary. But it all added up to the most fascinating woman he'd ever met. And the most dangerous.

He forced his gaze away from her before interest grew into desire and desire grew into arousal. He needed to get her key card and get going.

Her purse was on the kitchen counter. Reaching inside, he encountered a leather wallet, a small zippered bag that probably contained personal items, a pen, a small pad, the large, heavy key ring that must have held twenty keys and an envelope. He pulled out the envelope, his ears tuned toward the bedroom in case Hannah decided to get up.

The writing on its front was familiar. He'd just seen it on the back of the photo Hannah had showed him. It was her mother's. Stephanie Clemens.

She had written, *To My Daughter, Hannah Claire Martin.* Then in a different color ink—*To Be Opened in the Event of Stephanie Clemens's Death.*

Mack's heart twisted. He wondered why Hannah had the letter now, if her mother was still alive. He turned it over to look at the seal. It was self-sealing and ridiculously easy to open. Retrieving a small magnifying glass from a drawer, he examined the flap more closely. It was pristine, no wrinkles or tears. She hadn't opened it. He took out his pocketknife and carefully pried the flap up.

With a crooked smile, Mack pulled out the letter. He wasn't even pretending that there might be something in the letter that could help him with Hannah's legal case. He just wanted to know more about her.

He glanced toward the bedroom as he took out the letter and unfolded it.

My Darling Hannah, he read.

I've never told you anything about your family. I always told myself that it was for your own good. I think I wanted to believe that, but of course that's not true.

Mack skimmed the intimate words, looking for anything that would tell him anything about Hannah or the people she'd gotten herself mixed up with. But it was a very personal letter between mother and daughter, and as he read on, he felt guiltier and guiltier about invading Hannah's privacy.

Then, toward the bottom of the handwritten page, he saw something that stunned him to his core.

Your grandmother is Claire Delancey. She is the sister of Robert Connor Delancey—

Mack stopped. He blinked and read the words again, but they hadn't changed. *Your grandmother is Claire Delancey.* "Holy—" he whispered.

He turned and looked toward his guest bedroom again, feeling an urge to go back in there. He wanted to study Hannah's face in the light of this new knowledge, to see if he could see any resemblance. *Delancey.* Hannah was a Delancey. *Whoa.*

Or was she? Was all this an elaborate scam to get money from the Delanceys? It was pretty hard to believe that Hannah's mother happened to be best friends with Mack's mother and Mack worked for Dawson Delancey. But it was even harder to believe that Hannah was that deceitful—with her pale skin and its tendency to flush or drain of color at the slightest provocation.

Mack skimmed the rest of the letter, torn between believing and doubting. He needed to call Dawson and ask him about his aunt and whether she'd ever had a child. But not now. He reinserted the letter into the envelope and pressed the flap down. Good as new. He stuck the envelope back in Hannah's purse.

Then he dug deeper and found her phone. He'd been impressed that Detective Teilhard had let her have it. These days, cell phone service providers provided the police with CDs and transcripts of voice mail and texts, as well as address listings and anything else recorded on the SIM card of the phone. There was seldom any reason for them to hold on to the physical phone. For a minute, he studied the phone, familiarizing himself with its functions, reviewing the few names in her address book and recording his phone number in her phone and entering hers into his. Finally, he went to her voice mail. When prompted for the pass code, he tried the default, which was the last four digits of her phone number. It worked.

He retrieved the messages. The first one was from a Steve Rabb asking her to come to his office to sign the papers appointing her as her mother's power of attorney.

Rabb was obviously a lawyer, and his tone told Mack

that he felt as though Hannah's paltry legal needs were beneath him.

The next message showed the caller I.D. as B.J. That had to be Billy Joe Campbell. Mack pressed the play button. What spewed out was an angry tirade, punctuated by curses and epithets. Billy Joe called Hannah a bitch and shrieked at her for driving his *bleeping* car after he'd told her not to touch the *bleeping* thing. Then he told her that she'd better be home with his beer within ten minutes or her mother would *bleeping* pay for every minute she was late.

By the time the message was over, Mack's hand was shaking with anger. The guy was probably lucky that he was dead. Saved Mack the trouble of killing him or at the least beating him within an inch of his worthless life. He listened as the third message played.

Where'd you go, Hannah? I know you don't want to talk to me, but I need to see you, talk to you. I need to make sure you're all right. Call me as soon as possible and let me know where you are. I'm worried about you. Bye-bye, Hannah.

The electronic voice told him that was the last message and gave him a choice of options. He pressed Replay and listened to the last message again. There was something odd about the caller's voice. His tone and his words didn't go together. The words could be interpreted as concerned and friendly, but the voice was creepy, low in tone and volume, yet menacing.

Mack moved on to the skipped and erased messages. There was nothing there but an earlier tirade by Campbell. Was that it? Four messages? Two from Billy Joe, one from the attorney and one from the creep, whomever he was.

To be thorough, Mack checked everything a second

time and saw a tiny icon on the settings menu that he hadn't noticed the first time around. When he touched it, the words *voice memo* came up. He pressed the button, expecting to find nothing. But there was one recording.

He played it and heard the same menacing voice as in the voice mail message he'd just listened to.

Hannah had hit the record button. Smart.

Mack listened to the man trying to get Hannah to tell him where she was and to meet him. He kept insisting that Billy Joe had given her something. She kept insisting that he hadn't.

Hannah's voice sounded terrified as she said, "I don't know who you are and I don't have anything. Billy Joe didn't give me anything. Leave me alone!" The man insisted that Billy Joe had said she was the key, which meant she knew where Billy Joe had hidden everything.

Then the man said, "Oh, by the way, your mom says hi."

Mack heard Hannah's gasp. "Wait! You know where my mother is—?"

Mack heard an odd, short laugh, then there was a click and a dead sound on the line.

"Wait—please. No, no, no."

Mack knew it was the same voice. The low, menacing one. But Mack was focusing on the last thing he'd said before he'd said goodbye and how much it had obviously hurt Hannah, judging by the brokenhearted tone of her voice.

He'd said, "by the way, your mom says hi." The words sent a chill down Mack's spine. No wonder Hannah was desperate. But it was Billy Joe who'd abducted her mother. How would this man have found out where the woman was?

Mack played the recorded conversation a second time and was more chilled by the man's tone and words than he had been the first time he'd heard it. He thought about letting Teilhard know about the recording, but he wasn't sure the detective would appreciate it or use it if Mack was the one who gave it to him.

Once he was in his car and on his way to Metairie, Mack called Dawson. He wished he'd been able to bring the letter with him, but he hadn't dared. If Hannah had woken up and found the letter gone, he'd be in big trouble trying to explain why.

Dawson's phone rang until it went to voice mail.

"Dawson," Mack said. "I need to ask you something and it can't wait until y'all get back. Call me on my cell as soon as you pick up this message." He hung up, then thought about his message. Should he have left Dawson more information, maybe told him about the letter?

No. He wanted to talk to Dawson, not leave a cryptic message. Part of the reason he didn't want to put that information in a message was that he wanted to ask Dawson not to say anything to anybody until Mack had a chance to see what he could find out about Hannah Martin and her connection with the Delancey family. But he also wanted Dawson to check it out from his end, subtly, of course. It shouldn't be too hard to determine if Claire had borne a child and if that child had been a female named Stephanie.

HOYT DILLER SCRATCHED the back of his wrist. More than twenty years and the red dye in the tattoo still bothered him. He loved the tattoo. Had from the very beginning, when he and his old friend Marco Ficone had sat at Marco's kitchen table and designed it. It said everything. The red heart, the black letters spelling out *MOM* and especially the bullet-hole graphic in the center of the *O*. That had been his idea. He scratched at the red ink in the heart. It had itched from the first day. The tattoo artist had told him his body would get used to it. Now Marco, his friend and a fine gentleman, was long gone, Hoyt was working for Marco's oldest boy, Sal, who only cared about money, and the red ink on the back of his hand had faded, but it still itched.

He tapped a cigarette out of the pack on the dash. Just as he lit it, a white BMW pulled into the parking spot directly in front of Hannah Martin's motel room. The shiny German car was distinctly out of place in the dingy parking lot of the dingy motel. He unconsciously slid down in his seat as a tall man in a tailored sport coat and slacks got out of the car and pulled a cell phone from his pocket.

The sharp-dressed man stood for a moment behind the driver's-side door as he pretended to check the display and key in something with his thumbs. He was pretty good. It was almost impossible to see his head move as he checked out everything around him.

Hoyt smiled. The ploy worked so well it was almost a cliché. Pretending to text or talk made anyone look innocent and distracted while they scoped out a place or person.

Finally, apparently satisfied that no one was watching him, the man pocketed his phone, pulled out a key card and unlocked the room registered to Hannah Martin.

Now, that was interesting, Hoyt thought as he watched the man. His clothes were as expensive as Hoyt's own. Not the ridiculous T-shirt and black slacks the boss made his men wear on duty, but Hoyt's personal clothing. The suits he wore to the casinos and church. The linen pants and rope sandals he liked to wear on vacation in the islands.

The man didn't have on a tie, which made his coat and slacks look a tad sloppy, but maybe he'd had a long day. That wasn't the question, though. The question was, what was he was doing at this no-tell motel in this particular room?

Hoyt figured there were only two reasons a guy like him would be at a place like this in the middle of the afternoon. He was having a clandestine affair that he *dared not* risk anyone finding out about—maybe with a married woman. Maybe with a man.

But far more likely, considering where he'd parked, right in front of Hannah Martin's motel room door, he was exactly who Hoyt had been waiting for. He'd hoped that Hannah would show up. He'd have grabbed her and headed back to Galveston. But this could be almost as good.

He called Mr. Ficone to report. "A guy just showed up and went into the girl's room. He had the key card in his pocket. From his clothes I figure he must be the lawyer, Griffin. Your computer guy said court records indicated that he bailed her out."

"Lawyer? Hell. Do you know how much I hate lawyers? What's he doing?"

"Can't tell from here. My guess, he's cleaning out the room and checking out for her. Probably has her a better place to stay."

"And what did you say his name is?"

"Griffin. I think his first name's Mack. I've got his address, too. You want to send someone to check it out? See if the girl's there?"

"Nah. I got nobody to spare. You handle it."

"I'll follow him. See where he goes. With any luck, he'll lead us to the girl."

"Can you get the drop on him while he's inside?"

"Sure I can, but my best bet is to stay hidden and then follow him—"

"No! He's a lawyer. I want him roughed up good. Right there in the motel. Get his thin lawyer blood all over the place. Grab his wallet, take his cash and leave the wallet there. Convince him you're gonna kill him for his money. But don't let him know how much you know. Act like you're all about the money."

"That's a big risk, Boss. This isn't a fancy place with interior entrances. Every single unit opens onto the parking lot. I don't think—"

"That's good, 'cause thinking's not what I pay you for. I pay you to do what I tell you *when* I tell you—and no arguments. Surprise him. Knock him on his pretty face. And ask him his name. If he's a lawyer, he's got a yellow stripe down his back. Scare him good, and while you're at it, don't forget we want him to think we ain't too bright."

No problem there, Hoyt thought wryly. "I don't know, Boss. What if he calls the cops?"

"What if he does? What are they going to do? You won't leave any evidence behind. Just make sure he doesn't see your face and make sure you leave him flat on the floor. Then let him call the cops while he's dragging himself up off the floor. You'll be hightailing it to his place to grab the girl. Then get back here as fast as you can. I got to meet with my suppliers tomorrow, which means either I've got the money or the drugs or that's all she wrote. That bitch better have the answer."

"Boss, let me talk to her. I can get her to spill what she knows. Besides, the rest of that shipment's probably somewhere around Dowdie, and that's a long way from Galveston."

"Campbell showed me a picture of her. I think I need to talk to her myself," Mr. Ficone said, his tone changing, becoming thick and rough. "She'll spill what she knows. I got my methods."

A shiver ran up Hoyt's spine. He'd seen the results of the boss's interrogation tactics a time or two, and he'd be happy if he never saw that again. Hoyt himself had done some cruel things a long time ago, back when he'd first started working for Marco. Back when he drank and took out his anger on whoever was closest—usually a girlfriend. He wasn't proud of that.

Now, though, he was an enforcer, a much cleaner, tidier job. Shooting somebody as part of his job wasn't a big deal. It wasn't personal, like other, closer methods.

"Sure, Mr. Ficone," Hoyt said. "All I was saying is if you bring her back to Galveston, then find out your stuff's up in Dowdie… Hell, that's six hours from this Chef Voleur place over to Galveston then another four to Dowdie. A straight shot, here to Dowdie, is only about seven hours. And like you said, time's getting short."

The boss grunted, a response he used like the Hawaiians use *aloha*. The trick was, his employees had the job of interpreting it. This time, Hoyt took it to mean that he still intended to question Hannah Martin himself.

Hoyt hadn't made three million dollars in the past five years, and remained alive, by disagreeing with the boss. He liked his job and his life. But Sal sometimes drove him nuts. For one thing, if he were the boss, he'd invest in some micro-tracking devices. Hell, if he had one, he could stick it on this guy's jacket when he attacked him.

Still, he did have Hannah's cell phone number, because he'd had the foresight to take Billy Joe Campbell's phone off his dead body.

Mr. Ficone's computer guy should be able to track Hannah through the GPS in her phone. Although Hoyt had no idea how all that high-tech stuff worked, he knew about it, thanks to his obsession with TV cop shows. In several episodes every season, somebody tracked somebody using the GPS on the person's cell phone.

While he waited to see what the guy with the Beemer would do, he called George, Mr. Ficone's computer guy.

"Got a question for you," he said. "I think I already know the answer."

After hanging up the phone, he got out of his car and walked over to the end of the building that housed the motel rooms. He sneaked down the far side and crossed through the breezeway nearest Hannah Martin's motel room.

In his mind, Hoyt was already in the fight. He was quick and intuitive, which, combined with his bulk and the element of surprise, made him almost unstoppable. He figured the attorney would be clumsy, as many long-limbed guys were. Piece of cake.

From his pocket, Hoyt dug out his brass knuckles. They were his favorite accessory, other than a handgun. The brass knuckles weren't as impersonal as a gun, but, like he'd reminded himself earlier, he tried not to question Mr. Ficone's motives.

Chapter Eight

Mack had been away from Hannah for twenty-three minutes. That was twenty-two minutes too long. What if she hadn't gone to sleep? What if she'd decided to head back to Dowdie on her own? He couldn't see her renting a car or finding the bus station in her exhausted state, but then she was awfully independent and determined for the type of woman he'd concluded she was. He'd locked the double dead bolt, but he'd also left the keys in the lock. His purpose was to keep others out, not lock her in. He'd hung his hopes on her exhaustion being as real as it seemed to be. He hoped he wouldn't regret not forcing her to come with him so he could keep an eye on her.

Once inside the motel room, what he saw cut into his heart. The space was small and shabby and smelled of disinfectant. He didn't want to think about what odors the disinfectant masked. The threadbare spread on the bed was undisturbed except for about twenty-four inches on the side near the bathroom, where the covers were barely mussed. It looked as if a child had slid into the far edge of the bed for warmth and comfort after being told not to muss it.

There was no suitcase, no hanging bag. He remembered what she'd sleepily muttered about keeping everything important in her purse and about how she'd jumped in the car and run. Still, it was sad to see nothing personal at all in the room. The closest thing to a personal item was a couple of discarded protein bar wrappers in the trash can.

He checked the bathroom where a wet washcloth and a damp towel hung on a bar. There was no toothbrush, no makeup kit and the faucet dripped.

Then he noticed the small photo stuck into the corner of the corroded mirror. It was the same photo she'd shown him.

His heart felt torn as he looked at the photo. He didn't want to touch it. Hannah had put it there as her one touch of home in this sad, decrepit motel where she'd hoped to get a few hours of sleep. Had she put the photo up because it comforted her? Or as a constant reminder that every hour she delayed getting back to Dowdie was another hour closer to death for her mother?

He reached for the photo, but his hand halted a couple of millimeters from it. What the hell? There was nothing sacred or magical about the picture. It was a snapshot, a frozen moment in time. Two girls sharing a happy, carefree afternoon.

He snatched up the picture with two fingers and turned it over. He'd seen the back when Hannah had first shown it to him and he remembered what was written there—by Hannah's mother and his own mom.

Swallowing against a lump in his throat, he stuck the photo in the pocket of his jacket. He was getting to know Hannah Martin better than he wanted to. From the moment he'd opened his door and seen her standing there, he hadn't gone more than a few moments without thinking about her.

The more he found out about her, the more he felt

responsible for her and the less he liked it. He stuck the photo in his shirt pocket, not wanting to look at it anymore. His reaction to it concerned him. He was going to be in big trouble if he didn't get away from her, the sooner the better. Which reminded him of the question that she had asked. Why had he jumped in and promised to secure her bail?

He glanced around the bathroom, even checking behind the door. There was nothing else of Hannah's in there. He took one more look around the pitiful room, touched the photo in his pocket and then tossed the key card onto the dresser.

He opened the door and glanced around the parking lot. Nothing seemed suspicious. There was one other car and three semitrailer trucks parked along the outside edges of the lot.

A couple in the unit across from Hannah's room were loading suitcases and baby things into the car, getting ready to leave. He watched them fasten the car seat into the back and place the baby in it. Once they'd driven away, he glanced around one more time, then reached behind him to pull the door closed.

That was when the train slammed into him. His rational brain knew it wasn't a train, but at the second of impact, that was the closest he could come to rationalizing what had happened.

The blow caused the inside of his head to explode in pain. It knocked him off his feet. He fell back against the open door and, despite his desperate scrambling, he stumbled backward and hit the floor butt first. He couldn't control his momentum, so the back of his head slammed against the floor.

He immediately tucked his legs and arms, preparing to roll up onto the balls of his feet. He heard the door swing shut, then felt a hand groping at his back pocket. He rolled and kicked and got a second stinging blow to the head. His roll and kick had left him with his feet under him, so he tensed, preparing to push himself up and at the bigger man, but before he could rise, a mass of hard muscle landed on top of him. A meaty forearm pressed into the back of his neck, effectively paralyzing him.

"Who are you?" a low voice muttered in his ear.

Mack's head pounded fiercely from the two blows, but he compartmentalized the pain. Without that skill, honed over a lifetime, the throbbing pain would overwhelm him and he'd be defenseless, writhing on the floor holding his head, leaving his attacker free to beat him, kill him or anything else he wanted.

With the pain locked away, Mack concentrated on the man's steady breathing, the stale odor of cigarettes and the detached competence that told him that for his attacker, this was not personal. The man was just doing his job. Mack filed that information away to think about later, along with an impression that didn't quite register in his conscious brain. An impression of red that felt as though it burned his eyes. He had no time to speculate on what his subconscious had noticed, though. He was too busy defending himself. He jabbed his elbow backward, aiming for his attacker's ribs. He got a soft grunt out of the guy for his trouble, but that wasn't enough. He'd barely hurt the beefier man.

He readied himself to jab the guy again, but before he could move, the other man grabbed a handful of Mack's hair and slammed his forehead into the floor. The blow was only slightly lessened by the thin layer of carpet, and Mack felt the skin split above his left eyebrow.

Warm blood trickled over his eyebrow and down his

upper eyelid. In a matter of seconds, the blood would be in his eye, blinding him with a red haze.

"I said, who are you and why are you in this particular room?" the man riding his back repeated. All he'd heard the first time were the words, but now, Mack recognized the voice. It was unmistakable. It was the man on Hannah's voice memo, the man who had killed Campbell and who knew Hannah could identify him.

Mack ignored the man's question. He needed to turn the tables fast. His head was splitting with pain. He could tell that one more well-placed blow might knock him out. And if one more drop of blood dripped in his eyes, he'd be rendered essentially blind. As the man groped Mack's butt again and got his fingers on his wallet, he shifted slightly, readying himself to buck like a mule to get the large man off his back.

The man felt him move and tensed. Before Mack could change tactics, and with surprising speed, the bigger man rose and stomped on the side of Mack's face with his heavy boot. He turned his foot first one way and then the other, as if grinding out a cigarette on Mack's cheek.

"Now, you listen to me," he said in the unmistakable low monotone of the recording on Hannah's phone. "We know you're hiding Hannah Martin. Where is she?"

"Who?" Mack grunted.

The shoe came down harder on Mack's cheek. Blood roared in his ears with an ominous whistling sound.

"Don't give me that. Why else would you be here? You want me to crush the side of your pretty face?"

Mack didn't answer. Every bit of strength, every ounce of concentration he had, was channeled into getting the better of this bull of a man.

Reaching backward, Mack wrapped his arm around

the ankle that was grinding into his cheek. It was an awkward position and if the man kicked backward, he could easily break Mack's shoulder.

Luckily, this time, Mack had surprise on his side, plus the agility of his lean muscles against the bulk of the other man. He jerked the ankle forward.

The burly attacker tipped to one side, off-balance. Mack got his arms and legs beneath him and pushed himself up to a crouch, but the other man righted himself with his hands against the closed door. He delivered a crushing kick to Mack's ribs. Mack collapsed in pain and breathlessness.

This time, the man stomped on Mack's neck.

"Maybe you don't get it," he huffed as he bent and pulled Mack's wallet out of his pants. Mack heard paper rustling, then the wallet landed a few inches in front of his nose.

"Nice to meet you Mr. Griffin. Nice to know where you live. I was hoping you'd cooperate. I'm going to be really pissed if I drive all the way to your house and she's not there."

"Then don't—waste your time," Mack grated through clenched teeth. "She's in—police custody." He coughed, which hurt his ribs, and spit out blood from a cut inside his cheek.

"Yeah? So what'd you waste all that bail for?"

"Not in jail," Mack muttered. He coughed again, groaning, hoping his ribs weren't broken. "Safe house. Don't know where." There was no way the man would believe such a bald lie. In fact, Mack was counting on him not believing it, counting on it making him angry.

"You lying—" the thug started as he lifted his foot to stomp on Mack's face again.

This time, Mack was ready. Each time the man lifted

his foot, he raised it too high. So for a split second, he was off-balance.

Mack twisted enough to grab the heavy boot with both hands. He grunted in satisfaction when he felt the thug's weight come down on that foot.

He jerked. The man toppled against the motel door.

At that instant somebody banged on the door. "Hey!" a man yelled. "What's going on in there?"

Mack didn't waste time wondering who it was. He whirled and pushed himself upright, ignoring the pain in his ribs, and crouched in a defensive stance. "Call the police!" he yelled back. He swiped his forearm across his forehead, where blood was dribbling down over his eyebrows.

His attacker rolled over and scrambled to get his feet under him. "Get away from the door!" he shouted. "I'll shoot you!"

"What?" came the response through the door. "This is my motel. You can't have a gun here. Open the damn door and stop fighting. Hell, I'm calling the police now!"

The big man lunged for the doorknob. Mack tried to focus on the man's face, but the blood was seeping into his eyes. He wanted to wipe his eyes again but he didn't have time.

His attacker threw open the door. Mack dived for his feet. He got hold of them, but the thug was pumping up momentum as he bulldozed over the motel owner, dragging Mack until Mack was forced to let go. He pulled his money clip, which his attacker hadn't found, out of his jacket pocket and peeled off three hundreds. "Sorry about the mess," he said, thrusting the bills at the guy, then turned and grabbed his wallet off the floor. "You okay?" he asked the motel owner.

But that man was picking up the money, cursing a

blue streak and digging in his pocket for his phone, all at the same time. Apparently he was fine.

Mack vaulted into his car and pulled out of the lot, breathing shallowly. He was pretty sure his ribs weren't broken, but they sure as hell were bruised. But his injuries would have to wait. He had to make sure the man didn't get to Hannah. He caught sight of the maroon car as it turned left, toward the interstate.

Good. Mack nodded as he maneuvered onto the street. The attacker was probably using GPS. Therefore, he'd be directed onto the interstate. So Mack turned and headed down the back roads, praying he could get to Hannah first.

He sped up as much as he could, considering the traffic. With one hand on the wheel, he grabbed his phone with the other and dialed Hannah's cell number. The phone rang until it went to voice mail.

"No!" he shouted, slamming his palm against the steering wheel. "Come on, Hannah. Wake up." He tried not to let himself think of another reason why she might not answer. "Be there," he whispered. He left a quick message for her to call him right away, then he dialed her number again. It rang once, twice, three times, four.

"Hannah, come on!" Mack growled. "Answer, damn it!"

"Hello?"

He blew out the breath he'd been holding. "Hannah!" he said, "Listen—"

"Mack? Is that you? I was asleep. How'd you know my number?"

"Hannah, listen to me. Get dressed. I'm on my way." He looked at his watch. It couldn't have been more than ten minutes since the man had sped out of the parking lot. They had about that much time left before he got to Mack's house.

"Go across the street to the pizza shop."

"Why? What's wrong?" Hannah's voice rose at least half an octave.

"Don't worry. Everything's going to be fine. Just get dressed and go—now! Don't waste any time."

"But—"

"Hannah, go!" he yelled, then remembered something. He'd dropped three hundreds on the motel floor. "Wait! Hang on. Do this first. Stay on the phone and go into my bedroom."

"Into your bedroom?"

"Yes. Just do it. Just listen to me and do what I tell you, okay?"

There was a pause. "Okay," she said. "I'm in the bedroom."

"Go to the closet. Stand in the doorway and run your hand along the left inside wall, next to the door facing all the way down to the baseboard."

"Okay," she said. Her voice sounded doubtful, worried. "Mack, all this is scaring me. Tell me what's going on."

"Did you find something on the inside wall?" he asked, ignoring her question.

"An outlet?" she asked.

"Right. It's fake. Pull on it and take out all the money that's in there. All of it. Put the money in your purse and then get out of there and go to the pizza shop."

"Okay," she said. He could hear her fingernails scratching on the plastic of the fake light switch. "Oh, my God!" she cried.

"What? What's wrong?"

"No-nothing. How much money is this?"

"Damn it, Hannah, it doesn't matter. Just take it and get out of there, please. There's no time to waste. Get out and go to the pizza shop. Wait for me there. Do not go anywhere else. Do not talk to anybody. Do you understand?"

"I— Yes, but—"

"Hannah! Do it!" He hung up the phone and stuck it in his pocket just in time to shift down into second and make a sharp turn. He drove for another ten minutes in hell, counting every second as he darted in and out of traffic.

He was terrified that she wouldn't do what he'd told her to. But he didn't dare call her again. He didn't want anything to delay her. Nor did he want to scare her even more than she already was.

When he got to his block on St. Charles, he turned left into the pizza shop parking lot. He threw the car into Park and left it running as he ran inside. There were several tables of people but no Hannah.

"Have you seen a young woman with a long, blond braid come in?" he asked the girl at the order counter.

"Whoa!" the girl at the counter said, looking horrified. "Mister, you're all—" she gestured "—like bloody. Are you okay?"

"I'm fine. The woman with the blond braid?"

The girl just stared at him. Her face was pale. She shook her head. "I don't—I mean—I'm going to get my manager."

"No," Mack said. "No. There's no need for that." He was aware of people at the tables looking at him and whispering. One child pointed at him and called out. "Daddy, look. That man's all bloody. Look! Did he get beat up?"

The girl disappeared through a door in the back.

"Damn it!" Mack said, looking around the shop. Where were the bathrooms? Maybe that was where Hannah was.

At that instant, the bell over the entrance rang. It was Hannah. His relief at seeing her quickly turned to annoyance. "Where have you been?" he snapped.

"Oh, my God!" Hannah stopped in her tracks, her hands flying to cover her mouth. "What happened to you? You look awful! Are you all right?"

"Yeah," he said, his tongue flicking out to touch the small split in his lower lip. "I ran into an admirer of yours at the motel."

Her face drained of color. "An admirer? I don't—"

He shook his head. "Sorry. Did I mention that I can be a sarcastic SOB?"

"You're saying somebody *attacked* you?" she blurted out.

The door behind the counter opened. "Hey, fellow," a short man in a striped pullover shirt came around the counter. "I don't know what kind of sicko fight club you're in, but you can't stay here. You're upsetting the customers."

Mack didn't acknowledge the man. He nodded at Hannah in answer to her question.

"At the motel?" Hannah said, the full meaning of his condition dawning on her. "*You* got beat up?"

"Come on," he said. "We've got to get out of here," he retorted, then shrugged gingerly. "He took me by surprise." He grabbed her hand. "Come on!" He pulled her out the side door to the BMW and opened the passenger door for her. "Get in," he said.

"Where are we going? I hope to the emergency room, because you need stitches." Her eyes roamed over his face. "Lots of them." She climbed into the passenger seat, and he slammed the door, ran around to the driver's side, got in and put the car in gear. He pulled out of the parking lot onto St. Charles and headed for the interstate.

"No. We don't have time for that."

"Don't be ridiculous," she said. "You have got to see a doctor. I mean, have you seen your face? It's—" She made a waving gesture toward him.

He shook his head. "Hannah, I said there's no time."

"Okay," she said. "How about you tell me what this is all about. Why all the superspy stuff?" She changed her voice to mock his deep rumble. *"Meet you in the pizza place. Bring all the money. Hurry. Don't ask any questions."*

"The guy who beat me up is on his way here to get you," Mack said flatly.

"What? To get me?"

"That's right. Whoever beat me up was looking for you. What I need to know is why."

"You're asking me?" Hannah said. "I don't know anything. I didn't know Billy Joe was selling drugs."

"Selling? That's not selling. Not with that much Oxy. He was distributing. Your mom's boyfriend was hooked up with some big nasty guys, in case you hadn't figured that out yet."

"I figured it out, thank you. The gunshot into Billy Joe's chest pretty much spelled that out for me." She yawned. "I asked you a question," she said sullenly.

"Yeah?"

She sighed in exasperation. "Are you going to go to a doctor? Because your face looks like—like somebody stomped on it."

"Thanks," he muttered, but he lifted his head and glanced in the rearview mirror. "Damn," he whispered.

He did look like somebody had stomped all over his face. He hardly recognized himself. Splitting his attention between the road and the mirror, he cataloged his injuries. There was that nasty cut over one brow that had left a trail of blood running down his eyelid and into his eye, tingeing everything red. The white of his left eye was bloodshot and the skin around it was puffy and beginning to turn red. He was going to have a black eye.

He touched his brow, near the cut. "That's probably going to leave a scar," he said.

"Oh, you think?" Hannah responded sarcastically. She dug into her purse. "I've got some hand wipes in here somewhere," she said. "Oh, here." She dug out a wad of cash. "Here's your money."

"Keep it for now," he said.

She shrugged and stuffed it back into her purse. "Fine. You want me to try to clean your face a little? I'm surprised you can see anything with all that blood in your eyes."

He blinked and felt the dried blood on his eyelids pull at his skin. "Hang on," he said as he came up to the entrance onto the I-10. He downshifted and looked at the signs, wondering what to do.

Should he go east or west? If they went east, all they'd be doing was running. Going west would take Hannah back the way she'd come—back to Dowdie, Texas. Back to danger. But he was with her. He could protect her, he hoped. He sure didn't want to turn the other direction and doom her to running for the rest of her life. He couldn't live with himself if he allowed her to do that. Trying not to imagine what Teilhard would say and how loud he would say it when he found out Mack had taken her out of the jurisdiction, he turned west.

Hannah found the hand wipes, extracted one and reached over to clean his temple.

"Give me that," he said, taking the wipe from her. He kept one hand on the wheel as he rubbed his right eye, then his left. "Ouch, that burns," he said, looking in the rearview mirror again. His nose was bleeding and his right cheek looked as though it had been dragged across a basketball court. He carefully dabbed at his nose. "I guess I scared the people at the pizza shop, didn't I?"

"That's an understatement. You definitely scared me. I almost had a heart attack when I saw you." She looked out the window. "Where are we going? Why are we headed west?"

"Here," Mack said, ignoring her question. He pulled out his phone and handed it to her. "Take a look at the picture I took at the motel."

"I asked you a question," she said while she was pulling up the picture on his phone's screen. "Wait. What is this?"

"See the maroon car? That's the guy who attacked me. Can you see the driver? Does the car look familiar?"

She flicked her fingers to zoom in. "Oh," she gasped.

"What? You recognize the car?"

"I'd forgotten all about it. The day Billy Joe was murdered, there was a car parked at the curb about half a block away from the house. It might have been this color.

"I think it is the car, but I can't see the driver." Her voice was shrill and breathy. "So he's the man who beat you up?"

"Could you stop saying that? I got in a few really good blows, too. It was kind of a tie."

"A tie," Hannah repeated. "So he looks as bad as you do?"

Mack ignored her.

"What did he look like?"

"He wasn't real tall," Mack said, "but he was huge and muscled. His arms were like hams and he had on a tight T-shirt, like an arrogant weight lifter might wear. Brown hair, really thin on top. I couldn't get a good look at his face. I was too busy."

She took a short, sharp breath. "The man who shot Billy Joe was wearing a tight shirt."

Mack nodded grimly. "So that is him. What do you have that they want, Hannah?"

She looked at him sidelong. "I don't know."

"Come on, Hannah. From what you told me, it sounds like Billy Joe convinced them that you know where the rest of the drugs are."

"I don't. I didn't know anything about drugs," she said.

"Why do you think they're after you, then? Billy Joe stole money and drugs. Let's assume for a moment that you really didn't notice that your mother's boyfriend was transporting and selling drugs. Yet Billy Joe somehow managed to make Ficone's man believe that you have the missing money, or at least know where it is."

"But I don't. That's ridiculous."

"Tell me everything he gave you."

"Me?" she repeated with a laugh. "Billy Joe never gave me anything. I mean, he wasn't big on presents anyway, but occasionally he'd bring Mom something."

"Like what?"

"Well, one day after he got back from a *business trip,* he brought her a bottle of very expensive cologne."

"Is it at your house?"

She nodded. "The bottle is. It's empty, because he got mad and poured the cologne down the toilet."

"What else?"

"He said he was going to buy her a car, but he never did. Oh. He gave her a topaz pendant once. I don't think it was real. Mom and I both thought the stone was too large and gaudy, but he insisted she wear it."

"Where is it?" Mack said.

Hannah frowned. "I don't know. She might have it on. Now, will you please tell me why we're going west? Where are you taking us. To Dowdie?"

"Absolutely," he said.

"Really?"

The way her face lit up made his heart ache.

"Oh, thank you, Mack. You're going to help me find my mother."

"We're going to Dowdie," he repeated, "because we've got to find the rest of Billy Joe's drugs and money before Ficone's man tracks you down and kills you."

MACK TURNED HIS entire attention to the road. He read the signs for upcoming towns. Very few of them were familiar, but then he hadn't done much traveling by car west of the New Orleans area. He looked over at Hannah, who was slumped against the window, sound asleep. He was glad. She was so exhausted, and she probably hadn't gotten eight hours total since she'd driven in from Dowdie.

Her eyes were twitching, which meant she was dreaming. Mack didn't have to wonder what kind of dreams she was having. Her mobile face told him everything as it morphed from serene to nervous, from relaxed to fearful as she navigated her way through the dreams. He hated to see fear darkening her expression. He wanted her to be happy, not sad. Relaxed, not frightened. But no matter the expression, her face was so lovely it made his heart ache.

What was he doing, taking her right back into danger? He should have given Teilhard all the information he had and turned Hannah over to him to put her in protective custody. Teilhard, with all the resources he had at his disposal, could protect her. Mack knew he couldn't.

He'd rejected law enforcement for the same reason he couldn't be a defense lawyer. He took people's pain, emotional and physical, too personally, not to mention that he was constantly worried that he wouldn't be able to help them. It was the same old doubt and fear that he'd carried with him his entire life. But this time, even with the doubts and fears, he'd committed to keeping Hannah safe, and that scared him. The only other time he'd pledged a commitment to keep a woman safe, he'd failed, and the woman—his mother—had died.

Hannah deserved someone better. Too bad he was all she had.

He glanced over at her and to his surprise, she opened her sleepy eyes and smiled at him, then closed them again.

Mack kept an eye on her as he drove, amazed that she could be so frightened yet sleep so peacefully. He wished he were the kind of man who could inspire that kind of trust. *I promise I'll protect you,* he thought, *with my life.*

Mack arched his neck, trying to get rid of the nagging headache he'd had ever since the man who'd ambushed him had slammed his head into the floor. He must have moaned aloud because Hannah started, then opened her eyes and sat up, yawning.

"What's the matter?" she asked.

"Nothing. My head hurts a little."

"That place above your eyebrow is turning into a lump," she said, "so it's no wonder it hurts. How did you let him get the drop on you, anyhow?" Hannah asked.

Mack glared at her. "First of all, I didn't *let* him. And like I told you, he surprised me. I came out of the motel room and was just about to lock the door and head back to my car when something hit me like a freight train, right in the throat. I think he must have swung at me with his forearm. I twisted around and went down. I don't think I've ever been hit so hard in my life."

"You didn't see anything?" she asked.

"Anything like what?" he asked. "I told you, I face-planted and before I had a chance to turn over, much less get up, he jumped on top of me. I think he was using brass knuckles." He tongued a deep cut on the inside of his lip that matched the one on the outside, then pulled his lip down and strained to get a look at the damage in the rearview mirror.

As he rubbed his jaw where one of the man's blows had landed, a vague impression he'd gotten during the fight came back to him. He looked down at his hands on the steering wheel, then stretched out his right hand and examined the back of it for a second.

"The only thing I noticed was that there was something on the back of his hand," he said. "Something that looked—" He stopped cold. His stomach flipped over and his scalp burned. Had there really been anything on the man's hand, or was the image a weird trick of the blood obscuring his vision? He shook his head, trying to clear it. The only other explanation was that he was having a flashback to his childhood, brought on by the sight of blood and a raging man swinging his fists.

Hannah put her hand on his. "Oh, right. The red tattoo."

"What?" Mack said, as his brain slowly processed what she had said. His heart felt like a solid block of ice in his chest as his brain plummeted back in time to the worst night of his life. The night his worst nightmare had come true. "Red tattoo?" he rasped.

"What's the matter?" Hannah asked. "You look like you've seen a ghost."

He shook his head. "Nothing. I'm fine. It was probably the blood in my eyes."

She took her hand away and folded her arms, shrinking back into the passenger seat. "The man who shot Billy Joe had a tattoo on his hand. It was red."

Mack didn't know how his frozen heart was managing to pump blood through his veins—even if it did feel like ice water. His hands tightened on the steering wheel until they cramped. And his brain was racing. He wasn't sure he wanted to hear what Hannah was about to say. Despite his uncertainty, his numb lips formed the questions, "Where? What kind of tattoo?"

"It was on the back of his right wrist." she started, then swallowed audibly. Her voice was shaky with remembered fear when she continued. "A red heart, with the letters *M-O-M* inside it. And inside the *O* was something that looked like…" She paused.

Mack took a deep breath through lungs that felt as though they were filled with broken glass. "A bullet hole. Right through the center of the *O*," he finished for her.

Chapter Nine

Hoyt cursed and yawned as he turned right on St. Charles Street for the second time. It was late, after eight o'clock at night. As soon as he'd gotten on the interstate to race to Mack Griffin's house, he'd realized his mistake. Within five minutes it was backed up with rush-hour traffic. Then a tractor-trailer rig carrying PVC pipe turned over and the pipe rolled everywhere, blocking all lanes. He was stuck, practically not moving at all, for over two hours.

He just hoped Griffin was behind him and experiencing the same frustrating delay. The bad news, even if he was behind him, was that he could call Hannah and warn her—tell her to run and hide.

When he'd finally made it to Griffin's address, he'd driven by slowly, trying to see if he could tell whether Griffin was there and more important, whether Hannah was there.

If she was here, he'd manage one way or another to get in and grab her, hopefully before Griffin got home.

He wasn't looking forward to another fistfight. Even with his brass knuckles, the younger, fitter man had almost beaten him.

As Hoyt passed Griffin's house, he noticed the pizza shop directly across St. Charles. At the last second he whipped across the median and into its parking lot. Stepping inside, he went up to the counter, where two waitresses in T-shirts with the pizza shop's logo and towels over their shoulders were talking.

"And then Tom kicked him out," the first waitress said. "I'm telling you, Kelly, he looked awful. His face was all bloody."

"I'm Detective Norris," Hoyt interrupted with a friendly smile. "Someone called about a disturbance?"

"Yeah!" the first waitress said. "My boss must have called. A man with blood all over him came in here looking for someone. He looked like a-an ax murderer."

The other waitress laughed nervously.

"What about the woman?" Hoyt said casually, patting his shirt pocket as if looking for a pen and pad.

"The woman? Oh, she came in right about the time my boss came out. She was blond with a long braid in back. She looked scared."

"Where did they go when Tom threw them out?"

"They got in his car and drove off."

Hoyt took a step forward. "What kind of car?"

"White. A BMW, maybe?" the young woman said. "You probably want to talk to Tom."

"That's okay," Hoyt said, pulling out his cell phone as if he was about to call for backup. "I know the car. Thanks. You've been real helpful." Then he ran out of the shop and jumped into his car, slamming his palm against the steering wheel.

How had Griffin beaten him here? He must have taken a shortcut on some backstreets.

His best guess was that Griffin was probably either on the interstate by now, headed east, away from any danger to Hannah, or that he'd headed toward the bayou country. He couldn't imagine that the lawyer was helping her merely out of the goodness of his heart or his sense of justice. Griffin was probably in love with her, or at least in lust, and hoping to keep her and himself out of danger.

It was a damn shame he didn't have a way of tracking them. If he were the boss, he'd pay for micro-tracking devices. He could have stuck one on Griffin's expensive sport coat during the fight.

Then it hit him.

HANNAH SLEPT WHILE Mack drove for another couple of hours, doing his best to ignore the headache that had been getting worse every minute since Hannah had described the red tattoo that had haunted his dreams for almost twenty years.

He massaged his left temple, where the pain had settled, and winced. His vision seemed to be getting blurry, too. The halos of oncoming headlights were growing bigger and brighter by the minute.

He glanced over at Hannah, wanting to wake her up and ask her more about the man and his tattoo, but truthfully, he wasn't sure he wanted to know any more. At least not right now. He needed to digest what she'd already told him.

That red-and-black image was a symbol of everything it had taken him years to bury in the back of his mind. The thought of dredging all that up and trying to deal with it again made him physically sick.

What were the odds that two men in the world had the exact same tattoo in the exact same place?

He swallowed against the acrid taste that always seemed to accompany these bad headaches and pushed the tattoo back into the lockbox where he kept the unbearable memories. But locking the image away didn't help the headache. That plus the beating he'd taken and the painful glare from oncoming headlights all combined to make it impossible for him to drive any farther.

About a half hour after they passed through Shreveport, Mack exited the interstate onto a state road and drove about eleven miles, passing through a couple of small towns until he came to one that was big enough to have a Piggly Wiggly, a Walmart and, surprisingly, two motels. He stopped at the Walmart, figuring he'd get them some toiletries and pajamas and underwear. As soon as he stopped the car, Hannah woke up, so he gave her money to do her own shopping. He got himself a small bottle of ibuprofen, which he opened on the spot. He downed two of the tablets with a bottle of water from a vending machine, then put the bottle in his pocket. While he waited for Hannah to finish shopping, Mack called Dawson again, since he hadn't called him back. The phone rang again and again and again.

"Damn it, Delancey," Mack muttered just as Dawson answered. *Well, finally.* "Where have you been?"

"Jules and I took a raft trip. We camped overnight and there was no phone service. We're driving back now. I was going to call you in the morning."

"Remember the young woman that came to see me while you and I were on the phone the other day? She's in some trouble because of her mom's boyfriend."

"Yeah? What kind of trouble?"

"You know what? Forget that. What's important is, I found a letter in her purse. The envelope was sealed, but it wasn't mailed. It was from her mother. I opened it." Mack paused for a fraction of a second, waiting for Dawson to give him hell about tampering with other people's things, but he didn't. So Mack continued. "The mother's name is Stephanie Clemens. Have you ever heard that name?"

"Not that I recall. Who is she?"

Mack took a deep breath.

"What's going on, Mack?" Dawson asked, beginning to sound slightly concerned with a pinch of impatience.

"I'm getting to it. The letter, like I said, is from mother to daughter. Stephanie Clemens has liver disease and is on dialysis. The letter is one of those confessions before dying."

"Okay." Dawson sounded distracted.

"Daw, Stephanie Clemens claims she's Claire Delancey's daughter."

"What?" Dawson snapped. Mack had his attention now.

"Does your great-aunt Claire have a daughter?"

"Not—" Dawson paused. "I've heard that she originally went to France because she was pregnant. She ended up staying there for ten years the first time she went. When she came back to Chef Voleur, she was around twenty-six and she didn't have a child with her."

"That would have been too long ago, anyhow. This woman is forty-two and Hannah is twenty-five."

"Aunt Claire went back to France in—let's see. She was probably thirty-six or so. And now she's seventy-nine."

Mack added in his head. "That would work. Is there somebody you could ask other than your family? It would be good if you kept this to yourself for a while. I'd hate to hurt your family if this is just a scam."

"I agree. Aunt Claire was always the *bad girl* of the family. She's lived *in sin* with Ektor Petrakis, the wealthy Greek businessman, in France all these years. He died recently, which is why she's returning here.

And yes, you're right about keeping it from the family until we're sure. I'll do some research on my great-aunt and see what I can find."

"Thanks. I'm not convinced that Hannah is any kin to your illustrious family yet."

"Do you think she's trying to get money?"

"Not Hannah. I don't think she has any idea what the letter says. She was carrying it but she hadn't opened it. The flap hadn't been touched."

Mack saw Hannah rolling a shopping cart toward him. "I've got to go. I'll give you a call maybe tomorrow if I have any more information."

"Okay. Meanwhile, I'll see what I can come up with on this end. Stephanie Clemens, right? What's the girl's name?"

"Hannah Martin. Got to go. Thanks, Dawson."

Mack and Hannah put their purchases in the car and Mack headed toward the motels. By the time he got them checked into the nicer of the two motels, Hannah was asleep again. He roused her gently, then grabbed the Walmart bags and unlocked the small room, which wasn't much better than the one Hannah had rented in Metairie. He set the bags on the dresser next to the old-fashioned TV as Hannah came in. He opened his mouth to ask her which of the two double beds she wanted, but before he even got the first word out she'd disappeared into the bathroom, her shopping bags in her hands.

That was fine with him. He took a six-pack of soft drinks out of a bag and stuck it into the small refrigerator. Taking the half-empty water bottle with him to the bed closest to the door and farthest from the bathroom, he took a good, long swig, then flopped down onto the bed and threw one arm over his eyes.

"Ow," he muttered, immediately taking his arm

away. His face was way too sore for that. His head still pounded and the ibuprofen tablets hadn't helped his nausea any. He propped himself up on his elbow and drank some more water, this time slowly, then lay back down and closed his eyes.

Behind his closed lids, the memory he'd tried to lock away burned through his eyelids like heat lightning. A big man—as big as Goliath—was there, his hamlike fists were doubled and his face purple and distorted with rage. There was another person in the room. A woman crouched on the floor against the wall with a terrified look on her blood-streaked face. She was crying and shouting, "Run, Mackie! Run to Aunt Beth's house."

Mack felt as though he were watching a movie on a big screen. There, in the foreground of the shot, a boy, no more than twelve, yelled, "Leave my mom alone!" The Goliath ignored the child, except for a vicious snarl in his direction as he advanced on the woman.

The boy's line of sight was nearer to the big man's hands than his face. So the prominent black-and-red tattoo on the back of the man's hand was no more than a couple of feet from his face. To him, the ugly, crooked red heart with the word *MOM* spelled out in black letters was an obscene insult to his mother.

Then the man clenched his fists and the tattoo seemed to stretch until the *O* in *MOM* stood out. The boy stared at it. Finally, he made out what was drawn in the middle of the *O*. It was a bullet hole.

The boy took all this in during the few seconds while the giant was advancing on his mother, cursing and yelling and threatening her if she didn't get up. By the time he loomed over her, reaching for her with that huge, tattooed hand, the boy went into motion. He ran at the man, swinging his arms. He hit him over and over, crying, "Leave her alone, leave her alone."

Finally, the man backhanded the boy, sending him tumbling to the floor. Then he grabbed him by the arm and jerked him to his feet, and Mack heard the man's low, threatening voice. "If you try that again, your mom will end up a lot more bloody than she is now. Understand?"

The boy swung at him again. The man flung him against the wall while the mother screamed, "Run, Mackie, run!" Sweat formed on Mack's forehead and dripped into his hair as he remembered what happened next.

It took more effort than he'd expected, but he finally managed to open his eyes and sit up. Yet still, even though he saw the front window and door of the motel room, part of the vision remained—the image of a red heart with the word *MOM* in black with a bullet hole through the middle of the *O*.

He wiped his face and pressed his fingertips against his temples and squeezed his eyes shut, pushing as hard as he could to force the awful memory away.

At that moment, the bathroom door opened, releasing a cloud of steam into the room, and Hannah stepped through it like a water sprite from a misty lake.

"Oh," she said on a huge sigh, "I feel so much better."

Mack stared, thankful to have something beautiful to look at after all that horror. She had on pink-and-purple pajama pants and a little pink top with tiny straps holding it up. Her hair was wet and long and hung over one shoulder in cascading waves, and her cheeks were dewy and pink. She smiled at him, and his heart, which he'd have sworn was cold and shattered into a million pieces, began to warm up and heal. Goose bumps rose on his arms. He wasn't quite sure why.

He didn't know where to look, since every single inch of her was fresh and lovely and clean, so he pushed himself up off the bed. When he stood, he swayed as light-headedness came over him for a second and the edge of his vision turned dark. But it faded almost immediately.

"Mack, are you okay? You look pale," Hannah said.

"Sure," he answered quickly. "I'm fine. I'm just going to unpack." He carefully walked over to where he'd set the plastic shopping bags on the TV table. He'd bought underwear, a pair of Levi's, a couple of T-shirts, white socks, an inexpensive pair of jogging shoes, disposable razors, deodorant and a comb. "Damn it, I didn't think about luggage," he muttered.

"I'll bet you didn't think about your face, either," she said.

He held up the razors.

She laughed and shook her head. "Not exactly what I'm talking about," she said with exaggerated patience. "You probably won't be able to use those for a couple of days. Here." She handed him one of her bags, which was damp from the shower spray.

When he looked inside, he remembered. "Oh, right," he said, as he checked the contents. Rubbing alcohol. Bandages in several sizes. Sterile reinforced strips and a tube of antibiotic ointment.

She took the bag back and grabbed his hand. "Sit over here," she said, guiding him to a hard-backed chair in front of the dresser.

"Let me take a shower first," he said, trying to maneuver away from her and toward the bathroom. He definitely needed a shower, but not as much as he needed to

get away from her. He was still queasy from the dream/
memory and still fascinated with how lovely she was,
fresh from her shower. He couldn't tell if his racing
pulse was caused by nausea or lust.

"Okay," she said, smiling at him. "Try to get all that
dried blood off while you're in there, but hurry. Otherwise I might be sound asleep."

Once Mack had disappeared into the bathroom, Hannah sat down on her bed with a pillow propped behind
her head. She felt warm and clean and drowsy after her
hot shower. She'd almost drifted off to sleep when Mack
opened the bathroom door. Hannah opened her eyes to
a narrow slit and peeked at him. He wore nothing but a
pair of pale blue pajama pants from Walmart. He stood
in the doorway for a moment, backlit by the bathroom
light. His hair was wet and furrowed, as though he'd
raked his fingers through it. His body was sprinkled
with droplets of water that shimmered in the reflection from the bathroom, making him look covered in
stardust.

She saw that he was just as trim and finely muscled
as she'd suspected he was from the cut of his clothes.
He had broad shoulders and a lean waist, trim hips and,
if she could judge by what she could see of the fit of the
pajama pants, long, powerful thighs.

After a few seconds, she realized he was studying
her. She didn't move a muscle, not even a twitch of her
eyelid. He didn't move either, didn't change his neutral
expression as his gaze assessed her. Then, when she
thought she couldn't go another second without wig-
gling something, even if it was nothing but her big toe,
he brushed both hands over his wet hair and flung the
droplets of water at her. "Wake up, sleepyhead," he said.

"Hey!" she cried, wiping her face and chuckling. "What are you doing?"

He smiled, surprising Hannah. "Hey, yourself. Just checking to see if you were asleep. Time to dress my wounds. Get up."

She faked a yawn that immediately stretched into a real one. "They're fine, I'm sure. I think I'm going to turn over and go back to sleep."

"No problem. I'll take care of all this myself. Where'd you put the bandages?"

"Oh, no, you don't. I'll do it. You sit right there." She got up, pointing to the single hard-backed chair. "I need to see how bad those cuts and scrapes are."

Mack shrugged. "Yes, sir, Dr. Martin." He sat as she gathered up the supplies she'd bought. There was a mirror over the dresser, and seeing his reflection, he was startled all over again by the condition of his face. "Damn it," he said.

"What?" Hannah called from the bathroom, over the sound of running water.

"The bathroom mirror was foggy, but I can see my face now and it hurts."

She came back into the room with a steaming washcloth. "You might be more comfortable lying down. I'm going to put this over your face and I want it to stay there for a couple of minutes."

He was tempted, but he figured since Hannah was going to be leaning over him in that skimpy little pajama top, he wasn't sure he could control himself. Sitting up, he'd be better able to hide any physical evidence of that lack of control.

"Why do you even need that? I just got out of the hot shower."

"I just want to be sure all the scabs are soft." She set

the items on the dresser in front of him and told him to lean his head back. "Are you sure you don't want to lie down?" she said.

"Damn sure."

"Why?"

Mack opened an eye and peered at her. "Why what?"

"You said *damn sure.*"

"I said that?" He hadn't realized he'd said the words out loud.

"Yeah. But I don't see why you wouldn't. It would take the strain off your neck."

Right, but it might add strain somewhere lower down. As soon as the thought flitted through his mind, he glanced at Hannah, but she hadn't reacted, so he must not have said that one aloud.

"Okay, then. Tilt your head back."

He did and she applied the hot cloth.

He moaned.

"Am I hurting you?" she asked as her fingers smoothed and straightened the soft, hot cloth.

"No," he said on a sigh. "Moan of pleasure."

"Is the cloth dripping too much?"

"Nope. Not at all. It's great," he said, hearing the strain in his voice.

"Good. Now stay still." The light, teasing touch of her fingers sent thrills through all the tiny nerves of his body as she slid them around the side of his face and then to the back of his neck where, to his dismay, she massaged for a few seconds. The more she kneaded the muscles of his neck, the closer he came to embarrassing himself.

"I hope your neck isn't too sore. I still think you ought to lie down."

"No!" he snapped, then cleared his throat. "I'm fine."

Her fingers caressing the nape of his neck were about to drive him crazy. When had that area become so sensitive? Maybe it had always been. For the life of him, right at this moment he couldn't remember another woman ever touching him there.

"Okay," she said, taking her hand away. "I'm going to get the bandages and the sterile strips ready. Then I'm going to use a hot soapy cloth to clean your face."

Mack nodded slightly. Even with his neck tilted back, he was becoming so relaxed that he was about to drift off to sleep. "If you don't hurry up I may go to sleep and slide out of the chair."

"That's okay. I'll just take care of you on the floor," she said, a smile in her voice.

He spent the next couple of minutes trying to stop imagining how Hannah would go about *taking care of him on the floor.*

Chapter Ten

"Okay," Hannah said. "Your face is finally clean of blood. Now I can get to work."

Mack was grateful for her matter-of-fact statement. It helped him concentrate on something besides how she might take care of him on the floor.

"How do you know so much about first aid?" he asked once she finally took the washcloth off his face and he could straighten his neck. He winced. His neck was stiff and sore. Very sore. Probably from that thug bashing his forehead into the floor.

"This is not just first aid. Some of it is second aid." She smiled. "I was a lifeguard at the lake for three summers. I've handled my share of small emergencies."

Mack assessed her. "Ever dealt with a big emergency?"

She shook her head. "The worst thing I saw was a kid jump off the tall diving board and land on the low board. I didn't have to do anything, though. Someone called 911 and an ambulance came. The head lifeguard helped out in the meantime."

"What happened to the kid?"

"I think he bruised or severed his spinal cord. I didn't know him or his parents but I think the last I heard, they'd taken him to Dallas." She examined the cut over his eyebrow. "I'm going to use sterile strips on this. I need to pull the edges of the skin together." She touched his brow.

"Ow," he said, pulling away.

"You're going to have a nice bruise there. What did he do? Slam your head against the wall?"

"Floor." Embarrassed, he dropped his gaze.

"Oh." Hannah's face was about a foot from his. She touched an uninjured spot under his chin and urged his head up. "Sorry," she said. "Bad attempt at a joke."

He lifted his gaze to hers. For a moment, neither one of them spoke. Mack felt like this was a crossroads of some kind, as if what he did in the next second would change their relationship irrevocably.

But he had no idea what he should do. No. He *knew* what he should do. His problem was, he *knew* what he wanted to do. He wanted to kiss her. He was dying to find out if those vulnerable lips were as soft and sexy to the touch as they were to look at. But the part of his brain that was still rational was screaming, *Don't do it. She's everything you don't want.*

Before he could act on that excellent advice, her eyes changed. They went from clear blue to smoky and dark. Her gaze flickered down to his mouth and he forgot to breathe. Was she about to take the decision out of his control?

But instead of leaning forward and kissing him, she caught her lower lip between her teeth and blinked. "Okay, then. I—need to clean this cut on your brow with alcohol," she said. "It's probably going to sting." She soaked a corner of a washcloth in alcohol, then placed it against the cut.

"Ow!" he said. "That stings."

"I know," she said seriously. "Hence my recent statement regarding stinging."

Mack chuckled.

She began to gently scrub the cut and damn it, it did hurt. He sat still, his jaw tensed, as she finished with his brow and went to the cut on his lip, the scrape on his cheek, which stung even more, and a small cut inside his nostril.

Trying to take his mind off the stinging, not to mention the torture of seeing her fresh, lovely skin so up close and personal, he took the opportunity to survey her features. She wasn't exactly pretty. Her high cheekbones, defined jawline and small chin made her look stubborn, unless she was smiling. Her small nose kept her from looking too stern, and her wide eyes looked positively innocent, if you ignored the jawline.

She poured more alcohol and went back to cleaning the cuts and scrapes.

Mack couldn't make himself stop looking at her mouth. It was soft and turned up at the corners, not at all stern. It was that jaw that was the problem, although if she was completely relaxed, for instance when she slept, it softened a lot. As she worked, she bit her lower lip. Mack felt a stirring of desire inside him at the sight of her small, white teeth. He allowed himself a fleeting daydream of what it would be like to make love to her. He decided it would be very, very nice, but it would never happen.

"I'm done, I think," Hannah said, looking down into Mack's eyes.

He didn't say anything and he didn't move. He didn't dare. Her mouth was so close to his that all he had to do was raise his head a half inch and their lips would touch.

Her eyes were soft and her mouth was the sexiest

thing he'd ever seen. Just about the time he made the momentous decision to steal a kiss, she retreated.

"Okay," she said, too briskly. "There you are. I don't know how much better you look, but you're going to feel a lot better."

He cleared his throat and sat up. The beginnings of arousal faded as he set his mind to ignoring the sensation.

"Ah, hell," he muttered. "I forgot to buy a toothbrush," he said. "Damn it!"

Her eyes sparkled. "Nyah-hah-hah!" she said, twirling an imaginary mustache. Reaching into one of the bags, she pulled out two toothbrushes and a tube of toothpaste.

"You're a regular Boy Scout, aren't you?" he said.

"That's *Girl Scout* to you," she retorted, "in case you can't tell."

Mack's control dissolved like tissue in the rain. The dangerous sensations he'd finally managed to suppress roared to life. He willed himself to stop, but there were some temptations too difficult to resist and right at that moment, with Hannah so near, her cheeks as pink as the little top she wore, she was the embodiment of temptation.

"Oh, I can tell," he said, and even though he was trying to stoke the fires of resistance, his hand reached out and touched her flaming cheek. "I can tell."

She didn't move a muscle while the backs of his fingers brushed her hot skin, or when he pulled his hand back and lifted his gaze to hers. But when he stared into her eyes and ran his forefinger across the curve of her bottom lip, she did move. She lifted her face to his in silent invitation for him to touch her again.

"Hannah," he said, shaking his head slowly. "You don't want me to—"

Her chin rose another fraction of an inch and her heavy-lidded gaze met his. "Are you telling me what I want?" she asked, her tone a mixture of amusement and challenge.

"I just don't think this is—"

"What? A good idea? I can't really think in terms of good or not good right now." She angled her head slightly. "I'm tired and scared and worried, and tomorrow I'm sure I'll have regrets, but tonight I just want a few minutes of being held and cherished and…" The longer she talked, the softer and more sultry her voice became, until she was whispering, her lips so close to his that he could feel the air stirring with her breaths.

Then, before his desire-soaked brain could think of a way to convince her just how bad an idea this was, she kissed him. At first it was butterfly soft, barely brushing his lips. If he'd had his eyes closed, he might have thought he'd imagined it.

He waited, craving and dreading what she was going to do next.

She kissed him a little harder and a little harder, until she was pressing her mouth insistently against his and he was fast losing the ability to breathe evenly. Then she pulled back. "You know, Mack, I'd have made you as a player. What's the matter? Got some kind of lawyer rule against kissing a client? Or just too tired?"

He swallowed, unsure how to answer her. The thing was, he *was* a player—when the game was being played by his rules, which this game was not.

He allowed himself a small smile at her brazen challenge. Here was his way out. He'd steal the game from her and show her what being a player actually meant. It would terrify her and she'd back off. At that thought, his desire was already waning.

Watch out, Miss Martin, he said to himself. *This game's about to change.*

"Well?" she taunted, the mischief edging out the embarrassment in her eyes. She obviously felt very sure of herself at this moment.

"You don't know what you're doing," he said softly, the smile still in place.

A brief shadow crossed her face. "What do you mean?" she asked, feigning innocence.

He lifted his head and looked down his nose at her. "Oh, it's not your fault. You've only had boys to play with. It's understandable that you don't know what you're getting into by flirting with a man. I'd advise you to stop now."

"Stop?" she said as a flush rose from her neck all the way up to her cheeks. "I—don't want to stop."

"Okay, then," he said. Without taking his gaze from hers, he slid his hands in a caress up her arms to her shoulders. Then, without changing expression, he gave a flick of his fingers and pushed the tiny straps of her top down off her shoulders until the swell of her breasts was the only thing keeping it from slipping to her waist.

Hannah gasped as she felt the material slipping farther and farther down toward the tips of her breasts, tickling as it slid. "What—" she started, but she stopped herself when Mack's smile grew noticeably wider. She'd started this, and she was not about to be the one who chickened out. She lifted her face to his and touched his lips with hers.

"Is that all you've got?" she whispered against his lips. She heard the breathy nervousness in her voice, but with any luck, Mack's blood was rushing in his ears and he hadn't heard it.

"That's not even a taste," he muttered, sliding his

mouth from her lips to her chin, then to her jaw and along the jawline all the way to her earlobe.

Her shaky breathing threatened to turn into a complete inability to breathe at all. He bit down lightly on her earlobe and she gasped as a sharp thrill fluttered through her all the way to the center of her desire.

He whispered something that she didn't quite catch, then he wrapped his arms around her, pulled her to him and kissed her fully and deeply. She did forget how to breathe. But Mack was breathing for her, feeding her breath and life, along with an arousal so acute that she could scarcely stand it as he opened his mouth and teased her lips with his tongue.

Nothing Hannah had ever done with the boys she'd dated had prepared her for this—this total immersion into the erotic fire of a true, deep kiss. She'd been kissed before. But Mack was right. Those were adolescent kisses. She'd never, until now, had anything to compare them to.

But now she'd been kissed by Mack Griffin. And what a kiss it was. He'd started the same way she had, soft as butterflies. But then he'd parted his lips and kissed her with barely enough pressure to convince her that he'd done it on purpose. Then came the feel of his tongue on her closed lips. A tentative touching that seemed to say "Is this all right? I want to taste you but I'd be sad if I scared you."

It was only after she'd almost unconsciously leaned into Mack and given herself up to his superior strength, expertise and talent, that he actually slid his tongue along her closed lips, urging them open. At the feel of his hot, wet tongue licking her mouth, her insides began to thrum with a sensation that was familiar, yet much stronger, much more intense with Mack. And he'd barely touched her.

As if he'd heard her thought, he caressed the curve of her shoulders, then let his fingertips graze her collarbone, then down to the beginning swell of her breasts. The thrumming inside her began to vibrate as he slowly moved closer to the tips of her breasts. Then his thumbs touched the sensitized peaks and she drew in a long, shuddering breath. Her nipples tightened almost painfully, allowing the soft material of her camisole to slip down to her waist, leaving her breasts bare.

He made an appreciative sound as he bent his head to kiss her collarbone, the flat area just above the swell of her breasts, then touched the top of one breast with his tongue.

She gasped at the fiery wetness on her naked breast.

Then he stopped.

She stood frozen, waiting for a cue from him to tell her what came next. But he was as still as she, his breathing hard and fast but steady.

Finally, she met his dark gaze.

"I didn't mean to scare you," he said.

"But you—" She took a breath. "You didn't. I was—"

He hushed her with a fingertip against her lips. "Yes, I did," he said, taking her hand and holding it up so she could see it. To her embarrassment, she saw that it was trembling.

"I guess I'm just tired," she said, persisting in her pretense that he hadn't startled and frightened her when he tongued her breast.

He stepped backward and gave her a brief nod. "I guess," he said.

She felt her face burn. She groped for the straps to her camisole and started to tug them up. "You think I'm just a country mouse, don't you, Mr. Hotshot P.I?"

"No," he said with an upturn in his tone that made his answer sound like a question.

Hannah propped her fists on her hips and glared at him. "Oh, yeah? Then what do you think?"

He assessed her, his eyes still dark with longing. "I think you're a lot more sheltered than you let on."

She bristled, and he held up a hand.

"I'm not saying you're naive. You're not. But you lived an insular life, taking care of your mother, didn't you? Never went out to parties or events. You knew that you needed to be at home for your mom. And your only male role models were the men your mom brought home. Most of them were poorly educated, immature males who thought that their masculinity depended on how well their woman obeyed them."

"Could you stop with the Sherlock Holmes shtick?" Hannah said. His description of her mother, her mother's boyfriends and her cut very close to the bone. And she didn't like it.

"What you've experienced is not what a man is all about. A real man takes care of the woman he loves, sure. But he does it because he respects her, and he treats her with honor. A real man will never hurt a woman. That's the difference between boys and men, Hannah."

Hannah felt as though if she said one more word, she would burst into tears. And there was no way she was going to let Mack Griffin see her shed even one tear now. Not one.

"Come on," Mack said. "Get in bed. I'm going out to have a look around, make sure I don't see our friend or his vehicle out there anywhere, and then I'll be back to tuck you in. How's that?"

Hannah sent him a curious look, wondering if he was using *tuck you in* as a euphemism for sex, but he'd already turned and was slipping his feet into his loafers and grabbing a shirt. "I'll be back in less than ten minutes." He started toward the door, then turned. "Oh, by the way. There's a chance we might have to get out of here in a hurry. Let me have everything but your tooth-brush and comb. I'll put them in the car, just in case."

"I'd rather keep my purse," she said, picking it up and hugging it to her chest. When she did, the envelope popped out the top.

"What's that?" Mack asked, eyeing the white en-velope.

Hannah pushed it back down into her purse. "Noth-ing," she said shortly. From the look Mack gave her, she knew she'd answered too quickly and too abruptly, and she knew he wasn't going to let it go. But she hoped he would.

"What's the deal with the envelope, Hannah? I've seen sticking out before," he said, gazing at her steadily with a glint of challenge in his eye. "Does it have some-thing to do with Billy Joe's murder or your mom?"

Hannah's fingers tightened on her purse. "No," she said. "At least—no. Nothing to do with the murder."

"Your mom?"

"Why are you so interested in a silly envelope?"

He shrugged. "Probably because you're so intent on not telling me anything about it. Is it some kind of bad news?"

"Bad news?" she laughed. "Good question. Why don't you read it if you're so curious?"

Mack took the envelope and gave it a cursory glance. "You haven't read it?"

Thoroughly sick of his nosiness, Hannah shook her head in disgust. "No. I haven't. It's from my mother. When she found out she was going to have to go on hemodialysis, she was certain she was on her way out, so she wrote that. She joked that it was her deathbed confession. I told her there was no way I was reading it while she was alive, so that's why she added *in the event of Stephanie Clemens's death* on there."

"Maybe you should read it."

Her eyes widened. "Why? Why do you say that?"

Mack looked at the letter and back up at her. "Just a hunch. Maybe there is something that could help you." He held it out to her.

She took it, then stood there, staring at the writing on the front, then touching it with a fingertip. "Why would you think—" She stopped, lifting her gaze to his. "You know what's in here, don't you?" She waved the envelope at him. "What did you do? You *read* my letter?"

"I just… I saw the envelope and figured there might be something in there that could help your case."

"My case? My *case?*"

"You know what I mean."

Did she?

Hannah looked up. "What?"

"Did your mom ruin your life?"

She shrugged. "I don't know. It was my life, the only one I had. It doesn't feel ruined." She took a deep breath, tore the envelope open and took out the folded piece of paper. "At least it's not a *long* letter," she murmured as she began to read.

"You feel like reading it aloud?" Mack asked.

"Oh, why not. You've already seen it."

"My Darling Hannah,

I've never told you anything about your family. I always told myself that it was for your own good. I think I wanted to believe that, but of course that's not true. I kept it from you because I didn't want to have to answer your questions and listen to you begging me to take you to meet them. But that was selfish of me. You need to know your family and you need to get everything you deserve from them.

My mother, your grandmother, and I have been estranged for years and years. I was born out of wedlock, as they used to say. Mother had me in France. She's never told me who my father is, just as I've never told you who yours is. It strikes me as I write this that I'm a lot more like my mother than I ever thought I was. Surprisingly, I think that makes me happier than sad.

Your grandmother knows about my illness. I wrote her a letter similar to this, which I know she got because I received a handwritten acknowledgment. I actually think it might be nice to see her again, but I doubt I'll have the chance now.

Okay, here goes. The information you need in order to find your grandmother and her family. Your grandmother is Claire Delancey. She is the sister of Robert Connor Delancey, the infamous Louisiana politician. His grandchildren are your cousins.

The Delanceys live in Chef Voleur, Louisiana, on the north shore of Lake Pontchartrain. But I understand that several of your cousins live and work in the city.

I hope you get to meet your grandmother and, if possible, that one day we can see her together.
Love,
Your mother."

Hannah folded up the letter and put it back into the envelope, then stuffed the envelope back down into her purse. "Here. You can put my purse in the car," she said.

"What about the letter?"

"What about it? I've never known anything about my mother's family my entire life, so why should I get all excited because she wants to get everything off her chest before she dies?"

"Maybe she wants you to be taken care of."

"And why would a strange family do that?"

"Hannah," Mack said. "I happen to know the Delanceys. They're great people and they've welcomed strangers into their lives and family many times before. Did you recognize Claire's brother's name? You know who Con Delanccy is, don't you?"

"I've heard the name. The politician she was talking about?"

Mack nodded. "A wealthy and notorious politician and your grandmother's brother. He might have been governor of the state of Louisiana, if he hadn't been murdered."

"Murdered?" she echoed. "He was murdered?"

"Apparently by his personal assistant, Armand Broussard."

"You know them? The Delanceys?" Hannah said, feeling a sensation in her chest that she barely recognized and didn't like. It was kind of an empty feeling—a lonely feeling. She'd never had siblings or even cousins to play with. Never had a family she could call her own. "How? How do you know them?"

"Well, Dawson, my boss, is a Delancey."

Hannah rubbed her hand just below her collarbone where the lonesome feeling was. "Are you going to tell them?"

He nodded. "I've told Dawson."

"You told him?"

"Sure. He's helping us. I think he deserves to know that he's helping a member of his family, doesn't he?"

"He probably deserves to have a choice as to whether he considers me part of his family."

"Trust me, he's checking you out."

"Oh. Well, that's not going to go in my favor, is it?"

"Don't underestimate him or the rest of the Delanceys."

"They're nice?" she asked. "Have you met my—my grandmother?"

"No, I haven't. But some of the Delanceys think she'll be coming back to Chef Voleur from France."

"Coming back? Really? Why now, after all this time?"

"I think her long-term companion, Ektor Petrakis, just died recently."

For some reason, Hannah felt like crying. Her grandmother might return to the United States. She could get to meet her and maybe, just maybe, her mom could reunite with her mother, too.

But the other side of that daydream was that at any time during the past twenty-six years, either Claire or Hannah's mom could have made the effort to find the other. The odd lonely feeling grew inside her chest again, and she knew it would be only a matter of seconds before the tears started.

"Shouldn't you get that stuff into the car?" she said tightly.

He nodded and grabbed the rest of the items.

She watched him until he closed the motel room door behind him. Then she climbed into bed, curled up on her side and at last, let a few tears fall.

Chapter Eleven

Mack loaded their things into the car, then, after looking around at the parking lot, the cross streets and the other shops in the area, he got in and drove the car around to the back side of the hotel, where the trash bins and air-conditioning units were. Beyond that side of the motel was a large storage rental complex that also held rental trucks and tractor-trailers. The vehicles and the metal storage buildings made a fairly effective fence, hiding the back of the motel. Happy with his decision, he walked back around the side of the motel. As he did, his phone rang.

It was Dawson.

"Hey, man," Mack said. "I was just thinking about you. What did you find out?"

"I had Dusty search through birth records in France. Turns out my computer whiz speaks and writes six languages. She did find the record of birth of a daughter to a Claire Delancey. Judging by the date, that would be Stephanie Martin. Dusty said the last name would be pronounced Mar-tan, being French."

"Wow," Mack said. "So Stephanie would be your first cousin and Hannah is your second cousin."

"Yeah, I guess," Dawson said, sounding a bit as if he was still having trouble believing the relationship.

"Dawson, I know this is going to be hard, but can you keep this quiet? This is going to be huge news for your family, but until we have definitive proof that this woman is really Hannah Martin, I'm thinking it would be better not to upset your family."

"I haven't changed my mind. I agree with you completely. Now, you want to tell me what's going on with this alleged cousin of mine, Hannah Martin?"

"Yeah," Mack said. "It's a long story and it involves drugs and stolen money and murder. I'm going to need your help to get Hannah and her mother out of all this safely."

"Okay," Dawson said on a sigh. "Go ahead. I don't guess I'm going to get to bed within the next hour or two."

Mack took a deep breath and proceeded to give Dawson every bit of information he'd gotten from Hannah as well as everything he'd figured out himself. The only thing he left out was the red tattoo.

Within ten minutes, Mack and Dawson had put together the beginnings of a plan. Dawson would put Dusty to work setting up tracking on the phone of the man who was following Hannah. They had his cell phone information because of the threatening calls he'd made to Hannah. Mack wanted to turn the tables and follow and capture him and find out just how deep Ficone was into drug trafficking in Texas from him.

Dawson had a few suggestions and they argued about a couple of things, but basically, by the time Dawson hung up, Mack was fairly happy with the plan so far.

HANNAH SPENT A couple of minutes in self-indulgent crying, then turned over and lay there, staring into space. The information her mother had given her in the letter was a lot to take in, especially now with everything that was going on. She'd never had many people around her, never really wanted them. But suddenly she was the center of a lot of attention, controversy and drama, and she'd just discovered she was a part of a family she'd never known existed.

Then there was Mack. Her face turned hot against the pillow just thinking about him. Why had she flirted with him? She'd never been a flirt. Years of living with her mom's boyfriends had made her wary of attracting that kind of attention.

So what had possessed her to say even mildly suggestive things to Mack, like *Then I'll take care of you on the floor,* or *That's* Girl Scout *to you, in case you can't tell.*

And then she'd kissed him. She'd surprised herself as much if not more than him. Still, it was his fault. How in the world was she supposed to be so close to him as she tended to his cuts and scrapes and not want to kiss that beautiful, injured face? Being that close to him did things to her insides that she'd never experienced before.

Not that she was entirely innocent. She'd had a couple of boyfriends, the operative word being *boy.* But Mack was definitely no boy. He was a man, through and through. His confident kisses, his gentle, deft touch, assured her of that. He'd showed her a man's desire, and he'd touched and kissed her and tongued her breast to communicate that desire. If he hadn't stopped, what would have happened?

A thrill hummed along her nerve endings and sent her heart racing. Mack would have made love to her. He would have continued kissing and tasting her until she was begging him. Just the thought of him inside her fired her blood in a way she'd never dreamed of. She gasped as her insides throbbed and heat spread through her, all the way to her fingertips.

The sound of a key card in the door startled her. She shifted in the bed so she could see the door as Mack came into the room. He closed the door and for a moment he stood there, the sculpted planes of his face and body outlined by the pale light from the open window. Hannah's breasts tightened just watching him.

After a moment, he pulled the curtains closed, then walked over to the other bed, took off his shoes and lay down, sighing as he did so.

"Mack?" she whispered.

"Yeah?"

"Is everything okay?"

She heard the sheets rustle as he changed position. "Sure."

"Mack?"

This time he didn't answer her.

She swallowed as desire rose inside her. "Would you like to sleep over here?" she asked in a small voice.

He didn't say anything for a long time. Finally, she heard him draw in a long breath. "That's not a good idea," he said softly.

Disappointed and yet in a way relieved, Hannah let out the breath she'd been holding. "I know," she said regretfully. She turned onto her side and tried to ignore the sharp, aching awareness of him lying so close to her. After a few seconds of silence, she swallowed.

"Mack?"

"Yeah, hon?" he muttered.

"It doesn't have to be a good idea."

She heard him sigh, then he was quiet for so long, she thought he might have gone to sleep.

"I don't—" he started, then stopped. "We wouldn't work," he said finally.

She waited, but he didn't say anything else. She turned over onto her back and stared at the ceiling, where the light from the motel's parking lot made odd shadows. "I don't understand."

"I'd break your heart."

She glanced over at him. She could see his profile outlined by the pale light. "Really?" she said. "You think I'm that weak? You think you need to protect me from *you* because I can't take care of myself?"

He didn't answer.

"You do! You think I'm like my mom. You think I have no judgment when it comes to men." She paused, trying to control her anger.

"I think you've learned all the wrong things," he said. "Your mom is an alcoholic and you've been exposed to too much of the bad side of relationships. But I've seen even worse, been through worse."

"Worse?" Hannah said on a short laugh, thinking if that was true then what he'd seen had to be horrific. "You've been through worse than cleaning up after your mom's drunken binges? Worse than watching her get hit by her boyfriends? Worse than dodging their fists yourself?"

"I watched a man kill my mom when I was twelve."

Hannah gasped. "Oh, Mack—" she said, her voice breaking.

"Don't," he snapped. "I just wanted to warn you. I don't do relationships."

Hannah's mouth twisted into a wry smile. "I didn't ask you to marry me, just to—"

"Hannah, don't put yourself in that position," he said tersely, then turned onto his side, away from her. She listened to his breathing as it settled, slowed down and became more even. She concentrated on its rhythm, using it to temper her own breathing and pulse. With great deliberation, she kept her mind on his and her breathing and refused to allow any other thoughts in. Eventually, Mack's breathing changed. He was asleep.

Still matching her breathing to his, Hannah finally felt herself relax. She filled her inner vision with the image of him standing in the bathroom door in nothing but pajama pants, his skin sparkling with water droplets. It was a dangerous thing to do, to dream about Mack.

He'd made himself perfectly clear. He didn't do relationships. She believed him, because she'd seen the hard glint in his eyes and the stubborn angle of his jaw. He meant what he said.

That side of him broke her heart, though, because she'd seen the other side—the sweet, vulnerable side that he did his best to keep hidden. She knew that side would always lose out to the other, stronger side that he'd developed to protect himself.

If she could turn back time and go back to before any of the awful events that had filled up the past days had happened, would she? No. She knew she'd never choose to go back to the time before she'd known Mack. No matter what happened in the future, for tonight, she had him. For the first time, she realized she was becoming truly relaxed. As she began to drift into sleep, her last thought was that she could sleep, because Mack was there with her, his strong, warm body protecting her from danger.

THE MAN WITH the red tattoo raised his gun and shot, and Billy Joe fell right where he stood. But the man kept shooting and Billy Joe kept falling—

Hannah was halfway out of the bed before she fully

woke up. Her throat constricted as a scream tried to push its way out.

Mack was already up and at the window, his hand pushing the curtains aside. "It's okay," he said, peering out. "Bunch of drunks."

The scream still clawed at her throat, thrumming in the same staccato rhythm as her racing pulse. She couldn't get a full breath.

Outside their door, the noise sorted itself into fists banging on a door, shouts of "Open up, we've got beer," and from farther away, "Shut up or I'll call the police" and "I'm calling the manager."

Mack checked the locks, glanced through the curtains once more as the commotion began to wind down, then crossed the room to her. He touched her chin, coaxing her to raise her head. "Hey, Hannah," he said softly. "Are you okay?"

She shuddered as her heart began to slow down and her muscles relaxed. She took a deep breath, finally. "The man with the red tattoo was shooting Billy Joe," she muttered. "He wouldn't stop shooting."

"Okay," Mack said. He slid an arm around her waist and guided her toward her bed. "Sit down. I'll get you some water. Don't think about what you were dreaming."

Hannah sat, doing her best to relax. She felt as though her muscles were still tied in knots. When Mack brought her a glass of water, she drank it all. He set the glass on the bedside table, then sat beside her.

"How're you doing now?"

Outside, a couple of guys were still talking loudly. Then a door slammed and like an echo, two doors farther away slammed, as well. "I guess the excitement is over," she said shakily. To her dismay, as she relaxed, reaction set in and she began to tremble.

"Oh, no." Her eyes stung and a trio of little sobs escaped.

Mack put his arm around her and pulled her close. He kissed the top of her head. She slid an arm around his waist, her hand sliding across his taut back muscles and savoring the heat of his body. He straightened.

"I'll get you some more water," he said.

"No, please," she responded, pulling him closer. "Just stay here."

But he stood and she had to let go. He walked back over to the other bed. She followed him and caught his hand. When he turned toward her, his mouth set, his eyes hard, she wrapped her hand around his neck, stood on tiptoe and kissed him.

"Stop it," he muttered, but she ignored him. She let her tongue flirt gently with his closed lips, and smiled when she felt him begin to respond.

Mack couldn't stop his body from reacting to Hannah's kiss. He'd never gotten this close to anyone like her—never allowed himself to. She packed a lethal combination of innocence, sexuality and vulnerability that he instinctively avoided—normally. Although he couldn't remember ever having this much trouble resisting. It was all about proximity, he figured. He'd always been a master at steering clear of women like her.

But Hannah's mouth was so soft and sexy as her tongue played with his in an erotic dance that nearly pushed him over the edge. He was hard and growing harder, and he had to stop her before it was too late.

He pulled away, then pressed his forehead to hers and closed his eyes. "Hannah. This is such a bad idea. Don't make me reject you. Don't make me hurt you."

She lifted her head just enough to touch her lips to his. "You think I don't have a mind of my own?" she whispered, kissing him softly again. "Do you actually think you're the one in control here?"

He felt her mouth widen in a smile, then she slid her tongue across his lips. "You're in for a big surprise, mister."

He wrapped his arms around her and pulled her to him, turning her teasing kiss into the erotic dance she'd started earlier. "Don't make this more than it is," he muttered as he slid his hands down to her breasts and lower to catch the hem of her pajama top and pull it off over her head.

Hannah lifted her arms, then wrapped them around his neck and kissed him more deeply yet. She took his hand and placed it on her bare breast. Then she slid his pajama bottoms down and caressed his buttocks. "Come to bed," she whispered, pulling him with her as she lay down.

Then they were together, wound around each other. Mack was inside her and somehow, he had the feeling she was inside him. He'd never felt like this before. As if he'd finally found the missing part of himself. When he could no longer hold back, he sank himself deeply into her and heard her breath catch. He thrust again and again, until he felt her contracting around him, then his own climax overwhelmed him.

When the sensations finally waned and he lay with his head resting on her shoulder, he struggled to stay in the fantasy the two of them had created. But he couldn't. As he drifted off to sleep, a single rational thought pushed its way into his mind.

He was so screwed.

MACK WOKE UP when the sky began to lighten, around six o'clock. Right away, he was aware of Hannah asleep next to him. Hell, who was he kidding. He'd been aware of her all night. He'd woken a couple of times with hunger gnawing at his insides and arousal aching in his groin.

He held his breath for a couple of seconds and listened to her soft, even breaths. He was glad she was sleeping soundly. She'd been hysterical the night before, when those drunken idiots had banged on the door. He'd been scared, too. After all, there was a high probability that the man with the red tattoo would find them. But Mack was betting his own odds that the guy wouldn't want to fight him again. Certainly not by himself.

Once the drunks were gone, Hannah had flung herself at him, crying, her whole body trembling. He'd gathered her into his arms and held her, comforting her and reminding her that he was here, between her and the door, and that he'd keep her safe, no matter what.

Then he'd made a fatal mistake. He'd allowed himself to consider the possibility of making love to her. He'd quickly tried to banish the thought from his head, but it had been too late.

Hannah's crying had calmed, and her desperately tight hug had relaxed. He'd felt the supple changes in her body and face that indicated sexual arousal. She'd kissed him, not softly, not sweetly. No, her kiss had been hungry, passionate, demanding. In the soft, quiet darkness, Mack had surrendered and made love with her.

And now, this morning, regret weighed him down like a dozen anvils on his chest. He'd known in the back of his mind that this would happen. He'd tried to tell her. But she'd been too desirable and he'd been too weak to resist her.

He couldn't remember when touching a woman had

been so exciting and new. Or when he'd ever given up so much of himself to any woman. He'd had a lot of sex, but he felt as though last night was the first time he'd ever really *made love* with a woman.

And now, because his lust had overridden his ingrained caution regarding a woman like Hannah, who needed his protection, Mack had put himself in an impossible position.

There was only one way he could effectively protect her. By locking away his desire for her the same way he'd learned to lock away physical and emotional pain. As long as he kept his personal feelings separate from his self-imposed responsibility for her, he could keep her safe—he hoped.

For a while, Mack lay still, listening to Hannah's soft, even breaths. He had a plan, as far as it went. Most of what he'd done since she'd knocked on his door had been based purely on instinct. That wasn't his way. He'd never been good at going by the book, but he did have his own rules. And Rule #1 in the MacEllis Griffin Operations Handbook was "Always Have a Plan."

He threw back the covers and got up, carefully washed his bandaged face and brushed his teeth. Then he quietly dressed, stuck his wallet and his car keys into his pockets, grabbed the motel room key and slipped out the door and into the coolness of early morning, hoping he hadn't woken Hannah. Taking deep breaths of the pleasantly fresh air, Mack thought about the past three days. *Three days.* Had he only known Hannah for three days? It seemed as if she'd been with him for years.

After a short walk that made him feel a lot better, Mack went into the small front desk area of the motel to check out the continental breakfast they advertised. All he saw was a pot of coffee, a pitcher of orange juice and some rather stale-looking muffins on a tray. He downed a glass of orange juice, then poured two cups of coffee and put them and two of the muffins on a plastic carrying tray. He started toward the double glass doors to head back to their room, when he saw the early-morning sun's reflection on a big maroon sedan that was turning into the parking lot.

Reflexively, he glanced at his watch. Six-thirty. Then he took another quick look at the car. It was definitely maroon, and it looked familiar. His pulse hammered in his ears as he squinted, trying to get a glimpse of the driver.

As the car headed straight for the front desk of the motel, right where he was standing, he finally saw the driver. He was big and bald, with biceps bulging from a dark T-shirt. It had to be him. The man with the red tattoo. So he'd found them. That actually fit in with what he and Dawson had talked about, but if Mack was going to turn the tables on the man, he had to keep himself and Hannah alive long enough to do it.

MACK SET THE tray down on one of the tables. He stepped up to the front desk, but no one was there. He rang the bell furiously.

A woman with what appeared to be a permanent scowl came out of the back room. "Yeah?" she said grudgingly.

"Is there a back way out of here?" he asked quickly.

"What for?" she muttered, her keen, black eyes giving him a suspicious look.

He gave her a sheepish shrug. "See that maroon car? That's the husband of the woman I'm here with."

She gave Mack a world-weary look. "Like I never heard—"

"Please," he begged. "We were high school sweethearts."

She jerked a thumb toward her shoulder. "Through that door. Y'all get in a fight and I'll call the cops on you."

Mack winked at her. "We're already gone," he said.

Heading out the back of the motel, Mack breathed a sigh of relief. When he looked down the rear of the rows of rooms, he saw the Beemer and felt the tightness in his chest loosen. Thank goodness he'd parked the car around back last night.

Now if he could just get Hannah out of the room safely, they'd be in good shape. They might even be able to get ahead of the maroon car so they could get to Dowdie and get set up for the rest of the plan, which hadn't been completely worked out yet.

Mack pulled out his phone and speed-dialed Hannah's number, but she didn't answer. "Still asleep?" he muttered to himself as he dialed again.

"Come on," he whispered. "Hannah, come on. Where are you?"

He found the nearest breezeway that led from the back of the motel to the front and crept to the corner, trying to peer around without being seen. There, to his left, he saw the maroon car. The man had backed it into a parking space across from the motel entrance and was idling.

What the hell was he doing? Then he saw Hannah, dressed in shorts, a T-shirt and tennis shoes, walking toward the front desk. She'd already passed the breezeway where he was hiding.

Mack ran down to the next breezeway. He had to get

Hannah's attention, intercept her and head for the car before the guy made his move to grab her.

As Hannah approached, Mack called out in a stage whisper, "Hannah, over here."

She stopped and looked around.

"Keep walking. It's me, Mack. Don't look around."

She turned her head toward the sound of his voice. "Mack?" she whispered.

"Don't talk. Just walk," he whispered. "When you get to the breezeway—" An engine revved and the maroon car pulled out of its parking space. The transmission squealed as the driver slammed it into First and floored it.

"Run!" Mack shouted to Hannah.

She ran toward the breezeway.

"Run!" he shouted again. "I'm getting the car!"

Hannah had no idea what was going on and no time to think. She heard a car behind her, approaching way too fast. She ran as fast as she could. As she reached the breezeway, tires screeched as the car took the corner into the breezeway and hit the left concrete wall. Pieces of metal and glass flew everywhere.

Broken safety glass peppered Hannah's skin but she couldn't stop. Mack had sounded nearly panicked.

She pumped her legs harder and gasped for air. Then over the noise of the car's engine and her own footsteps crunching on the asphalt, she heard a more ominous sound. It was the slamming of a car door.

Suddenly, she was thrown into déjà vu. The man was going to shoot her. She knew it. She doubted she'd be so lucky as to dodge his bullets for a second time.

Then she saw the white BMW pull up to the end of the breezeway and stop. *Mack.* She forced her aching legs to push harder, forced herself not to think about her spasming, oxygen-starved lungs or the bullet that could stop her at any second.

Behind her, she heard the unmistakable sound of a gunshot. Her muscles contracted automatically and she almost lost her footing. The bullet hit the wall beside her head with a thunk, then zinged past her. Or was that a second bullet?

In front of her, Mack flung the BMW's passenger door open. For Hannah, the next few seconds went by in slow motion. She felt the impact through her whole body as her right foot came down on the asphalt. Then her left foot hit the hard ground. She concentrated on going as fast as she could, no matter how jarring each stride was.

Two sharp reports sounded behind her and her neck muscles tightened, sending pain up through the top of her head.

That had been too close. In front of her, from the shadow of the car's interior, Mack was yelling something, but all she could hear was the zing of bullets echoing in her ears. A deep dent appeared in the white-painted metal of the BMW as if by magic, and in the next instant, Hannah felt a searing heat on the inside of her right elbow.

She had to slow down. *Had to.* Not only because she had no more breath, but also because if she didn't, she'd hurtle through the open passenger door of the Beemer with no control and dive headfirst into Mack, who was revving the engine in preparation for speeding away as soon as she was inside the car.

As she slowed, her perception of time sped up, so that by the time she hit the leather passenger seat of the white car, she was able to grab the door frames, lessening her impact on Mack by forcing her arms to take the recoil.

The next thing she knew, she was right side up, sitting in the leather bucket seat, heaving uncontrollably as Mack burned rubber getting out of the motel parking lot.

Mack drove silently, intensely, until he got onto the interstate and managed to put fifteen minutes between them and the motel. Hannah spent the time regaining control of her breathing and checking behind them for any sign of the maroon car. After a couple of minutes, she sat with her head back against the headrest and her eyes closed, trying not to think about anything. Trying merely to be grateful she was alive and grateful that she hadn't tripped or miscalculated and run into the Beemer's door instead of managing to aim correctly for the opening into the car.

Finally, after a long time, Hannah said, "Mack, he's probably tracking us through my phone. Can't people do that these days? I should turn it off."

"That's exactly right," Mack said. "He is tracking us through your phone. But actually, we're tracking him, too."

"We're what? How?"

"Dawson got his computer whiz to set it up. Piece of cake, since the guy called you twice."

"Called me twice? How do you know that?"

"You left your access code to your voice mail set at the default. The last four digits of your telephone number. Anybody could get in."

"You listened to my voice mail?" She frowned, thinking of Billy Joe's telephone tirades. She felt her face grow hot. "I can't believe you did that."

Mack shook his head. "I could have gotten the transcripts from the Metairie Police. Same difference."

She huffed and crossed her arms, turning away to look out the passenger-side window. "Well, then, you should have. A person's phone messages are private."

Mack laughed. "Not really. Not these days."

For a moment, both of them were silent, but Hannah wanted to hear what Dawson and his computer person were doing with the man's phone. "Okay, fine. So what's happening with tracking the man?"

"Dawson's getting the info from Dusty and texting me his position," Mack said. "By the way, the man's name is Hoyt Diller."

Hannah heard a hard, brittle tone in Mack's voice, but within a couple of seconds, he reached over and squeezed her hand briefly. "We've turned the tables on him and we're leading him to Dowdie, hopefully to trap him and, if we're lucky, Ficone. But we've had to bring in the sheriff. We need him and his deputies to help us. There's no way we can handle this ourselves."

"The sheriff? But won't he arrest me? I mean, not only am I accused of drugs and maybe murder, I also fled the jurisdiction, right?"

Mack nodded. "Since we both swore in writing that you wouldn't leave the jurisdiction while out on bail, you're in violation of a court order, at the least. At worst, there will be a warrant out for your arrest. I could be brought before the bar, but I'm not too worried about that. I was planning to let my license to practice lapse anyhow."

Hannah took a deep breath. "So what now?"

"I'd like to think that the desk clerk heard the gunshots and called the cops, but even if she did, there's a good chance they're just now getting there."

"Do you think the cops will arrest him?"

Mack took out his phone and glanced at the screen. "Looks like he's back on the road, about twenty minutes behind us."

Hannah looked in the passenger-side mirror again, then turned around to get a good look. "I don't see him," she said. "That's good, right?"

"Yeah, for what it's worth. We're on U.S. 49. It's a pretty good road."

Mack looked up at the stretch of road in front of him, then glanced in his rearview mirror. "I'd rather be on the narrow county roads. That car he's driving is awfully low to the ground. A couple of good bumps and he'll knock a hole in the radiator and be stuck on the road while we just drive right on into Dowdie."

"This car is too low, too," she pointed out.

"The shocks are probably four times as good as his car."

Hannah shook her head. "The chassis is too low. It'll be as bad as the maroon car, trying to drive fast on those rough roads. We need a pickup."

Mack considered their options. There weren't many. "Okay, then," he said, looking around him at the town they were passing through. "Look. There's a used-car dealership up ahead. Let's trade the Beemer for a pickup."

Chapter Twelve

It was after nine o'clock at night when Hannah drove the teal-blue Ford pickup into Dowdie and turned onto the road to her mother's house. "The house is about two miles down this road," she said.

"I see what you mean about your neighbors."

"The closest one is Mr. Jones, about a mile away. But out here, there's not much light pollution, so you can see car lights or a porch light from a long way away.

"We have forty acres. Mom didn't realize the place was that big when she bought it ten years ago. The house is on the center lot, so we have plenty of room on either side. And with those tall spruces that line the road as a windbreak, you can't really see the house or much of the garage from the road."

"It's a two-car garage, right?"

"Yeah," she said. "But Billy Joe's Mustang takes up one whole side, and his tools and equipment take up the other. It'll take us all night to move his tools and equipment so we can hide the pickup in there."

"I'll take care of that while you make sure we can stay in the house without anyone knowing we're there. And think about where Billy Joe hid the money."

"And where my mother is."

Mack nodded grimly and Hannah knew what he was

thinking as clearly as if he'd said it aloud. Mack didn't think her mother was still alive. With Billy Joe dead, she'd probably been tied up or confined for two days without food or water.

"Here's the house, on the right."

"I can see why Billy Joe liked this place."

Hannah nodded. "It was perfect for him. I don't think he ever cared for my mom. I think he saw our place and it was just gravy that a single woman owned it. He wasn't happy to have me around, but he had to put up with me to get all this." She'd shut off the truck's headlights before she'd turned onto their road. She pulled into their driveway and drove around behind the garage so the truck couldn't be easily seen from the road.

"Where's Hoyt?"

Mack checked. "We made lots better time in the pickup than he is. He's about two hours behind us and—" he paused as a buzz announced another text "—hah. He's turned and headed south. He's going to Galveston, I'll bet. Maybe he'll bring Ficone back here."

"You're happy about that?"

"It falls in with our plan. We're hoping not only to catch Hoyt, but Sal Ficone, a pretty big drug dealer on the Gulf Coast."

She nodded. "I think we can safely stay in the basement without being seen," she told Mack as she shut off the engine. "The sliding glass doors face the woods. Mom put up blackout curtains to keep the sun off the patio. The whole front of the house is open, though. You can see into the living room and dining room at night. We won't be able to go upstairs for anything." She climbed out of the driver's side of the truck as Mack got out of the passenger seat.

"Then the basement it is. Can you fix us up places to sleep?"

Hannah nodded. "There's a couch down there that opens into a double bed. It's kind of old but it's not too uncomfortable."

"Okay, why don't you head on inside. I'm going to start on the garage."

"Do you want something to eat?" she asked.

"Damn it," Mack said. "I meant to stop and get us something."

"There's a freezer full of food in the basement. We'll be fine."

He nodded. "I'm starving. Is there something easy you can fix for tonight? What time is it?"

"It's kind of late. After ten."

Mack studied her. "You're exhausted. Forget food. I'll find us something, even if it's crackers and coffee."

"Don't worry about me. I've been more tired than this. Earlier this week." She smiled shyly. "I feel pretty good now."

Mack winced at the implication. She was referring to their lovemaking the night before. He had been doing his best to put it out of his mind. It was a sign of his weakness that he'd given in to his desires and made love with her. It didn't matter that it was the best thing, the most wonderful thing, he'd ever experienced. He'd compromised her safety by allowing himself to get involved with her.

"It's no problem making you some dinner," Hannah continued.

As she spoke, Mack's phone rang. He looked at the display. It was Dawson. "It's Dawson. I need to talk to him. I'll be inside in a few minutes."

"Come around the back and through the basement

door. Watch your step. The sidewalk going down the hill is cracked. You could trip."

Mack watched Hannah navigate the old sidewalk and then answered the phone. "Dawson?"

"Mack, we found Stephanie Clemens."

"Found her? Is she all right?" Mack asked, hardly breathing.

"She's alive. She's dehydrated and in shock. But she's being rushed to Dallas for emergency hemodialysis and the doctors are optimistic."

Mack was relieved, for Hannah's sake. "Good," he said. "Where'd you find her?"

"In an apartment just outside of Paris, Texas, that was rented to Campbell. About the time we tracked it down, the police received a call complaining that loud music had been playing for three days. They found her locked in the bathroom. She'd gone into liver failure so she was unconscious. The paramedics said she'd probably been out no more than six hours."

"And what hospital is she going to?" Mack asked.

Dawson told him.

"Thanks, Dawson. If her mother dies, I'm not sure Hannah could stand it."

"Trust me, Mack. I understand. Now listen, since Hoyt has turned south, you've got overnight to be ready for them. We have no idea exactly what time they might be there tomorrow, or even if they'll make it back to Dowdie that soon, but at least you can be ready. I've already talked to the sheriff."

Mack and Dawson briefly discussed the rest of the plan, then Dawson hung up and Mack ducked under the crime-scene tape crisscrossed over both the overhead garage door and the side door.

When he turned the knob on the door, it opened and

he stepped inside. Pulling a small, high-powered flashlight out of his pocket, he shone it around.

On the other side of the garage, he saw the distinctive shape of a vintage Mustang Cobra. He looked at the polished red finish, the chrome cobra on the side along with the letters *SVT.* Hannah had mentioned that Billy Joe had a Mustang, but she hadn't told him it was a *Special Vehicle Team* Cobra.

"Nice," he muttered as he examined the car. It was in beautiful condition. As the flashlight's beam played over the shiny surface from the rear to the front, he saw that the hood had been removed, leaving the engine exposed.

From what Mack could tell, and he certainly knew very little about working on cars, the engine was partially disassembled. A soft blanket was thrown over the car's fender to protect the paint job from scratches.

Mack turned his attention to the rest of the garage. As Hannah had said, there were tools and supplies everywhere, and right inside the side door was a wooden workbench that stuck out about four feet from the far wall. If he moved the workbench, rolled a couple of car-lifts over in front of the Mustang, then picked up empty parts boxes and toolboxes and moved two large trash cans outside, the truck would fit easily.

It took him about forty minutes to take care of everything. Finally, he was able to open the garage door, ripping the crime-scene tape to shreds in the process, and drive the truck into the garage in the dark. It fit almost perfectly. With a sigh of relief, he closed the garage door with a passing glance at the ruined crime-scene tape, closed the side door, then headed down the sidewalk to the basement and slipped in through the sliding glass doors.

Inside, Hannah had turned on a lamp, which lent a dim glow to the room. Hannah had already folded out the couch into a double bed and made it up with crisp white sheets. The mattress looked droopy but serviceable.

"Mack?" Hannah called. "I'm in here."

He followed her voice through the closest of two doors on either end of the wall behind the couch. The room was a laundry room with a washer, dryer, sink and a small chest freezer. On top of the dryer sat a microwave and a coffeepot. The air held the delicious smell of fresh coffee.

"I got those from upstairs," Hannah said. "I think I've fixed us a pretty good setup here. Want some coffee?"

He nodded gratefully. "But first, is there a bathroom down here?" he asked as she handed him a mug. "I want a shower more than coffee."

"I understand." Hannah nodded toward the interior wall of the laundry room. "It's right there on the other side of that wall. Go ahead. I'm about to dig in the freezer and see what we've got for dinner. I'm thinking it's going to be pizza."

"Works for me," Mack said. He took his plastic bag of clothes into the bathroom with him. The bathroom was large and had a window that opened out onto the side of the house. Rather than take a chance of somebody seeing the light and investigating, Mack hung a towel over the curtain rod.

While Mack showered, Hannah found two frozen microwavable pepperoni pizzas, a package of frozen chopped green peppers and onions and a bag of Italian-style cheese, so she embellished the plain pizzas, then cooked them according to the microwave directions. They wouldn't taste as good out of the microwave as if she'd baked them in an oven, but they would definitely be filling and more nutritious than coffee alone.

She'd taken the first pizza out of the microwave and was inserting the second when Mack came out of the bathroom. She looked up and the sight of him made her knees weak and her mouth dry. He had on jeans with no shirt. He'd flung his wet towel around his neck. His hair was dripping wet and every so often a drop would slither down his cheek or get caught in his long dark eyelashes.

Hannah swallowed a gasp at the sheer beauty of his body.

He met her gaze and sent her a mocking smile, as if he knew and was amused by what she was thinking.

She moistened her lips with her tongue. "Did you have a good shower? Plenty of hot water?" None of that was what she'd wanted to say. She'd wanted to say *You are the most beautiful man I've ever seen.* Instead, she turned away from the enticing sight of his bare shoulders, his lean, hard abs and the jeans riding low on his hips. That wasn't what she'd wanted to do, either. She wanted to forget about food, sleep and danger and bury herself in his hot, hard body. Lose herself in the pleasure he roused in her.

But the things she wanted were not practical, probably not even possible. So she took a deep breath and sent up a brief prayer that Mack couldn't read her mind. "The pizzas are ready," she said, feeling self-conscious. "Are you hungry?"

Mack's hooded, smoky eyes were watching her. They didn't waver when a droplet of water slid over his brow and balanced, shimmering, on his ridiculously long lashes. Finally, he blinked and the droplet and the smokiness disappeared.

In the next second, Hannah couldn't be sure if any of that had happened or if she'd imagined it.

"Hungry?" he said quietly, putting all sorts of meanings into the word. "Yeah, I am."

Doing her best to pretend that his answer was not a double entendre, Hannah handed him a plate filled with slices of pizza and pointed to the living room. "Sit on the end of the bed. Use the coffee table. And if you want, turn on the TV and we can see what the local news has to say about Billy Joe's death." By the time Hannah had brought her plateful of pizza and cup of coffee to the couch, he'd found a network channel that was showing local news. He had closed captioning on and the sound turned low.

They ate in silence and listened as the reporter listed community events and praised the football team. Finally, he turned the camera over to a second reporter.

"Thanks, John. We've been following an incredible story of a local resident, Stephanie Clemens, of Dowdie, who has been missing for several days. Ms. Clemens is a hemodialysis patient and according to her physician's office, as of this morning, she has missed one of her lifesaving treatments. Sheriff Harlan King told our reporter that he's mounting a countywide search for her and her daughter, Hannah Martin, whom he's seeking for questioning in the murder of Billy Joe Campbell, Ms. Clemens's boyfriend. The sheriff has asked that anyone with information regarding the murder of Mr. Campbell or the whereabouts of Ms. Clemens or Ms. Martin call the sheriff's office immediately. Back to you, John."

Mack turned off the TV. "Someone might hear it," he said around his last mouthful of pizza.

"The sheriff is going to mount a search," Hannah said. "You know the first place they'll look is here. Even if we leave, they'll know we've been here. What are we going to do?"

While Mack took their paper plates into the laundry room and threw them into the wastebasket, he debated how much to tell Hannah about what he and Dawson were planning. "I don't think the sheriff is our enemy," he said carefully.

"Maybe he's not, but if he finds me, he's going to arrest me."

"That might not be such a bad idea."

Hannah's mouth dropped open. "What?" She crossed her arms and began pacing back and forth in front of the glass doors with the blackout curtains. "That's not funny."

"Wasn't meant to be."

Disbelief and hurt crossed her face and she wrapped her arms around herself, as if to protect her heart.

"I'm worried about you. I need to know that you're safe."

"Well, I need to know that my mother is safe. Only she's not. She's out there somewhere, sick. Close to dying."

Mack couldn't hold her gaze. He got it. Hannah was terrified for her mother. And as long as her mother was missing, Hannah would never give up. She'd never put her safety ahead of her mom's. He wished he could tell her that her mom had been found and was safe and sound in a Dallas hospital.

But Dawson had provided the voice of reason and

Mack had to agree with him. If Hannah knew her mother had been found and was in the hospital, she'd fight him until he let her go to her. And that was too dangerous.

"Hannah, all I can tell you is that I'm very sure your mom will be all right. What I'm trying to do is stop Ficone and his hired hit man from grabbing you. You do understand that these people are ruthless, don't you? They won't stop until you tell them where their money and drugs are."

"But I can't. I don't *know* where they are."

Mack spread his hands. "*I don't know* is not an acceptable answer to a man like Ficone. Didn't you tell me the man told Billy Joe that Ficone was meeting with his suppliers in three days? That was today. That means if Ficone isn't dead, he's desperate. He's being squeezed from both sides. That makes him dangerous, but I'm betting it will also make him careless. It should be easy to take him and his goon down."

Mack saw in Hannah's face that she'd already moved on to the next logical conclusion. He set his jaw.

"Oh, my God! That's what you're doing. You're not concerned about me or my mother. You're not even interested in stopping Ficone. All you want is revenge for the man you think killed your mother."

"Hannah—"

She laughed, a harsh sound without amusement. "This is great. I'm such an idiot. Of course it's about the man with the red tattoo."

"It's not. You need to listen—"

"I don't need to do anything," she said, swiping her hand through the air in a dismissive gesture. "Don't talk to me unless you're ready to respect me enough to stop lying to me. For someone who demands the truth from others, you sure don't reveal much."

He gave her an ironic smile. "Then we make quite a pair, don't we?" he said.

Chapter Thirteen

Mack took a walk around the house to be sure the basement lights couldn't be seen and that no one was hanging around, he told Hannah. But when he got outside and far enough away that she couldn't hear him, he called Dawson.

"Do you know what time it is?" Dawson asked when he picked up the phone.

"I always know what time it is. Have you talked to the sheriff?" he asked.

There was an infinitesimal pause before Dawson answered. "I have. I've talked to the FBI, too. We're going to have to discuss a few changes. I was going to call you around 5:00 a.m."

Mack frowned. "What kind of changes?"

"I know you want Hannah out of harm's way. But think about this. What if she's there, just like Ficone's man expects? And she shows him that she's looking for the key—the answer to where Billy Joe hid the drugs and money."

"You want to use her for *bait?*" Mack interrupted. "Oh, hell, no."

"Listen, Mack. She'll be safe. You'll have the sheriff and his deputies all around. You'll take them down before they can do anything."

"I said no. What happened to the FBI?"

"They're out now that Ms. Clemens has been found. They were always in it just for the kidnapping."

"Listen to me, Daw. We are *not* putting Hannah in more danger. She's not an agent. She has no idea how to handle herself in a life-or-death situation. Use me. They can question me. I can be the one who figured out what Billy Joe was talking about."

"Come on, Mack. You know that won't work. They'll never believe you. It's got to be Hannah. I'm guessing he hasn't called her again."

"Nope."

"All right. Like we said earlier, we're going on the assumption that they'll be at the house early in the morning. I figure Ficone will probably send two men at least, but you'll have four."

Mack argued with Dawson for a while longer, but he knew he was already defeated. No matter how much he didn't like it, he knew that Dawson's plan was a good one—as long as the bad guys did what they were expected to do.

When Mack got back inside, Hannah had changed into pajamas with a robe that looked like a kimono and he could tell that she was still angry about his idea of letting the sheriff put her in jail.

"Well?" she said.

"What?" He looked at her sharply. Had she seen him talking on his phone? Worse, had she heard him?

"Did you see anything?" she asked. "Wasn't that why you went out?"

"Everything was quiet and dark. No traffic. But you were right. You can see headlights or even a lightbulb from a very long way away." He paused, looking at her. "Why don't you get some sleep? We're going to be up and getting ready by six o'clock. Take the couch. I'm going to keep an eye out."

"Or you could call the sheriff and he could stick me in the *tank*. That'll give you plenty of time to get a good night's sleep without having to worry about me."

"Trust me, I'm tempted," he said wryly. "But Dawson and I talked again and we've given up the idea of locking you up. Too much trouble."

She raised her brows. "Really? I'm thinking I might like this Dawson."

"I made the decision. I decided I want you where I can keep an eye on you. Want more coffee?" he asked casually.

She followed him. "Mack, what's really going on here?"

He sighed. "Nothing's going on. I'm just trying to figure out the best way to handle Ficone."

"No. It's something."

"It's nothing you need to be concerned about." He walked over to the bed and sat down on it, leaning back against the pillows.

"It's about the man with the red tattoo, isn't it?"

Mack sipped his coffee, feeling Hannah watching him. He kept his eyes on the coffee's liquid surface, studying it as intently as if it were tea leaves that might reveal the future.

"Tell me about the tattoo. Ever since I first mentioned it, I've felt like we're headed for some big *High Noon* shootout between you and that murderer. You knew exactly what it looked like. You've seen it before. Talk to me about it. It's obviously eating you up inside."

"I—" He stopped. He'd never talked about what he'd seen. Not to the police when he'd called to tell them his mother was dead. Not even to Dawson. The most he'd

ever said about it was to her when he'd told her he'd
watched a man kill his mother.

"Oh, Mack," Hannah said, touching his arm with
her fingers. "Is this about your mother?"

He closed his eyes for a second, then went back to
staring into the coffee cup. "The first time I remember seeing my mother hurt and bloody was when I was
about six. I don't remember what the man looked like
who hit her. All I remember is that I tried to hit him
and he just tossed me aside."

Hannah's fingers tightened on his arm. He thought
she was going to say something, but she didn't.

He swirled the coffee around in the bottom of the
cup. "It happened at least one more time, with a different boyfriend." He looked up at her, then back at the
cup. "I think she actually got one guy put in jail for assault. Then years later, I came home from school one
day to find her new boyfriend, a big man with a receding hairline, yelling at her, 'Didn't I tell you not to wake
me up with that damned vacuum cleaner?' He yelled,
then he hit her with his fist."

Mack stopped, feeling his stomach churn with nausea. He remembered now why he'd never talked about
it. Every time the memories tried to push their way into
his conscious mind, they made him physically ill and
stripped him of his confidence and control, so he shoved
it as far to the back of his mind as he could.

His eyes began to sting. He rubbed them with his
finger and thumb and noticed that they were damp. He
cleared his throat. "Then he picked her—up off the floor
and kept on—" He swallowed and cleared his throat
again. "I tried to stop him. I was twelve and I was sure
I could beat him up."

Hannah made a choked noise and when Mack looked at her, tears were gathering in her eyes.

"I couldn't protect her. I couldn't save her," he said, then shrugged.

"Oh, Mack, you were a child. Of course you couldn't."

He got up and took the cup into the laundry room. Hannah followed him.

"Come on, Hannah. You asked. I told you. Now drop it."

"Mack. You do realize that you couldn't possibly have stopped him, right?"

He turned to her, his jaw tight. "I don't need pop psychology, Hannah. I know all about it. Just drop it," he grated. "I'm not talking any more about it."

Hannah's heart was breaking. She knew what he had gone through. She'd seen the same pattern with her own mother, and she'd sworn to herself that she'd live alone rather than allow a man to treat her that way. No wonder Mack shied away from relationships. No wonder he did his best not to get involved.

She lifted her arms toward him, but he just glared at her and walked away.

"Mack, damn it." She stomped around and stood in front of him just as he was about to unlock the sliding glass doors. "Stop being so stubborn. I just want to hold you."

At that instant, everything about him changed, so suddenly and completely that she was shocked. He gave her a steady, emotionless look like nothing she'd seen from him before, not even when he'd opened his apartment door and seen her standing there. His expression then had shown his irritation at being interrupted. But this—this was as if a machine with a human mask for a face were looking at her. She took an involuntary step backward and lowered her arms.

"I told you, Hannah. I suck at relationships. I usually date women who don't want one. It works out well for both of us."

"You don't mean that. You're the strongest yet most gentle man I've ever known," she said. "You are—"

Before she could even finish her sentence, he turned on his heel, opened the sliding door and left.

Hannah stared after him for a long time. Her hands were still spread palms out, as if entreating him to come to her for comfort. She blinked and shook her head, trying to figure out what had just happened.

Who was Mack Griffin anyway? Was he the broken, vulnerable man who'd watched his mother get beaten to death? The way he'd been so reluctant to help her or even have anything to do with her made sense now. He was afraid he would fail to protect her like he'd failed his mom.

But this emotionless robot of a man who'd just spoken to her as if he were swatting a bothersome fly, who'd told her he cared nothing for love or tenderness and liked women who felt the same, was a totally different creature. But in a way, that made sense, too. If she believed that he'd never wanted to help her in the first place and had only done so because—

Because? *That was the problem.* Why? If he was that man, why would he have helped her at all? She didn't hesitate. She knew the answer. To get the information he needed about the man with the red tattoo. He'd done what he had to do—taken care of her, come to her rescue, had sex with her. And she'd believed it all. The tenderness, the sweetness. Because when he was close to her, she couldn't think straight.

Somehow, when he touched her, she saw the best in him. Promise, safety, temptation, even love. Was that the truth? Or was the truth that it had all been a lie? Had he just used her to find the man he believed had killed his mother?

Now that he had the information he needed about the man with the red tattoo, he had no further use for her. He'd tried to warn her, in his own way.

Hannah felt a sadness and a grief that she doubted anything would cure. She understood him now. He was both men. He was everything. Broken and unbreakable. Vulnerable and stoic. Full of revenge and full of heartache.

She turned out the lights and got into the bed, closing her burning eyes. She'd thought she would cry—for him and for herself. But she didn't. She went right to sleep.

Much later, Mack came in, stripped off his clothes and got into bed with her. He took her in his arms, the coolness of his skin giving her goose bumps at first. He kissed her and caressed her, and she did the same, until they were both hot and panting. Then he made love to her as if she was the most precious, fragile, beautiful thing he'd ever held.

After the lovemaking was over and both of them had cried out in climax then collapsed, drained and satiated, he tucked his head into the curve of her shoulder and whispered in her ear.

"I love you, Hannah. So much." His breath was hot and sweet against her ear. "As much as I can. But it's not enough. You deserve so much better than me."

THE NEXT MORNING, Mack and Hannah were in the kitchen before six o'clock, talking about the plan for the day. In front of Hannah on the kitchen table were her laptop, Billy Joe's key ring and a flat, plastic key holder that advertised an insurance company.

Hannah sipped hot coffee with sugar. "I can't even think about this," she said. "Me acting like I know about computers? I couldn't fool a four-year-old. Are you sure this is a good plan?"

"You don't have to fool anyone. You just have to be confident. You'll be sitting in front of the laptop as if you've been trying passwords all night, as if you're sure that Billy Joe hid the information about the drugs and money on his computer somewhere. I'll get the computer set up for you."

"Fine." She stood and started to pace. "Mack, my mother's appointment for dialysis was yesterday. She's going to die."

Mack caught her by her upper arms. "Listen to me," he said. "Your mom is going to be fine. You've got to believe that. And panicking doesn't help anything."

Hannah stiffened. "Let go of me," she said through clenched teeth. He did, thank goodness, because even in the middle of a panic attack, his touch rattled her. His warm fingers held too much promise, too much safety, too much temptation. And she couldn't go there. Not even if last night was real. Not even if he'd told her the truth, that he loved her. Because she knew what he'd said after that was also true. It wasn't enough.

She chafed her arms as if he'd hurt her. He hadn't— at least not physically. He'd never do that. He'd seen his mother hurt and eventually killed by men who abused women. He was the perfect protector, precisely because he had spent his life learning how not to get involved. And that broke her heart.

Mack would never admit or even believe that he needed love. He believed all he needed was revenge.

His goal was to find the man who'd killed his mother, the man with the red tattoo. Once he'd done that, he'd have no further use for her. He'd told her he didn't do relationships.

"Do you know what this is?" He showed her a tiny black plastic square.

She nodded. "I've seen them."

"It's an SD card. It stores data, like a jump drive." He inserted it into a slot in her laptop. "When the man comes in and demands to know what you know about the money, you tell him that you've been up all night trying passwords, but a little while ago you noticed something funny about the plastic key fob that held Billy Joe's keys. So you split it and discovered the SD card hidden inside. But you haven't had a chance to try it."

"That plastic holder wasn't on his key ring," she said.

"No, it wasn't, but Ficone's man won't know that. Now look. The plastic was split lengthwise and the SD was slipped right between the two layers."

Hannah examined the piece of plastic.

"Tell him you can't believe Billy Joe thought of that on his own."

"This? Oh, I can believe he thought of this. What I can't believe is that it will fool the man with the red tattoo or Ficone for more than a moment."

"A moment is all we'll need. We need to go over the rest of the plan so I can get out to the garage. I want to take a look at it in daylight. That's where the sheriff and I are going to be hiding to wait for Ficone's men. Now, Sheriff King should be here any minute, along with three of his deputies."

"Sheriff King? But he'll arrest me." Hannah's eyes went wide.

"Dawson has talked to him. We know that Hoyt, the guy in the maroon car, followed us almost all the way here before he turned south toward Galveston. Dawson's computer whiz has been tracking him using the GPS locator on his phone. What we're betting on is that he's bringing Ficone here to find the money and drugs himself."

"I don't get it. We don't know where they are. How will we convince Ficone that they're here?"

Mack folded his arms and gave her an ironic glance. "The more we act like we're searching for them here, the more Ficone will believe that we have proof of where they are."

"And the deputies are going to be in the basement?"

Mack nodded. "And you'll be right here, where we can see you and the deputies can hear you."

The kitchen table faced two large windows that looked out over the side yard, the driveway and the garage. Her mother had left them bare of curtains, and that meant that anyone who drove into the driveway or who was looking out the side door into the garage could see someone sitting at the kitchen table. "When he—or they—drive in, you'll be working on this laptop, trying passwords to get into it. You think Billy Joe stored a file in there with information about where he hid the money and the rest of the drugs."

"So all I'm doing is looking at the plastic key fob when they come in? Hopefully they won't run in firing their guns. What do you think Hoyt—or Ficone—is going to do ?"

"I *hope* he's going to take the SD card and sit down at the computer himself. That would be the best scenario. If he starts retrieving what's on the SD card, he'll be distracted and we can get the drop on him."

She looked at him. "What's the worst scenario?"

"He gets pissed off and thinks it's a setup and you're lying to him. But by then we'll be in position to get the drop on him and Sheriff King will arrest him."

"Okay," she said. "Let's do it."

Mack studied her for a moment. "You're ready?"

She shrugged. "Does it matter?"

His mouth curled. "Not a bit," he said. "Is your earpiece in place?"

She touched her ear and nodded as he checked his own.

"Go ahead and turn it on. Sheriff King has the others. We'll get them synced to the same channel when they get here."

Hannah pressed the remote control in her pocket and a faint buzzing told her the unit was on.

Mack walked to the back door and opened it. "Watch how loud you talk," he whispered, "when you're this close to the other person. You could get feedback."

She nodded again as he headed toward the garage.

She sat and inserted the SD card into the proper slot on the laptop. As she did, she wondered just how much the man with the red tattoo, or Ficone, knew about Billy Joe. Probably not as much as she did.

During the past few months while Billy Joe and her mom had dated, she had gotten the definite impression that he was hardly a great technological mind. For him, setting a reminder on his cell phone had seemed challenging. Yet Mack and his friend Dawson were banking on Ficone's people believing he had stored vital information on an SD card and password protected it.

On the laptop's screen, a window with a blank area came up with the words *enter your password*. She looked out the window toward the garage. If the card was asking for a password, did that mean that Mack or someone had put a password on it?

Mack said all they had to do was fool Ficone's man for a moment. She supposed it would help if the man saw some evidence that she'd been working on getting into the data on the card. She thought about what Billy Joe would choose as a password. Certainly nothing too complex, because it was Billy Joe. Maybe Stephanie1? Or Mustang1? Or June 11, her mother's birthday?

Then, in the distance, she heard the sound of a car engine. She froze; her breath caught in her throat as she listened. Her mouth went dry and her heart pounded. Was it the man with the red tattoo? Her rational brain said no. The sheriff was due to be here any minute. It was probably him.

She hadn't known where she was going when she'd run away from a killer five days ago. But now she did. She was headed toward this. The next minutes or hours were a matter of life or death.

MACK WENT INTO the garage by the side door. Moving all the equipment last night had probably played hell with the crime scene. He hoped the crime-scene techs were finished gathering evidence.

He looked at the place on the floor where the workbench had sat before he'd moved it. The concrete floor had been wiped down, but not cleaned thoroughly, and there were streaks of blood still there. Mack saw two places where crime-scene technicians had swabbed samples. The small streaks of their cotton swabs were clearly visible.

Mack figured the guy with the red tattoo was a professional, and if he'd had time, he'd have cleaned up Billy Joe's blood, maybe even using bleach in hopes of confusing the techs and possibly even corroding the techs' instruments.

Mack figured it wouldn't be difficult to prove that someone had bled out on the concrete floor. The hard part for Mack—or whoever Hannah hired as her lawyer—would be proving that it hadn't been Hannah.

Mack straightened. The sheriff should be here within the next ten to fifteen minutes. Meanwhile, he wanted to take a look at the workbench and see what the blood spatter looked like on it, so he walked toward the back wall of the garage.

He went over in his mind the plan that he, Sheriff King and Dawson had worked out. He was confident that they'd definitely be able to handle one or two or even three men. They should be able to handle as many as half a dozen, if they were able to get set up in place in plenty of time.

They were dealing with several unknowns. First and foremost, that Ficone's man or men would even show up this morning. That assumption was based on the man with the red tattoo telling Billy Joe that Ficone had forty-eight hours to give the money to his suppliers and the drugs to his distributors.

Mack examined the workbench. Despite some smears where he'd moved the bench the night before, the pattern of blood spatter on the workbench matched the floor and wall near the door, and matched Hannah's description of the one that had gone through Billy Joe's chest and out his back, which was why she'd seen the blood blossoming on the back of his shirt.

Now the question was, where was the bullet? Mack tried to picture exactly where the man with the red tattoo had been standing, where Billy Joe had stood, what the trajectory of the bullet had been and which way it had been traveling when it had exited Billy Joe's back. He knew that the crime-scene techs had probably measured and estimated the trajectory. He wondered if they'd found the slug. If they hadn't, maybe he could.

Chapter Fourteen

Hannah clutched at her chest as if the pressure of her hand could calm her heart. The car's engine she'd heard had not gotten louder, but had gone past and faded. It was obviously someone going by on the road. She looked out the window at the garage, wondering if Mack had heard it. She started to ask him, but they had talked about not using the earbuds for idle talk. The units were extremely powerful and therefore the batteries tended to run down very fast.

She picked up her coffee cup, dismayed when her hand trembled. She needed to calm down. It was going to be a really long, terrifying day if she jumped at every sound.

She checked the time on the laptop. It was twenty minutes to seven. Hadn't Mack said that the sheriff would be here by seven? So the next sound she heard would probably be the sheriff's truck.

She drained the last drops of coffee from her cup, wishing she'd thought to bring the coffeemaker upstairs this morning, then picked up Billy Joe's heavy key ring and dangled it from a finger, thinking how heavy it was.

Just how many keys did Billy Joe have on that ring? There had been times during these past four days when she'd have sworn that the keys added five pounds to her purse. She sct her coffee cup down and counted them.

"Eighteen, nineteen," she whispered, handling the last key, which was clad with black rubber. It was the key to the Mustang. Too bad it was up on blocks. It would be a great car to drive.

She tried to remember how Billy Joe had brought it to the house and gotten it into the garage, but she couldn't. He must have brought it while she was at work or in the neighboring town of Paris for the art class she'd been taking at the community college. She'd never thought about whether he'd driven it or had it hauled. She closed her eyes and tried to remember whether it had tires or if it was literally up on blocks. If it did have tires, was it drivable?

When she opened her eyes, she was looking at the words that had come up on the computer screen when she'd inserted the SD card. *Enter your password.*

She dangled the keys, staring at the plastic key fob. Would the trick fool them? She shook the keys like cymbals, listening to their metallic clatter.

She knew Billy Joe as well as anyone. Where had he hidden the money and the drugs? She should be able to figure out his hiding place. She was a *lot* smarter than him.

And that quickly, she knew. She closed her fist around the Mustang key. She wanted to tell Mack, but not through the earbud. She wanted to show him.

They were in the Mustang! They'd been right there, behind the man with the red tattoo the whole time. That was why Billy Joe had laughed. He'd thought he was putting something over on the man, up until the instant he'd been shot.

Hannah hurried outside and headed across the driveway. The yellow crime-scene tape was ragged and torn and fluttering in the breeze like a parade of tiny yellow flags across the overhead door. Hannah saluted them as she skipped, nearly giddy with excitement that she'd solved the mystery. She couldn't wait to tell Mack.

Just as she reached for the doorknob, she heard something behind her.

MACK HEARD SOMETHING through his earbud. He stood still and listened. Had Hannah coughed or said something out loud? Then he heard it again. It was a quiet scream, this time cut off in the middle.

"Hannah, what's wrong?" he said quietly as he rushed toward the side door. But the earbud went dead. Then he saw her, through the glass panes. He stopped short.

She was in the clutches of a man who had his hand over her mouth. Mack stared at the hand. It was large and the back of the wrist was covered with a red heart tattoo with the word *MOM* in black letters inside the heart.

"Get rid of your earpiece," the man yelled. "Now!"

Mack pulled the earbud out of his ear, held it up and then tossed it on the ground. "Now open the damn door!" the man yelled. "And be careful or I'll shoot her."

Mack looked at his other hand. He was holding a gun, and the gun's barrel was sunk into Hannah's stomach. Mack opened the door.

"Back up!"

Mack backed up. He was trying to think, to improvise a plan to get the gun away from the man with the red tattoo and save Hannah, but his brain seemed frozen with shock. All he could do was obey the man's orders.

"I said back up! More!"

Mack took a couple more steps backward, doing his best to jump-start his brain. Yes, the man had a loaded gun aimed at Hannah. Yes, Mack knew that he would shoot her—but maybe not yet.

Did he still believe that she knew where the drugs and money were? Would he hold off on killing her until he'd gotten the information from her?

"Open the door," the man commanded Hannah. When she did, he sidled inside, pushing her ahead of him. Then he nudged the door closed behind him and let go of Hannah's mouth. With lightning-fast movements, he reversed the hand holding her around the waist and the hand holding the gun, then he pressed the gun up under her chin.

Watching him, Mack knew he was a professional. He knew that the best place to hold a gun for maximum impact and minimum chance for error was directly under the victim's chin, propped just inside the jawbone so she couldn't turn her head and dodge the bullet.

"Let her go," Mack said.

"Mack, I'm sorry—" Hannah started, but the man jabbed the gun more deeply into her flesh.

"Shut up!"

She nodded, her eyes on Mack, wide and wet and terrified.

Mack clenched his fists. "Damn you. There are law enforcement officers here. They probably have you in their sights right now, just waiting for the perfect shot."

"Oh, please, Mr. Griffin. Don't give me that lawyer bunk. There's nobody here. I've been looking around the area for the past hour. We're going to be done long before they arrive. I can guarantee you this is not going to take long. I just need to get rid of you and start convincing Hannah that it's in her best interest to tell me where the money and drugs are."

"She doesn't know. Nobody does. You killed the only person who could tell you."

Hannah opened her eyes wider and, without moving her head, she shifted her gaze behind him, then back at him, then behind again. Then she moved her lips.

He frowned.

The man with the red tattoo jabbed the gun into the soft flesh under her chin again, hard enough that she cried out. "What are you doing, Hannah? Why don't you tell me what you just tried to tell Mr. Griffin?"

She didn't move.

"Hannah?" He jabbed again.

"Ah!" she cried. "Nothing. It was nothing!"

The man squeezed his other arm more tightly around her waist, then turned the barrel of the gun toward Mack. "I'll kill your lawyer friend here," he said. "I promise you that."

Hannah's jaw throbbed where the gun's barrel had been pressing. It was a relief not to have the hard steel pushing into the top of her throat enough that she had trouble swallowing. But now the man was pointing the gun at Mack.

She shook her head. "No! Please, no. I'll—" Her breath caught in a sob. "I'll tell you."

"Hannah, no!" Mack cried. "You can't believe a word he says. Don't worry. I'm fine. I'll be fine. Please, Hannah, just hold on. The sheriff will be here any second."

"For what good it will do," the man said. "Come on, Hannah. Tell me."

She nodded, still looking at Mack. "Okay," she said, her chest heaving with her panicked breaths. "I told him I love him," she said. "I—just needed to say that before you—"

The man laughed. "That's so sweet, Hannah."

She felt his arm muscles tense as he lifted the barrel of the gun.

"No—please don't—" she gasped.

"Shut up," the man whispered in her ear.

Mack's face went still and he moved his gaze from her to the man holding her. He'd morphed into the emotionless robot she hated. "What's your name?" he asked the man, his voice level and detached.

Hannah felt tears fill her eyes and slip down her cheeks. "Mack, don't. Don't give him the satisfaction."

"Satisfaction?" The man's low, creepy voice sounded more animated than she'd ever heard it. Mack had intrigued him. "What in the world could give me more satisfaction than killing the two of you?"

"I asked you a question," Mack said, still no emotion in his voice.

"My name? It's Hoyt. Hoyt Diller. Why?"

"I've waited twenty years to meet you," Mack said, still no inflection in his voice. "You killed my mother."

Hannah felt Hoyt's body go tense. Mack had surprised him. He laughed. "I doubt that. In my line of work I don't get an opportunity to assassinate women very often."

"I don't think this was work," Mack said. "I think it was purely entertainment."

The man tensed even more. "Oh, yeah? What the hell are you talking about? And if all you're doing is trying to buy time, it's not going to work. I've only killed a couple of women in my life, so you've got two chances to get it right, and then—Hannah? You can say good-bye to your new boyfriend."

"No," she cried, sobbing. "No. Please don't. I'll tell you. I'll tell you everything—"

"My mother!" Mack's voice rose above hers, pulling Hoyt's attention back to him. "My mother was Kathleen Griffin, and you beat her to death right in front of me."

Hannah put her hands on top of the man's arm that was wrapped around her waist. "Please!" she sobbed. "It's in the Mustang. Everything. Billy Joe hid the money and the drugs in the Mustang. Take them to your boss. That's all you want, right? Just go and leave us alone. We'll never tell anybody—"

"Hannah!" Mack yelled, his voice no longer steady and emotionless. "Stop! My mother was your girlfriend, *Hoyt,* in Chef Voleur—"

"Oh, shut up," Hoyt spat. "Stop boring me with your pathetic story. Do you think I care about your whore of a mother? I've never been to that dumb town before. Never even heard of it."

Mack's eyes turned a peculiar color, like tarnished silver. He dived at Hoyt's feet.

"No! Mack!" she cried as a gunshot rang out. Her legs dropped right out from under her. Hoyt's arm squeezed her so tightly she couldn't catch a breath. Another loud report sounded. She screamed.

Then it seemed to her that the world exploded into volleys of gunfire. Hoyt let go of her.

The next thing she knew, she was on the ground with the smell of gun smoke in her nostrils and her eyes burning like fire. She rolled up into a ball and lay there, trying to make herself as small as possible.

"Mack?" she sobbed quietly. "Where are you? Are you okay?" Her eyes stung with smoke and tears and she couldn't hear anything except gunfire and incoherent shouts.

Mack, please be okay.

THE NEXT AFTERNOON Hannah kissed her mother on the cheek. She whispered, "'Bye, Mom. I'm sorry I have to go. I'll see you tomorrow." She didn't like her mother's color. The liver failure and dehydration had taken its toll. But the doctors assured her that the hemodialysis was doing its job and within a few days, her mom would be well enough to be discharged.

They'd also told her that because of the trauma of her abduction, her mother had been moved forward on the liver transplant list. There was a real possibility that she'd receive a liver within the next few weeks.

Her mother smiled wanly. "'Bye, sweetheart," she whispered. "Don't worry. I'm feeling better already. It's you I'm worried about. Nurse, are you sure she's ready to be discharged?"

Hannah shook her head and smiled. "There's nothing wrong with me except a cut on my forehead." But when she straightened, her head throbbed in pain and she swayed.

The nurse caught her arm. "Okay," she said. "That's enough. Sit back down in the wheelchair. I was supposed to have you downstairs five minutes ago."

Hannah sank into the chair, her head spinning. She touched her forehead where a large bandage covered what she'd been told were five stitches.

"Thanks for bringing me by to see her one more time. I don't know how long it will be before I can get back here."

"Oh, you're welcome, honey," the nurse said as she turned the wheelchair and rolled it out of the room and down the hallway of the dialysis unit to the freight elevators. "I'm taking you down the back elevators to avoid the reporters and the gawkers. There's a police car waiting for you in the basement of the parking garage."

Hannah let the nurse help her out of the wheelchair and into the backseat of the police car. During the nearly two-hour drive from the hospital to Dowdie, Hannah alternately dozed and replayed the past twenty-four hours since what she thought of as the *Shootout at the Mustang Garage*.

She had no recollection of being in an ambulance or getting the five stitches. She did remember Sheriff King visiting her in the E.R. cubicle. He'd asked her about a million questions and told her that Hoyt Diller had been taken into custody, as had Sal Ficone, who'd been picked up in the maroon sedan about a quarter mile from Hannah's house. He'd supposedly been waiting for Hoyt to take care of the dirty work. Then Ficone had planned to sweep in and take possession of the drugs and money that Billy Joe had stolen, which were found in the Mustang, under the seats, exactly where Hannah had said they had to be.

The sheriff had also told her that her mother was upstairs in the hemodialysis unit and was apparently doing fine.

He hadn't offered anything about Mack, though, so Hannah had asked.

"He's okay. Took a bullet in his left arm, but that's it. He was discharged. I'm not sure where he is tonight, but tomorrow he'll be at my office, just like you, answering questions and filling out forms."

She'd been discharged from the E.R. and had spent the rest of the day and overnight in her mom's room.

She'd hardly slept at all. She'd spent most of the time talking to her mom or holding her hand while she slept.

Hannah was dozing in the car when the change in engine sound told her the police car was slowing to a stop. The officer driving got out and came around to help her out of the backseat and into the Dowdie Sheriff's office.

Sheriff King met them at the door and guided her back to a room with a big wooden table, a refrigerator, a microwave and a coffeepot full of what smelled like fresh coffee.

"Want a cup?" the sheriff asked her.

"Please," Hannah said. "With lots of sugar."

He poured the coffee and set the cup, a spoon and a box of sugar cubes in front of her. She dropped seven cubes into the cup and stirred it, watching the dark bubbles rise and burst on the coffee's surface. She was just taking her first swallow when the door to the room opened.

She looked up and nearly choked on the coffee. It was Mack. He had on blue scrubs and his left arm was bandaged and in a sling. She breathed deeply. The sheriff had told her he was all right, but it was a huge relief to see him for herself. The last time she'd seen him he'd been diving at Hoyt.

He took in the room with a quick glance, nodded briefly at her then walked over to the coffeepot and clumsily poured himself a cup. He sat down opposite her.

She lowered her gaze to her coffee again, but she could feel his eyes on her. She looked up, clearing her throat quietly. "Hi," she said.

He took a swallow of coffee. "Hi," he muttered. "You're okay?"

He nodded. "You?"

"I'm fine." She touched the bandage on her forehead with a sheepish smile. "Five stitches. Hardly the badge of courage you have there. What happened to you?"

He grimaced and gave a little shake of his head. "Took a bullet. Went straight through the biceps without hitting anything. It's fine." He paused. "I heard your mom's going to be okay."

His casual mention of her mother made her angry. Her scalp tightened and a place in her chest burned. "She's going to be fine. Why didn't you tell me you'd found her? I had to find out from Sheriff King that she was safe on the hemodialysis ward. The nurses told me she'd been there for almost twenty-four hours."

Mack's jaw tensed. "Your life was in danger. I couldn't risk you running off to the hospital in the middle of everything because you had to see your mother."

"What did you think would happen?" she asked sarcastically. "The bad guy would grab me?"

Mack sent her a disgusted look.

Part of why she was so angry with him was because she knew he was right. She definitely would have wanted to rush to her mother. Would she have? She couldn't say. "Where was she? And how did you find her?"

"Dawson had Dusty, his computer person, looking all over the area for an apartment rented to Billy Joe Campbell. Dawson's wife called all the hospitals. When neighbors complained about loud music coming from an apartment in Paris, the police found her. She'd been locked in the bathroom."

Hannah nodded, her eyes stinging.

"Thank you for saving her," Hannah said politely, although inside, she felt as though she was about to explode. How long were they going to sit here like two people discussing last night's game around the water cooler? She was sick of his calm exterior, his even tone, his carefully studied disinterest. She had to do something to provoke a response in him—positive or negative, it hardly mattered.

"So, Mack, did you get what you wanted from the man with the red tattoo?" She tried to emulate him. Tried to keep her voice as steady as she could.

She saw his jaw muscle tense and flex. She waited, holding her breath, but he didn't answer. He drank his coffee without looking at her.

"Well?" she prompted. "Was him calling your mother a whore what you were going for?"

Mack set his coffee cup down carefully. "Hannah," he said warningly. "Don't—"

"Don't what? I want to know, Mack. I'm curious. You found him—the man who killed your mother. Did it help?"

He shook his head, then looked up at her, and what she saw broke her heart. His green-gold eyes were dark and bottomless with pain. "It wasn't him." He grasped the cup at the rim and twirled it on the table, watching it spin around and around.

This time when he looked at her, his mouth was twisted into an ironic smile. "Ficone has the same tattoo. Apparently, the patriarch, Marco, I think was his name, designed the tattoo as a tribute to his mother, and had all his hit men get it so rival families would know who they were dealing with. His boy, Sal, has continued the tradition. There may be a dozen guys who have the same tattoo."

"Oh, no," Hannah said. "I'm so sorry. You must be devastated."

He stood and turned away to put his cup in the sink. "I've got to go. I just wanted—" he cleared his throat "—a cup of coffee before my turn to be grilled by the sheriff."

Hannah stood, too, and watched him as he turned toward the door. She waited, hoping against hope that he would turn around. But he didn't. Just at the moment when he was about to step across the threshold of the door, she spoke. "Mack?"

He stopped, but didn't turn around.

"Mack, turn around and look at me, please."

Nothing.

She swallowed and her throat tried to contract. "I love you," she said softly. For a long time, nothing happened.

Then Mack lowered his head and rubbed the back of his neck.

"I love you," she said again.

He made a sound, deep in his throat. It was a groan or a moan.

"I love you." To her chagrin, her eyes began to sting. "I love—"

Mack turned. "Hannah, don't do this, please. I've tried to explain—"

"I love you, Mack," she said. "And I know you love me. *I know it.* You have to trust me. And you have to trust yourself. I don't know why you don't. You were born to be a protector. You saved me."

She saw his throat move as he swallowed and shook his head. "I nearly got you killed."

"If you hadn't helped me, I'd have died," she said. "You saved me."

He shook his head. "It's not—"

"I love you," she interrupted. "And you love me."

This time, to her surprise, he nodded. "I do. I love you. But it's not enough."

She smiled at him. "It will always be enough."

Mack took a step toward her.

She lifted her head and smiled at him.

He took a second step and wrapped his good arm around her and pulled her close. He buried his nose in her hair and held her, so tightly that she found it hard to breathe. He kissed her hair gently, then the bandage at her forehead, then the tip of her nose and her mouth. His kiss was soft at first, but when she opened to him, he kissed her more deeply and intimately, until both of them were panting with desire.

Hannah heard footsteps, which paused in the doorway. Sheriff King cleared his throat. "I'll come back later," he mumbled.

She chuckled, breaking the spell of the kiss. Mack pulled back, a smile on his face and a glimmer of wonder in his eyes. "I guess we've got to take care of this business before we can deal with *us*."

She nodded. "Should we go find the sheriff and tell him he can come back now?"

Mack nodded, his smile fading. "Hannah," he said, "This isn't going to be easy."

"I don't think either one of us expects easy."

"I'm kind of a mess," he went on. "I've got a lot of issues."

Hannah kissed him lightly on the cheek. "Then we make quite a pair, don't we?"

Epilogue

Two weeks from the day they caught Sal Ficone, Mack smiled at Hannah as she hung up from talking to her mom.

"How is she?" he asked. "Just fine. Right?"

Hannah nodded reluctantly. "Yes, she's fine. Yes, she's in the hospital. Yes, she's safe. But I'm still not sure…"

"Shh," Mack said, pulling her close in the confines of the taxi that was speeding through the streets of Paris. "You're doing exactly the right thing. Your mom would be all over you if you'd refused to take this trip."

She sighed. "I feel so torn. I know Mom's okay right now, but how much longer can she wait for a new liver? My grandmother sounded well, but it's only been a few days since her heart attack."

Mack looked out the taxi window. "Which is why we're going to her house, rather than having her take a taxi to the hotel. You'd never forgive yourself if you hadn't come and something happened to Claire."

"That's what's tearing me apart. I could lose either of them in a heartbeat." She touched Mack's arm. "And what if a liver becomes available, like, tonight?"

"You know what the doctor said. That's why she's right there in the hospital. And we can be in Dallas within several hours."

"And we'll be there four days from now, on Monday anyway, for Sal Ficone's arraignment," Mack reminded her as the taxi spun in a U-turn and pulled to the curb in front of a lovely old house.

"Oh. Is this Rue de Jonge?" Hannah put her phone in her purse. She got out while Mack paid the driver. Then the two of them walked up to the door.

"Oh, Mack," she said, practically speechless with emotion. "This is so unbelievable. I have—no, *we* have a new family, and I hardly know any of them."

Mack kissed her forehead, where a small bandage had taken the place of the large one. "I've already told you, the Delanceys are quite a crowd."

"And now we're meeting the grandmother I never knew." She patted her hair then turned to look at him. "Where's your sling? You're not supposed to take it off."

Mack's eyes sparkled. "Probably in the bed back in the hotel room."

"You can't just ignore what the doctors said. You're supposed to wear it all the time.... It's going to be quite a while before we're able to settle down in Chef Voleur," Hannah said.

"Don't worry about that. I'm fine as long as I'm with you," Mack murmured in her ear as the front door opened and a petite woman with a gray braid wrapped elegantly around the crown of her head, and wearing a gorgeous couture pantsuit and four-inch Jimmy Choo shoes, stood there, beaming. "Hannah? And Mack?" she said. Hannah just stood there smiling, seemingly unable to speak.

"Hannah, I'm your grandmother," the tiny woman said. "You're welcome to call me Grandmother, Grandmere or Claire." Claire took a step back and gestured for them to enter. The living room appeared to take up the entire first floor. It was sparsely furnished and a hand-painted mandala was the focal point on the expanse of hardwood on the floor.

Hannah felt Mack's hand on the small of her back, warm and reassuring. She stepped inside, with him at her side.

Then she held out her arms. "I want to call you Grandmother," she said, wrapping her arms around the smaller woman. Her grandmother had a strong, vital presence, but in Hannah's embrace, she felt tiny and frail. Hannah's heart twisted.

Then Claire pushed her away to look at her. "Oh, my goodness, you look just like your grandfather."

"M-my grandfather?"

"Ektor," Claire said. "Ektor Petrakis. Stephanie was the spitting image of him when she was a baby." A shadow crossed Claire's face. "How is your mother?"

"She's actually doing okay. She's in the hospital, due to receive a liver transplant any day now."

"Oh, I'm so glad." Claire stared into space for a few seconds, then turned her attention back to Hannah.

"My dear, you are so beautiful." Claire took Hannah's hand in hers, then she reached out her other hand for Mack's. Hannah glanced at him and found him grinning as if she was his newfound grandmother. "Come in. Come in. We have café au lait or tea, and I have madeleines from the bakery on the corner. Sit and let's talk."

She pulled them to one corner of the large room where two sofas faced each other in a small conversation area near a window.

"I want to hear everything, Hannah, from the moment you were born." She laughed, and the sound of her laughter was like a chorus of small bells. "I need enough information to hold me until I can get my doctor to let me fly to Texas to visit my daughter, and have another, hopefully longer, visit with you."

"As soon as Mom can travel after her liver transplant, we're going to take her to live in Chef Voleur with us. We've decided that the hometown of the Delanceys will be our home, and I want my mom and you, if you'll agree, with us," Hannah said. "And so does Mack."

Hannah glanced at Mack, who had not sat, but was walking around looking at the art pieces placed strategically around the room. He smiled at her, then at her grandmother. "We'd be honored, Ms. Delancey."

"Oh, child," Claire said. "Call me Claire or Grandmother."

Mack sent Hannah a quick look, then grinned at Claire. "Ma'am, it would be my great honor to call you Grandmother."

Hannah felt tears sting her eyes. Something felt odd in her chest, too. She pressed her hand there, right below her collarbone, and realized that the empty, lonely spot under her breastbone no longer felt empty. It felt full, with love and happiness. With her grandmother and her mother. With Mack.

And the desolate, uncertain future she'd seen before her just a few days before now stretched like the beautiful, mighty Mississippi River, drawing her to the town of Chef Voleur, where her family was. Where she would always be safe and loved.

* * * * *

THE DELANCEY DYNASTY *comes to an end with BLOOD TIES IN CHEF VOLEUR, on sale next month*

A sneaky peek at next month...

INTRIGUE...

A SEDUCTIVE COMBINATION OF DANGER AND DESIRE

My wish list for next month's titles...

In stores from 18th July 2014:

❏ Evidence of Passion – Cynthia Eden

& Hunted – Beverly Long

❏ Bridegroom Bodyguard – Lisa Childs

& KCPD Protector – Julie Miller

❏ Secret Obsession – Robin Perini

& Blood Ties in Chef Voleur – Mallory Kane

Romantic Suspense

❏ Cavanaugh Strong – Marie Ferrarella

Available at WHSmith, Tesco, Asda, Eason, Amazon and Apple

Just can't wait?

Visit us Online

You can buy our books online a month before they hit the shops! **www.millsandboon.co.uk**

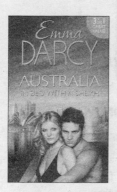

Discover more romance at

www.millsandboon.co.uk

- ❤ WIN great prizes in our exclusive competitions
- ❤ BUY new titles before they hit the shops
- ❤ BROWSE new books and REVIEW your favourites
- ❤ SAVE on new books with the Mills & Boon® Bookclub™
- ❤ DISCOVER new authors

PLUS, to chat about your favourite reads, get the latest news and find special offers:

- 🔘 Find us on facebook.com/millsandboon
- ➤ Follow us on twitter.com/millsandboonuk
- ❤ Sign up to our newsletter at millsandboon.co.uk

The World of Mills & Boon

There's a Mills & Boon® series that's perfect for you. There are ten different series to choose from and new titles every month, so whether you're looking for glamorous seduction, Regency rakes, homespun heroes or sizzling erotica, we'll give you plenty of inspiration for your next read.

By Request

Relive the romance with the best of the best
12 stories every month

Cherish™

Experience the ultimate rush of falling in love.
12 new stories every month

INTRIGUE...

A seductive combination of danger and desire...
7 new stories every month

Desire™

Passionate and dramatic love stories
6 new stories every month

nocturne™

An exhilarating underworld of dark desires
3 new stories every month

For exclusive member offers go to
millsandboon.co.uk/subscribe